W9-CKH-006

April
is
Forever

***Also by Doris Elaine Fell
in Large Print:***

Always in September
Before Winter Comes

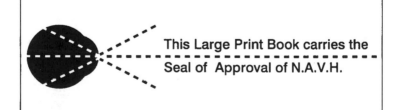

This Large Print Book carries the
Seal of Approval of N.A.V.H.

April is Forever

Doris Elaine Fell

Thorndike Press • Thorndike, Maine

Henderson County Public Library

Copyright © 1995 by Doris Elaine Fell

All rights reserved.

Published in 1998 by arrangement with Crossway Books, a division of Good News Publishers.

Thorndike Large Print ® Christian Mystery Series.

The tree indicium is a trademark of Thorndike Press.

The text of this Large Print edition is unabridged.
Other aspects of the book may vary from the original edition.

Set in 16 pt. Plantin.

Printed in the United States on permanent paper.

Library of Congress Cataloging in Publication Data

Fell, Doris Elaine.
    April is forever / Doris Elaine Fell.
      p. (large print) cm.
    ISBN 0-7862-1362-0 (lg. print : hc : alk. paper)
    1. Vietnamese Conflict, 1961–1975 — Secret service
— United States — Fiction. 2. Intelligence service —
United States — Fiction. 3. Intelligence service — Laos
— Fiction. 4. War widows — Fiction. 5. Large type
books. I. Title.
[PS3556.E4716A9 1995b]
813′.54—dc21   97-48789

Henderson County Public Library

In the prime of my life
must I go through the gates of death
and be robbed of the rest of my years?

Isaiah 38:10 (NIV)

Dedicated to those
who for love of country
finished life's journey early,
whose names are engraved
not just on memorial walls
but in our hearts

• • • •

Jordan, Jon, Anthony,
my cousin Ray
and especially in memory of
First Lieutenant George Jonathan Hill
Sam and Sopie's son

Prologue

Luke Breckenridge eased back the flap of the tent and stared into the darkness. The jungles of Laos lay foreboding — a spattering of stars, a sliver of moon, endless shadows that stirred in the forest around him. Night had swept in eerily over the forested mountains, leaping from daylight to blackness without warning. Far down the tree-lined hillside, faint moon gleams sent shimmering streaks across the Mekong River. He brooded as the waters lapped angrily at the tree roots. The songs of the night played off-key, the hawking cries of birds muffling the sounds of the river, the crunch of leaves, the snapping of twigs on the trail.

Luke stood motionless, empty, homesick, his body damp and sweaty from the humidity. His *cammies* looked as battle worn as he felt, his scruffy beard shadowed like the night. Canvas-top boots pinched against his blistered heels, the jungle rot eating between his toes and inflaming the balls of his feet.

As he watched, a night patrol crept out through the shadows — the spirited poorly clad Hmong troops in the lead, men who barely came to his armpits. A handful of South Vietnamese, hardened by war, followed. But Luke worried most about the small platoon of marines in the rear who weren't supposed to be there — fresh recruits in battle dress, camouflage markings on their boyish faces, heavy rucksacks on their backs, M16 rifles clutched in their hands. Luke's men, all of them, fighting together, dying together. They'd patrol the trails until dawn, crossing deep into Pathet Lao territory to hunt down the Communist-backed soldiers who were better equipped and better trained than the Hmong.

The haunting beauty of Laos remained veiled in an unending, bitter conflict. He hated his role: noncombatant. Military advisor. The threat of death was always there, snatching away Luke's thoughts of yesterday, his dreams of tomorrow. Life seemed ill-defined, a far cry from his days at Annapolis where he had learned the stratagems for winning wars and leading men into battle, not sending them. War coursed through his arteries and stirred him to thoughts of a gallantry that eluded him with a noncombatant assignment, but his hopes for victory would never come without a political revival in Washington policy.

Luke shifted on his swollen feet and stifled the hacking cough that gnawed at his lungs. He was sick and he knew it, but even if he went back inside the tent to lie down, would he sleep? These days he dozed better standing on his feet or sitting braced against a tree trunk. Now all he could do was lean against the tent and suck air into his ravaged lungs. And wait and watch.

Clouds covered the moon sliver, leaving its outline shrouded in gray. He longed for a full moon, the familiar sights of home, the touch of Sauni's hand in his own, the taste of her lips on his.

He swatted at gnats buzzing at his ear and grabbed blindly at the memory of flying to Santa Barbara on their honeymoon. He remembered a full moon rising in splendor over the Pacific Ocean, of standing on the shoreline with Sauni, the cold waves crashing over her polished toes. The aroma of hot dogs was suddenly so real that he salivated at the thought of them sizzling on an open beach fire — the flames illuminating Sauni's delicate features for him even here in the jungles of Laos.

As quickly, the rat-a-tat-tat of gunfire higher on the mountain slope thrust him back into reality, into darkness, into silence — back to the smell of dampness, of his own

9

sweat, of the Laotian forest around him. He listened intently. Had one of his men fallen — one of the young Hmong or a marine fresh from boot camp dead before he could write home and brag about his first baptism of fire? Surely the Pathet Lao soldiers had been waiting for Luke's patrol to come over the ridge.

Another distant sound broke the stillness. He cocked his ear to the grinding whir of a chopper drawing closer, a fool's mission at this hour. The pilot winged low over the treetops, stirring a wind that swayed the branches as he daredeviled a night landing. Luke tensed for the crash, waited for a burst of fire from the fallen aircraft. The swaying of branches stopped. The whir of the rotary blades ceased. Hank Randolf, his commanding officer, would be checking it out. Five minutes. Ten minutes. An hour. Still Luke waited outside the tent. A twig snapped behind him. He spun around, his hand on the .45 at his side.

"Captain, it's Hank," came his C. O.'s whispered warning.

"Sir?"

"You have company."

"Me?" *Dear God, not the admiral, not my dad. Not out here.*

His C. O. stood beside him now, his breath

tainted with the smell of cigarettes. "We have a mission for you, Captain."

"Bangkok?" Luke asked hopefully. "A medical reprieve?"

"No, a trek across the mountains. A special mission."

Further into the hellhole, Luke thought. *What's happening to me? A year ago, even a month ago, I would have jumped at a challenge. Now I feel as hopeless as the people in this land.* He scowled at the stranger behind Randolf. The intruder stayed in the shadows, a man with a stocky build, not much taller than Hank, not much older than Luke. The major's *cammie* shirt fit too tightly, and even in the darkness Luke could see his neck bulge at the collar. It was a face Luke could barely see, one he would not remember. The man's helmet shaded his eyes; the tight chin strap distorted the shape of his jaw and mouth. A thick moustache covered his lip. Luke had an immediate uncanny mistrust of the man. *You stand there in battle dress,* he thought, *but you're CIA. I know it.*

"It must be important for you to fly in low like that," Luke said to the stranger, "and risk pointing out our camp to the enemy."

There was a brief stilted laugh, gravelly, humorless. "I was a passenger, Captain Breckenridge, not one of those fly-for-hire

11

pilots risking a night run for an extra buck."

"Is Air America back to flying you boys around?" Luke challenged. It was no secret that in this part of the world Central Intelligence had access to its own airline — its own chartered planes and pilots.

Luke felt certain there was a smirk on the man's face as he said, "We have a man being held in a Laotian village a few days from here. We want you to get him out before the Viet Cong snatch him away and transfer him across the border to the Hanoi Hilton."

"Or before Saigon falls?" Luke asked bitterly.

"That will never happen. We'll win this, one way or the other."

"Tell that to Washington, sir. By the way, you know my name. I don't know yours."

"You don't need to."

"Listen, Luke," Hank intervened, "I suggested that the major use a Hmong scout to bring the man back, but he wanted a marine."

Me in particular? Luke wondered.

The rough voice sounded determined. "You know the language and the area, Breckenridge. You're quick and agile on your feet."

Not lately, Luke thought. *Not with these feet.* His melancholy mounted. "I'm only weeks from a scheduled R&R in Bangkok. Will I be back in time?" *Will I be back at all?*

"You'll be taking a mail drop for me," the major said.

"I'd rather be taking a company of men and rescue helicopters."

"Secrecy counts."

"Counts for what?" Luke asked.

"Just bring our man out."

"I'll leave you two." Hank hesitated, then added, "Luke, your replacement arrived on the same chopper."

Alone, Luke waited for the major to draw closer. The man remained in the shadows. "This weather is unbearable," he said.

Luke wiped his own brow. "The monsoons will cool it."

"Yes, they *are* coming soon, aren't they?"

"The trails will be washed out when they come and the Mekong River swollen." *Like my feet.*

"You *were* trained for this job, Breckenridge."

The words cleared his mind. *The Farm.* The months of training outside Washington. The cutting of red tape to shorten his time there to get him back to Vietnam for a third tour of duty. He had volunteered for the special assignment under military cover. A career marine assigned temporarily to the

13

CIA. He hadn't expected to end up in Laos. "Is this a downed pilot?" Luke asked.

"He's station-chief for American Intelligence in Thailand."

"Then how'd he get lost in the mountains of Laos?"

"That's what *we* want to know. Rumors have it that he had an agent there, possibly a woman, probably a double agent." The major choked on the words. "I want that agent snuffed out. Quickly. Quietly."

"For honor, God, and country, I presume?" A hacking spasm tore at Luke's rib cage and left him sweating profusely. He leaned toward the major and sucked in some air, trying futilely to snatch a clearer glimpse of the major's face.

"Take some sulfa with you for that cold," the major advised. He had taken something from his pocket and was grating it against his fingernails. "This reconnaissance mission has Washington's approval. Top secret. Direct from the president."

Which president? Luke wondered. *Past,* present, future? Or is this direct from Langley? "When do I leave, sir?"

"Before dawn."

Luke's protest died in his throat. By dawn some of his men would find their way back to base camp, exhausted and aged beyond their years. The Hmong would eat their rice and the marines their C-rations, but none would remember eating. A few would venture down to the river to bathe and then climb wearily back up the hillside, their eyes hollow, their thoughts and longings for some bamboo hut in a mountain village or a shingled two-story home in Pittsburgh or New York — as homesick as Luke was at this moment for Sauni. His men would pillow their heads on rucksacks and sleep fitfully, their rifles beside them, their hellish dreams on fallen comrades and on the officer who had deserted them without a goodbye. Would his replacement understand them? Weep with them?

"How long will it take, Major?"

"A week. Ten days at most."

"And if we don't get back before the fall of Saigon?"

The major tipped his helmet lower. "We'll withdraw our combat troops before that." The gravelly voice was hostile, monotone.

"I'll need a map," Luke said. "And a description of the man I'm to bring back. And the woman —"

"Your C. O. has your orders. Burn them before you leave."

The moon crescent escaped from its cloud cover, sending streaks of light across the major's face, revealing his piercing eyes. "As soon as you're ready, Captain," he said.

"Do I go in full garb, sir? Take my M16 with me?"

"No." The answer was emphatic. "Go lightly."

Go permanently, Luke thought.

"Take your .45, nothing else except —" He inched forward, lifted Luke's hand, and pressed a capsule into his palm. "If something goes wrong, take that."

"Cyanide? That's not the way we do it at Annapolis, sir."

"This isn't Annapolis. You'll be going partway with my pilot. He has some cargo to deliver."

"And I'm to be dumped out with the sacks of rice?"

His laugh was mocking. "Don't sound so worried, Captain. He can set that baby down on a mountaintop." Again Luke was certain a smirk covered the major's face. "You'll go on from there alone, Breckenridge, by foot to the village of Xangtiene."

"Major, that's out of our war zone — out of our area."

"That's right."

"If I don't get back, what about my family?"

"What about them? If anything happens,

16

we'll notify them."

That I'm dead? That I deserted over the lines? That I sold out to the enemy? Luke's mind stayed hazy, his distrust of the major growing by the minute. He longed to sit down on the cot in his tent and prop up his feet. But the major rejected the offer to talk inside; he had grown impatient, anxious to detail his orders — brief concise plans that left Luke no room for questions or for error. The major's voice stayed hushed, mordant, as he talked.

No, I won't remember him, Luke decided.

Finally the major said, "There's a downed American aircraft a quarter of a mile from the village. A navy Phantom jet with a twisted wing sticking out above the ground. That's your dead drop." He pulled a metal disk from his pocket and handed it to Luke.

As Luke wrapped his fingers around it, negative emotions ran wild inside him again. He coughed, a dry annoying spasm this time — a fever, not humidity, drenching him.

"Leave this by the wing tip, Breckenridge, and then get out of there. Stay low. When the agent picks it up, follow her. She'll lead you back to our man. If he's alive, bring him out."

"Not both of them?"

"I've already told you what to do with the woman."

Luke followed the riverbed for miles and then cut across a narrow trail into the safety of a dense thicket. Along the way he foraged for food and drank the last drop from his canteen. His chlorine pills were gone, but he couldn't risk a fire to boil the stagnant river water. On the third day he stumbled behind bushes, ravaged with fever and delirium, and slept. He awakened hours later, hellbent on getting out of there alive.

At daybreak Luke staggered across the final stream a quarter of a mile from Xangtiene and took the forty steps north, then twenty due west — and there she was! The plane's nose burrowed into the earth, one twisted wing protruding above the ground. *For love of country. Oh, God, what a forsaken burial ground. For nothing. All for nothing.*

Belly-crawling through the thicket to the plane, Luke secured the ciphered message under a rock, his hands clammy and mud-caked as he left it there. Coughing racked him again, immobilizing him. He lay exhausted under the tropical sun, its rays dry and barren like a California summer. *Sauni. Sauni. Sauni.* The cry was his own. He longed to hold his wife and tell her that he would resign from the military, that he'd forget the war and his commitment to it. A trickle of blood stained the ground. His blood. In surprise Luke cried out, "Sauni, I'm sick. Really sick."

Behind him someone spoke softly in English, her voice heavily accented. With great effort Luke rolled over, still coughing fitfully. Through blurred vision he saw someone towering over him with a rifle in her hand — a pretty woman with dark hair and thick-lashed brown eyes, *but not the soft corn silk hair that flowed gently around Sauni's face.* The stranger wore a khaki uniform, its ugly fullness partly concealing her graceful figure.

Luke felt no fear as she prodded him with the butt of the rifle, only fury as he lay sprawled by the wing tip. With uncanny in-tuitiveness he knew that he had been framed, betrayed. Luke coughed again; this time a violent, bloody spasm choked him. He drifted, unable to stay alert.

The woman kicked him to wakefulness, forcing Luke to meet her gaze. *Captain, U. S. Marine Corps. Admiral Breckenridge's son.* His cracked lips moved, but the words were a muddled phrase in his own mind. Silent, feverish words. She stared down at him, the sensuous smile on her lips spreading. In a low, sultry voice she said, "I've been expect-ing you, Captain Breckenridge."

Chapter 1

Saundra Breckenridge waited alone on the second floor of the bustling tearoom in Schaffhausen. Her corner table overlooked the crowded street with its quaint shops and a flower-rimmed fountain that spouted streams of sun-ribboned water. Tiny rainbows of color, tiny ribbons of memory — Luke and Pierre. She felt uneasy now wearing the red suit that had once been a favorite of Pierre Courtland. Nostalgically she fingered the gold locket Luke had given her twenty years ago.

Sauni had chosen the Swiss side of the bridge instead of the German town of Busingen for this painful reunion with Pierre. *Keep it neutral,* she told herself. *Meet his bride. Be friendly. And then say goodbye, a final goodbye.*

Her thoughts shocked her. She had never been in love with Pierre, but since his phone call inviting her to his wedding, Sauni found herself suffocating in unbearable loneliness. The emptiness was like having Luke die in Laos all over again.

Luke was the link between them: Luke and Vietnam. Luke and Pierre's brother were both casualties of the Asian conflict. Early in their acquaintance, she had reminded Pierre that her doctorate separated them; she held faculty status at the school where they met; he was a student. But the problem that plagued her was the age difference, at least a dozen miserable years that robbed her of a second chance for happiness. To Pierre, age hadn't mattered; he had fancied himself in love with her. *Attracted was a more accurate description,* she thought now. But it had ignited a marvelous friendship, an Asian connection that they both needed. They shared hours over cups of tea, Pierre's intense interests stretching like her own from skiing to French literature, from an aversion of war and politics to a love of classical music, Schubert and Strauss in particular. Sauni had cried for days when Pierre left school and went back to his executive job in Geneva. His absence thrust her into isolation — forcing her to reflect once again on memories of Luke and his shameful death.

Luke. Dear Luke. So long ago. So difficult to forget.

Sauni brushed the ruffled curtain aside and glanced out the cafe window as the Courtlands came down the cobblestone

21

street hand-in-hand. Pierre looked as striking as ever with his muscular build and confident stride, that intellectual brow of his ridged with happy crinkles. He was neither handsome nor homely, just a friendly middle-of-the-road kind of guy with a beguiling grin and a pleasant sun-bronzed face. She allowed her gaze to stray to Pierre's bride. Even in heels Robyn looked petite beside him, wisps of her auburn hair shimmering in the sun. She had legs to envy, a cute upturned nose, and eyes only for Pierre.

They disappeared through the cafe door. Moments later Pierre barreled through the tearoom, pushing his way eagerly toward Sauni, his hand gripping Robyn's and tugging her along. "Saundra Breckenridge, you look as lovely as ever."

I should, she thought. *I'm wearing your favorite color.*

He pulled her to her feet, snuffing out her breath with a hug, and whirled her around to face his bride. The two women stood at eye level, studying each other intently. Pierre kept grinning, his arm still resting on Sauni's shoulder. "Saundra, this is Robyn," he said proudly. "And, darling, this is *the older woman in my life.*"

His words cut through Sauni like a saber. She swallowed, wanting to shout out, *It*

22

didn't matter when first you knew me. It was obvious that at forty-five she was eighteen, maybe even nineteen years older than Robyn.

She forced herself to take Robyn's hands in her own and felt a slight tremor. *Had Pierre's bride dreaded this meeting too?* Sauni made another quick appraisal — blue eyes sparkling like the Rheinfall, a captivating smile, and a rippling lilt in the voice as Robyn said, "Dr. Breckenridge, we're sorry you missed our wedding."

"Call me Sauni, please." *Lessen the pain of my years.*

As Robyn pulled her hands free, Sauni tried to remember what Pierre had told her about his bride. She was an artist. No. Not that. A museum curator? An art historian? An art gallery owner — that was it. She thought of the Childe Hassam painting in the school library. "Do you carry many French paintings in your gallery?"

"It's Mother's gallery. She carries French Impressionists."

As they chatted over lunch, Sauni felt a growing warmth toward Robyn, a genuine friendship. The Courtlands looked radiant, stealing glances at each other between bites — the way she and Luke had looked at each other when they first met. She fingered her heart-shaped locket, pensive with the long-ago memories.

Pierre drew her back. "Sauni, what happened on your last trip to Washington?"

"The usual threats when I pushed for information on Luke."

"From?"

"In a roundabout way from the White House. More openly from Dad. Anytime it gets close to reelection, he gets edgy." To Robyn's frown she said, "My dad's been a senator for many years. He won by a small margin in the last election. It was enough to keep him involved in the social whirl of Washington for another term. Dad thrives on it."

"So what stirred up the ruckus about Luke this time?"

"An old family friend was in Washington recently. When she went to the Vietnam Memorial, she didn't find Luke's name there, so Myrna stormed into Daddy's office and demanded answers. Then she called me. I understood. I remember how shocked I was when I didn't find his name there myself. I told her that it was too late. To let it go. She wouldn't, of course."

Pierre whistled. "How did your dad handle that one?"

"With his usual political savvy. 'I'll look

24

into that, Myrna, right away.' He didn't count on Myrna contacting an editor friend at the *Washington Post*. That blew things wide open again. There's even talk now of removing Luke's body from Arlington Cemetery."

"What did friend Myrna say about that?"

"She went from trying to immortalize Luke as a hero to championing the petition to have him removed from Arlington."

"He should be allowed to lie there in peace," Robyn said quietly.

"In the beginning, Luke's mother insisted he wasn't buried there anyway. But someone lies in a grave marked with Luke's name."

Pierre reached across the table and squeezed Sauni's hand. "Come on, doc. They won't ostracize him from the cemetery."

"They will if the media stirs up the old rumors. Dad would rather have that happen than have his own name blackened in the Senate." She glanced hastily at Robyn, then back to Pierre. "Dad never wanted me to marry a marine. Daddy was opposed to the war in Vietnam, but at first he was proud of Luke in his own way. Then when they accused Luke of betraying his country, my father refused to defend him. Dad never asked for proof of Luke's guilt. He could have you know; he's one of the insiders in Washington."

She pushed her cup aside. "Forgive me. Here we are celebrating your marriage, and I'm burdening you with my problems."

Quickly Robyn said, "We want to help you clear Luke's name."

Sauni shook her head. "That's what I've always wanted — to squelch the awful rumors. Now I'd be happy if they'd just let Luke's body lie where it is." She covered the locket with the palm of her hand flat against her breast as though she could protect Luke that way. "I guess it was only natural for my husband to choose a military career. He would have done so even if there hadn't been an undeclared war in Vietnam. It was part of the Breckenridge tradition. But if they remove him from Arlington, it will kill his mother. Amy has grieved enough already."

Pierre beckoned to a waitress and ordered more tea for all of them. "Bring a tray of your pastries too," he added. Turning back to Sauni, he said, "We really want to help you."

"How? Can you bring Luke back? Or can you patch up things between my dad and me? We parted with pretty stiff words this time, Pierre." She brushed furiously at her tears. "My husband was a good marine, not a traitor. If Dad can't remember Luke for what he once was, what can I expect from strangers? Dad won't allow me to mention Luke's name in his presence anymore. He's family. Dad should defend Luke's memory, but he'd rather sacrifice it for votes."

"Call him," Pierre suggested. "Tell him you're sorry."

"But I'm not. That's what frightens me. I talk to my students about God's forgiveness, and I can't even show it to my own father."

"Then give yourself time to heal, Sauni."

"I've had more than twenty years. Shouldn't that be enough?"

Pierre peered over his teacup and smiled. "I'm not worried about you. This threat to remove Luke's body from Arlington has opened old wounds. It's hard on you and your dad, but you'll come to terms. You've lived under the shadow of God's wing for a long time, Sauni. You'll find your way again."

"I want to, Pierre, but those rumors about Luke threaten my father's popularity in Washington. Luke's name is an embarrassment to him now. We're like two strangers."

"Perhaps my father-in-law could help," suggested Pierre.

"Dad's an intelligence officer with the CIA," Robyn said proudly.

Saundra shrank back, a wall rising between them. "The CIA sent my husband on that fateful mission into Laos knowing he'd never come back."

"But you're not certain," Pierre reminded her. "You've wanted to know what really happened for twenty years. Maybe Robyn's dad can dig into the Langley files and come up with the answers."

"Someone would stop him. They stopped Admiral Breckenridge when he tried to investigate his son's death. The CIA proved most evasive. They denied ever knowing Luke."

Pierre avoided Robyn's eyes as he spoke. "Sauni, I'm not a fan of intelligence agencies myself. My father-in-law and I have a go-around on it often, but at least we can ask Drew's advice."

"I'm afraid to face the truth."

"On the contrary," he argued, "you're afraid of the unknown."

"What if the rumors are true? I couldn't bear that."

"Would it be any more painful than what you've gone through?" Robyn asked. "My dad is leaving for Washington next week. He's spending the weekend with us before he leaves. Come join us in Geneva," she urged. "At least talk to him."

Sauni glanced shyly at Pierre. "I'd like to see Geneva again."

"Then it's settled. We'll call you the minute we hear from Drew."

Sauni turned to Pierre's bride. "Are you liking Geneva, Robyn?"

"Oh, it's exciting to be there, but shopping is beyond me even though I speak the language. Cooking for Pierre is the real challenge; I only have one or two menus down pat." She laughed, a delightful little ripple, and Sauni smiled back.

"I burned most of Luke's first meals, too. My dad said that's why Luke put in for reassignment to Vietnam. Actually, Luke hated being at the Pentagon when his classmates from Annapolis were serving aboard ships and flying missions in Vietnam. I just couldn't hold him back."

"My brother Baylen was like that," Pierre said. "They were both devoted to the Corps, both committed to winning the war in Vietnam. But there was no retired admiral in our family. Baylen didn't have that tradition to live up to; he was just trying to please Uncle Kurt."

"I married into tradition," Sauni said. "Luke's parents boasted that as far back as the Breckenridge family could trace, there had always been a military officer in the family, a hero to brag about."

She looked away, lost in her own thoughts. "Luke wanted to be a hero. He would never disgrace that uniform, never betray his country. It's so unfair that he died for nothing." Her laugh turned brittle, bitter. "The Breckenridges listed a genealogy of officers dating back to the Civil War; some served on each side. Luke's paternal grandmother bragged that if she had a mind to do it, she could prove her right to belong to the Daughters of the American Revolution. She scolded me more than once because I never gave the family another heir." She pushed aside her teacup, smiling faintly. "If I had, my son would have surely been one of those casualties in the Persian Gulf."

"Can we give you a ride back to the college?" Pierre asked.

"Not this time. It's pleasant to walk along the Rhine. It's just three miles." *A lonely walk from now on,* she thought.

"I understand."

Did he? she wondered.

As they stood, Robyn said, "Sauni, I've been admiring your gold locket all through lunch."

"Luke gave it to me," she whispered snapping it open. "This is the way we looked when we married. A couple of young kids."

30

9266 07

"Yes, you were young."

"Twenty when I met Luke, barely twenty-one when we married. He was so dark and handsome — just back from Vietnam and assigned to the Pentagon. All he wanted was to go back and take up the cause in Vietnam again. At first my dad tried to pull strings to keep Luke in Washington, to keep him alive for me." Sadly, she whispered, "It's hard to think of Luke always being in his twenties, just twenty-five. We planned to grow old together."

"You never thought about marrying again?" Robyn asked.

Sauni blushed and glanced at Pierre. "Actually Luke and I were divorced. But I still think of myself as his widow. It never seemed right for me to marry again — not when I still loved him." She closed the locket. "I promised Luke I'd wear this until we met again."

She tried to ease Robyn's embarrassment with a smile. "I loved Luke, but I threatened him with divorce if he went back to Vietnam. I thought he'd leave the Marine Corps rather than lose me. I was wrong. In spite of what the government says, the admiral still thinks his son went back on a special mission. If that's true, then I let Luke down when he needed me most."

She linked arms with Robyn as they left the tearoom. "When Luke was overseas, I dreaded the possibility of two marine officers coming to my door. That never happened to me. They notified Luke's mother of his death instead. When she called me, I think I already knew. Time shattered for both of us the day Luke died."

Chapter 2

Drew Gregory loved Geneva, that international city surrounded by hills and the towering Alps — a city that hosted diplomats and watchmakers with equal poise. It was a thriving metropolis with the Rhone River flowing by historic buildings on its way to the Mediterranean. Toward the north, castles and vineyards dotted the towns along the lake shore. Over the years he'd stopped many times in Geneva, pleasant visits, but now with Robyn and Pierre living there it was like going home.

He hadn't seen them since the wedding — his own choice. "Give yourselves some time alone," he had told them. But Drew hadn't counted on two whole months. He was eager to see Robyn again, even more since last night's frantic phone call. "Dad, I really need your help," she had said. "No, I can't explain over the telephone." He called the airport immediately and grabbed an earlier flight, not even taking time to call Robyn back to tell her that he was flying in on Wednesday.

From the moment of takeoff at Heathrow

Airport and the flight across the English Channel, he counted the minutes until the plane circled wide over the crescent-shaped Lac Leman. As they banked into the rain-filled sky, the glittering lights of Geneva and the Palais des Nations rose to meet him. Somewhere down there — an hour from the airport — was the gray stone apartment where Robyn lived.

The muscles of Drew's stomach tightened. He had piloted planes for years, even for the Agency on rare occasions, but fatherhood gave him a peptic tightness. He conjured up countless problems that might be bothering her: homesickness, a lack of funds, her first quarrel with Pierre. No. That would have come sooner, he decided with a chuckle, but he still worried about the marriage turning sour. Pierre and Robyn had only known each other a few weeks — a romantic whirlwind courtship much like his own with Miriam. And he knew all too well how that marriage had shattered.

The Swissair jet touched down on the wet tarmac and skimmed the runway, jolting to a stop. Grabbing his briefcase and raincoat, Drew headed for the exit before anyone could block the aisle. He was tall and broad-shouldered enough to barrel his way to the baggage counter ahead of others, but his thoughts remained on those hectic days before Robyn's wedding. When others had tried to plan the ceremony, she had threatened to call it off or wait for springtime to marry when the snows of winter had melted.

Drew smiled about it now as he hailed a taxi, but it wasn't just Robyn's prenuptial jitters. Miriam had demanded a fashionable wedding, the best of everything for Robyn while Pierre's aunt insisted that her home in Paris was the only place for a stylish wedding. Adding to the tension, Pierre and Drew had argued heatedly about politics and the Swiss Reformation. Finally, for Robyn's sake, they called a truce — no more arguments about religion or intelligence work. At the last minute friends of Pierre had offered their home near Montreux for the ceremony. Their living room window faced the dazzling snow-white Mt. Blanc, Robyn's touch with Heidi's Alps.

It had turned into an international affair with guests flying in from Paris and London. The guest who surprised Drew the most was his old friend, Uriah Kendall. Uriah appeared as the ceremony began, a well-groomed man, his sandy hair a powdery gray, the grief lines around his eyes deeper now. But Uriah slipped away before the reception — before Drew could even speak to him.

As Drew's taxi sped through the rain-splattered streets of Geneva, he smiled at the memory of that special moment when he had stood at the top of the stairs with his daughter's arm tucked in his. She had indeed looked like a princess, exquisite in the lace-trimmed gown Miriam had purchased. They had walked slowly down the spiral stairs to the sounds of a violin playing Schubert's Unfinished Symphony. Pierre had waited for them at the foot of the stairs, his smile widening as Robyn reached him.

No, Drew thought as he stepped from the taxi to the rain-swept sidewalk, *too much love exists between Robyn and Pierre to have soured so quickly*. With an unexpected burst of generosity, he tipped the taxi driver, grabbed his luggage, and raced beneath the dripping elms to the apartment complex. He buzzed, and as he heard Robyn's voice, he said, "Princess, it's Dad. I couldn't wait until Friday to see you."

Drew dropped his luggage as Robyn ran down the steps straight into his arms. "You should have called us," she scolded. "We could have met you at the airport."

"I'm glad I didn't. My welcome here was worth it all."

They climbed the steps, arm in arm. When they reached Pierre, he took Drew's luggage.

"Sir, good to see you."

Pierre looked as if he had dressed hurriedly. His hair was unruly, his shirt only partly buttoned. They followed Pierre into the apartment. "Well, here it is," Robyn said.

The living room rug was a burnt orange with flecks of bright green and purple all through it, the fluorescent colors so shocking that Drew stared in disbelief. Still, it was a man's room, the expensive furnishings practical. Three unmatched occasional chairs, a hassock, and a large leather sofa blocked out some of the wild pattern in the rug. He wondered if the place came furnished or if his son-in-law, like himself, had little flair for interior decorating.

"We're looking for another place, Dad. We'd like to settle in one of the small towns facing the lake."

Pierre ruffled her hair. "Your daughter has definite ideas. A house that faces Mt. Blanc. A big yard for kids. Bathrooms, lots of bathrooms. And a room reserved for you and another one for Miriam."

"But we'll hate to leave here," Robyn said. "You kind of get used to the rug after a while. Besides we don't spend that much time in the living room — not yet at least."

Robyn stole a glance at Pierre. He winked

back as she led Drew across the room to the portrait of Pierre's parents hanging on the wall beside the stereo. Pierre definitely resembled his father.

"Come on, Dad. I'll show you where you're going to stay."

She coaxed him into a narrow room with a rollaway bed, a small dresser, a lounge chair, and a huge desk cluttered with her art books. She bounced on the mattress. "It's comfortable. You won't mind?" She seemed alarmed now. "Would you rather use our room? Pierre and I could rug out."

"Sleep on the floor?" he asked. "No, this is fine." He tossed his briefcase on the bed and looked around for a clothes closet.

"You'll have to hang your things in our room."

He followed her into the bedroom, and there the masculinity of the apartment was gone. French perfume permeated the senses. Crisp lace curtains hung in the windows. Even the lamps were trimmed with wide bows. And in the middle of the pink queen-sized comforter lay a tiny kitten purring softly.

"I never had a cat before," she said happily as Drew hung his clothes in their closet. "Mother despised them. But I found this little fellow prowling around in the yard. So he's mine now. Keepers. Do you like his name?"

Drew acknowledged the kitten with a pat on its head before he stowed the suitcase back in the corner of the closet next to Pierre's army uniform and rifle. The sight of them startled him. He had forgotten that Pierre was committed to the Swiss military until he was fifty. "I hope that thing's not loaded," Drew said.

"Pierre is very careful, Dad. And before you go to bed, be sure your pistol is unloaded."

He cupped her chin. "*I'm* very cautious, too."

"Dad, I wish you were as vigilant at keeping old friends."

"What's that supposed to mean?"

"Mother worries that you lost touch with Uriah Kendall."

"It's a dead friendship since he lost his wife Olivia."

"Then you really haven't heard from him lately?"

"Since your wedding? No. He won't return my phone calls, and so far he's ignored my letters. I wanted to thank him for coming."

"Did you know he buys paintings from Mother's gallery?"

"He does? Before the wedding or after?"

"Both. She never sees him, but one of his sons flies out, chooses an expensive painting, pays cash — thousands — and is gone again. Uriah gave us a place setting of china and a copy of his wife's last suspense novel for a wedding present." Robyn pointed to her desk. "Olivia was very gifted."

Drew picked up the book and read the inscription: "To the Courtlands — May your lives together be as joyful and full as mine with Olivia. Uriah T. Kendall."

"He was devoted to her. At least, it looked that way, but her death was shrouded in mystery and made a recluse out of Uriah. We lost touch after that. I was surprised to see him at the wedding."

"Mother invited everyone."

Again Drew fingered the cover of Olivia's book. "Is that why you sent for me, Robyn — so I'd make amends with an old friend?"

She frowned. "Not really. But it's a good idea, isn't it?"

"I'll try phoning him again when I'm in the States. He lives on the Maryland side not far from Langley."

Her frown deepened. "Do that, Daddy. Coming to my wedding may have been his overture to friendship. Or is he an old CIA buddy who needed to get in touch with you?"

"Hardly. He's British. Remember?" Her

question annoyed him. Uriah lived near the intelligence community, but he had never been part of it. From the living room Pierre had upped the stereo. The powerful strands of Meyerbeer's "Coronation March" vibrated through the apartment, drowning out the need to explain Uriah's friendship.

She smiled. "Sorry, Dad. Pierre likes classical, loud when he wants my attention. French composers. Austrians. Germans. All of them."

"That should please your mother."

"The volume doesn't." She patted his cheek. "I'll go make some sandwiches while you freshen up. You must be famished."

"I am now that you mention it."

Robyn pointed to the bathroom as she left him. Again the room and the fragrance seemed feminine. A pastel shower curtain and towel sets blended; a row of scented bottles lined the counter beside Pierre's shaving lotion. Two toothbrushes lay side by side; two silk dressing gowns hung on the hook behind the door. Drew sensed happiness in this home, but still he worried. Why was she so reluctant to spring her problem on him?

Back in the living room, Drew found Robyn sitting on the floor by the sofa, her well-shaped legs curled beneath her, her head resting against Pierre's knee; gently his fingers brushed her shiny auburn hair. Drew felt like an intruder, as though he had stepped into a romantic hideaway that needed no guests.

"Sit down, Dad, and have a sandwich."

The occasional chair was surprisingly comfortable as Drew eased his lanky body into it. Pierre and Robyn smiled, their faces untroubled. He waited, but the conversation steered quickly to Pierre's executive job at the medical corporation and then to Robyn's culinary failures in their tiny kitchen. "We've gone out to eat a lot," Pierre said. "It's that or a burnt offering."

"My cooking was not the only reason."

"No," he admitted. "I keep long hours at the office, almost as many as Robyn spends at the Museum of Art and History studying Italian and Dutch paintings."

"Robyn," Drew cautioned, "maybe you ought to buy a cookbook and concentrate on that instead."

"Is that what you told mother to do?"

"Your mother was a good cook when I married her."

"I like museums better than cooking. Besides, Pierre wants me to learn everything I can at the Petit Palais."

"She's right, Drew."

"It's an old mansion that's been turned into a museum," Robyn said excitedly. "The fortification rooms and crypts are filled with French Impressionists, Postimpressionists, and Fauve artists."

"This is your father, Robyn," Drew said dryly. "Not your mother. Go slowly when you're throwing the art world at me."

"It's not the artists so much, Dad. We're impressed with the way they've utilized the rooms at the Petit Palais. We want to do the same thing at the von Tonner mansion and put the baron's magnificent art collection on display."

"She's right again, Drew. The baron's place may become a national monument after all, thanks to your brother's good advice."

"Aaron? Lately my brother's advice only leads to trouble."

"The lawyers here were pushing for proof of ownership of the von Tonner estate. And Aaron — well, he was tied in with Ingrid von Tonner, so I talked to him."

"Aaron doesn't know anything about German law."

"True, but he knew enough to realize that the divorce settlement between Ingrid and the baron might be illegal. Felix signed it less than a month before Ingrid committed him to the clinic in Cannes with a diagnosis of dementia. If we can obtain the records, we can verify that Felix wasn't mentally capable of signing those divorce papers."

Drew drummed his fingers on the end table as Pierre continued, "If the courts throw out Ingrid's divorce agreement, then the baron owns everything, and his will would still be in effect."

"Dad, the baron may have left everything to Pierre."

Pierre ruffled her hair in a gentle reprimand. "Felix had many interests. Show horses, racing horses. The preservation of the Black Forest. His concerns included reseeding the land and the care of the show horse when its use ran out." His eyes shadowed. "I only wish the baroness had cared as much for Felix."

"I still think Pierre's the heir to a mansion."

He grinned. "I'm an heir to a mansion all right, Robyn, but not necessarily one on the Rhine." He looked squarely at Drew. "I really do own a place in Heaven, and I intend to occupy it someday."

That's it. That's the problem that Robyn referred to on the phone. They've brought me here to saddle me with a sermon. But the threat slipped away as Robyn said, "I still think Felix will leave his art collection to you,

Pierre. He promised you."

"Honey," Drew said dryly, "trying to possess the baron's art collection in Felix's lifetime destroyed Ingrid and your uncle."

"What destroyed them, sir, was art fraud."

"And so far, Pierre, my brother has gotten by with it."

Pierre's grip tightened on Robyn's hand. "Interpol is still gathering information against him. It may take another slip-up on his part, but he'll be held accountable for the von Tonner fraud."

A troubled frown appeared on Robyn's brow. "No matter what happens to Uncle Aaron," she whispered, "we obtained a reprieve for the baron. The courts assigned Pierre as his guardian, and they let us take Felix back to his own home to live, at least for now."

Pierre nodded. "The Klees are taking good care of him."

Drew felt no hunger, but he leaned forward and took one of Robyn's sandwiches. *Come on, Princess,* he urged silently. *Tell me. What was it you couldn't discuss over the phone last night? Not my brother Aaron. Was it really Aaron?*

He almost choked on the last bite of roast beef. *A yard for kids,* Pierre had said. *Oh, no, Robyn. Not that. You're not pregnant? You a mother. Me a grandfather. No, you two need more time — more time to get acquainted.*

Robyn watched him in silence, her eyes glowing. Miriam's eyes had shone like that the day she discovered she was pregnant, pregnant with Robyn.

"What's wrong, Dad? You look like you've lost your best friend."

"Or was it the sandwich?" Pierre teased.

Drew wiped his mouth. "You haven't asked me why I came early."

"We didn't have to, Daddy. You came because of my phone call." She reached her hand up, and Pierre took it. They exchanged glances.

"Is this some kind of an announcement?" Drew asked.

Robyn giggled. "No, Dad. Nothing like that. Not yet. We just want you to get into the files at Langley for us."

Drew actually laughed. "Some particular file, Robyn?"

"Yes, the one on Luke Breckenridge."

"Luke Breckenridge? Am I supposed to know him?"

"We don't know him either," Pierre explained, "but we promised a friend that you'd help us."

"You're talking about one of the most formidable buildings in the Washington area.

46

One doesn't just walk into Langley and check out a file. It's not a public library. Who is this man?"

Robyn looked visibly disappointed. Pierre winced, his hand on her shoulder. "Breckenridge served in Vietnam. A captain in the Marine Corps. He died in Southeast Asia — like my brother Baylen did — more than twenty years ago."

"A marine? Then why would Langley have a file on him?"

"His wife thinks he was on a mission for them when he died."

"If so," Drew said quietly, "the records are classified."

"I'm sure they are, sir. But rumor has it that Luke committed treason on that mission. You have friends at Langley —"

"I want to keep their friendship. I can't ask them to look into classified material. It isn't done that way. Documents like that — if they do exist — are available to very few."

Drew thought of the sprawling CIA complex and its state-of-the-art monitoring system: closed circuit television cameras and chain-link fences topped with barbed wire. He slumped deeper into the cushions of the chair. *I've got two problems. A brother who hates my guts and a dead marine who sold out his country. No, four problems — with these crazy kids wanting me to do the impossible for them.* "Who told you he was on an intelligence mission?"

"His widow, sir. Or the one who would have been his widow. They were divorced shortly before his death."

"Pierre, perhaps she got the facts wrong."

"One thing is certain — he went to Vietnam in a marine's uniform. Three tours of duty actually. He died there. Saundra Breckenridge has copies of his death certificate. But Luke's name isn't on the Vietnam Memorial Wall."

Drew hid his irritation. "Why not?"

"She was told that traitors don't get their names on memorials. Surely your friends at Langley will know if he was a traitor. Can't you find out that much for us?"

He tried to out-stare Pierre as his son-in-law asked, "Tell me, Drew. Things like this do happen, don't they? Men sacrificed for some mission and then a government coverup?"

Wait, Pierre. Don't press me. We called a truce, remember. No politics. No religion. We'd stay clear of those topics. "Sometimes men sacrifice themselves — their right to life and family for the good of the Corps or the Agency. A willing sacrifice or a heroic moment of putting their life on the line."

"What if someone deliberately sacrificed Luke in a CIA coverup?"

Coldly Drew said, "Pierre, I'm still not in a position to help you. I'm with the London embassy, remember?"

"And we're family. At least be honest with us. Admit who you are and what you are. We know it anyway."

Drew couldn't explain his commitment to a code of silence. He rubbed the back of his neck. "When you called yesterday and said something was wrong, I was worried. I came at once because I thought something had happened between you two."

"Just good things," Pierre said. "Robyn is the best thing that ever happened to me." He picked up the last of the sandwiches and nibbled at it. "Luke Breckenridge's death and betrayal was the worst thing that ever happened to Sauni. If she could just know where he died — how he died. Is that too much to ask?"

"Dad, please help us trace Luke's final hours. Can't you think of anyone in Washington who might help us?"

Chad Kaminsky kept coming to mind. And Porter Deven in Paris. He felt relieved to offer them something. "I can ask Porter before I leave for Washington. He might have some suggestions."

"Drew, Sauni is coming Friday to meet you. If there's nothing you or Porter can do, then I'll talk to my uncle at Interpol."

Why not the president? Drew thought. *Start with the top and work down.* He sighed. "Princess, I have a problem for you, too. I'd like to see your mother while I'm in the States."

"Do you need an excuse to do that?"

"A better one than I have," he admitted.

"Pierre and I ordered a wedding album for Mother's birthday. You could hand deliver it for us."

He laughed. "A fly-for-hire postman. That's six thousand extra miles round trip from Langley. Do you think it would work?"

"It's worth a try. At least it will get you to the door of Mother's art gallery. But it won't guarantee getting inside."

"And it won't build a lasting relationship," he said woefully.

"Mother says it's too late for that."

Pierre laughed. "It's never too late. In the morning I'll ask my secretary to call the airline and revamp your ticket. But, sir, are you planning to see your brother this trip, too?"

"Not intentionally, but I'm putting the old farm up for sale. If Aaron gets wind of that, we'll run into each other."

"That's not a good idea, sir."

"Selling the place? Or seeing my brother?"

"Both. Interpol and Swiss and German Intelligence are still trying to wrap up a case against him for art fraud."

"Dad, Uncle Aaron blames you for everything. If you take the farm away from him, too . . ."

Drew wanted to reach out and take her hand to comfort her. Aaron wouldn't need the farm for long, not if Interpol had its way. Drew's voice sounded strained as he said, "Princess, your uncle would only gamble the farm away. Your mother doesn't want it; she never did. She despised the cold, snowbound winters. And it's unlikely that you and Pierre will ever want to live there."

"What about you?"

Drew shrugged. He loved the farm, even the winters when the night skies were clear and brilliant, the stars within reach. But the farm would be empty without his Irish mother there. "Honey, I've spent so much of my life in Europe now that I'll never go back."

"But you love the old place."

"I love the memories."

"Uncle Aaron wants the farm."

"He wants it because it belongs to me, Princess."

"Drew," Pierre warned, "Aaron's threats against you are real. If you see him this trip,

51

don't turn your shoulder blades to him. He can't reason where you're concerned. He'd rather have you dead."

"Yet you accepted his legal advice?"

"Yes," Pierre admitted, "and it helped us. But in Aaron's twisted thinking, he blames you for Ingrid von Tonner's death and Miriam for the humiliating art fraud scandal."

"That sounds like my brother. He's an expert at twisting justice." Drew smiled wanly for Robyn's benefit. "But he's been good to my daughter, Pierre. That's my only good memory of him."

Chapter 3

Saundra Breckenridge unlocked the apartment with Robyn's key and stepped inside. Drew Gregory stood as she came into the room, a polite, composed expression on his face. She sensed the restraint in his greeting — a guarded man, reluctant to meet her, perhaps uneasy about his daughter's promises. Sauni regretted coming, regretted trying to lure this towering stranger into the fight to honor Luke's memory. Gregory with his intelligent eyes and thick brows could no more chisel Luke's name on the Memorial Wall in Washington than she could.

Her gaze went to the masculine hand shaking hers. There was a sense of security in that firm grip, a strong hand with a black onyx ring on one finger. Gregory didn't fit her image of an intelligence officer — gruff, shrewd, devious, a shifty cloak-and-dagger man. Instead, he appeared nonchalant, even casual in his gray flannels, a dress shirt unbuttoned at the neck, a dark blue cardigan, and highly polished shoes like Luke had always worn. She forced herself to look at his intense gray-blue eyes, sympathetic now as they appraised her.

"I'm sorry," she said. "I didn't realize anyone was home."

He looked around the compact room and pointed to a chair. As she took it, he eased into the one facing her, gently scooping the kitten onto his lap. His actions were unhurried, an ordinary man caught in the middle years, older than she, wiser perhaps.

"Dr. Breckenridge, I will vacate my room so you can have a place to stay. I'll take the sofa," he offered.

"Don't do that. I've already checked into the Mon-Repos. It gives me easy access to the airport and metro station. I've stayed there before when I visited —"

"Pierre?"

"Yes," she said, embarrassed.

"Then you've known each other for some time?"

His tone stayed on an even keel, neither threatening nor accusing, but she felt obliged to explain. "We met when he came to Busingen to study."

The crinkle lines around Drew's eyes deepened. "Then you're a theology professor?" He visibly retreated.

"Oh, no. French literature mostly. Pierre was an excellent student, an avid reader."

54

He seemed to be waiting, her explanation not enough. "We both lost someone in Vietnam," she said softly.

"Yes, Robyn told me." He was scratching the kitten behind the ear, and the purr rose between them.

Shyly, she said, "It's been more than twenty years, but at times it seems like it just happened. Pierre understood. He invited me to holiday in Geneva. I — I wanted to ski and see more of Switzerland. He was such a gracious host."

"Did my daughter break up something special?"

"No. No, Mr. Gregory. Pierre and I could never be more than friends. We were bound by our loss, nothing more."

She felt herself flushing under his scrutiny, certain that he only half believed her. "Mrs. Breckenridge, how long have you and Robyn been friends?"

"We met only once."

A hint of a smile formed on his lips.

"She's so easy to know."

One thick brow arched. "And she made promises to you that I may not be able to keep."

"And that bothers you?"

"Yes. I want to please Robyn. We've been reunited only these past few months — after sixteen years' separation."

"Robyn mentioned it."

"I've been an absentee father for all those years, but now I'd do anything for Robyn. Anything in my power."

"She said you have connections in Washington."

He nodded. "Mrs. Breckenridge, Robyn tells me your father and Luke's father have been unable to help you. What do you think I can do?"

She went rigid, sucking at her lower lip, wishing that the Courtlands would crash through the door. She wanted to scream at them, *What have you gotten me into?*

"When you put it that way, Mr. Gregory, nothing. If a senator and an admiral couldn't crash the fortress in Washington, you certainly won't."

Suddenly her legs went jellyfish wobbly. *This man knows all about Luke. Knows exactly what happened. That guileless face is only a mask. Pierre, Robyn,* she repeated to herself, *what have you gotten me into?*

"Mrs. Breckenridge . . ."

She blinked against her pain, her disappointment.

"Your husband was a marine," Drew said. "I'm an old army man myself. I go back a war or two."

"But you lived in Washington. I understand you've been part of the intelligence community for years. You know the political scene. Perhaps you've heard Luke's name tossed around."

"Perhaps," he said.

"Luther Walton Breckenridge the fourth. Does it ring any bells for you, Mr. Gregory?"

"Luke — for whom the bells toll. War creates many casualties," he said quietly. "Unfortunately, their names are forgotten too quickly."

"I want people to remember Luke, but not in dishonor. There's been a long line of Breckenridge heroes." Her voice rose with indignation. "But not Luke. He's a traitor according to Washington. Yet I know he was a good decent marine who loved his country."

"I don't know much about the Marine Corps, Mrs. Breckenridge. I just have a few friends who served with them. That's all."

"Luke died on an intelligence mission."

"You're certain of that? Marine intelligence?"

"No." Her tone fell flat. "Central Intelligence."

"How would you know that?" he asked kindly.

"Luke's friends. Some of the men who

served with him called me when they rotated back home. They told me what happened."

"Perhaps Luke's friends wanted to ease your pain."

"Their pain, too. They were classmates at Annapolis. All of them honorable men, especially Allen Fraylund. Allen knew that Luke and I were divorced. He didn't have to look me up, but he did."

Drew waited in silence.

"Allen was guarded in what he said, but he told me Luke didn't die in Vietnam. He was killed in Laos. It didn't make sense. Why did the government lie?"

"Were any of Luke's friends with him when he died?"

She leaned against the chair. "None of them saw him die, if that's what you mean. Luke had been in Vietnam. For a long time that's where we thought he was killed. But Allen and another friend, Craig, swore that Luke had been sent to Laos a few weeks before his death."

"Confirmed?"

"Yes, after Luke's dad stormed Capitol Hill for weeks. Then my dad got involved reluctantly. Finally the government reissued a statement that Luke died behind enemy lines in Laos." Her sigh erupted from deep within her. "Mr. Gregory, that was two years *after* he was killed."

"A simple error in paperwork. Things like that happen."

"Simple? Luke was our whole life. They didn't say Luke was killed in action, not the second time. *He died behind enemy lines.* This seemed to be quite significant to the government."

"That's mere terminology. You're relying too much on what Luke's friends said. Bits and pieces of information."

She dug her long polished nails into the cushion. "Luke's father wouldn't give up. He bombarded Washington for information. All he ever got were doors slammed in his face. Then he was pressured into retiring."

"Early retirements are common after long years of service."

"Are they? Then why did the government wait until after his retirement to call him in and warn him against pursuing information on Luke? When the admiral refused, he was told that Luke had carried classified material across the enemy line to a foreign agent — secrets that wrought unbelievable damage to the war effort. Imagine, telling a father that his son was a spy."

Drew leaned forward frowning. "Was he?"

She wanted to shout back, *No, no, no. Not Luke.* One of her nails split on the cushion.

She picked at it.

"Mrs. Breckenridge, was your husband a spy?"

"I don't know," she whispered back. "Not the Luke I knew. Not the Luke I loved." She faced Drew again. "He had been buried with military honors, and now they were telling his dad that his son was a traitor. An investigative reporter in Washington got wind of the story and made front-page copy of it. The shame and humiliation almost killed his parents and me."

"They believed it?"

"No, but others did."

The blue of Gregory's eyes darkened. "Luke's friends never told you anything about that final mission?" he asked.

"Not until we talked to Duc Thuy Tran, a Vietnamese soldier who had served under Luke."

"In Vietnam?"

"In Laos. Duc Tran was out on patrol the night Luke left. When Duc got back to the base camp, Luke was gone. The C. O. told the men that Luke had been transferred for his health. According to Duc, at least that's what Allen told us, Luke was having trouble with his feet and chest. Jungle rot and pneumonia probably."

"Were you able to confirm that?"

Why go on? she wondered. *Drew doesn't believe me. He never will. I'm feeding him information to use against me when he goes to Washington — to Langley. If Drew's part of the coverup, he could make it more difficult for Luke's parents.*

"Mrs. Breckenridge," she heard him say, "do you have proof that he was rotated out for his health?"

She focused on him again, drained at the relentless questions. "There's no record of Luke being sent to an evac. station or into Tokyo or Clark Air Force Base or anywhere else for that matter. No records at all. Later Luke's commanding officer told Tran that Luke had been flown home." She smiled faintly. "For several years Duc didn't know my husband had died, not until Duc moved to the States."

"Did you ever speak personally to this Duc Tran?"

"Yes, after Allen told me about him, we located Duc in a refugee camp in Thailand. It took Luke's parents five years to get through the red tape, but they finally sponsored Duc's move to Los Angeles. That's when we learned for certain that Luke had left the base camp in Laos under mysterious circumstances."

"Your in-laws paid the man's way to this

country. He'd tell them anything they wanted to hear."

"Duc respected my husband. I think he told us the truth."

"Still Tran was your husband's friend. It would be within his culture to protect Luke. You told me Luke was not well. Perhaps his illness sent him over the deep end. It happens in war. Maybe Luke sold out to win a conflict he had come to hate."

She struggled for words to convince him. "Tran would have despised a traitor, but he agreed with me — Luke was not the kind of man to go off the deep end."

She fell silent until Pierre and Robyn burst through the front door. Sauni leaped out of her chair, tumbling briefly into Robyn's arms and lingering for a moment more in Pierre's.

"Well," Robyn said excitedly. "I see you two have met. Is Dad going to help you?"

"No," Sauni said. "Mr. Gregory is able perhaps — but reluctant for sure."

Pierre's face clouded. "Really?"

The kitten was in Robyn's arms now, purring contentedly. "Keepers, I thought you were going to keep peace between these two." The kitten stopped purring and licked its paw.

"Did you tell Drew everything?" Pierre asked. "Does he know your husband trained at The Farm before his third tour of duty?"

Sauni shook her head. "He didn't ask about Luke's training with the CIA."

"And *she* never mentioned it," said Drew.

Robyn put her hands to her hips. "Enough is enough. It's okay, Dad, if you can't help us, but tell *us* what to do."

"Robyn," he said gently, "there's really nothing I can do. Nothing any of us can do. It all happened a long time ago."

"I know," Saundra said. "But since they left Luke's name off the Wall, the pain never seems to go away. And now with this cry to remove his body from Arlington, the humiliation is unbearable."

"Dad, Sauni attended the memorial dedication at the National Cathedral. When volunteers read all 58,000 names, she kept hoping, praying that Luke's name would be included. It wasn't, Dad."

"The admiral and I took turns dozing," Sauni added, "but for the most part we stayed awake for those fifty-six hours. They never read Luke's name, Mr. Gregory. We heard name after name — even some of Luke's friends — but they never read Luke's name."

She was surprised that she didn't weep. She had always wept at that memory before, but this time Drew Gregory had tears in his eyes. "None of this would have come up again, Mr. Gregory, except for that petition being circulated in Washington — the attempt to have Luke's body removed from Arlington Cemetery."

He frowned in disgust. "They won't do that."

"I think you're wrong," Pierre said. "The public outcry against Luke is growing ever since the rumors of his betrayal surfaced again."

"The White House will stop it, Pierre."

"Why, Drew? Right now the media is off your President's back and blasting a dead war hero instead. Reburial won't affect Luke. Nothing can ever hurt him again. But it will destroy his family."

Chapter 4

Sauni Breckenridge's slender fingers tugged at a strand of hair caught in her heart-shaped locket. She was attractive and vulnerable with skin as smooth as satin and lipstick that blended with the velvet rust suit she was wearing. Flaxen hair — like corn silk — fell to her shoulders, softly around her pensive face. Drew expected her to cry, but perhaps there were no tears left.

He softened as he studied her movements. "Mrs. Breckenridge, why don't you start from the beginning? Tell me everything."

"From the day I met Luke? That's ever so long ago."

"Then it's a good starting place. I want to know as much as I can about your husband before I go to Washington."

"Oh, Dad, you're really going to help her?"

"I can't promise that, Robyn. I can't do anything unless I know the whole story — exactly as Sauni remembers it."

Sauni lifted her face until their eyes met. "Drew, did you ever see Washington when the cherry blossoms were in full bloom?"

65

"Many times. There's nothing more spectacular, is there?"

"It looked just that way the day I met Luke. I was twenty, a junior at Georgetown University with little more to worry about than going to the spring dance. The Potomac flowed like always. Visitors swarmed along the broad streets of the city. The Capitol's dome gleamed in the warm sun. And pink and white cherry blossoms reflected in the shallow waters of the Tidal Basin — the Thomas Jefferson Monument in the center, the trees framing it on either side." A fragile smile touched her lips. "Time stood still for me only twice in my life, Drew. The day I first met Luther on the steps of the Capitol and the day I heard he died."

Washington, D. C. April, 1971

Washington looked brilliant in cherry blossoms as Saundra Summers rushed into her father's office on Capitol Hill. Glenn Summers sat hunched at his desk as though even in solitude he were apologizing for his willowy form. At moments like this, she pitied him, sitting alone, surrounded by paperwork and political problems. The senator was seldom home, rarely at play — a serious, apathetic man with sallow skin from too much indoor living.

66

"Dad! Dad, may I come in?"

He looked up startled, his permanently ridged brow furrowing more. His deep voice boomed across the room. "What's wrong, my pet?"

"Dad, my date for the spring dance fell through."

A twinkle brightened his gray eyes as he leaned back against his chair. "I thought you were going to tell me the war was over."

"It's the war that ruined my date. He'll be shipped out to Vietnam *before the dance.* Can't you do something?"

"Why not get yourself another date?"

"All the handsome eligibles are shipping out to Asia."

Outside, they could hear the familiar shouts of the protest marchers, the draft-card burners. "Go out there and get one of those young demonstrators and dress him up for the ball. At least it would keep him off the street for a few hours."

"Be serious, Dad. The President will be at the dance. And the First Lady. All of Washington will be there."

"I hope not."

"I can't miss it no matter what's going on in Southeast Asia."

He tapped his pen against the desk, his eyes sad and unsmiling now. She knew that look. His million-dollar lecture on her self-centeredness would follow. "Men are sacrificing their lives for us, Saundra. Does the young man who's going to Vietnam mean so little to you, nothing more than a dancing partner?" His tone sharpened. "If the dance is so important, go with Mother and me."

"I want my *own* date." She slumped into the chair. "The war is ruining everything for me."

An acquiescent smile crossed his face. "I know just the man for you. The junior senator from Georgia."

She brightened. "Who?"

"I can't remember his name right now. And I must get back to work. My constituency is creating a ruckus about this war. They want us out of Vietnam, and I have to come to a working agreement with my voters if I'm to be reelected in the fall." More worry lines puckered his brow. "President Johnson was so bent on stamping out communism he couldn't keep his focus on our horrendous losses. And Nixon — Nixon wants to bring the boys home diplomatically. He just won't say which year. I won't oppose him, but I want votes in the fall."

"All I want," she said, "is a date for next Saturday."

"And more money for a new gown?"

"That would be nice. Can you spare some?"

"Impossible. Your mother hit me for two hundred this morning."

"Just thought I'd try."

"Try getting a job instead."

"I'm at university full time."

"May I remind you, my pet, I —"

"I know. You worked your way through law school."

The senator stood and shoved some papers into his briefcase. "Come along. Walk me over to the Capitol building. It'll do you good to spend some time with your old dad."

They linked arms. "Dad, are you in session the rest of the day?"

"Every day," he said. "It's my job, remember? It keeps you and your mother in stylish clothes and you at the university."

She had grown up in this city, yet never ceased to thrill at the gleaming white Capitol nor to take pride in her father's position. She had, he often reminded her, everything she wanted. *Except a proper escort for the ball.*

For a few moments after mounting the steps to the Capitol, they browsed through the Rotunda from one marvelous oil painting to another. Suddenly, her father leaned down and kissed her on the cheek. "I will see you this evening, my pet."

Would he? His hours were erratic, his devotion more to the job than to his marriage. Her parents followed separate lifestyles, coming together mostly for meals and the Washington parties. They seemed content with this arrangement, rarely arguing, rarely together long enough to do so. But they both doted on her.

As her father disappeared, she rushed down the corridor past the security guards and out of the Capitol. Racing down the steps, she tripped and tumbled forward. Herculean arms broke her fall and steadied her. "Whoa there," the young man said as though he were reining in his favorite mare.

You can let go now, she thought indignantly. But as he held on, his uniform's rough wool felt warm and protective against her cheek. She bent her head back and looked up into the strong handsome face of a six-foot-two marine — with a row of ribbons across his chest. She stood there mesmerized by his hypnotic dark eyes.

"Well," he said, still gripping her arms, "my time in Washington may have meaning after all."

"Really?" she asked, pulling free.

He whipped his dress cap back into place, a rim of sandy hair showing beneath it, and guided her the rest of the way down the steps, his hand firmly holding her elbow.

"I can make it on my own," she said.

"But I don't want you to go alone."

And I don't really want to. She blushed. "I must go, Lieutenant, before you forget what you came for."

"Oh, I'm Luke Breckenridge, the Pentagon errand boy. And you?"

"I'm Sauni. Just Sauni."

"Sauni, don't go away. I'll be right back after I deliver a message to a pompous senator, a stodgy old boy. The Pentagon wants more money to keep the war in Vietnam going, and the senator wants us out of there — before I can get back to the war and be a hero."

His voice stayed chipper as he said, "Men like Senator Summers anger me. They're as big a hindrance to the war effort as those protest marchers across the street."

He gently pushed her mouth closed with the back of his hand. "You'll catch a fly," he said. "What's wrong?"

"Nothing. Just go see your stodgy senator. I'm going home."

"Not until you promise to go to the Ford Theater with me on Friday. I've got tickets for two — and the weekend free."

Did they ship your date out, too? she wondered. "The Ford Theater Friday? I can do

71

that — on one condition."

He saluted. "Name it."

"Go to the spring dance with me — next Saturday."

"Me? Why, I would be honored to take you. That is — if my transfer orders don't come through before that."

"To where?"

"Back to Vietnam. Where else? If it hadn't been for my dad, the admiral, I'd be there with my outfit now." His eyes shadowed. "Some of my best friends and classmates are still out there on ships; others are advising the south Vietnamese on how to win the war. Several of my buddies have died." He glanced back up the Capitol steps. "And for what? Certainly not for Senator Summers."

She turned abruptly. "Wait," he said. "Where do I pick you up?"

"You already did."

"But I mean for Friday — for our evening at the theater."

She wrote down her name and phone number, laughing as she handed it to him. "We live in Georgetown. Call for directions."

He did a double take. "Saundra Summers?"

"Yes. Or Saundra Pompous Summers, if you prefer."

Luke recovered quickly. "You're stuck with a senator! I'm stuck with an admiral. I'll see you Friday. Seven o'clock."

She waited on the tree-lined street and watched him march up the steps — straight, tall, and handsome. She pictured him in his dress blues, her friends seething with jealousy as she arrived at the Saturday dance on the arms of Lieutenant Breckenridge.

Luther Breckenridge charmed her completely. The Ford Theater was only the beginning, the dance even more memorable. After that he began phoning two and three times each day, and within a week he was meeting her on campus or at the house in Georgetown on a daily basis, even at the midnight hour when he came off duty. Six weeks after she met Luke, they drove out toward Langley. He parked as close as he dared.

"This is the spooks' hideaway," he said.

"I know. The spy network of the world."

"Sauni, I've been inside on errands for the Pentagon. It's top secret all the way. They practically fingerprint you before you can use the men's room."

She had the feeling that deep inside, he was fascinated with the Agency. "Don't tell me you want to be one of them?"

"Maybe, someday. After I'm a general. These guys are company-minded, like the Corps. They're committed. They've got that old *semper fidelis* spirit. They'd do anything for this country."

"Even die for it?" she asked.

"Yes, this country is worth fighting for — worth dying for."

She didn't speak to him for several minutes, not until they drove back to the George Washington Memorial Parkway. He was everything she wanted, and she feared losing him. Still she grew up in those first two months of knowing Luke.

He was right — she was spoiled rotten. He tore up her credit cards, made her balance her checkbook, and even made her take back two new pairs of shoes she didn't need. "I want you debt free," he told her, "because I'm going to marry you."

"You haven't asked me yet."

He winked. "I'm asking you now." And without waiting, he teased, "You won't need a dowry to marry me, but you will need my parents' approval. I called Mom and told her we'd be there this weekend."

"What about asking my parents?"

"I already did, Sauni. Your mother cried and then started calling her friends to tell them. Your father made it clear that he is opposed to the uniform, the military, and the war. But," he said smiling, "your dad said you always get your way."

As they crossed the bridge into Ocean City, New Jersey, Sauni felt the chill of the sea breeze tempered by her own excitement for the young marine by her side. Luke pulled to a stop in front of one of the houses on Asbury Avenue, yardless and flush with the sidewalk, a white two-story structure.

He pointed to the three small windows in the top loft. "That's my corner of the place," he said. "This is as close to a permanent home as we've ever had. Grams and Mom were born here. With Dad's job, we were always moving, but when I was a high school sophomore, Mom put her foot down. 'No more moving, not until Luther finishes school.' So Mother and I came here to this old place."

The Breckenridge home with its board-and-batten siding and pitched roof looked a little wider than most of the narrow houses in town. A sturdy old tree touched the house, its thick top branches partly covering the fish-scale shingles. A woman leaned against the lattice-trimmed railing, smiling and waving at them.

"Go on in, Sauni. I'll park the car in the alley."

She was left to introduce herself to Luke's mom, to clasp the soft hand extended to her. "So you're the special gal Luther met seven weeks ago. You apparently made quite an impression on my son. Come, I might as well show you the Breckenridge heroes."

Their portraits lined the walls of the small living room and the hall leading to the kitchen. Men in uniforms, with the blue and the gray of the Civil War hanging together. Grandparents and great-grandparents. Uncles and cousins. The admiral and Luke. They were all there. All in uniform.

Mrs. Breckenridge blew across the top of one frame. "Dust collectors," she said, but Sauni sensed her pride in being an officer's wife, an officer's mother.

Barreling through the back door, Luke dropped their luggage on the kitchen floor and gave his mother an undignified whirl around the room. She flushed as he planted a kiss on both cheeks. There was a quiet dignity to the way she faced Luke. "Are you trying to tell me that your orders came through?"

"No orders. Not yet. But soon."

She kept her arms around her son. "Saundra, do you know Luke plans to be a general someday?"

"Yes, he keeps telling me. But I'm still surprised that he didn't go navy so he could be an admiral like his dad."

"Oh my, no. Luke's his own man. Besides, there's only room for one admiral in this family." She sighed as she glanced at Sauni. "I've grown fearful of sending my men off to war again, especially the only son I have left, just for a promotion."

Mrs. Breckenridge looked sixty, a little older than Sauni's own mother. She was carefully groomed, a soft white cashmere buttoned around her shoulders. Luke had her smile and some of her gentleness, but none of her fears. Her dark premonitions for her son winged across the room to Sauni.

"Luther, dinner won't be until seven," she said hastily. "There's time to take Sauni down to the boardwalk if you like."

But they stayed, and Luke showed Sauni through the house to the top loft where most of his trophies and boyhood memories were hung on the wall or stored in the closet. "Mom keeps everything."

Sauni tried not to look at him because she blushed when she did. Gently, she fondled each trophy and put it down again. They were all there: sports and spelling bees, Sunday school pins and diplomas. Luke excelled in everything — football, baseball, tennis, dancing, and scholastics.

"Wow, you were valedictorian in high school and Annapolis."

"The admiral expected it. It's the Breckenridge tradition. Dad had a rigid law: low grades, no sports. Top grades, all sports."

"Luke, what happens when you don't excel? Or what if you never get another promotion?"

"A fate worse than death," he teased. But his eyes clouded. "If I really failed, I could never face my dad. I feel like I owe it to him, kind of for my brother, too. I just want my dad to be proud of me, Sauni — the way he was proud of my older brother Landon."

"Well, I'm proud of you, Lieutenant, *just the way you are*."

He grinned. "I love you, Sauni."

"Don't let your mother hear you."

He blew on her ear. "Don't worry. You already passed the test. The admiral's the last hurdle. I've got your ring in my pocket. It's yours as soon as you charm him. Yours regardless."

As they reached the living room again, Luke's father marched up the porch steps, handsome in his uniform. There was only a slight lifting of his brow when he saw Luke.

He shook hands with his son, kissed his wife, and acknowledged Sauni with a polite smile.

The admiral was an austere man with a stern expression and rigid stance. He was as tall as Luke but more stockily built; he had silver hair and eyes as bright and dark as Luke's. There seemed to be no camaraderie between them, only verbal fencing that subsided during the meal but resumed in the evening hours. They challenged each other at the intellectual level as though father-and-son love was nonexistent.

Admiral Breckenridge had come up through the ranks, gaining most of his military prestige and popularity in the Pacific. His wife kept the house shipshape, but Luke gave no indication of bowing to his father's commands. Surprisingly enough, the admiral seemed content and well adapted to the old-fashioned home. His smoking jacket and unlit pipe fit in with the maroon leather chair that overpowered the room.

"Mom wouldn't let him smoke in the house," Luke explained, "so he gave up smoking, but he's still attached to his pipes."

It wasn't until they prepared to leave for the trip back to Washington that the two men gave each other a strong embrace, going beyond their facade and revealing two people deeply committed to each other as man to man — father to son.

Sauni sat in the Courtland living room feeling in limbo as though she were floating between long ago and now. One moment Luke's presence seemed intense, the next far away. "Before I met Luke, I planned on graduate school and a teaching career, not on saying marriage vows. But a week after finishing my junior year at Georgetown, we were married in the chapel at Annapolis."

As she tried to describe Luke to them, she seemed to know him less: Luke the gentle, caring man, the lover. Luke the family hero, the son forcing himself to carry on the Breckenridge military tradition. Luke the patriot, the marine. Luke the warmonger, the traitor — no, no, a thousand denials. Luke loved his country.

She sat silently, so many images of him in her mind: Luke in his dress blues gliding with her across the ballroom while others stood on the sideline watching. His unexpected anger when she smeared his mouth with bridal cake. Luke the gentle lover on their honeymoon. Luke, shouldering his duffel bag, hating her tears as he left to go back to war. Dear, dear Luke pained when she asked for a divorce. Which memories did she dare reveal to Mr. Gregory? Which ones might destroy even Luke's memory?

Drew waited for her to go on. Robyn had slipped from the room, and now she was back placing a delicate teacup in Sauni's hands. Sauni felt warmth from the hot, steamy tea and sipped, barely aware that it scalded her throat as she swallowed. She glanced around the room at Pierre, his gaze anxious, sympathetic, as though he were warning her to say no more.

Again Sauni's thoughts strayed to those marvelous days spent on the Santa Barbara coast with Luke, their mutual choice for a honeymoon. Without ever asking — without his ever saying — Sauni knew there had been other girlfriends, serious relationships. But that first night, as he swept her up into his arms and carried her into the bedroom, Sauni knew she was the only one he had ever loved. He was gentle, tender, and she trusted him.

She sighed as she faced Robyn. "I was so terribly, terribly in love with Luke," she said aloud. "But war changed him. He brooded as though the weight of Vietnam rested on him. He had come home with his captain's bars from that second tour of duty, but it wasn't enough. He wanted to accept a special assignment and go back to Vietnam for one more year."

She put the teacup on the table beside her, her eyes searching Robyn's for comfort. "Robyn, I threatened to leave Luke if he went back to the war. I don't think I'll ever forgive myself for sending him away."

They had stood in the living room of their small Georgetown apartment, Luke looking more handsome in his uniform than the day she had met him. He couldn't take his eyes off her. "Sauni, let's don't quarrel about Vietnam anymore."

"I mean it, Luke. If you go back," she told him, "I'll leave you. I won't go through the loneliness and stress of waiting. Waiting for what? For two marines to come to my door and tell me —" She choked and went on. " 'We regret to inform you —' "

"I'm not dead, sweetheart. I'm here. I'm alive."

"But you're married to a conflict across the ocean, Luther Breckenridge. I want you to be here married to me. Please, leave the service while you have the chance."

He started toward her. She backed away. "I'm serious, Luke. If you go back, I won't be here when you come home again."

"Just one more year over there. I'll be back a year from April — in time for my twenty-sixth birthday. I promise, Sauni."

"I won't be here — I hate your old war. I'm sick of crying myself to sleep every night." She ran to the desk and picked up the papers from the lawyer's office. She shoved them at Luke.

"What's this?"

"Divorce papers."

He stared at her, the hurt in his dark eyes glaring. "Is there someone else, Sauni?" he asked.

"No one."

"Then why are you sending me away like this?"

"I want to set you free and be free myself. You believe in the cause across the ocean. I hate it. You belong there. You don't belong to me."

He took two steps and crushed her against his broad chest, his chin touching the top of her head. "But I love you, Sauni. I promise, when this assignment is over, I'll leave the marines."

The rough wool of his uniform against her face muffled her words. "You can't. You're going to be a general. Remember?"

"I'd be nothing without you." He pulled her closer. "Don't send me away, Sauni. Not tonight. I planned a candlelight dinner for the two of us and a quiet evening to-gether."

She heard herself say, "No. It's best to say goodbye now."

His tears surprised her. "This is my last night," he said. "I have to report back to the base by midnight."

For an instant she almost went back into his arms, her resolve crumbling. But it would only make things harder for both of them.

"Did you ever see your husband again?" Drew asked quietly.

"No. Luke flew out the following morning."

Drew reached out and touched her hand. "Don't keep blaming yourself, Mrs. Breckenridge. You were young and frightened."

"And foolish," she said. "Foolish enough to think he could break with the Breckenridge tradition. In a way I blame his father. Luke was always trying to please the admiral — to make his father proud of him. But that isn't fair either. I guess we always want to blame someone."

She smoothed her skirt and stood. "I can still see Luke as he turned and walked out the door. The click of the latch sounded like thunder in my ears. I thought he'd come rushing back and take me in his arms. He didn't, of course. Two months later Luke went on that fateful CIA mission."

Chapter 5

An hour after Sauni insisted on taxiing back to Hotel Mon-Repos alone, Drew kicked off his shoes and stretched out on the bed. But sleep couldn't penetrate his racing thoughts. It wasn't like the old days. Back then they knew who the enemy was — communism and the Cold War. But the pieces to this puzzle with Luke Breckenridge lay hidden in the jungles of Laos.

Drew had promised Robyn that he'd call Porter. He sat up and dialed. Porter came on the line on the fifth ring. "Deven speaking."

"Drew here. I'm at my daughter's."

"Geneva? When do you leave for Washington?" Porter's voice was too light and good-natured, a warning for Drew to be on guard.

"I'll be airborne before the sun comes up. Soon enough?"

"You're clear on what I want you to say?"

"You know that I am."

"Run it by me once more, Gregory."

"I'm to meet with the Director of Operations and Chad Kaminsky and lay it on the line. I've got my speech memorized. 'Gentlemen, Porter wants you to beam your satellites on the mercenary training posts in Spain before they get out of hand.' "

"Tell them there are stockpiles of weapons and mortar batteries there. They're preparing military strength for some foreign government. Tell Kaminsky I'll work with the station-chief in Madrid, but I think Burdock is dragging his feet on this one. Emphasize that."

You're lying, Drew thought. *You're after this one yourself, and you'll come out looking clean.* "Why don't I just tell Chad another political avalanche is about to sweep over Langley unless we move in. That should get their attention."

"Forget the snowdrifts, or you'll tumble with the avalanche. Just get them to beam one of those million-dollar satellites on Spain. Be specific. Point out the target areas and danger points to the U. S.; get those new technology boys on our side."

Drew attributed Porter's rise in volume to too much wine. "Porter, I don't trust the new breed with all their technology." *Laser beam star gazers, cellular phones, computer chips, digitized photography,* he scoffed to himself. Would these really keep America top dog in the spy world, ten feet ahead of the British spooks?

"Come on," Porter said, his voice slurring. "There are more ways to gather intelligence than dead drops and secret mailboxes."

Still, as far as Drew was concerned, nothing could replace the old CIA operatives or the one-on-one-agent contact. Let the new-tech boys spy out corporation secrets and drug cartels and terrorist buildups. But who did the ground work? He was convinced that high-tech machinery, as valuable as it was, might miss the enemy that still existed in the new Russia. How could a billion-dollar satellite ever substitute for gut ingenuity?

"Drew, tell Kaminsky those mercenary camps in Spain trained combatants for that civil war in Yugoslavia."

"What was once Yugoslavia," Drew corrected.

Drew's own world had been torn apart in Croatia, his cover blown. But he hadn't met up with any of the soldiers of fortune rumored to be there. Twenty or thirty thousand of them at final count, Americans included. "Trained for which side?" he asked.

Porter's contempt for the dog killers of war rose in his voice. "You know they didn't swear allegiance to any political group. They just took up arms with the Serbs or Bosnians or the Muslims — as long as it was the best price." His expletive boomed across the wire. "Tell Chad an American is heading one of those camps. I plan to stop that bloody mercenary before he ends up sending American-trained commandos to Russia during the elections. That's all we need to blow our fragile peace."

"And if Kaminsky's answer is still no?"

"We'll go in anyway. Now how can I help you, Gregory?"

"I've met a war widow."

"That's a new wrinkle."

"It's not what you think, Porter. This one is looking for someone to inscribe her husband's name on the Vietnam monument."

"Tell the widow to take that up with an engraver."

"Can't. They left his name off the black granite on purpose."

"What purpose did that serve? He's dead, isn't he?"

"Killed in Laos more than twenty years ago." Drew let the memory of Vietnam bite into Porter's memory; it was Porter's war.

"Then don't get involved, Drew. It's not CIA business."

"According to his wife, he was on a CIA mission when he was killed. Guy's name was

Luke Breckenridge, a marine captain . . . Porter . . . are you still there?"

Now Porter's voice grated like loose gravel pouring from a cement truck. "Forget it, Drew. If the man betrayed his country —"

"I never said that."

"Don't bother Langley with this one. That's an order." He hesitated, then changed the subject. "Will you see your brother this trip?"

"I'll probably run into Aaron at the family farm."

"Call me if you have problems."

I just did, and you kicked it under the table. Drew wanted to forget it, too, although it needled him that Porter dismissed the Breckenridge issue so abruptly. What if Sauni Breckenridge had told the truth about her husband? A hero had the right to lie in peace and his family to live the same way.

On Monday Drew rolled out of bed at the crack of dawn and was waiting for a taxi when Robyn shuffled groggily past him with a coffee mug in her hand. "I hate to see you go," she said.

He winked at her. "I've been trying to reach Porter again this morning, but he's not answering. You'd think that old basset hound of his would nudge him from his stupor."

But on the fourth ring, the answering module kicked in. Perplexed, Drew risked dialing Porter's secretary. He couldn't decide whether Brigette's "hello" was professional or seductive. She was a dainty bombshell who always wore her blonde hair swept back from her pretty face. "Sorry to bother you. I'm trying to reach Porter."

"He's not here, Mr. Gregory. He left for Washington last evening on an emergency. I thought you knew."

"No. No, I didn't." He cradled the phone scowling.

"Dad, what's wrong?" Robyn asked.

"Porter flew to Washington last night."

"Is that so unusual?"

"It was unplanned. Otherwise why did he ask me to go for him? He must have decided I can't handle it alone."

"You can handle anything." She stood on tiptoe as the doorbell rang and kissed him goodbye. "You won't forget to check on Luke?"

He smiled. "You won't let me."

Drew stepped into the blinding lights of the airport. Had it really been three years since he had hit Washington National? If anything, the terminal seemed more crowded than ever, the noise level piercing. With the time difference, he had arrived long before the supper hour. While he waited for his baggage, he found a phone and called Chad Kaminsky. Chad's secretary ran interference.

"Kaminsky is expecting me," Drew reassured the woman.

But he grew impatient waiting for Chad to come on the line. *Okay, okay, lady. Quit dragging your alligator shoes*, he thought. *Get Kaminsky for me before Langley shuts down for the night.*

Finally he heard his old friend's familiar bulldog growl. "Drew, good to hear from you. Sorry to keep you waiting. Have a good flight? When did you get in?"

"I just arrived. I'm caught out here in this hustle and bustle, but I wanted to confirm our morning appointment. Is eight good for you?"

"Eight?" The pause was obvious. Chad seemed to be conferring with someone. He had muffled the phone. "That's not good, Drew. In fact, tomorrow is out."

"What's the matter, Chad? Did the secretary forget to write it down? I'm on a tight ten-day schedule. You know that."

Again Drew heard the muffled sound as

Chad planked his chubby hand over the mouthpiece. The appointment had been worked out days ago. Drew switched to his other ear and flipped the pages of his Pocket Planner. Yes, Chad had made the mistake.

"Look, Gregory, we'll have to hold off until Friday. Sorry to mess up your schedule, but things are tight around here." The words came fast, not Kaminsky's usual Arkansas drawl. "Yeah, that's the best bet. You can catch Harv and me at the same time."

Drew didn't like it. Porter had been emphatic. *See Harv and Chad with this mercenary problem separately. Swing them to my side one at a time.* "Did Harv cancel my eleven o'clock with him?"

"Afraid so. It's Friday with both of us. The best we can do."

Drew saw the trip to Miriam's in Los Angeles slipping away unless he took a flight to L. A. one day, a flight back the next. More jet lag. Anger began in the pit of his stomach; he felt as if a crescent wrench had gripped his gut and tightened. Drew hated a foiled mission — hated it more when it was his own plan. "Chad, can you and Harv spare just a few minutes tomorrow? I'll keep our business to a minimum."

"Impossible!" Chad's tone had turned harsh, his voice crusty.

Drew kept pushing. "Is Harv there?"

"No. No. Haven't seen him all day."

I bet, Drew thought. *He's right there leaning on your desk directing traffic.* Or was it Harv? Someone was there deliberately stalling, changing everything. "So what time on Friday, Chad?"

"Make it closer to eleven. We'll catch lunch together." Chad had slipped into low gear now. "Is there anything that can't wait until then? Anything in particular?"

Like Luke Breckenridge? Drew thought. No — that one can keep. He wasn't going to risk his in-coming call being monitored. When he brought up Luke's name, he wanted to watch Chad's expression. Kaminsky had a lot of rough edges, but his body language always gave him away. If he'd ever heard of Breckenridge, Drew would know it by the look in Chad's eyes. "No, I'll keep everything on hold."

"Be good to see you." Kaminsky was trying to put his old enthusiasm into his words, but was falling short. "Sorry about the mix-up, Drew. Huh — why don't you go on to upstate New York while you're waiting? Then I won't feel so bad about rescheduling."

Chad knew about that? "Have you seen Porter?" Drew ventured.

A noticeable pause. "Deven? You know he doesn't get this way often. In Paris the last I knew. Attending all the embassy parties."

Had Porter's secretary made a mistake? No, Porter always chose people who gave him the most mileage. Brigette kept a calendar of Porter's appointments that was more accurate than his own. If Brigette said Deven had flown to Washington, then chances were he was sitting in Chad's office even now. Brigette didn't make mistakes.

"Have a good trip to New York, Drew. See ya Friday. It'll be good to have you on board for the day." Kaminsky managed a grumpy chuckle, but it felt more like a right to Drew's jaw. The call ended, and Drew stood there wondering who severed it first.

Upstate New York, is it? And how did you know about that one, Kaminsky? I didn't send you my itinerary. In spite of his irritation with Chad, he'd take the man's suggestion. He'd check into the hotel now and catch a shuttle flight to New York in the morning. A few good hours on the interstate, and he'd be back at the family homestead.

It was a crisp wintery day, typical for this time of year. A gusty wind made kites of the clouds as Drew's taxi squealed to a stop in front of the Capitol Hilton. When you're

94

mad as a hatter, you go for the best. To ease his annoyance, he decided on a luxury room with a view, signed up for a sauna and a massage, and ordered room service for a late dinner — cost be hanged. He'd use the expense account that Porter had allotted to him this trip, maybe even go all out and invite Uriah Kendall over for steak. Drew wasn't a drinking man, but he considered emptying the liquor bottles from the room's refrigerator down the bathroom drain to run up the tab. Just the thought of it helped cool his fury, leaving him so upbeat that he tipped the bellboy as if he had cash to burn.

The hotel placed him within walking distance of the metro station, but his window gave him a good view of Pennsylvania Avenue without leaving the room. The city spread out before him — the White House two blocks away, the Mall and the Washington Monument, the white-domed Capitol. A spectacular city. Drew had loved it when he lived here — basking in the political scene.

As he stood by the window, nostalgia swept over him. On his last visit, he had handled his business at Langley and caught an earlier flight back to Europe. He hadn't even gone back to the farm to see his mother. Drew hated painful goodbyes. A second one would be wrenching. They'd just spent a week together, and he hated seeing her sick and slowing down. He had called from Washington National, his luggage already checked in for the flight back to Europe. "Hey, sweetheart, I finished up here in Washington."

He had heard her suck in her breath with excitement. Even as he held the phone in his hand, he could picture her — fragile ten years before her time, her thin yellow-gray hair pulled back severely from her face into a single pigtail. She looked so ravaged with cancer that her once-smiling Irish eyes bulged a sickly blue.

"Are you coming back, son, to visit me a little longer?"

He stopped the rest of her invitation before she could give it. "I'm heading back to Paris, Mom. We'll have a longer visit the next time I'm here."

"Drew, Drew, I'm not contagious. I'm just dying."

"No, you're not," he had said. "Just get well and fly over to Paris and spend some time with me."

"Yes. Yes, I'll do that."

He had heard a tremor in her voice as she added, "We'll make that a very long visit next time."

He never went home for the funeral.

Where was he then? Croatia? Somalia? North Africa? Someplace, somewhere on Company business. For a moment he tried to remember. Feared doing so. Flowers? Yes, he had sent flowers. Roses when he flew back to Europe early. A massive floral tribute when she died. He admitted it to himself now — he couldn't hack memorial walls. Couldn't face his mother sick and dying, had refused to see her dead. Drew had, as he realized now, let his mom down when she needed him most, a woman he admired to the hilt. And she turned around and rewarded his absence with the family inheritance.

He grabbed a hankie from his back pocket. She'd been dead three years, and this was the first time he allowed himself to cry over the empty void she'd left behind. This must be the way Sauni Breckenridge felt — serving divorce papers to the man she loved and having him dead two months later.

Drew had an hour before darkness. He reached for his coat and scarf and left the hotel. The bellman hailed him a taxi. The gum-smacking driver grinned. "Where to, mister?"

"To the Vietnam Veterans Memorial Wall."

"It'll get dark soon."

"Then hurry."

The driver — fortyish and of Italian extraction — shoved another wad of gum into his mouth. "You could walk it from here. I take ya and it'll cost you. I've got me a minimum fare."

No, my knees would buckle. "Will you settle for twenty?"

Drew braced himself against the car seat as the driver roared off. "Got someone there, sir?"

"Yeah," Drew said. "My friend Luke."

"Me, too. My older brother. Got himself killed in that unfriendly war. A rocket exploded. Only our neighborhood called him a hero — until this. That wall has been healing." He pulled up to the curb. "My mother still goes there once a month to leave a flower for her Tony-boy. That blasted war."

Drew stepped from the taxi and held out his twenty.

"Keep it, sir. We've both got someone on that wall."

Drew protested. The young man wiped his sweater sleeve across his eyes. "The ride's on me. That blasted war," he repeated. "Tony-boy Giardini. Don't forget. His friend Trippkins is there, too. Died the same day. If you see the name Tony Giardini, mister, that's my older brother. Trippkins is right below him. Same panel."

Drew walked down the gently sloping path, already worn from the pilgrimage of others. He stopped inches from the wall. His calloused indifference to memorials softened as he stared at the names on the black granite slab. Thousands of them — Jackson, Shine, Diaz, Thornton, Hill, Jordan, Waloski.

"Incredible!" Drew said. "So many."

Two bronzed statues added to the somber setting. Soldiers and nurses with youthful faces and realistic expressions. The soldiers in battle fatigues held weapons — instead of the hand of the girl or wife left behind. The nurses held the wounded, anxiety and caring in their faces.

As dusk settled in, a young man in an olive drab jacket and worn jeans — his clothes too thin for this kind of weather — ran his bare hand over a name on the wall, caressing it with his touch. Unabashed, he wiped his nose with straggly strands of his shoulder-length hair.

The bottom of the wall was cluttered with scattered memorials: A snapshot. A bouquet of flowers still in the green tissue. A lone rose taped to the wall, frozen in time and memory. Tiny flags that the wind fluttered like the clouds. A rosary. And somebody else's Purple Heart.

The young man stepped back and saluted.

Saluted his friend for what? For dying? For being missing? *No,* Drew thought, *for being American. For being young. For going when all too many wouldn't go with you. For giving me this country to believe in.*

As Drew turned back, a girl bundled warmly against the weather walked up to him. Her I. D. tag marked her as a National Park Service guide. She held a book of names against her chest. "Can I help you find someone before I go off duty?" she asked.

"Giardini," he said, remembering Tonyboy. "And Trippkins."

"Missing?" she asked softly.

"Dead — killed on the same day. I'm not sure of the year."

She found them and pointed Drew in the right direction. She gave him the panel and line numbers. "Is there anything else, sir?"

Luke. Yes, Luke, he thought. He pronounced the name slowly, spelled it out clearly. "Luther Walton B-r-e-c-k-e-n-r-i-d-g-e the fourth. Killed in Laos in '73."

The wind whipped against the pages of her book as she searched for Luke's name. Her voice somber and reverent, she said, "His name just isn't here, sir."

"It should be." Drew was shocked by the intensity in his own voice. Did he really mean it? Had his daughter's faith in Luke Breckenridge brought him to this? Or had a widow's grief?

"Are you sure of the date, Mr. Breckenridge?" she asked.

He didn't correct her. Instead he flipped through his address book to Sauni's name. "Yes," he said. "The date matches."

She looked more distressed. "Do I have the right spelling?"

He leaned over her shoulder. "That's it."

"It just isn't here. They left space on the wall," she said nervously. "In case someone's name was inadvertently missed. You should check with the veterans or one of the senators."

Senator Summers? he mused. "Yes, I'll do that." He'd like to see Summers squirm at the name of his son-in-law. He patted the girl's shoulder. "Before you go off duty, the family over there needs help," he said. He pointed to an older couple staring up at the granite wall, blindly searching for a name.

"Yes, I'll go." Still for a moment she hesitated, her eyes sad as though she had failed him. "Was it your son?"

"No."

She waited, her face sympathetic as he groped for a relationship. "It's the husband of a friend," he told her.

Then she rushed off, almost gladly. He

looked down at the paper in his hand where she had scrawled the panel and line numbers for Trippkins and Giardini. *But none for Luke Breckenridge.*

Chapter 6

Drew caught the first morning shuttle and was in Albany with a car rental at his disposal before the city became snarled in go-to-work traffic. He nosed the Toyota Camry onto the fastest route northeast, bypassing Troy, on through flat terrain that rose slowly in sloping hills toward the distant mountains. Drew still felt exhilarated by the nippy morning drive when he reached the turnoff to the Gregory Dairy Farm that hugged the Vermont border.

The taste of nostalgia wet his mouth and tugged at his throat. He pulled off the road onto the crusty snow that still covered the serene hillsides. The tiny town lay nestled in a snowbound valley, veiled in part by the morning mist that had blown in from the frozen lake. Drew remembered it being like this often in the wintery months of his boyhood — his town veiled in snow and mist. He gazed at the familiar: the cubicle post office, Haynes' Corner Store where he had bagged groceries at fourteen, a one-pump gas station, the country school, and the massive Grange that served the surrounding communities. He'd learned to square dance there and had stolen his first kiss from the Montroe girl before joining the army. They made a pledge to love forever. Her pledge lasted two months. While he rode the English Channel toward the Battle of Normandy, Carla married the boy with the Greek name. Drew wondered now whether they still lived on the farm or if she had dragged him off to the oil fields of Saudi Arabia.

As he blew on his gloved hands, the hot vapors from his mouth steamed up the car windows even more. He wiped a spot clear, his gaze settling on St. Bonaventure's where he had been an altar boy too many years ago to count. Beyond St. Bonaventure's stood the steepled Community Bible Church — the hellfire and brimstoners who had been good to his mother in the closing days of her life.

It struck him now that Carla Montroe had gone to church there, so their relationship would never have worked out. She had told him she planned on being a missionary or an opera singer — definitely not a farmer's wife. In turn, he shared his desire for the political scene in Washington — definitely not the farm scene.

Drew chuckled, his dry humorless

chuckle, the lump in his throat easing now. Spread out from the town were the farms — the Montroes' well-kept homestead; the old Remington place, bought out now; the Wallingfords' silo looking in need of a paint job; and Phil Gadberry's place with the rusty water tank where Aaron had climbed to the top once — on Drew's dare — and panicked.

He recalled the blistered bottom he'd suffered on Aaron's account. Drew had climbed that old water tank dozens of times himself, but it was off-limits after the firemen rescued Aaron. As Drew looked at it, he had an old yearning to climb it again. To prove to himself that he still could — to fan his boyhood back into reality and cut the years piling up on him.

His gaze turned homeward now, a quarter of a mile to the right, where the sprawling Gregory Farm stood as proudly as ever. He took in the familiar landmarks, each one stirring a memory. The picket fence outlined the three hundred acres of property, ample grazing land for the cattle. The fence curved in an uneven pattern across sloping hills, past the far corral where Drew had learned to ride, and lowered down through fields of barren fruit trees toward a frozen river and the woods that lay behind the farm.

Aaron never got the hang of farming, never

saddled a horse nor rode one, but he did help their mother plant some trees in the orchard. The rest of Aaron's time went to fishing for trout for dinner or trekking those woods, mimicking bird calls. Drew wondered why he had never credited Aaron with these strengths; instead, he saw him as a scrawny weakling, as an object of scorn. Is that how their mother had seen him, too? Is that one of the reasons she deprived Aaron of the farm, the farm that he wanted?

Putting the car in gear, Drew drove slowly onto the property, his sights on the hayloft and the red barn that had serviced a thousand head of Holsteins at its peak. Caring for those black-and-whites had cost his father hours of hard work and, in the end, his life as well. In the distance stood the machine shop and his mother's chicken house, a tractor and truck, and the unoccupied handyman's cottage. Thick limbs of an old elm shaded the spot where they'd built their treehouse — off-limits to girls, even to his mom.

Now he allowed himself to face this homecoming as he parked the car behind a Mercedes Benz. Home: the two-story farmhouse where he'd grown up, a wrap-around porch where his mom used to rock, the attic window where he'd had his own room. Drew had grown accustomed to his dad being dead, fifteen years now, but not his mother. This was his first visit since her death, and he'd come home to sell the farm, to sever these memories, and cut himself off from all that was familiar.

Again the miserable lump in his throat swelled. It was as though he could hear her voice clearly saying, "Drew, darling, buy me a dress from that shop on the Bahnhofstrasse."

"In Zurich?" he had asked.

"You know how I love to shop there."

He had almost choked as he asked, "Some big date, Mom?"

"Yes, darling. My funeral. I want to look my best."

He stepped from the car, his eye on the Mercedes. So his lease farmers were doing well. A woman, fortyish perhaps, opened the door and stared at him. "Hello," she said. "I'm Loyal Quinwell."

The greeting held the question, *Who are you? I wasn't expecting anyone.* But she smiled, and the smile and her rosy cheeks reminded him of that stolen kiss at the Grange when he was fifteen. "I'm Mr. Gregory," he said walking up the steps.

"I thought you were out in the barn with my husband."

He nodded toward the rental. "I just arrived."

A curious towhead peeked around her apron. Small-fry size, four at most, frowning like his mother. She hugged the child as she said, "But Stan called up to me when I was making the beds. He told me you had arrived, that you were going to the barn together."

"No, I just came," he repeated.

"Well, Stan will tell you we can't afford to buy the place now. Not yet. We're just beginning to get ahead."

"Buy the place?"

"You told us if we didn't make up our minds, you'd sell the farm to someone else. We may never be able to afford it."

"I'm thinking of selling, but no one knew that."

She shivered. "Come in," she said apologetically. "I'll have one of the boys run out to the barn and get Stan."

Drew stomped snow from his shoes and stepped inside, grateful for the warmth. She took his coat and scarf, and before he could even follow her to the kitchen, she said, "We love this old place, Mr. Gregory."

And so do I, he thought, soaking up the familiar rooms.

"If you could only wait another five years,

maybe we could swing a loan then."

"Why don't we sit down and you tell me what this is all about, Mrs. Quinwell? But first, how about a cup of coffee?"

"Oh, do have some." She poured it, overflowing the cup, and again she apologized. "Stan always handles the business, Mr. Gregory."

"*Drew* Gregory. I'm the owner. We've never met, Mrs. Quinwell."

"Isn't it your law firm that manages the farm for you?"

"I'm not a lawyer, Mrs. Quinwell. My brother Aaron is. He arranged for Bryan and Caldstein to handle the farm after our mother died. After I inherited it."

Little puzzle wrinkles framed her eyes again. "We've never heard of you, except in town, of course. They spoke of the Gregory brothers there. Mainly at the grocery and Grange. We thought Aaron owned the farm. We've been leasing from him."

"You've been leasing from me. I'm sure it's just a matter of paperwork. I'll speak to my brother about it." *I'll wring his neck,* he thought. *But I can't see him now. I won't miss my visit with Miriam.* "You've kept everything in mint condition," he said.

"We work hard. Stan's a good worker. We'd never consider it otherwise. We Quinwells had nothing. No money. No prestige. Just nothing. But our pastor —"

Somehow Drew knew what she was going to say. He pictured her here at the farm caring for his mom in those closing days of her life, long after the dwindling population had forced St. Bonaventure's to move its parish to the city. "Was it your little church that came by with food and visits when my mother was ill?"

She nodded. "Community Bible. Stan and St. Bonaventure's priest were friends. The priest came back once a month for a Sunday mass. But your mother was too ill to go."

"My mother hadn't gone to church for a long time."

Her face flushed. "Father Carlos and Mrs. Gregory got on well, but he worried that she would die between his visits. Stan promised him that we'd look in on her."

She chose her words saying, "Toward the end we wanted to send for her family, but she wouldn't let us. She was a lovely lady. Always talking about her boys, especially the one —" Her jaw sagged. "You're her older boy, the one who worked for the government?"

"Hardly a boy," he said.

Loyal stared up at him. "She often called

you her patriotic agnostic — and me her guardian angel."

"And what did she call herself?"

"A very lost sheep. But she really wasn't, not in the end."

"Did she want you to take over the farm?"

"Mrs. Gregory thought Stan could make a go of it and keep the farm in good condition for her son. We thought your mother meant Aaron. But if what you're saying is true, then —"

Lightly, he said, "She left it to her *agnostic* boy."

Stan Quinwell clumped into the kitchen in rubber boots. His son raced ahead of him; Aaron lagged behind. Stan kicked off his boots by the door and kissed his wife on the cheek. "It's all right, honey," he said. "Tad told me what's going on."

Quinwell was a foot taller than his wife, a big man in a flannel jacket, his long johns showing at the wrists, his jeans ragged at the knees. He wrapped his burly hands around the mug she gave him and eyed Drew coolly. "You must be the other Gregory," he said as Aaron joined them.

Drew nodded. "I'm the older brother. I own this farm. You are leasing it from me."

Aaron had crossed the threshold too late to turn back and high-tail it to his Mercedes

Benz. "Drew," he sputtered, "I wasn't expecting to see you, not here at the farm."

"Apparently not."

Aaron's dark eyes flashed, his pallid face an exact image of his father's: gaunt cheeks, thin lips, a studious expression. Avoiding Drew's outstretched hand, Aaron brushed the snow from his leather jacket, forgetting it was Quinwell's kitchen now — not their mother's.

Pointedly Drew said, "I've been thinking about selling the farm, Aaron, not having it sold out from under me."

Aaron managed a stoic composure. "Bryan and Caldstein's asked me to look into it. If it turned out promising, they were going to contact you about selling."

"At whose suggestion, Aaron? Yours? Since when have you been part of their firm?"

He hesitated. "I've been part of the firm all along. We left my name off our letters to you to avoid any problems."

"I expect you to be up front with me, Aaron. I asked you to handle my affairs, not to meddle in them. Dale Caldstein is the head of the firm, isn't he?"

"Yes."

"Then I'll talk with him."

Loyal Quinwell looked anxiously from one

brother to the other. "Could I get you something?" she asked.

Drew smiled. "More coffee would be nice."

As they took their seats at the kitchen table, Aaron toyed with his cup, sloshing the coffee. "I want this property, Drew. I haven't got anything left. This business with Miriam's Art Gallery will ruin me unless she defends me."

"You've got it wrong. The von Tonner art fraud ruined you."

"I was Ingrid von Tonner's lawyer. Nothing more."

Drew was convinced of Aaron's guilt. So was Interpol. But with Ingrid von Tonner dead, Aaron might do what he had often done — slip through the fingers of justice.

"I want the farm," Aaron said again. "I intend to get it."

Drew turned to Quinwell. "You have a written lease, don't you?"

"Yes, sir," Stan said. "Written up by Bryan and Caldstein."

"I'll have a new lease drawn up, one that will protect you for the next year. It will probably take me that long to sell."

"That won't give us time enough, Mr. Gregory. My wife and I love this old farm, but we can't swing it financially."

Drew stared out the kitchen window. The morning mist had lifted, but the sky still threatened more snow. The stillness outside was breathtaking, the solitude that his mother had always loved. That he loved. He didn't have to ask twice what his mother would do. She would continue to lease the farm to the Quinwells because their hearts were here in this place.

"Don't sell the farm to them," Aaron begged. "It's the only place I ever felt really happy. Don't take it away from me."

Aaron did look like the final prop was being kicked out. But coldly Drew said, "Aaron, Mother left the farm to me."

"Yes. And I hate her for it."

Loyal Quinwell's cup rattled in the saucer. Drew turned to her. "Would you mind showing me around the old place?" he asked.

She seemed grateful for an excuse to leave the room. "My other children will be coming home soon. Please don't mention selling in front of them. They're so happy here."

He followed her. The walls of the rooms were familiar, but the Quinwells had added so many touches that it was clearly their place now. The pictures on the walls, the lamps in the rooms, the rugs on the floor — these were different. Here and there he touched the familiar: the solid oak table in the dining area, the four-poster bed in the back room, the built-in desk and book shelves that his dad had made for him.

"Thank you," he said when they reached the kitchen again.

Turning to Stan, he added, "I'm staying at the Capitol Hilton in Washington. I'll leave my number. Call me there, say next Monday. That will give me time to have a new lease drawn up."

"But what about Bryan and Caldstein?"

"I think they'll see their way clear to a new agreement. If not with them, with someone else. Their reputation is in question. Selling my property without my permission — not good."

He looked around. "I see my brother is gone."

"He's waiting for you outside," Stan said.

Drew slipped into the coat that Loyal held for him. He took his scarf, still smiling at her. "Don't worry, Mrs. Quinwell. I own a good-sized property here. We'll work something out so you'll still be on the land, at least until all your children are grown."

He walked down the porch steps and over to Aaron's car to stare down angrily at the half-brother he had always considered weak and spineless. Cold, bitter eyes stared back. Drew had always been the stronger one —

tall, muscular, and mature enough at fifteen to deceive the army recruiter. Aaron, with his gaunt appearance and sticklike extremities, had been an uncoordinated kid, the last one chosen for the kickball or soccer team. Even now, as a grown man, Aaron still compensated with high-class clothes, flashy cars, and a keen intellect.

"I'm leaving, Aaron. I'll be in touch with your law firm. Tell Caldstein he can reach me at the Capitol Hilton in Washington."

"You'll ruin me."

"Not purposely. Now tell me, do you see your father often?"

"Good ole David Levine? *Your* father was the only dad I ever knew. That's why I changed my name to Gregory. To please him. To please Mom."

Drew felt a moment of pity. Aaron had been short-changed. A flamboyant actor for a father, who couldn't even give a command performance on his greatest role in life: husband and father. Drew understood that kind of failure. "Did you ever tell David about Mother?" he asked.

Aaron nodded. "Right after she died. I was crazy enough to think he'd care. He sent a potted plant too late for the funeral. But as old as he is, he's still doing two-bit parts on Broadway."

Drew wanted to part without harsh words. "Thanks for standing by Mother during her illness."

"What good did it do me?" Aaron asked. "She practically cut me out of her will. Just because I was David Levine's son."

Drew knew that wasn't the only reason, but there was no need to alienate Aaron further. He looked troubled enough. "She didn't forget you. Mother left you a sizable fortune."

Aaron's face twisted. "It's gone. Every dime."

Drew didn't ask where. He guessed: Atlantic City, Las Vegas, Monaco, the Kentucky Derby. He shrugged against the freezing weather and slipped his gloves on. "Aaron, I'm catching a plane to Los Angeles later this evening."

Fresh anger raged in his brother's face. "To Miriam's?"

"Yes. I'm delivering a gift for the kids. By the way, I spent the weekend with Robyn and Pierre. They're doing well."

"Are they?" Aaron asked bitterly. "Now that you're back in the picture, Robbie won't even take my phone calls."

Biting his tongue, Drew turned and crunched over the snow. As he opened the door to the rental, Aaron roared his Mercedes Benz alongside Drew. "I won't give up this farm. One way or the other, I'm going to have what should be mine."

Drew's anger exploded, his cool gone. "Over my dead body."

"If that's what it takes!"

Don't turn your shoulder blades to your brother, Pierre had warned. Drew slammed the door and rolled down the window. "Move, Aaron, so I don't put a dent in that ostentatious little car of yours."

The Quinwells stood on the porch, their bodies taking the wintery winds, worry lines cutting their faces. Drew waved, then followed the speeding Mercedes Benz that had already put distance between them. He cut cautiously along the winding country road past the old stone mill and rhythmic waterwheel, refusing to look back once more at the old homestead.

Chapter 7

As Drew opened the door to Miriam's Art Gallery, melodious chimes resounded — as though sending a warning signal to Miriam. Floy Beaumont rushed toward him, hands outstretched in welcome. "Drew Gregory! Miriam didn't tell me you were coming."

"She didn't know."

He set his briefcase down, crushed Floy's hands in his, and then leaned forward to kiss her well-rounded cheek. Embarrassed, he said, "That's from Robyn. She sends her love."

"I hope she sent the wedding pictures."

He tapped the briefcase. "I've got them."

Floy's eyes twinkled. "That's your entrance key."

"Thanks." He squared his shoulders, feeling suddenly thirty-six again and tongue-tied with a diamond ring in his pocket. But back then Miriam had been glad to see him.

She eyed him from her plush glass-encased office and waved, sending unexpected warmth through his body. "Here goes," he said to Floy and made his way toward Miriam.

He envisioned a double image — the young, beautiful girl he had married; the mature, impeccably groomed woman she had become. He focused on the latter, searching for the right words, pacing himself into a casual approach with an unhurried stride.

Miriam stepped into the hall to greet him, looking lovelier than ever, her oval face perfectly shaped, her eyes brilliantly alive. Dangling gold earrings caught the sunlight as she faced him. She extended a ringed hand, her smooth slender fingers touching his.

He wanted to brush his hand on his trouser leg to wipe away the clammy dampness, but it was too late. "Well, Drew, as always you're a most unexpected surprise."

"I'm on a business trip."

"Washington, of course. You missed it by three thousand miles."

"Guess I took the wrong plane."

She gave him her guarded half smile. "You always had trouble with planes," she said. "Catching the right flight home especially."

"I'm sorry." She had already reduced him to an apology, and he resented it, his surface smile hiding his agitation.

She backed off. "You didn't come to buy one of my paintings, did you? They're all genuine now. No frauds." Her voice had slipped to a whisper, her eyes begging him to understand.

"That's all over, Miriam," he said gently. "You were cleared of that von Tonner scandal."

"I wish my conscience knew that." Then flippantly she said, "So *do* you want a painting? I'd be surprised. Or have you learned to distinguish a Monet from a Pissarro finally?"

Her intended dart struck. He resented her superiority in the art world, but he controlled his tongue. "Any of these famous works would look out of place in my London flat."

"I'd help you choose the right one," she said quietly. "Robyn said your place needed a bit of color."

What it needs is someone to share it with me. "It's a drab, lonely place," he admitted.

"Come in, Drew. Sit down and tell me about Robyn. Is she happy?"

"She's well and happy — and she sent you something."

Miriam clapped her cheeks. "Oh, Drew. The wedding pictures!"

"An entire album." He took the wrapped satin-covered volume from his briefcase and handed it to her. "It's your birthday present from Robyn and Pierre. Actually, I threw in my business trip so I could deliver it in person."

He watched her remove the delicate tissue and smiled as she ran her hand over the soft fabric. Her face glowed as she turned to the first page, a picture of the bride. Her daughter. His daughter. A forever reminder of the love they had once shared.

"Oh, Drew, is she really as joyful as she looks?"

He thought of Robyn, a constant pink glow to her cheeks. Those frequent eye contacts with Pierre — reaching out across the room to send a message of love without words. "She's radiant."

"I'm glad. I was so afraid she'd be lost without her art."

"She lives at the museums and just sleeps at the apartment."

Miriam looked up, her eyes sad and distant. "I really miss her."

"Then why not move to Europe, Miriam? Start a gallery there."

She shook her head. "Oh, no, Drew. They didn't take a picture of us dancing together?"

"Yes. Remember, I asked them to take several."

She seemed to sense his reaching out for togetherness. Her eyes misted as she met his gaze. "Don't, Drew. We can't draw back the years. They're gone."

"Don't you like our picture?"

"Yes. We look happy there talking and dancing together. But you have such a startled look on your face."

"That's when you told me how much the wedding was costing me."

"But there weren't any extras — except flying Gino and Floy over for the ceremony. You didn't really mind, did you?"

He chuckled, a dry monotone, but a chuckle nonetheless, a small break in his no-nonsense personality. "It was worth every dime to see those hectic days come to an end."

"It was rather a bad scene, as Robyn would say. But I hated cutting the cord."

"I know. But she wants you to visit as often as you can."

"I owe it to my customers to stay here, to build a trusting relationship with them again. The art scandal was not good for business; it'll be a while before the gallery is doing well again."

Gently, he said, "You haven't asked about Pierre."

"No, I haven't, have I? Robyn writes about him all the time, and when I call or she calls, it's Pierre this and Pierre that."

"Right now he's her whole life."

She sighed. "That's as it should be." She closed the album. "I shall treasure this."

He heard dismissal in her voice. Had he flown an extra three thousand miles to be turned away so quickly? "Would you have dinner with me?"

"I'd rather not this evening."

"I'll be gone in the morning."

"Another one of those planes to catch? Do you still fly, Drew?"

"Just commercially. I let my pilot's license run out."

"I never thought you'd give up flying."

"Miriam, I gave up everything when you left me."

Her thinly arched brows lifted. "Everything but the Company. Did you ever crash land? Friends in Washington said that you did."

"Once," he said. "A long time ago in an Alpine village. I slammed right against a mountain slope. I would have died if it hadn't been for the village priest taking care of me."

Father . . . Caridini . . . yes, that was his name. The priest had dragged Drew from the burning plane, risking flames and an explosion. There had been gunfire and gunshot wounds, but Father Caridini never asked any questions. No questions from the priest. No answers volunteered by Drew. He had been sheltered in the church rectory in a tiny room beside the chapel where he awakened each morning to the sound of cowbells.

Miriam's hands rested on the album. "Are you going to tell me it was just a pleasure ride — just a friendly little crash?" she asked. "Isn't that the way you always viewed danger?"

"Is any crash ever friendly? What about dinner, Miriam?"

"It's still no."

"Not even if Floy joins us."

She considered. "Not even then."

He snapped his briefcase shut. "Have you talked to Aaron lately?"

"No. Have you?" she asked as they both stood.

He nodded. "For half an hour yesterday."

"I didn't think you two had that much to say to each other."

"We didn't plan to meet. He was at the farm when I arrived."

She touched his hand. "Oh, that was your first visit back."

"Since my mother died."

"Did it go all right?"

"Better than I expected until I saw Aaron. He still wants the farm, but I plan to sell it."

"But you love that old place."

"I always planned on retiring there with you."

"I know, but I wouldn't have made a good farmer's wife."

"Aaron won't need the farm either, Miriam. He's fighting extradition. He denies any partnership or wrongdoing with Ingrid von Tonner in the art fraud scandal. Says he was her lawyer and nothing more. I'm sure he's guilty as sin, but with Ingrid dead and without your testimony, he'll go free."

"Then let him."

"He deceived you, Miriam. You could have lost everything, including this gallery."

"I'm lucky, I guess," she whispered. "Luckier than some."

Was she thinking of Ingrid? Of Monique Smith's loss? He considered saying, *You're a fool.* He shrugged instead. "It was good to see you." It sounded like a final goodbye, the last act of a play with the curtain going down.

"You can't forgive Aaron, can you, Drew?"

A peptic tightness gripped him. "He tried to destroy you."

"Yes, but hasn't he been punished long enough? We should never have excluded him from Robyn's wedding."

"The guest list was your department."

She stood beside him as he opened the

door. "If I go to court to speak against Aaron, in time you'd hate me for doing it. And I can't forget — he was good to Robbie all her life."

Their raised voices carried out toward Floy now. "Interpol is still gathering evidence against him."

"I know. Kurt Brinkmeirer called me twice to tell me." She sighed. "It's as if I'm being caught in a firestorm. You coming at me from one side, Aaron raging on the other."

He touched her cheek. "I'm sorry, Miriam."

"You're brothers, Drew. Mother Gregory loved both of you. I know she left most of her inheritance to you, but for a reason. Your mom knew that Aaron could not be trusted. She was wiser than both of us. We trusted him too much."

"Aaron was never in serious trouble until this art scam."

"Wasn't he? You were away. Your mother refused to worry you about Aaron. But she'd want you to help him now regardless of what he's done."

Drew recoiled at the thought. He wanted to ask, *What were those secrets that troubled Mother? Aaron's gambling? His women? Defending notorious criminal cases? The wild spending?* But instead he said, "I'm overnighting at the Beverly Hilton."

"That's a gem of a hotel."

"I chose it because it was close to you. They have French dining in the Penthouse and dancing — in case you change your mind."

"I eat lightly in the evening." She stood on tiptoe and kissed him gently on the lips. "Take care of yourself and give Robyn and Pierre my love."

Drew dragged wearily into the Hilton, claimed his passkey, and went straight to his room. *She didn't even thank me for delivering the album,* he thought as he flopped on the bed. *Three thousand extra miles, and she didn't even care about seeing me.* But what had he expected?

He half dozed, his thoughts on his brother — David Levine's kid, the free spender with everything — the nattily dressed criminal lawyer. Interpol couldn't pick him up too quickly. But would they?

Drew had been asleep for hours, stretched out on the bed in his clothes, when a persistent tap at the door awakened him. The maid, he decided, with fresh towels and a candy mint for his pillow. He rolled off the bed, mumbling, "Use your key, you fool."

As he opened the door, Miriam smiled and

held up a picnic basket. She had changed into winter-white slacks and a matching cashmere sweater with flecks of gold in it. She wore a soft silk scarf at her neck and designer sandals on her slender feet.

"I was afraid you might skip dinner this evening."

"I did," he said sheepishly, wondering if he looked as messy as he felt. Hair uncombed. Shirt unbuttoned. "I've been sleeping."

"I can tell. But I had to come — for Robyn's sake. We're her parents. We parted poorly when I sent you away this afternoon."

"So you came — just for Robyn?"

"And Pierre. And for you."

"Then we can be friends? For Robyn's sake, of course."

"And for our own," she said softly. "May I come in?"

"The room's a mess. I'm a mess," he said running a hand through his rumpled hair. "I haven't showered or shaved." But he stepped back and smiled as she entered.

"Go ahead and do both if you like." She looked around, her eyes settling on a round table by the window. "I'll set the food out."

He whistled as he showered, hurrying lest she slip away again.

"Did you pick up your towel?" she asked

as he padded out of the bathroom in his stocking feet, a pile of dirty clothes under his arm.

She remembers my bad habits. "Yes, just in case you planned an inspection tour," he teased.

"You certainly pass inspection. I like the shirt. The color's good on you, Drew."

She was always a sucker for powder blue. "Robyn said you'd like it."

"I do."

She passed inspection, too, stirring old memories. He began to sing their old song. His rich tenor voice filled the room. He held out his arms. The familiar embrace, the scent of her perfume erased all time as he swirled her gracefully around the room. His arms tightened around her waist. "I wish it could be this way for the rest of our lives."

Flushed, she pulled away. "Drew, let's eat. I'm — I'm hungry."

Miriam had brought a small coffee pot, and the rich aroma of coffee mixed with her lingering scent. He noticed now that she had spread a cloth on the table and set it with her own dishes and red linen napkins. As he pushed in her chair, his lips brushed the nape of her neck. He sat down across from her, grateful that the table was small — and her hand within reach. For now he restrained himself and said quietly, "Thanks for coming, Miriam."

"Thank Floy. She said if I didn't come, she would come and apologize for my rudeness. So I'm here, and I'm sorry for being unkind. But I should have called ahead, not appeared on your doorstep."

He smiled. "I like surprises, especially nice ones. You look so lovely. Are you certain you don't want me to take you out to dinner?"

She met his gaze evenly. "Quite certain."

Miriam had thought of everything — thick roast beef sandwiches with mustard and lettuce the way he liked them. Carrot and celery sticks. Plenty of tossed salad. Cheese strips and olives. A baked potato still warm in its foil. Sliced apples and oranges for dessert. And she hadn't forgotten his taste for sparkling cider. He popped the cork for her and filled their goblets. "To you. To our friendship," he said, lifting his glass.

"To our friendship," she repeated shyly, her eyes shining.

As they finished the meal, she asked, "Will you be in Washington tomorrow? Or Langley?"

"Yes to both questions."

"Company business?"

"Partly. Robyn asked me to help a friend of hers."

"At Langley?"

"I'll start there."

"Please, don't let her get involved in Company matters."

"It isn't my choice, Miriam."

She began putting the dirty dishes in the basket. "How much longer, Drew? How many more years before you retire?"

"I would be out already if it hadn't been for Porter Deven. He's dragging his feet on my retirement."

"Do I dare ask why?"

"I can't even venture a guess. But I look forward to getting out and settling down in Scotland someday."

"I thought you'd live closer to Robyn."

Pensively, he asked, "Would that be wise?"

"One of us should be near her."

"We *both* should be."

She closed the basket and stood. "I have to go, Drew. Floy is waiting for me in the lobby."

"All this time?"

"No. She promised to come back for me in two hours."

He flexed his Rolex band. "Were you afraid of coming alone?"

There was an almost indiscernible stiffening of her shoulders, a defiant tip of her well-sculptured chin — those old warning signs that she was on the defensive. "I was afraid you wouldn't let me go . . . no, that I might not want to leave," she whispered.

He stumbled to his stocking feet, almost knocking his chair over, but she was inching toward the door, grabbing up her purse and coat, her lovely complexion flushed with embarrassment.

"Don't go. Stay here with me . . . tonight."

"Floy is waiting. Praying, I might add."

"That you won't stay?"

"That we'd be able to talk things out and be friends."

"Will I see you again?" he asked.

"Someday."

"Not *some*day, Miriam. I want to marry you."

"Again?" She touched his lips. "It's too late for us, Drew."

"I'm serious. As soon as I close out the business at Langley, I'll fly back. We can get married."

"I'm too old for marriage."

"That's ridiculous. We all need companionship."

Her deep-set eyes were wide and beautiful, darker than he remembered. He knew by her expression that she recognized the intensity and longing in his gaze. She lowered those long, thick lashes, teardrops making them glisten. "I want more than just companionship."

He grinned. "It might not be as romantic this time."

"Maybe not," she agreed.

"I've never stopped loving you, *Liebling*."

"I'm afraid."

"Afraid of what?"

"Of living with you. Of waiting for you to come home each night, not knowing if you will even get there. Not knowing if you are in danger. I couldn't go through that again." She brushed furiously against a tear.

"Afraid of the memories?" he asked quietly.

"Afraid — of sleeping with you again. Of our feelings. Maybe they won't come back."

"I think they will." He ran his fingers over her arm.

She turned. He tried to block her way now, standing in front of the door. "Don't leave. Don't go back to your house. I need you. I love you. Stay, please."

"Floy is waiting."

"I've been waiting for years, Miriam. Surely you feel something for me —"

"I always have. For me, Drew, there hasn't been anyone else."

"And you think there has been for me?"

"Weren't there other women for you?"

He was quiet, thoughtful, his fingers sliding down her arm again. He leaned closer. "No one that ever meant anything to me."

He kissed her gently, then with growing intensity. For a moment she yielded, then abruptly thrust him away. "Friendship, Drew. That's all I can offer."

Wiping *her* tears from his cheek, he stepped aside reluctantly and let her open the door. *You do love me, Liebling,* he thought.

As Drew checked out of the Hilton, a man in a gray business suit tapped him on the shoulder. "Mr. Gregory?"

"Yes," Drew said, half turning.

The stranger seemed tall for a Vietnamese, his dark eyes inquisitive behind wide horn-rimmed glasses. His thick, black hair was cropped closely around his ears and neck. Drew pegged him at forty, a couple of years older perhaps.

The man licked his thick lips. "I'm Duc Tran."

"Tran?" Drew kept studying the stranger's face, trying to place him. It was a full pleasant face, apprehensive at the moment, with a broad forehead, wide nostrils, and round protruding cheeks. He looked well-groomed, a narrow green tie knotted tightly against his neck.

"Am I supposed to know you?" Drew asked.

"Sauni Summers sent me."

Bingo! "You're Luke's friend."

Tran glanced around warily, his thick lips dry again. "Yes."

Drew pocketed his credit card and glanced at the clock. "Let's talk. I have twenty minutes before the airport limousine is due."

He guided Tran toward two empty lounge chairs in the corner of the lobby where they could face each other. "Why did Sauni Summers — Sauni Breckenridge — send you?"

"I don't know. Yesterday I refused to come."

"But you came."

He nodded. "This morning when I backed my car out, I saw graffiti all over the garage door. 'Laos liar,' it said."

"Laos liar? What kind of gibberish is that? Racial?"

"Perhaps . . . or another warning."

Drew rubbed his wrist, bouncing over his watch, his eye on the time. "Tran, only my daughter knew I was coming to Los Angeles."

The dark head bobbed. "She gave Sauni your number."

"Tell me about Captain Breckenridge."

Tran squirmed. "So many years ago. I've forgotten."

"You've forgotten your friend? You must remember something to get graffiti on your walls." He checked his Rolex. "My limo is coming. If you want to help Sauni Breckenridge —"

Tran's natural bronzed skin blanched, the deep brown eyes narrowing even more behind the horn-rimmed glasses. "I've not seen the Breckenridges for a long time."

Yeah, you ingrate, Drew thought.

"I was warned I'd be deported if I stayed in touch with them."

"You became an American citizen, didn't you?"

He nodded miserably. "Thanks to Luke's parents. But they threatened to send me back —"

"They? Luke's parents?"

"No. Two men. No names. And they would not send me back to the refugee camp in Thailand, but to my own country."

"*This* is your country now."

"Yes," he quailed. "I am an American. My

137

children were born here, but I would have lost everything. I would be dead."

"Dead for going back?"

"I fought with the Americans against my own people. For two years afterwards I worked for the Americans, and then they fled. I almost made it on the last American helicopter out of Saigon, but I was thrown from the steps of the plane."

"Accidentally?"

"No, CIA, I think. For a long time I was interned in a labor camp in Thakhek before I escaped across the Mekong River — only to become a refugee."

Drew glanced at his watch for the third time. "Tell me about Luke."

"We were friends. He was very sick."

Drew pointed to his temple. "In the head?"

Tran's hand went briefly to his chest. "In here," he said. "Luke had trouble breathing. And walking. His feet were bad." Duc moistened his lips again. "There's no way that Captain Breckenridge could have made it to Xangtiene from our base camp. He was too sick."

"The records place him there — deep in enemy territory."

Tran looked uncomfortable. "He would have had to fly there — at least partway. But we were told he went out for medical care, then home. I never knew he died. Not for long time."

"Would you swear to that?"

"Never." He looked like he was fast developing a cold-weather lip — dry and cracked — his round cheeks sagging as though numbness had set in. "I can't let anything happen to my family."

"Why would it? Breckenridge is a dead man."

"But maybe someone killed him."

The limo driver entered the lobby. "A Mr. Gregory?" he called.

Drew stood and waved. "Over here. I'm Gregory. Coming." He glared down at Tran. "How do we keep in touch?"

"If you need me, leave word at your wife's gallery."

"No, that's not a good idea."

"My company will start an account with her. It will be a simple matter to pick up messages."

"I'll be going back to Europe in a week."

Duc offered a toothy smile. "Miss Summers — she will fly my wife and me to Switzerland if we're needed."

Drew spun away in disgust. Bribery. This whole charade was bribery. Another free trip and Duc Tran would tell Luke's family anything they wanted to hear.

"Gregory," the driver called out again im-patiently.

"Coming." He strode quickly to the desk and picked up his luggage. When he turned back, Duc Tran was gone.

Chapter 8

The first streaks of dawn brightened the Businger skyline as the Courtlands pulled up in front of Saundra's gray frame home. For a second she held back before opening the door to Pierre. What lay behind their invitation to the von Tonner mansion? Did they have news for her? She was certain of it. *Bad news about Luke.*

Pierre seemed preoccupied as he faced her, his easygoing smile restrained. "Did you find someone to take your classes?" he asked.

"Annabelle Vandiver."

He almost chuckled. "I remember her."

"And she remembers you." *She warned me not to fall in love with you nor care too much. Annabelle knew we had nothing in common but classical music and Vietnam. I should have listened to her.*

He grabbed Sauni's luggage and hurried her out to the car. As he packed the trunk, the opened trunk lid shielded their faces from Robyn. He kept his voice low. "Who knows that Drew is helping you?"

"No one except you two."

His hand was on the hood now, hesitant. "Sauni, what about your friend Vandiver?"

"She knows about Luke. That's all. Nothing about Mr. Gregory."

"And Duc Tran?"

"I did call Duc Tran, but no one else."

"Not your dad?"

"No. I was afraid he'd interfere. What's wrong, Pierre? Is there more bad news from Washington?"

"There's no news at all about Luke. My father-in-law's Monday appointment at Langley was cancelled."

Sauni smothered her disappointment as Pierre said, "He rescheduled for Friday. But Drew wants to know why you called Duc Tran without telling him."

"Was Drew angry with me?"

"He makes his own moves, Sauni. He doesn't want this Duc Tran showing up at Miriam's Art Gallery."

Robyn tooted the horn. "Come on, you two."

"Wait, Sauni. How much can we trust Tran? The man is frightened or gives a good appearance of being so. Why?"

"I don't know, Pierre. He didn't even want to talk to me. He said it wasn't safe — that he's been threatened."

He touched her hand. "It's not just this

142

Duc Tran encounter. Drew feels that he's being set up, that his appointment in Langley was deliberately rescheduled. It may have nothing to do with Luke, but we don't want anything to happen to Robyn's father."

"Then why did you invite me to go with you this weekend?"

"Robyn thinks you need a weekend holiday." He slammed the trunk lid and opened the door for her.

Robyn reached around and squeezed her hand. "Sauni, don't let Pierre worry you. My dad's not a quitter, but he is in charge. Don't run ahead of him. Now . . . I'm glad you're going with us. You'll love the von Tonner place. Pierre and I do."

As Pierre drove through Schaffhausen and turned north into Germany, his mood lightened. "Wait 'til you see the von Tonner art collection. It's indescribable. By the way, isn't your friend Vandiver interested in famous art pieces?"

"Mostly in stolen ones. Her favorite was the Mona Lisa taken from the Louvre and the Rembrandt-Monet heist from the Isabella Stewart Gardner Museum. Since she's been living in Busingen, she's kept up on the von Tonner art scandal, too."

"Did you tell her the collection is intact

except for a few major pieces sold by the late baroness?"

"Million dollar sales," Robyn said mournfully.

"When Annabelle learned I'd be at the mansion this weekend, she sent her camera with me. I'm to snap pictures of everything."

"You'd better take that up with Albert Klee, the caretaker there. He's against people photographing anything on the property."

"Oh, dear. Annabelle will be disappointed."

"That's the way I'd describe my parents' visit in Los Angeles. I phoned both of them yesterday. All Dad said was that he delivered the wedding album. When I called Mother, all she did was cry."

"Then she probably cried in her soup," Pierre teased. "They had dinner together at a plush hotel, Sauni. Romantic, huh?"

"A picnic in Dad's room," Robyn corrected. "Of course, Pierre thinks that's ridiculous, but my parents loved picnics."

For miles they drove along the Rhine River in silence. Robyn's bubbling excitement at the prospect of seeing the mansion again seemed to have subsided. Sauni felt a formidable sense of sadness for Robyn's mother, a kinship with a woman she had never met.

The searing memory of thrusting divorce papers in Luke's face crashed in on her. She rarely allowed it to surface. It was too painful. She wondered if Miriam Gregory had also used divorce papers to gain her own way. For Sauni, it had backfired.

She could never erase Luke's look of utter disbelief nor the words he had whispered. "But I love you, Sauni."

"If you go back, I won't be here when you come home again," she had told him.

A childish statement, she thought now. As though she could ask a career marine to ignore a war or a military assignment. He had needed her strength, not her rejection. But back then, her own desire to keep him from going back to a battlefield had been reinforced by her father's opposition to the war. With Luke's cleft chin nuzzling the top of her head, he had promised to give up the marines *after one more tour of duty.* Later, with the divorce papers still in his pocket, he had asked to stay with her one more night. She had turned him away; she recalled it now as the cruelest thing she had ever done to Luke.

She saw his handsome face again now through blurred vision: disbelieving, wounded, the strong jaw sagging. But he had kept the proud Breckenridge stance, his shoulders squared even as his eyes misted.

"This is my last night. I have to report back to the base by midnight."

She heard herself refuse him again.

Luke had tossed his winter service jacket over his shoulder and left without looking back. She'd been too proud to call after him to tell him she loved him. Was that the way it had been with Miriam Gregory? Too proud? Too stubborn? And now, too late?

"Sauni — Sauni Breckenridge . . ."

She looked up. Robyn had turned in her seat and was staring at her. "Are you all right? I've repeated the same thing three times."

"I'm sorry. My thoughts wandered."

"Then you probably didn't hear what Pierre said. His aunt and uncle will be visiting the baron this weekend. You'll finally get to meet them."

"Isn't that the uncle who works for Interpol?"

"My only uncle," Pierre said proudly. "Before that Kurt spent twenty years in the States. Served in the U. S. Marines. He's got that old *semper fidelis* spirit. You'll like Kurt and Ina."

Pierre gunned the motor. "There she is!" he cried out. "The von Tonner mansion. It's like coming home."

"It *is* home to you, darling," Robyn said.

Saundra leaned forward, her head close to Robyn's as they rode high above the Rhine, wending their way up a steep, narrow road. Toward the top stood a majestic structure, its grayish-white stone almost blinding in the winter sun; its turrets jutted from a slate blue roof. "Pierre, it's a fairyland castle."

"Impressive, isn't it? I've loved this place since I was a boy."

"And you never invited me here?"

"I rarely came myself when the baroness was alive."

Sauni stared ahead. A brick wall and semi-barren trees surrounded the property; animal-shaped hedges lay beyond that. Even a few winter flowers dotted the yard in reds and yellows. "You'll have to come back with us in the spring or summer," Pierre told her. "Hedwig's garden is worth the trip."

As they neared the ornate gate, Pierre blared his horn. The gate swung open, and a gray-haired man waved them through.

"That's Albert Klee," Robyn said.

Sauni peered back out the window and watched him secure the gate. Then Albert turned, his hand shading the hawk eyes that stared back at her. "Is he the caretaker?" she asked.

"He's more than that," Pierre said. "He and the baron have been lifelong friends, so much more than master and servant. Albert has always been good to me, too."

Robyn laughed. "When I first met the Klees, I liked Albert right off, but I found Hedwig most formidable. The baroness was alive then and very much the mistress of her castle."

"Now," Pierre said, "Hedwig is in charge."

As the car stopped, the old man rushed up in quick, agile movements to swing the door open. His wrinkled face broke into a grin, spreading the thin lips wider. He pulled Pierre from the car and gripped his arms. "Boy, it's good to see you. We told the baron you were coming — and reminded him numerous times since."

"And?" Pierre asked hopefully.

"Have patience. We're getting some meat on those bones. Can't fatten up the memory, but he'll recognize you."

"Is he still asking for Ingrid?"

"All the time. We've stopped telling him she's gone though. It was like having her die all over again each time he heard it. So we just talk like she's away for a little while."

Albert trotted around the front of the car to hug Robyn and extend his rough, work-worn hand toward Saundra. Her own felt small in his as he cupped them with his callused palms. "The boy here told me about you," he said.

This trip? she wondered. *Or a long time ago when Pierre and I were first friends? Friends — that's all we have ever been.* She chided herself for futile memories and smiled up into the weathered face hooded by bushy brows.

"Hedwig made soup and homemade bread for us," Albert said.

Pierre glanced toward the double doors and started toward the steps where a new wheelchair ramp rose beside them. Klee held him back. "Before you go inside, boy, there's been a change made in the sitting room. Herr Brinkmeirer's doing. You may not like it."

Worry lines hit Pierre's brow. "What's wrong?"

"Your uncle hung the baroness's portrait beside the baron's."

"Is he crazy? That oil painting isn't even finished."

Old Albert looked down, his servitude returning. "Your uncle arranged for the artist to complete it. Now Felix sits in there for hours at a time gazing up at her. It seems to comfort him."

"Is Uncle Kurt here yet?"

"No, not until morning." Klee grinned broadly, his stained teeth ugly and uneven.

"Do you wish to see the baron before we eat?"

"Is he up?" Robyn asked anxiously.

"Up?" he chortled. "He's with Klaus and the horses."

"Out in the stable in this weather? Oh, no, Albert."

He patted her face. "Hedwig insists on it. No arguing with her. She says Felix needs good food and fresh air. She feeds him herself and then wraps him in warm blankets for his trips outside."

"He's better then, Albert?"

He shook his head sadly. "He's put on a few extra pounds and has more color in his cheeks, but we can't extend his life."

Pierre started off toward the stables on a run. Then he turned back. "Come on, ladies. Let's go see Felix."

They set out after him walking rapidly over the crusty ground, the chill of the mountain air whipping against them. When they reached the stable, Pierre was kneeling on one knee embracing the frail old man tucked warmly in the wheelchair. Felix clutched a carrot in his trembling chalk-white hand. Gently, Pierre said, "Baron, it's Pierre. I've come to see you."

The gaunt face lifted, the watery eyes so pale they looked a sea-foam blue; puffy pouches hung beneath them. Pierre wrapped his strong fingers around the old man's and steadied them so the chestnut stallion could nibble the carrot. The horse neighed. Felix smiled.

Sauni choked up watching them: the magnificent horse with powerful chest and elegant mane, the fragile baron with slumped shoulders and tufts of thinning gray hair, the younger man hiding his tears. The horse stood proudly on sturdy, muscular legs. The old man would never stand again, but Pierre stood in the gap between them reaching out to both of them.

"That's Monarch," Robyn whispered. "He's a Persian Arab, a really spirited horse. The baron gave him to Ingrid — his two wild ones, he called them. Ingrid handled Monarch well. And so does Klaus the stable boy. Pierre has ridden him a few times — while I anxiously held my breath. Other than that, Monarch has thrown everyone who tries to ride him."

"But he obviously likes the baron," Sauni said.

"Yes, he seems to know Felix is his friend, doesn't he?"

Pierre turned and waved for them to come. When Robyn hugged Felix, she caught a smile in return. Sauni took the old man's icy hand in hers. "I'm a friend of Pierre's," she said.

Felix's watery eyes turned back to Pierre, a fragile smile still lighting his face. "Did Ingrid come with you?" he asked.

"No, Baron."

Felix leaned forward to stroke the stallion's neck. "He misses Ingrid. She always had peppermint sticks for him." Then he muttered unhappily, "Take me back to the house, Pierre."

Monarch neighed as Pierre rolled Felix out of the well-kept stable. Maneuvering the wheelchair up the ramp and into the house, Pierre asked, "Where to, Baron?"

Felix pointed toward the sitting area where two portraits dominated the room. Sauni barely recognized the sharp, well-chiseled features of the baron, a playful smile around his thick lips. It was like staring into the face of a stranger and having him stare back at her. She allowed her gaze to move to the portrait that captivated the baron. His eyes teared as he stared up at the baroness, a woman with shimmering silvery hair and dark enticing eyes. She had a regal bearing, an engaging smile, her graceful ringed hands resting against a brocaded chair back.

The portraits were overpowering, diminishing the antiquity of the room and its ornate furnishings. Pierre turned away first.

"Do you like it, Pierre?" the old man asked.

"Yes, it's a lovely surprise. Ingrid would be pleased to see her picture hanging there beside yours."

Felix folded his gnarled hands and stared up at his baroness once more. "She will never see it, Pierre. She's gone, you know."

"Gone?" Pierre asked, a catch in his voice.

"Dead, I think. You never liked her, son."

"No," Pierre admitted. "I'm sorry about that now."

"Yes, so am I."

Robyn squeezed his thin shoulders. "She loved you, Felix."

"No," he lamented. "She loved my money. But it didn't matter. She was all I ever wanted in a woman." His words faded. "For a little while, I thought we were very happy."

The canopied bed and the spacious luxury of the quiet room were lovely, but Sauni did not sleep well. One moment she saw Luke's face. The next, two portraits side by side in the sitting room downstairs. The baron's face blurred, and she saw Luke's. Ingrid's face blurred, and she saw her own. Sauni buried her head beneath the pillows, but she could not block out the images nor the sound

of the baron's voice saying, *For a little while,
I thought we were very happy.*

Her pillow was soaked with her own tears.
At dawn she padded barefoot to the window
and looked down toward the Rhine. In the
loneliness of the von Tonner mansion with
the wind hitting against the narrow shuttered
windows, she cried out, "Oh, Luke, we were
very happy for a little while."

On Sunday Robyn and Sauni waited by
the packed car as Pierre said his goodbyes
in the privacy of the baron's bedroom.
When he joined them, Kurt Brinkmeirer
clapped Pierre's shoulder. "It gets harder
to leave him each time. But he is happier
here, Pierre. The Klees are taking good
care of him."

"I know, Uncle Kurt. I just wish he could
live with Robyn and me. We could get a big
enough place."

Kurt winked at Robyn and jammed an
unlit Marlboro between his lips. "That's not
practical, Pierre. Felix spent so little time in
Geneva. Nothing would be familiar. This is
home for him."

"What happens if the courts take over the
mansion?" Robyn asked.

Kurt smiled amiably, the Marlboro in the
corner of his mouth distorting his smile. "I

wanted to hold off on my good news until everything was settled, but the lawyers have the records from the clinic now. It looks like things are in the baron's favor; the Cannes clinic confirmed his dementia diagnosis on admission."

Pierre grabbed Robyn and whirled her around triumphantly. "Didn't I tell you? The divorce papers were illegal!"

"Slow down, Pierre," Kurt warned. "They'll contact us as soon as any official decision is made. That could be months."

"But it looks like a green light for the museum," Robyn exclaimed. "I wish Felix understood so we could tell him."

"He's content the way things are, Robyn. Don't clutter his thoughts with legal matters." Kurt hugged her before she eased into the car beside Pierre. "Ina and I are enjoying having a niece," he said. "We should get together more often."

"Let's do," Robyn answered for both of them.

Kurt pocketed the unlit cigarette and glanced back at the mansion. "So you two are still thinking about a national museum?"

"Someday," Pierre said.

"I think more about it than Pierre does," Robyn admitted. "Art is my dream. I'd hate leaving the von Tonner art collection lying neglected in the tunnels for another fifty years."

"Then why don't we hang some of the pictures up in the mansion — so the baron can enjoy them?" He winked. "Ina was thrilled to see the baron's favorite Rembrandt hanging back in its old place on the landing."

"You didn't do that?"

"No, Pierre. Ina and I thought you did."

Pierre rubbed his square jaw and grinned. "So Albert put it back where it belongs."

Uncle Kurt nodded politely to Sauni in the back seat. "I'm sorry we didn't have more time to talk about your husband, but that sort of problem is out of Interpol's control."

The big, burly six-footer leaned down and smiled at her, his gaze sympathetic. "If things don't work out with Drew Gregory, I'll call a couple of my old marine buddies. We old leathernecks stick together, but if your husband broke faith with the Corps or his country, we won't be able to help you."

His eyes seemed as piercing as Pierre's. "My nephew and his wife are inclined to believe that Captain Breckenridge kept faith with his country."

Sauni sounded less than confident even to herself. "My husband did. I know he did."

Kurt reached through the open window

and squeezed her hand. Thin threads of hope leaped inside her, then tumbled again. She looked back several times as the car wound around the twisting roads until Kurt and the mansion slipped from view.

Then she lapsed into silence. *Luke would have loved the old mansion — particularly the tunnels,* she thought with a chilling uneasiness. As she stared out at the gathering storm clouds, she tried to imagine Luke racing through the labyrinthine tunnels, alert and curious. Instead, in the cloud formations, she saw a marine captain limping over the trails of Laos toward Xangtiene, a metal box marked TOP SECRET gripped in his hand.

Dear Luke, she cried silently, *even strangers want to believe in you now, but did you betray us all? Did you really betray your country? Were you trying to punish me for the divorce?*

Chapter 9

For Drew cloud nine had collapsed, but he still drove through the gates at Langley, riding high with his thoughts on Miriam. When the guard asked for identification, Drew almost said, Miriam's Art Gallery, but he caught himself in time.

Unknown by the new breed at the gate, he was directed to the visitors' parking lot. He stepped from the car and glanced at the sprawling complex before him, shaded in part by massive oak and magnolia trees. Deep inside the headquarters in a windowless room, a safe contained Langley's ultra top secrets, classified documents that were closed to him. Did they contain the mission to the village of Xangtiene nearly a quarter of a century ago? Even if he had the right to know what that safe contained, he didn't know Luke's designated code name.

As he made his way toward the entry, Drew passed the curving Kryptos sculpture in the courtyard between the old and new buildings. A maze of letters covered the stone scroll, its secrets encoded on copper plates, secrets symbolic of the life Drew led.

Every time he walked through the doors into the main lobby, he was struck afresh with the code of honor that existed with Company men, a secrecy commitment that had ruined his marriage. He still had trouble defining honor and integrity and the need-to-know principle that governed CIA officers. Side-stepping the circular mosaic emblazoned with Central Intelligence Agency, he asked himself again, *What right do I have to know about Luke Breckenridge?*

To his left was the statue of Wild Bill Donovan and to his right the memorial to fallen CIA officers. He paused there and looked up at the rows of unnamed stars. These men and women had operated under-cover, their names withheld even now for security reasons. Drew considered the possibility that one of those stars might represent Breckenridge. If it did, then he knew why Luke's name had been omitted from the Vietnam Memorial Wall. Things happened that way sometimes — a CIA man under military cover. It had been done in several wars, definitely in Vietnam.

A hand slapped his shoulder. He turned, surprised to see Chadsworth Kaminsky standing there. Kaminsky, a hunk of a man, was lugging around twenty extra pounds and a dozen new wrinkles. He'd been a fair and square man to work with, but he looked as uncomfortable as Drew felt when they shook hands.

"The receptionist told me you were here, so I came down to meet you. What are you doing — checking out the honor roll?"

Drew's eyes went back to the rows of stars. "It's sobering — a wall full of *unknown* warriors."

"You know it has to be that way. We still operate under deep cover in some places," Chad said. "Some of these stars are new. Somalia, for one. Are you looking for someone in particular?"

"A young marine."

"You've got the wrong memorial wall."

"Do I?" Drew ran his hand over the shiny marble surface, his fingers touching one star. "What happens if one of our officers serves under military cover? Do we omit his name on both walls?"

"Are you on a fishing expedition, Drew?"

"Yeah, and I feel like I'm swimming against the current. Kid's name was Luke Breckenridge. Three tours of duty in Vietnam. Divorced. No kids. Annapolis grad. Apparently ended up in Laos on a CIA mission. Killed in a village that people say doesn't exist."

Chadsworth flexed his fat fingers. "He's buried in Arlington."

"I'd like to see the files on him."

Chad's gravelly tone lowered. "You and the media! You're the third one in three weeks trying to unlock the Breckenridge files. Forget it. You know that's all classified stuff, if it does exist."

"Then tell me — do we have a star up there for Breckenridge?"

Kaminsky's answer erupted vehemently. "These honorable men and women died for this country. They didn't betray it."

"Did Breckenridge?"

"Let it go, Drew."

"The *Washington Post* said —"

"If the newspaper is your source of information, then ask them." He cracked his knuckles and said more calmly, "When you were in Croatia, our first reports had you dead. Neilson and I thought we'd be starring you on this wall. We hated the idea."

"That's another false report where I want answers, Chad."

"We all make mistakes. You just blew your cover. You're lucky you got out of it alive."

"Someone else blew my cover." Drew pictured his thick file marred only by the time in Croatia. "I was luckier than Breckenridge."

"Did you know him?"

"I know his wife, Saundra."

"I've met Mrs. B. a couple of times when she was defending her husband's reputation. She's a determined lady, but not half the problem that Breckenridge's parents have been. His father is a retired admiral, a well-decorated hero. They've fought this rumor thing about their son for twenty years." He sighed. "They should have let it go. Captain Breckenridge was buried with honors — before anyone knew what really happened."

"Tell me, were the newspaper facts accurate?"

Chad glanced around the lobby. "Some of them. The military did cut through red tape in a big hurry after he was killed in Vietnam."

"In *Laos*."

"That error has been corrected. Haste was important in the beginning, so Breckenridge's sealed casket was shipped home immediately and his burial given full honors at Arlington."

Drew frowned. "His casket? Not his body?"

They advanced slowly around the lobby. "It took months of investigation to quell rumors in Southeast Asia. Like the *Washington Post* said, some classified secrets fell into the wrong hands during the war. After Luke's disappearance — his death, if you prefer — nothing else turned up missing during that era."

"The Agency labeled him a traitor on circumstantial evidence?"

"Not at first. Try to understand, Drew. He wasn't on patrol. The kid traipsed into the jungles on his own — behind enemy lines."

"But his wife said Luke was sick with pneumonia, his feet full of jungle rot."

"Her story! There's nothing in the records to confirm that."

"But he was under CIA cover, right?"

"That's just his wife's opinion."

A long silence passed between them. "Chad, what's kept this story of treason fueled for more than twenty years?"

"The press and Breckenridge's parents. The rumors die down periodically. In the beginning, out of respect for the admiral, we kept it under wraps. Classified. Then the Memorial Wall went up, and the White House faced a hassle over the Breckenridge omission. That's when the Agency called the admiral in and squared away with him. We told him his son was guilty of treason. He walked out with his chin on his boot top. Never saw a man so devastated."

"The admiral accepted the accusation — just like that?"

"He fought for details at first, but the truth about Luke's betrayal was too much for him. Admiral and Mrs. Breckenridge went into seclusion after that. So things stayed relatively quiet until recently. Then, like the newspaper said, a wealthy widow from Florida came on holiday — an old family friend to the Breckenridges. It made her mad that Luke's name was left off the wall, so she stirred up a ruckus scuffling off to an editor friend at the *Post*. Now she's on a crusade to get Breckenridge's body removed from Arlington." Kaminsky swore softly. "Some family friend, huh? That woman won't stop until she gets her way. She's got money, power, and senators behind her."

"Why not transfer Luke's body and close this case forever?"

Chad's pace quickened, his agitation evident in thudding steps. "The Agency can't allow that. Arlington represents government control for us. If Luke were buried elsewhere, his father could do what he's wanted to do for years — exhume his son's body. And if there's no body, then what?"

The muscles in Drew's neck tightened. He did his best to keep his voice even. "What are you saying, Chad? Isn't Luke Breckenridge buried there?"

"How could he be? He walked into the

jungles on his own and disappeared behind enemy lines in the predawn hours. We don't know what happened to him."

"Didn't his commanding officer have an explanation?"

"Luke's C. O. committed suicide."

Drew almost stumbled. "Good grief . . . Is it possible that Breckenridge is still alive?"

"Doubtful, after all these years. And we don't want the media getting wind of that rumor. It lends credence to the belief that he sided with the enemy. You wouldn't like taking that kind of message back to Mrs. B., would you?"

They finished circling the lobby a second time before heading toward the elevator. "Drew, if Porter sent you to Washington just over this Breckenridge case, then we might as well skip the meeting with Harv Neilson. Harv has enough problems."

"I've barely discussed Breckenridge with Porter. Porter's primary interest is a mercenary camp in Spain."

Chad lunged at Drew like a linebacker. "Porter knows about that? You'll set Harv on edge when he hears that one."

They rode Neilson's private elevator to the seventh floor in silence. As the doors slid open, Chad warned, "Harv wants to keep good ties with Spain. Personal reasons. He doesn't like intelligence reports on mercenary camps in Europe, and he opposes any covert activity, especially in Spain." Chad winked as they reached Neilson's office. "Maybe you can persuade him differently."

Neilson sat behind his mahogany desk surrounded by telephone hot lines to his senior officials. A bookcase crammed with history and law books rose to the ceiling. His life was framed on the walls — family photographs and an impressive assortment of degrees and military honors. Neilson's smile of welcome came slowly as though his thoughts were not contained within these walls.

He'd hit the sixty mark, sixty-three, if Drew remembered correctly — a reserved, well-groomed man with thinning silver hair and mild good looks. A dynamo on the tennis court, he fought to win and cursed when he didn't. Drew knew him to be an intelligent man, his memory chips as good as any computer.

"Sit down, gentlemen," he said, his voice impersonal. "I got in late from the Daily Brief with the President. I'm due back there again early this afternoon."

Drew took Neilson's hand, remembering the friendship that had once existed. "I won't keep you long, Harv."

"Long enough for lunch," he encouraged,

his tone more friendly. "I'm expecting another guest."

Kaminsky wiped his brow and planked himself in the softer chair, leaving the straight-back one for Drew. Neilson and Kaminsky both hailed from the Bible belt, but Neilson's churchgoing was political, Kaminsky's more genuine. Neilson acted far more polished, coming as he did from a wealthy Charleston family. By contrast, no matter how Kaminsky tried, he couldn't shake his weight or his country background. But he was a good man, with a more easygoing personality than Harv's.

Neilson folded his arms. "So what's this plan that brought you to Washington?" he asked.

"Porter wants to infiltrate a mercenary camp in Spain."

"Sounds like one of Porter's usual bombshells. Go on."

Drew took advantage of the opening and for the next twenty minutes briefed them on the mercenary camp, pointing out its growing threat to American safety. He summed it up saying, "Porter wants to put some men on the inside to see what we can discover."

"Does that include you?" Neilson asked.

"That's the plan. Victor Wilson will go with me."

"Tell Porter he's out of line. We have men in Madrid."

"He said to tell you he'd work with them."

Harv actually smiled.

"An American may be running the camp. Porter first got wind of it months ago when the Serbs turned over three prisoners to the French government. They turned out to be soldiers for hire — said they had been trained by an American in Spain."

"Not Africa?"

"No, Spain."

Neilson rubbed his jaw. "Chad, I want satellite confirmation on this." Harv was already looking at his watch. "I can't go to the President with rumors or some cock-and-bull scheme of Porter's. Does he have an exact locale?"

"The camp moves periodically."

"You know I won't authorize men or funding for a covert operation in Spain. Neither will Congress. Besides, King Juan Carlos is a personal friend of mine. Go back and tell Porter to turn over his information to Spanish Intelligence."

"You're not interested in the American?"

"Drew, Americans do a lot of crazy things. If the man wants to get himself killed training mercenary soldiers, let him."

Drew had an uncanny feeling that the

American was already identified, already expendable. Surely Neilson knew an American-run camp spelled trouble.

Neilson guffawed. "No need for Porter to risk sending men in. I'll let the satellites nail down the camps for us. Then we'll pass that information on to Spanish Intelligence. Don't worry, Drew, I've come to appreciate those big boys in the sky. Laser satellites can orbit the earth faster than it would take you to weasel your way into camp as a hired soldier."

Neilson's hands flattened and tented at an amazing speed. "Congress and most Americans fight any military intervention or covert operation that risks lives and weapons. If Congress kicks up a fuss about putting troops on the line for an African bread basket, they won't thank us for risking a covert operation in a friendly country — nor budget for it."

Kaminsky wiped his chubby hands on his thighs. "Some of the senators even scoff at the need for our Agency anymore."

"Is Senator Summers involved in the cutbacks?"

Chad shot Drew a warning glance as Neilson said, "Summers is always at the center of controversy. He thinks handshakes are ample between foreign powers. Have you had a run-in with him, Drew?"

"I never met the man."

"Then why ask if he's involved?"

"His daughter and mine are friends."

"Summers's daughter?" Harv asked. "Then you know she's a war widow. Her husband was killed in the Vietnam conflict."

"Yes, in Laos. I understand the senator tries to keep rumors about his son-in-law under cover. Why, Harv?" Drew challenged.

A trickle of sweat formed on Kaminsky's brow as he sent another warning signal to Drew. Neilson's strong, firm hands went flat on the desk. "Summers hates having a traitor for a son-in-law."

"If young Breckenridge is guilty of treason, why all the hush-hush? Are we protecting the Agency for some reason?"

Neilson grabbed one of the phones. "Send David Shipley over here."

Minutes later a breathless Shipley bounded into the room, a stocky, curly-headed man in his mid-forties with a boyish grin, bright intelligent eyes, and two packs of gum in his shirt pocket.

To Drew he looked like one of the new breed, an Ivy Leaguer from Harvard with four degrees behind his name. A satellite wizard who wanted to set Drew straight about traitors.

In a pleasant modulated voice, Shipley said, "Good to see you again, Neilson. How may I help you?"

"Mr. Gregory here is interested in Laos."

Shipley turned to Drew, a stick of gum in his hand. "I'm your man. I know the jungles of Laos and Vietnam as well as anyone."

"You're with the Company?"

"Spooks? Not me. I spent twenty years in the army. Several of them working with the Joint Casualty Resolution Center before I retired. Now I'm doing a similar job with a corporation in Thailand — in Bangkok to be exact. I'm just another civilian now."

Drew gambled on the man's knowledge. "I'm interested in a marine named Luke Breckenridge."

The smile remained fixed as Shipley glanced first at Neilson and Kaminsky, then back at Drew. "One of the MIAs?"

"No. He was killed in Laos twenty years ago."

"Did they find his body?"

Hurriedly, Kaminsky said, "He's buried in Arlington."

"Then I'm not sure why you called me in to meet this gentleman. My work is with the men who were left behind."

Neilson forced a smile. "Gregory thinks there's some question about the mission

Breckenridge was on when he was killed. Have you ever heard of the village of Xang-tiene in Laos?"

"I've been in several villages. The names all sound alike." Shipley turned his alert eyes on Drew. "I don't think you understand my job. We try to locate missing men; we don't track the mission or patrol they were on. We follow every clue or faked photo, every false sighting and rumor. In a few cases we've been able to return the remains of some of our men home, confirming their death and resolving their identity."

"But you've never heard of Luke Brecken-ridge?"

He hesitated. "Not that I recall."

Drew plunged on blindly. "His father-in-law is a senator, and he's on a committee to have Luke's body removed from Arlington National Cemetery."

"Because of something that happened in Laos? Sounds like the kind of man who would sell you down the Mekong River."

"He's interested in reelection."

Harv interrupted. "Gregory knows Breck-enridge's widow."

Shipley seemed confused, uncertain now. "Neilson, when we spoke earlier, I thought . . . look, there's nothing to resolve in this case — not if he's buried in Arlington."

An uncomfortable silence settled over the room. From the expression on Neilson's face, Drew discerned that things were not going as planned. Or maybe Shipley had missed his cue. A fresh stick of gum seemed to revive him. "Gregory, I'll keep your friend in mind," he offered. "If I ever hear anything —"

"Forget it," Neilson said. "Dead marines are not Drew's responsibility. Congress wants our Agency to keep tabs on the military hardware that's rusting in Russia and on terrorism."

Drew flicked the lock on his briefcase. "You're right, Neilson. The stockpiles of plutonium around the world are far more important than war widows and mercenary camps."

"You're sounding like your old self, Drew. Power politics or potential war zones — that's our focus. One crazy country with a nuclear weapon — that's all it would take."

Shipley smiled wryly. "I'm for removing sanctions against old enemies and forming good trade agreements with them. Then there'd be no need to worry about nuclear threats."

Drew couldn't tell if the young man was serious or not. He mixed everything he said with a boyish grin. Was he pushing for more

American corporations back in Vietnam or for full, free exchange with that country, too? "So you don't want to hold out for an accounting of the men we lost in Vietnam?" Drew asked.

"We'll never have that, sir. But improved relationships between our countries will open doors for me — and help me in my search for the remains of missing men. I've trekked those jungles on mission after mission with little help from old Saigon." He shot a glance at Kaminsky and Neilson. "There's no way we'll ever get an accurate accounting. But I can assure you, none of our boys are still alive over there. For all the trips I've made, we have less than a hundred men accounted for. And Luke Breckenridge was not one of them."

Drew felt he was parroting what Chad and Harv wanted him to say. "I don't believe you," Drew said. "And I won't until every rat-infested labor camp and every isolated village is searched. The instinct for survival may have kept some of our men alive."

"Impossible!" Harv said. In his smooth articulate manner, he added, "Drew, the MIA/POW issue is dead."

"Tell that to the families who still have missing men there."

Neilson's hands flattened on the desk

again. "You've forgotten something, Drew. Our operatives are busy fencing with drug kingpins and terrorists these days."

"Yet Congress won't approve of our investigating a mercenary camp that trains terrorists?"

"Come on," Kaminsky said, "that kind of scouting expedition doesn't get votes here at home. Be content, Drew. You hold a good position at the embassy in London."

"I've had my fill of pretending to be a diplomatic attaché. Train me in the computerized tracking of terrorists. Let me work with the technology boys here at Langley for a while before I retire. I've still got a good mind. And London is not where I want to be."

"Tell that to Porter."

"I've told him several times. Did you talk to him about it when he was here? His secretary said he flew over for a few days."

"Porter wasn't in town," Neilson snapped. "His secretary gave you the wrong information. That old bachelor is probably on the Riviera with some bathing beauty."

Drew knew better. Porter Deven was more apt to be holed up in a room with his favorite French wine.

For the sixth time, Neilson looked pointedly at his watch. He pushed back his leather chair and rose to a straight five-ten. "Let's have lunch. Come along, Shipley. You were good enough to come by — twice now to fill us in on your work. You've earned a meal in the director's dining room."

"What's the final word for Porter?" Drew asked.

Neilson smiled slyly. "No funding. No permission. But tell him to keep me posted. And when that one's over, check back with me, Gregory. Maybe you still have enough years left to track some terrorists — by computers. You could keep your eye out for your old KGB opponent. What was his name?"

"Nicholas Ivan Trotsky."

"He never did resurface, did he?"

"He will someday."

"Not with the new Russia."

"I may not live to see it, Neilson, but he's out there somewhere. A clever man. A clever sleeper."

Neilson chortled, a hard, cruel laugh. "Give Porter my message on Spain. Now let's hurry. Like I told you, I'm due back at the White House this afternoon for another briefing with the President."

"What's the hot topic this time?" Drew asked.

"Mercenary training camps, for one. But let's talk about that later. My lunch guest is anxious to meet you."

Neilson strolled into his private dining room ahead of Drew, his hand extended to the reedy, loose-limbed guest waiting for him. "Senator Summers," he greeted warmly, "we're sorry to keep you waiting. Kaminsky tells me you're going to run for office one more time. You've got my vote."

An hour later, Neilson stood at the window and watched Drew Gregory stepping briskly toward the parking lot. The visit in the dining room had not gone well. He turned slowly and faced Glenn Summers. "What do we do now, Senator?" he asked wearily.

"Do everything you can to get that man out of the country and back to London."

Chapter 10

When Gregory reached his Washington hotel, the room was in shambles — his clothes strewn across the rug, the bed torn apart, the mattress slit, drawers dumped on the floor, chairs overturned. He forced the door hard against the wall to brutalize anyone hiding behind it. As the wall vibrated, a pastoral painting swayed on its hook, then slipped as if in an inebriated stupor to the floor.

He crouched, fingers outstretched, ready to spring, his own heavy breathing pounding in his ears. The drapes hung motionless. The Beretta, *if he still owned one*, was in the briefcase under the bed. Five seconds. Ten. Drew crept across the room to the bathroom. No one. The closet — empty except for his clothes dumped on the floor. Behind him someone gasped. He whirled and stared at the maid trembling in the doorway, fresh linen toppling from her arms.

As she stumbled over the towels, he grabbed her. "It's okay. Here, sit down. You'll be all right."

"Has someone been murdered?" she cried.

"No, thank God! Not murder, a robbery," he corrected.

The name tag on her uniform read "Maria." She was college age, a petite young woman with a mole on the side of her nose. Her long black hair was pulled back with a ribbon. The maid's uniform and flat tie-shoes magnified her plainness, but her eyes, darting fearfully from one corner of the room to another, were lovely. Slowly, as her trembling eased, she unclenched her fist revealing the mint for his pillow crushed in her hand. Drew grabbed a clean hand towel from the floor and gently wiped the chocolate from her fingers.

"Did you call the house detective?" she whispered.

"Not yet. I'll check to see what's missing before I notify anyone."

"Will you be all right alone?"

"Of course." He guided her to the door, smiling reassuringly.

"You must report it, Mr. Gregory."

"I will."

Drew pushed the door shut and bolted it even as she clutched the linen cart. He'd better hurry and sort through his possessions before she had time to spew out her story, bringing the management to his door. He made a beeline for the bed and stooped down to retrieve the briefcase that had been kicked almost to the center. Snapping the broken lock open, he found his passport, traveler's checks, and ticket back to Paris. Even the Beretta lay safe at the bottom of his shaving kit. But snapshots of Robyn along with some personal papers were missing.

Drew righted the chairs, slid the drawers back into the dresser, and rehung his suits. While he was scooping his underclothing and socks from the floor, the phone rang. Although the voice sounded deeper over the telephone, Drew recognized it as David Shipley's.

"Yes," Drew said sharply. "What do you want, Mr. Shipley?"

"I thought we could have dinner together, Gregory."

"No. Someone just tore my room apart. It's a mess here."

"Are you all right?" The concern sounded genuine.

"Yeah, but I'm madder than a pit viper."

"Have you called the police — about your room?"

"I don't intend to." He kicked at some loose papers on the floor. "But I'm going to call room service and order up dinner."

"If tonight is out, then let's have supper at the airport tomorrow. Neilson thought you were flying out in the evening. And I'm scheduled to leave at midnight for Bangkok."

"No again. I don't leave for another few days."

The fractional pause annoyed Drew. Then Shipley suggested, "Would you consider changing your ticketing? I'd do the same."

The question trumpeted like a warning. But why this desperate urge to meet with Drew? "No, I have plans for my time here." *And some things to check out, like who tore this room apart.*

Drew wanted the young man off the line. "Have a good flight back to Thailand."

"I could delay twenty-four hours. I'd like to stay longer myself and visit some friends . . ."

Then why don't you?

"And get in some sightseeing."

"Forget that. A storm front is moving in with heavy snows predicted." *Come on, come on, get off the line, Shipley.*

"You could go with me to see the Vietnam Memorial Wall."

The suggestion infuriated Drew. "Why? Did you and Kaminsky scrawl Luke Breckenridge's name there for me — so I'd back off?"

"I told you in Neilson's office, I don't know him, sir."

"It seems like no one does."

"I'd have time to meet you at Arlington Cemetery before my flight. Maybe early in the morning?"

"You don't get it, do you, Shipley? I'm busy."

"Some other time then. My wife and I might vacation in Europe one day. She's been hinting at Paris in the springtime."

So he's married, Drew thought. Actually, he knew hardly anything about Shipley. Harv and Chad had been vague. "Do that. If London is on your itinerary, look me up."

"Good luck then," Shipley said.

Drew slammed the receiver down and went back to straightening up the room. Why this sudden friendliness from Shipley? He didn't have long to muse. In less than five minutes, he heard a determined knock on his door. Drew grabbed his Beretta and peered through the peek hole. He didn't recognize the stranger, but a bellboy stood behind the man.

Drew slid back the lock, opened the door, and glared at a lean man with a hotel I. D. badge in his hand.

"Mr. Gregory, I'm Oscar Radcliffe, the house detective."

Hardly the muscular type, Drew thought. *You'd never make a bouncer.* A flicker of interest stirred in the man's face as Drew slipped the Beretta into his coat pocket. "I have a permit."

"And did you register it at the desk?" Radcliffe asked coldly.

Drew glanced beyond him to the expressionless bellboy standing patiently by the luggage cart. *Good grief. Am I to be tossed out?* "Is there a problem, Radcliffe?" *Besides the gun.*

"We had a call that you might need our services."

"The maid?"

Slowly Radcliffe lifted his drooping eyelids. "We've talked with her, but the call came from your friend, Mr. Shipley."

Drew hooked his thumbs in his belt and stared back. *Friend, eh?* "Dave shouldn't have done that. Nothing is missing."

Radcliffe barged forcefully into the room and eyed the unmade bed and torn mattress. "You're certain nothing was taken?"

"A few papers." He didn't mention the snapshots, unsure why anyone would want them. "And the directions to my wife's art gallery."

"You needed directions?"

"We're divorced," Drew said stiffly, but he determined to be cooperative now rather than be delayed at checkout time.

Radcliffe snapped his fingers, and the bell-boy pushed the cart into Drew's room. "We're moving you across the hall, Mr. Gregory," Radcliffe said. "For your safety."

"To a room without a view? No. No thank you."

Radcliffe picked up the phone, muttered some orders, and then said, "We'll transfer you down the hall instead — three doors. Same view. We've upgraded you, sir, for all the trouble — the inconvenience that this robbery has caused."

And miss the thief returning? "I'll stay right here."

"Impossible. You must transfer. There will be an official investigation. The police will want to cordon off this room."

"And keep me at bay? *I'm* the one that was robbed."

"Sir, you said nothing was missing."

"Two or three hundred dollars I kept in my suit jacket."

"Cash? I see. But no way to trace that."

"And my address book. A new one. Personal numbers."

"Women?" Radcliffe asked.

Tight-lipped Drew said, "My wife and my daughter and the couple running my farm in upstate New York." In case Radcliffe already knew about London, he added, "And my

184

secretary's number at the embassy in London."

"Yes, we know about London. Is your passport missing?"

"I've checked. My passport and traveler's checks are safe."

Drew felt an intense dislike for Radcliffe. He grabbed up his clock and briefcase, tossed his raincoat over his shoulder, and gave the room a final sweep with a practiced eye. "Have the bellboy bring my luggage and my —" Remembering his computer, he looked around. It was gone, disks and all.

"Add my lap computer to the list. My Macintosh is missing."

The house detective stepped back, allowing Drew to storm from the room. He followed, saying quietly, "We've sent Maria home."

His voice lowered to a subdued monotone, and he seemed to take pleasure in saying, "She let the thief into your room. The man claimed to be you. You know — the usual. He'd forgotten his key. Her actions were against hotel policy, so we may have to let her go permanently."

"You can't do that, not if she knows what the man looked like."

"We have her description of the man."

Radcliffe opened the door to Drew's new quarters and again stepped back to let Drew go first. Diplomatically he said, "May I suggest that you register your weapon downstairs before the police arrive."

"Of course." *No way,* he thought.

"And you will be available? They'll want to talk to you."

"I'm having dinner in my room. Is that good enough?"

"If there's any problem — if we can help you in any way —"

"I'll call."

Radcliffe hesitated. "We hated calling in the police, but there's been another unfortunate incident in the hotel. Perhaps Maria mentioned the guest in the room on the floor below you?"

"Another robbery?"

"She was less fortunate. She arrived back while the assailant was still there. After an apparent struggle, he strangled her."

A murder? Maria had asked. No wonder she seemed so frightened. "In the room beneath mine? Are you considering a possible connection?"

"Should we? The police may think so. They'll question you."

"Well, I'll be here, as I said, having supper in my room."

"And you will call if there is any further disturbance?"

"Yes, I told you, I'll call."

Radcliffe paused in the doorway scratching his ear. "By the way, Mr. Gregory, do you know a Mr. Uriah Kendall?"

"We're old friends."

"I see." Again Radcliffe scratched his ear. "Mr. Kendall left word at the desk that he's been trying to reach you."

As Drew showered and dressed the next morning, he still felt irritated about the two hours of questioning, the repeated implications as though a rephrased question would be rewarded by the response they sought. At first the police had not mentioned the dead woman in the room below. Drew sized up their reasoning — just a couple of tough detectives checking out another Washington homicide — but this time in a first-class hotel instead of a rundown section of town.

Drew kept his information to a minimum. "I'm an embassy attaché — from London. *Not a bona fide member of Central Intelligence.* I'm here on holiday. *Not a thwarted business trip.* I'm sightseeing — you know, the familiar spots." But he didn't specify Langley or the Vietnam Veterans Memorial Wall. Nor did he mention the dead marine, not when

he believed that the secrets of Luke Breckenridge were somehow involved in his ransacked room.

Finally, he gave them the number that
would ring directly to a CIA hot line, a
Washington office number that could not be
traced back to Langley. A number that
would confirm his holiday status from the
American embassy in London. Drew was
playing a rough game of chance, but he was
better off being an unknown on holiday than
a long-time member of the intelligence community.

He was just short of shutting the door
behind the detectives when the heavier of the
two men asked, "Were you acquainted with
a Nell Ashcroft, a guest in this hotel?"

"Nell Ashcroft? No, I don't know her. Is
she important?"

"She's dead. Murdered on the floor beneath this one."

"What makes you think I knew her?" *Good
grief*, he thought. *They're trying to level a murder rap on me.* "Do you think my intruder
and her assailant are one and the same?" he
asked.

"It appears that way." The officer adjusted
his hat. "You and Miss Ashcroft are both
from London."

"A number of people are."

"About your missing address book — could her name be in it?"

Drew's voice hardened. "I — said — I — didn't — know — her."

The officers tipped their hats and were gone without even reminding him to keep in touch. Or was somebody already on duty outside his room ready to track his every move? *Nell Ashcroft.* He'd forgotten to ask whether she was young or old. Pretty or plain. On business or vacation. But did it matter? Whoever — whatever she was — had been snuffed out.

Obviously, the detectives wanted to link them. Was there some connection? But he didn't even know a Nell Ashcroft. Did Porter? Or could she be a friend of Sauni or Luke? Or Aaron? Drew contemplated his room phone, but he didn't dare risk it. The management had selected this room for him; they may have bugged it. He'd hold off on calling overseas until he got to an outside phone booth. He wouldn't even risk returning Uriah Kendall's call — no need to involve an old friend. But if he saw Radcliffe again, he'd ask — no, demand — information on the woman who might have died in his place.

His mood hit rock bottom. Outside, dark clouds hung low over the city threatening to engulf Washington in a blizzard. He'd never been one to take up a grave watch, but he decided to outrun the storm — if he could — and visit the Arlington National Cemetery.

By the time he reached it, thick, milky snow flurries dotted the grass with patches of white. He asked for a temporary pass to drive to the grave of a friend. Luke's name didn't stir a reaction. After a few twists and turns, Drew ended up on foot in front of Luke's grave. Breckenridge shared a final resting place with soldiers from every war and with poets, Presidents, generals, politicians, and ambassadors — Drew's old friend Mac for one — and hundreds of young men little known except to their families.

As he stood there, the tips of his ears felt frostbitten. The bitter cold temperature and his somber memories whipped like wind around him. Snow adhered now, a thin blanket of whiteness covering the earth, blending its color with row upon row of matching headstones.

"Breckenridge," he said, "I'll do my best to find out what happened to you. It must be out of the ordinary, judging from my ransacked room — and the death of Miss Ashcroft."

As he brushed the snow off the top of the

headstone with his gloved hand, nature painted it chalky again. "If Chad Kaminsky is right, then I'll tell your wife. If you are innocent, I will have to prove it and still get your name on the wall. If that fails, I'll personally come back and blow a bugle over your grave."

As he turned, he saw an elderly woman kneeling on the frosty ground. Her knees would be numb, arthritic if she lingered there. He started toward her.

"Don't, Drew. She's all right."

David Shipley stood fifteen feet from him, his head bare, a thick woollen scarf at his neck. "She has a right to grieve her own way."

"I thought you were going to Bangkok. How did you find me?"

"I followed you from the hotel. Let's just walk along." He nodded toward the older woman. "In case we're being monitored."

They turned toward Drew's car. "Did Kaminsky send you, Shipley?"

"I don't work for the Agency. They call me in periodically to discuss my search missions in Vietnam and Laos. This time they asked me about Breckenridge."

Drew stopped walking and glared down at Shipley. He was a runt of a man, stocky in build, his grin forced. Snowflakes clung to his curly hair and heavy overcoat.

"You said you didn't know him."

Shipley adjusted his collar against the wind. "During my visit with Kaminsky the other day, he brought in another man. There was no official introduction except Dev— Dave."

"Dev?" Drew asked. *Porter Deven?*

"He reminded me of a walrus with his thick moustache and icicle eyeballs. I wouldn't want to be interrogated by him. I'd probably end up spilling my gut. He acted nonchalant, but I felt he was there to size me up."

"You think so?"

"He didn't take notes — didn't even ask many questions, but his mental calculator clicked every minute. Drew, if our meeting is to appear casual, let's keep ambling among these headstones. Arlington is impressive, isn't it?" He shivered. "But I'll be glad to get back to Bangkok. My family often asks why I'm so content living abroad. I can't explain it. Can you?"

"My job took me away."

"Mine, too. As it turned out, I'm quite happy living in Asia. My wife is Thai. She was homesick and wanted to go back there to have our first child. I dragged my feet long enough for our son to be born in the States.

But our daughter is Thai."

Drew didn't want to hear Shipley's family history. He was too busy watching the woman as she went back to the empty tour-mobile and climbed aboard. "Shipley, you deliberately met me here today; you even delayed your trip home. Why?"

"I don't like being used. Kaminsky knew that Breckenridge was on my list. I wasn't to tell you."

Drew spun around again. Endless snow flurries pelted his face. He blew against them. "What are you talking about?"

"The village of Xangtiene does exist in Laos," he said. "An American Phantom jet is still burrowed into the ground there, nose down. I've seen it. I'm willing to wager that Kaminsky and his friends knew about the village and that plane before I told them."

"Breckenridge wasn't a pilot. He walked in."

"If he did, then he walked into big trouble. When I mentioned the plane, you could feel the tension at Langley mount. For just a second, Dev's gaze turned brutal. So I just backed off. I'd gone there as a courtesy; I'm not government or military anymore."

"You backed off. Why?"

"I don't want to run into trouble on the back streets of Bangkok someday. You boys don't always play fair."

"Why are you telling me all this?"

"In case something goes wrong. I've trekked the jungles of Southeast Asia three dozen times, and in spite of Kaminsky's denial, Xangtiene does exist; there is a downed aircraft there. I even filed a report on it."

"Then it's in the records."

"When I was with the military, we salvaged some items from the plane — enough to establish the pilots' names and to at least close the questions for their families."

His breath vapors rose like ringlets of smoke. "Identity was determined mostly by records — the names of the men who left the carrier that morning and by the few remains we dug up. When I filed my report, my C. O. blacked out the name of the aircraft and village and substituted an area far to the west."

They had gone past the car, walking along Memorial Drive. As they turned back, Shipley stomped his feet against the cold. "I challenged my C. O., and he told me to leave it alone."

"What does all this have to do with Breckenridge?" Drew asked.

"Rumors say Breckenridge left a message by that plane. Your Agency has insisted there was no such village and no such plane. Later, as a civilian on my second search-and-rescue mission there, I proved them to be liars."

"Your word against theirs, Shipley."

"I have photographs of the downed aircraft near Xangtiene. If something happens to me, the negatives are safely tucked away in a bank vault in Switzerland, thanks to my maiden aunt."

"I'd like to see the pictures."

"Sorry. Unfortunately, they could be harmful to Captain Breckenridge. He supposedly used the plane for a drop — classified material. I speak the dialect fluently, Mr. Gregory. The people in Xangtiene told me that an American was held there briefly."

"Of course. The pilot and co-pilot."

"No, he was not a member of the crew. The pilots either died on impact or were burned to death. Villagers buried them in a shallow grave near the plane. But the people said another American arrived in Xangtiene a few weeks after the crash. He was alive for awhile — at least until the second monsoon."

"As a prisoner of war?"

"He was in captivity according to the Hmong. But they also insist that a foreign woman had been expecting the American."

Drew looked back toward Luke's grave, distant from them now. "More rumors.

That's all Mrs. Breckenridge has lived on for years."

"We didn't have much more to take back to the families of those pilots either. We couldn't even give them bodies to bury — a few bones and ashes. But those pilots faced an honorable death."

"And Luke didn't? Must I go back and tell his wife that?"

"I wouldn't tell her anything. Let it die as these men here in Arlington died." The tiny bald spot on the top of Shipley's head had turned white with snow, the tips of his protruding ears a frosty red. Still he kept walking, his hands thrust deep in his pockets.

"On my second trip there I found one of the village leaders wearing an American wedding band. It cost me plenty of rice to buy it back from him, Gregory."

"And did you turn it over to one of the families?"

"The ring didn't belong to the pilots," he said. "I wish it had. It would have given me great comfort to take something like that back to them. No, the ring belonged to a third man. Earlier this week I considered turning it over to Kaminsky."

"Why didn't you?"

"I don't trust him or your Agency. I suspected the ring might belong to Breckenridge, but Kaminsky and Neilson still deny that he worked for them. So I kept the ring."

"And you really think it's Luke's?"

Wind ruffled Shipley's hair, adding to his boyish appearance. "Inside the ring, the last letters of the man's name are worn thin, but — tell me, Gregory, what is his wife's first name?"

"Saundra — Sauni."

"The date and the words 'from Sauni to Luth' are clear."

"Luth, not Luther? What are you going to do with the ring?"

"If I were still in the military, I'd turn it over. But I'm privately employed now. I've made so many trips over there that it's beginning to tear me up inside. I sure would like to give something to one of those families."

He glanced defiantly at Drew. "I don't even care whether or not he betrayed his country. War can destroy a man. I just want to extend some measure of healing to one family and give them back something that once belonged to their son or husband."

"Breckenridge was divorced."

"I know. I called his parents last night — after talking with you. I knew you intended to find out what you could about Luke. Perhaps his parents would be willing to talk with you." He paused. "I promised them I'd stay over and meet them before I went back to Bangkok. Would you like to go along? They're living in Ocean City, New Jersey, a couple hours from here."

"What are they doing there in the middle of winter?"

"Luke's mother was born there — on Asbury Avenue. She shies away from crowds now, so they're staying there year round."

"Does Kaminsky know you're going to see them?"

"Why tell him? I just plan to show them their son's wedding ring. If they can identify it, I'm going to leave it with them."

As Drew crunched through the snow, he wasn't certain he should trust Shipley. But how could Shipley have reached the hotel room first? No, someone else had ransacked Drew's room.

Shipley extended a bare hand toward Drew. Slowly he opened his fingers to reveal a large gold band in the palm of his hand.

"Luke was a big man," Drew said.

"Big hands at least," Shipley agreed. "Want to check it out?"

"Dave, I can't identify it. You know that."

"Well, do you want to go to Ocean City with me or not?"

Drew scanned the sky. "We'll get caught in this blizzard."

"If we move fast enough, we'll beat it. Besides, I'm hauling chains in my car."

"I need to go back to the hotel first."

"Forget that, Gregory. Let's go now. I don't want anyone to follow us to Ocean City. I know a parking garage where we can leave your rental. Then we'll use my car."

Drew kicked at the slush. "What if we get snowed in?"

"Then we'll just borrow some of the admiral's clothes."

"They may have some wild driving in Bangkok, but can you drive in this weather, Shipley?"

"I did in Kansas when I was a kid."

Chapter 11

Drew recognized the Breckenridge house from Sauni's description: a bit wider than the neighbors, blue shuttered windows, a lattice-work railing, the top branches of a narrow, weather-beaten tree blowing too closely to the snow-covered shingles.

"Slow down, Shipley. There it is," he said.

Dave skidded over the sheet of ice to the curb and turned the front wheels in. "If this weather keeps up, we're stuck here. Look at the stalled cars. This town isn't prepared for snow like this."

They risked crossing the street in the middle of the block. Shipley stomped his feet on the porch so loudly that Mrs. Breckenridge opened the door without waiting for them to ring.

"Ma'am," he said politely, "I'm Dave Shipley, and this is my friend Drew Gregory. We're a bit late."

She glanced at the weather. "We rarely have a storm like this. I was afraid you wouldn't even get here. Come in, and get those wet coats off. We'll just go right to the kitchen. It's warmer out there."

The smell of pot roast permeated the hall as they followed her to the cozy kitchenette. "This is my husband," she said, nodding toward the stately man at the table.

He rose slowly. And again Sauni's description of him had already filled in his strong features for Drew. Some of the old spark and sense of command were gone, but when he extended his hand, the grip was firm. "Admiral, I'm Drew Gregory. Shipley invited me to come along."

"Did you know my son?"

"No, sir. Just know about him."

The eyes clouded. "So you're Shipley?" he said turning to the younger man. "Sit down. Both of you."

Mrs. Breckenridge was already there with coffee mugs and a tray of cookies. "We eat backwards," she said. "Dessert first."

There was something soft and gentle about her, and again Drew remembered Sauni's words — a dignified, well-groomed woman with Luke's smile. He couldn't take his eyes from her smile; it was generous and full, sincere and friendly. *Luke's smile.* For a moment, he felt like he had a glimpse of the man whose name was not on the Vietnam Veterans Memorial Wall.

In that moment, Luke took on personality.

Drew rejected the emotion, not wanting to face the fact that Luke had once existed. He heard Shipley saying, "Gregory here is with the CIA."

Luke's smile faded from his mother's face. "Then what do you care what happened to my son?" the admiral asked stiffly.

"Ah, but I do care. That's why I'm here, Admiral."

"Does Washington know you're interested in Luke?"

"Yes, sir. They do now."

"Then, Gregory, you're running a high risk coming here."

"I had to come. No, I really wanted to come. Saundra and my daughter are friends."

"Oh!" Mrs. Breckenridge exclaimed. "How is Sauni? The dear child. We wish we could see more of her. Don't we, Luther?"

He nodded halfheartedly. "She's the one who moved away."

"Yes," she sighed. "We miss her. After Luke died, we told her that she should marry again — find happiness with someone else. But she said Luke was the only one she would ever love."

Still loves, Drew thought. "Then why did she divorce him?"

She shook her head. "It was a foolish thing

to do. Luke wouldn't give up his career, and Sauni resented it interfering with their times together. She prayed he wouldn't go back overseas."

The admiral's eyes turned cold. "And as soon as he left — before Luke could even get jungle rot again — my daughter-in-law drove to Elkton, Maryland, and finalized the divorce. She's lived to regret it. If she had waited three months, she would have been his widow."

Drew heard the bitterness in the admiral's voice, the sense of injustice paid his son. His wife patted his hand and said, "Sauni wasn't the admiral's choice."

"Nor did Luke please *her* father," the admiral snapped. "Her father opposed the war in Vietnam. He offered to pull strings to keep Luke from going back. Imagine suggesting that to my son. As long as Luke was stationed at the Pentagon, Summers was placated. But my son and the senator never saw eye to eye. Did they, Amy?"

She winced. "What hurts us the most is the way Senator Summers turned against Luke when the rumors started." Her voice stayed even and calm. "You do know about the rumors, Mr. Gregory?"

When Drew hesitated, Shipley spoke up. "Yes, we both know. And we know about the threat to remove his body from Arlington."

For several minutes, only the tick of the kitchen timer broke the silence. Finally, Luke's mother said, "A few years ago it wouldn't have mattered. I always thought Luke was still alive."

The admiral's gray head bobbed sympathetically; he reached for her hand. "They were so close — my boy and his mother."

"That wasn't the reason, Luther." She looked at her guests. "I believed they sent home an empty box — filled with rocks perhaps, but not my son. The casket was sealed, under constant military supervision until it was lowered into the ground at Arlington."

Drew noticed the defiant tilt of her chin and was amazed at the quiet way in which she spoke — as though she were rehearsing a bit of family history that no longer held meaning for her.

Quietly she said, "Ten years ago my son called me."

"Don't, Amy," the admiral begged.

"I know it was Luke. I'd know that voice anywhere."

Helplessly, the admiral said, "Amy was ill. Hospitalized."

"For a nervous breakdown," she said softly. "And then the doctors found out I'd had a mild heart attack instead. You've heard of the Posttraumatic Stress Syndrome, haven't you, Drew?"

"A lot of the servicemen and prisoners of war experience it."

"That's what I had. Posttraumatic stress from the death of my sons. Grief, the medical journals call it. No — don't try to stop me, Luther." The crystal eyes blazed. "The doctors had me heavily sedated for days, but I know Luke was by my bedside."

"Amy, it was the medicine."

"How would you know, Luther? You were out at sea. But my son was there." She patted her chest. "If only in my heart. Gentlemen, do you know what it's like to have the same dream over and over and hear your son begging you to rescue him from the jungles? I tried, but I could never reach him."

Gently the admiral said, "Mother, if Luke were alive, he would have come home to us."

"Not if he thought he had failed us or broken the Breckenridge tradition." She turned to Drew. "Luther here never believed me, but someone visited Landon's grave while I was in the hospital. It had to be Luke."

She avoided her husband's eyes. "The grave marker had been scrubbed clean and the grass cut away. Someone had pounded a kite stick into the ground, but the kite had caught in the tree and torn. Only Luke could have remembered how much Landon loved flying kites."

She stood and checked her roast. "Another hour and we eat. Have some fruit to tide you over." Her gaze rested on Drew. "You didn't come because of the Arlington affair, did you?"

"I asked him to come," David said, covering a sneeze. "Drew wanted to know more about Luke, and I wanted to deliver something to you." He sneezed again as he pulled the ring from his pocket and put it on the table between the Breckenridges. Amy sat back down, tears welling in her eyes. "Was it Luke's?"

"We think so, ma'am. I found it in the village where he died."

"In Xangtiene? Then he really *is* gone." She picked it up and read the worn inscription. "Yes, this belonged to my son."

The ring passed from hand to hand. Clutching something that had once belonged to Luke seemed to revitalize them. And without permitting their tears to flow, the Breckenridges spoke about him for the next thirty minutes. The admiral with obvious pride, his wife with a steady eye as she said, "Luke always took risks as a boy."

"Yes," his father agreed. "He was a kid with nine lives. It didn't matter whether we moved to a new base or a new country, Luke would dare anything for attention. So much so that he often had to learn the language to stay out of trouble. But languages came easy for him," the admiral boasted. "And mountain hiking."

Amy smiled at that. "Luther refused to worry, and I worried enough for both of us. Luke was only ten the first time he struck out on an overnight hike alone — and got lost on the trail."

"Admit it, Amy. By sheer perseverance, he endured that night in the forest. He was plenty scared, but he made up his mind to come out of it alive. High dives. Speed. Racing. Anything for a thrill. That was our son. That was the Breckenridge spirit in him."

"Luke survived all those wild adventures," she added sadly. "No matter what, he always came back. When those two marines came to our door that day, I didn't believe them. Something inside of me said Luke was still alive. For years I clung to that hope. Even when they told us he had betrayed his country, I didn't believe them. We still refuse to believe them."

Their hands locked now, the admiral looking pained as he watched his wife. She smiled at him. "Luther here worried about me, but rarely about Luke. But neither one of us wanted to face the loss of a second son. Only our faith in God kept us from falling apart. And now with this latest threat to dig up Luke's grave site — to humiliate us more — it's better that my son is gone. *Dead.* Yes, I allow myself to say that now."

His affectionate grip tightened. "The admiral and I are getting on in years. He doesn't like to admit it, but I turned seventy-eight my last birthday — and Luther is pushing eighty-one. The rumors can't hurt us much longer, but we are so concerned about Sauni."

Drew leaned forward. "She doesn't want you hurt either. I think she'd like you to visit her in Europe."

"Is she happy there?" the admiral asked.

Drew chose his words carefully. "She seems content."

Outside, wind-blown snow built drifts against the house; the branches of the old tree scraped at the shingles. Shipley's eyes watered as he sneezed again. "We'd better be on our way," he said. "Or we won't get through."

"No," Amy Breckenridge told him. "You're not leaving the house in this weather."

"My wife's right. You should stay overnight. Give the snowplows a chance to clear the roads to Washington."

"We didn't come prepared to stay all night," Drew said.

She glanced at her husband. "I'll take them to the attic and get them robes and pajamas."

There was a flicker of pain in his face, but he nodded as she stood. She led them up the narrow steps to Luke's room and laid out robes for both of them.

Kindly, Drew said, "Downstairs you mentioned two children."

"Yes, we had a son older than Luke. We lost Landon when he was twelve." As she bit her lip, it turned a chalky white. "The admiral was away with the Pacific Fleet that time — he was often unavailable in an emergency. The navy finally flew him home two weeks before Landon died of leukemia."

Her voice caught. "The admiral had such grandiose plans for our firstborn: military school, Annapolis, a navy career. He never accepted that Landon was a fragile child, caught up with books and classical music. Landon spent hours curled up on the sofa, shutting us all out, absorbed in his fantasy world. I didn't realize at first that he wasn't well until I noticed the bruises on his arms that never seemed to heal. When I accused the boys of fighting, Luke said, 'No, Mom. His nose bleeds just happen. Nobody hits him, especially not me.' And from the sofa Landon cried out, 'You promised, Luke. You promised not to tell.' "

She kept blowing at a dust particle on the dresser. "Landon had been shooting up taller, his voice changing to deeper tones. For weeks I had thought my boy was approaching manhood; instead my son was dying. He looked so thin and peaked lying there, and I remember thinking, *My son is ill.* I knew it even before I heard Luke's frantic whisper. 'He's sick, Mom. Do something, please. We can't wait for Daddy to come home.' "

She looked away. "I piled the boys in the car — Landon on the back seat covered with blankets — and drove to the Naval Hospital. We sat on benches for hours, Landon's head pillowed on my lap. When the doctor told me the diagnosis, I couldn't pronounce the medical words, let alone understand them. Landon was gone in a few weeks."

As fresh grief creased her face, Shipley took three strides to her side and hugged her. "I've got a twelve-year-old," he said. "I don't know what I'd do if we lost him. My son likes music, too. Classical — of all things."

"Then encourage it. Do you have other children?"

Shipley had already opened his wallet. "That's Davey on the left. Named for me," he said proudly. "Maylene is in the middle. Our only girl. And Rockboat is the two-year-old terror."

"Rockboat?"

"Samuel really, but he's been rocking our lives ever since his arrival." With another warm glance at his children, he pocketed the wallet. "In the beginning, Mrs. Breckenridge, we considered an alternate plan, an abortion — because we panicked at the thought of providing for three kids. But we just couldn't do it, not and please God. We look at Rockboat now and thank God for him. We know life would be empty without the little rascal."

"We so wanted grandchildren," she said softly. "The admiral looked forward to having youngsters around when he retired."

"Did he want another generation of soldiers?" Drew teased.

"No," she whispered. "I think he wanted to make up for all those times he missed being home when our own sons were small."

Shipley held her at arm's length and smiled. "Adopt my kids, Amy. They'd love another set of grandparents. You'd be long distance, but they'd love getting cards and phone calls."

"And gifts?" Her eyes brightened. "I'll talk to Luther about it. I know it would do him good. Even though we have each other, we're lonely. We grew sick of yacht clubs and whispers about Luke."

Shipley whipped out his wallet again and slipped the snapshot from the plastic insert. "Here, take this until I can get you a better picture. By the way, it's going to be four kids soon. Can you handle that? Another boy according to the doctor."

Drew could see by her broad smile that it was more than okay. But she asked, "Will the real grandparents mind?"

"No. My parents won't anyway. They'll be excited. Would you mind if we named our baby Luther Landon Shipley?"

"Are you sure?" Amy asked, cupping her mouth, crying. "That would be so special. It would really fill a void in our lives."

"I'll check with my wife first, but she usually gives me my way." He winked. "We could call the baby L. L. for short. We'll be your family's Asian connection."

"You'll be our lifeline," she whispered.

Drew's neck muscles began tightrope-walking. He decided to keep in touch with Shipley, and if the man broke his promise to this woman — or if he deceived her — Drew would personally make Shipley crawl. But he smiled as Amy said, "David, you'll let little L. L. be what he wants to be when he grows up? The admiral and I won't be here then — but any *grandson of mine* must be free to follow his dreams."

Shipley nodded in agreement.

"I've always thought that after Landon died, Luke felt an obligation to follow in his dad's footsteps, to be the family hero from his generation." She stared at the snapshot of David's children. "I think Luke was our Rockboat — and left to his own devices, who knows what he might have become? He was such a wonderfully robust child. Into everything. Curious about everything. Always bent on winning."

She nodded toward the open closet. "Those shelves are full of trophies. Sometimes I think Luke won them so there'd be enough for Landon's memory too."

"It's hard to try and fill someone else's shoes," Drew said.

"Yes, I know. But whatever Luke's dreams might have been, he put them aside in his junior year in high school. It was a beautiful sunny day when he came home and announced that he was going to Annapolis. He wore a shiner and his knuckles were skinned.

'Just a disagreement, Mom,' he said. 'I ran into a couple of cowards who don't want to defend this country.' "

She managed a smile for both David and Drew. "Our country was involved in Vietnam — his dad already there. Luke read everything he could about the conflict. He insisted that we put a flagpole up in the yard so he could raise the flag each morning. He was a wonderful boy. But I do wonder if he ever wanted to be something else besides a four-star general."

Certainly not a traitor, Drew thought. *No, the son she describes would never be disloyal to his country.* Mentally, Drew filled in Luke's features again: his mother's smile, the admiral's eyes, a profile like the Breckenridge side of the family. Drew reflected on Luke's boyhood and on the devastating loss of his brother Landon. Luke had been an achiever, a young man with a sensitive nature and a strong, independent personality. But had the Breckenridge traditions and his brother's death robbed him of his own dreams? Vague images, Drew admitted to himself, but as the puzzle pieces came together, he still formed a strong, favorable impression of the young man who had lived in this room.

A photograph of the boys hung crookedly on the wall. He reached out and straightened it. Good-looking boys. He recognized Luke from the pictures that Sauni had shown him. He was taller and stronger, his arm around Landon's shoulder. He looked dark and serious compared to Landon's fairness and smiling blue eyes.

"We took that picture about a month before Landon's death. He begged us to take him home before he died. The doctors fought it, but he wasn't *their* son. Luke was only eleven, but he was devoted to his brother — he carried his meals to him, emptied his urinal, read to him, sat with him. And tried to get him to eat. But Luke rarely spoke of his brother after Landon died."

"You don't have to go on, Mrs. Breckenridge."

"Oh, but I do, David. That's why Mr. Gregory came. To hear about Luke. To find out what made him a traitor."

"I never said that."

"You didn't have to," she told Drew. "I sensed it when you walked in the door." Her eyes strayed back to the picture of her sons. "They were only a year apart — very close like you see in that photograph. And then months later, we found out that our sensitive eleven-year-old repeatedly hitchhiked over to the Seaside Cemetery to stand by his brother's grave. Maybe to promise Landon that he'd keep the family tradition."

She looked up dry-eyed. "I can't tell you how many times the admiral spanked that boy for coming home late and not telling us where he'd been. And when we found out that he had gone to visit his brother's grave, we begged his forgiveness." She smiled — *Luke's smile.* "Luke simply shrugged and said, 'I loved him, too, Mom.' "

"Why didn't you bury Luke next to his brother?" Drew asked.

"I wanted to — but the admiral insisted that he be buried in Arlington with the rest of the Breckenridge heroes."

Early the next morning as they prepared to leave for the trip back to Washington, Mrs. Breckenridge protested, "I hate to see you leave now. The storm is only going to get worse."

"We don't have a choice," Drew said. "We're flying home soon."

She chuckled. "You sound like Luke. Home was always somewhere else, some faraway land where he could earn his battlefield promotions."

"That's not fair, Amy," the admiral said.

"Isn't it, Luther?"

"Your boys are both *home* now, ma'am," Shipley said.

Her eyes misted. "I wish I knew for certain about Luke. He grew up in Sunday school, but he drew away from God after Landon died. He didn't even believe that his brother was in Heaven — didn't believe that Heaven existed. Nor could he understand how a loving God could take his brother away. I don't think he ever resolved that."

Using the corner of his handkerchief, Shipley gently wiped the tears from her cheeks. "Now that your boys are together, I'm sure Luke is at peace."

She nodded, but Drew saw pain in her eyes. He felt as if he were in Luke's camp — lost and uncertain about the existence of Heaven, but Amy Breckenridge smiled up warmly at him. "Mr. Gregory, come back again sometime."

As they stood by the front door, she handed them wool caps and earmuffs, a thermos of hot coffee, and a sack of sandwiches. "I threw in some of my cookies," she said. "Please call us when you get to Washington. Drive safely, David. We're praying that God will give you protection over those icy streets."

Pray about driving? That was a new one to Drew; he'd always left driving to his own good judgment.

"I'll call when we get there," Shipley said.

Amy pulled his face down and kissed him. She was more restrained with Drew. "I hope you found the answers you wanted — that you've come to positive terms about our son."

She took a small box from her apron pocket and pressed it into his gloved hand. "Please give Luke's ring to Sauni."

"But, Mrs. Breckenridge, Shipley gave it to you."

"It's best this way. The admiral and I talked long into the night. It was Luther's suggestion that we let it go. After all, Saundra gave it to Luke during one of their happier moments."

The admiral's arm wrapped tightly around her waist. "We have many treasures of our boys, many good memories," he said. "And Sauni has so few."

Chapter 12

The New Jersey Expressway looked a snarled mess with cars going at a snail's pace and a three-foot snowbank piled at the edge of the highway. For the last ten minutes, the wind had whipped and buzzed, hurling the fallen snow from the ground and slamming it against the windows. Above them, the clouds darkened, putting nightfall in a noon sky and threatening to unleash hail on the already hazardous roads.

Still Shipley took the icy roads too fast, doing almost forty-five when everyone else had slowed to a crawl. The windshield wipers squealed and swished in a monotonous rhythm.

"David, let me take the wheel," Drew grumbled. "I'd like to get to Washington in one piece."

Shipley blew on his gloved hand. "I'm okay."

Drew leaned forward. "Hard to tell which cars are stalled, isn't it? A person could freeze to death out here."

"Sure could. My wife Namlee hates our

rainy season. But she'd go berserk in this."
He seemed amused at the thought, that silly
grin of his plastered on his face. "Hey, Drew,
that Dodge stopped up ahead, hazard lights
blinking — isn't that the one that tried to cut
us off an hour ago?"

"Same car," Drew agreed. "Same crazy
lady driver."

David eased up on the gas. "We should
stop. She's having trouble getting the hood
up."

"Too risky to stop for strangers these
days."

They crept several car lengths past her. "I
wouldn't want my wife caught out in this
storm all alone."

"Well, then pull over."

The tires scratched through a sheet of ice
as the chains cut a fresh path toward the
shoulder of the road. David swung his door
open and tossed the keys on the seat. "Stay
with the car if you want."

"No, if it's a highway trick, you'll need my
trusty Beretta."

Shipley took off at a run, struggling against
the swirling snow and slipping and sliding
like a kid on his first pair of skis. After stumbling twice, he slowed to Drew's cautious
pace. Suddenly, a Snugtop Ford Ranger with
tinted windows swerved from the expressway

and showered them with slush.

Drew spun around as it skidded to a stop behind their rental. "What's that fool doing? I hope he didn't hit our car."

The doors swung open, and two men stepped down. The driver waved cheerily and started his own slip-slide sprint toward them.

"It's okay, Drew. Just two more Good Samaritans."

They reached the stranded motorist first, the van driver right behind them. The stranger raced to the driver's side and tapped on the foggy window. "Where are you?" he demanded.

"I'm . . . over . . . here."

Drew found the young woman kneeling by the back tire, her teeth chattering, the wind whipping at her long blonde hair. Snow chains lay in a kinked pile beside her. "You okay?" he asked.

"I had a fight with my boyfriend," she cried. "He refused to put my chains on, and now I'm stuck here in this blizzard."

The girl's lips had taken on a purplish hue; her pug nose looked red and swollen. He reached down and pulled her to her feet. "Do you have something besides that ski sweater to keep you warm?" he asked.

"A wool . . . jacket . . . in the trunk."

"Get it while we put these chains on."

The stranger stomped his feet and turned up his collar. "I've got a jack in my Ranger — I'll get it," he offered. He set off, crunching over the snow.

"Don't bother," Drew called after him. "We won't need it."

Drew knelt and stretched the chains in place, his fingers so numb he could barely control them. "Now roll the car a bit, Shipley."

As he pulled the chains snugly around the tire and snapped the hook in place, the Ford Ranger plowed backwards, burned its wheels for traction, then cut out wildly over the icy surface. It gunned its way into the expressway traffic and disappeared.

"Some Samaritan. What was that all about?" Shipley asked.

"Forget them. Lend me a hand, David." He smiled up at the girl. "Good — you put that extra jacket on. It's okay now. We'll stay with you until your car is running again."

It took several minutes before the Dodge quit sputtering and hummed enough to bring a big smile to the girl's face.

"This heap's pretty old," she said. "Bob was going to work on it this weekend. How can I ever thank you for helping me?"

Drew patted her hand. "You just did with that smile."

As she pumped the pedal, the car sputtered again. "I'll get off at the next off-ramp and find a motel room for the night."

"That's great," Shipley said. "You can call your boyfriend from there. He got you into this mess; he can come rescue you."

She laughed at the idea and with a quick little wave gripped the wheel with both hands. Drew ran interference as she nervously made her way back into the line of bumper-to-bumper traffic. When he reached the rental, Shipley was in his seat waiting.

"Is everything okay, Shipley? I just found somebody else's footprints on my side of the car. I don't like it."

"Nothing's missing. The tires are okay. I've got the keys."

"I'd better check under the hood."

David shivered. "Forget it, Drew. It's too cold to stand out there any longer. Come on, let's get out of here."

On the Turnpike, an hour outside of Washington, a popping thud erupted under the hood of their car; then came a flapping sound like a belt gone loose. The dashboard lights flashed red — the alternator, the battery, everything giving out.

Shipley gripped the steering wheel. "I can't control it."

He slammed on the brake, sending them into a skid.

Drew pressed against the dash. "Ease off the brake."

David complied. Then confused, he lapped at the gas and spun the car, the back wheels making snow flurries instead of traction. They skidded over the ice, careening wildly back and forth across the lane as Shipley fought to keep on the road.

One second Drew swore under his breath; the next his altar boy prayer pushed at his memory. He braced from his side of the car, grateful that they weren't airborne and plummeting from a snow-laden sky. He tried to grab the wheel as the car whipped across the middle lane, scraped the back bumper of another motorist, and plowed violently into a snowbank. The impact blanketed the windshield with snow, blinding them both.

"Let's get out of here, Shipley."

"Fat chance. My door won't budge."

"Force it. I'm snowed in on this side."

With a loud Tarzan cry, Shipley pressed his shoulder against the door and shoved. He climbed out, with Drew right behind him. Shipley's knees buckled. As he swayed, Drew steadied him. "What happened, David?"

"The power steering went out on me."

An oncoming truck pulled to a stop, blocking the snarled traffic even more. The driver leaped down from the cab and hurried to them. "You boys all right?" he asked. "Then let's get you back on the road. Where you headed?"

"Washington."

"Good luck. They're still plowing the main streets there."

Grinning good-naturedly, he went toward the front of the car and took command. They heaved together. Pushing. Shoving. The wheels spun mockingly. They kept trying. Moments later the Buick was out of the snowbank and headed in the right direction. The front end was dented, but the trucker managed to open the hood. Still grinning, he peered under it, and his face turned solemn.

He jabbed his finger down. "The serpentine belt was cut," he said. "Deliberately, I'd say. Looks like somebody didn't want you two to get to Washington."

"That's impossible," Shipley snapped. "We've been visiting friends. I'm sure no one tampered with the car there."

"Unless those friends don't think too much of you."

Drew stepped up beside the driver and ran his finger under the belt, tapping the frayed ends together. "How far could we have driven with the belt like this?"

The trucker's brows and shoulders seemed to shrug at the same time. He flicked some snow from his sandy hair. "A few miles. Maybe even a half hour. Can't really say. Depends on whether someone just nicked the belt or slit it midway."

"We stopped a ways back to help a woman motorist. There was another car — a van with two men."

"Did you know them?"

"No. They came up to help. At least one of them did."

Shipley slammed the hood closed in disgust. "Why would anyone damage this car intentionally?"

Drew felt certain his lips had turned white, not from cold but from rage. The car was not the target. He was. First his ransacked room. Now this. What did this rented car have to do with Luke Breckenridge? *Get hold of yourself, Drew,* he chided himself. *Aaron's a greater threat. Don't turn your shoulder blades to him.*

Quietly he said, "Maybe someone wanted me dead."

The trucker yanked a wool cap from his jacket pocket and tugged it over his head and ears. "Nah! They just wanted you to come to a screeching halt."

They. The nebulous they. It was too freezing cold out here to think clearly or to try to put the puzzle together. Drew hadn't liked Kaminsky's evasiveness nor Neilson's warnings against pursuing the Breckenridge case. He couldn't get back to Paris and Porter soon enough. Right now infiltrating a mercenary camp seemed more appealing than ever.

Shipley glared up at Drew. "So now we're stranded in this blizzard."

The trucker offered a farcical grin. "Nope, your luck's still holding. I've got a cellular phone."

Bucking the wind, he stomped off toward his unmarked truck, climbed up into the cab, and grabbed his phone. Then with an apathetic shrug, he reported the towing company's answer. "Said to leave it. They'll be towing cars out of snowbanks for the next five days. Come on. It's against rules, but hop in. I'll truck you as far as I'm going."

"Wait," Shipley said. "Let me get my keys and briefcase."

"Grab my things, too," Drew told him.

They climbed into the cab, Shipley reluctantly taking the cramped space on the bedroll behind the black leather seats. The driver honked his horn for right of access, then wove the big wheeler into the ice-crusted fast lane.

"Be good to have company," he said. "Name's Warren Mackey."

He freed one hand long enough to grip Drew's.

"Criss," Gregory said. "The name's Criss."

Shipley covered his surprise. "Call me Dave."

Mackey took the storm in his stride, increasing speed and whistling as he drove around stranded motorists. "Another swerve like that one," Drew said, "and this thing is going to jackknife."

"No sweat. This rig is some baby to maneuver," Mackey bragged.

"Yeah, you drive like there's no tomorrow, Mackey."

"Might not be." He patted the wheel and honked again. "The tonnage holds this sucker to the road." He gulped the coffee that Shipley handed him.

"How far you going?" Shipley asked.

Mackey winked at Drew as the truck rolled around a curve. "McLean, Virginia. That's far enough, don't you think, Criss?"

The lights of Washington were a welcome sight as Mackey pulled off the Turnpike into a gas station. "Sorry, but like I told you, it's against company policy to have passengers. So this is as far as I can take you," he said cheerfully. "You're on your own from here."

Shipley groaned. "Catching a cab in this weather is hopeless."

"Walk. Can't be more than twenty blocks to your hotel."

My hotel or Shipley's? Drew wondered. *How would you know that, Mr. Mackey?* He pulled his collar snugly around his ears. "Come on, Dave. Let's go. Mackey wants to make Langley before dark."

A guilty smirk crossed Mackey's face. "McLean," he corrected.

"My mistake. Thanks for the ride."

Mackey pulled from the station, swung the big wheeler back into the traffic lane, and rumbled away — the car phone in his hand.

He's reporting in, Drew thought angrily. *But to whom?*

Drew struck out along the slippery sidewalk.

"Wait," Shipley called. "Twenty blocks. Maybe we should at least try to call a taxi."

"We'd just waste more time."

Plowing into the chilling wind energized Drew. Several days had passed since his last morning jog — and weeks since that last game of tennis with Vic Wilson in the embassy gym in London. Drew liked to think of exercise as his version of finding the fountain of youth. That and an aspirin a day would keep his blood flowing. But he jammed his gloved hands deeper into his pockets, convinced that his blood was turning to ice chips in this blizzard.

Shipley's stocky body lagged behind. "Are we in a race?"

"We are — against darkness and this storm."

"Then let's take a subway train."

"They'd hardly be running on schedule — or running at all."

Three blocks later, Shipley took a couple of jogging steps. "Drew, how come you used the name Criss back in the truck?"

"It's an old nickname. Reserved for strangers. I think Mackey got the message."

"That you don't trust him?"

"Something like that, Shipley."

"Didn't you trust the girl either?"

"I think she was a genuine stranded motorist."

David inched his way to the curb and scanned the on-coming headlights for an empty taxi. By the time they reached the tenth block, the pedestrian traffic had dropped considerably. People stood huddled in alcoves. Others had slipped inside of cafes.

A few were taking refuge in the massive cathedral across the street.

"The next church I see on this side I'm going in."

"You do that, David. They tell me it helps to pray."

They were almost there. "Hey, Drew, what about dropping into a cafe and letting me thaw out."

"I'll do that at the hotel. By the way, where are you staying?"

"I'm not. I checked out of my hotel yesterday. Took my things out to a locker at the airport."

"That's crazy."

"So are Kaminsky and Neilson. I want them to think I'm gone."

"Then spend the night in my room. I've got two bunks."

"Thanks, I will. If I make it through this," he joked.

"Thought you trekked the jungles all the time."

"Not in sub-zero temperatures."

As the snow flurries started again, Drew's cheeks felt raw, his earlobes numb. Finally they reached his street just three blocks from the hotel. The Capitol and many of the buildings, stark white in the daylight, looked a muted gray in the darkness. An uneven pattern of lights shone from the windows of the half-empty office buildings. Straight rows of rounded street lamps glowed on either side of the wide boulevard. Motorists had left their cars stranded along the way, their emergency blinkers still flashing. Those still driving paid no attention to the stop signs or signal lights as they skidded through the icy streets.

Drew stepped off the curb first and made it safely across to the median. Behind him he heard the grind of an engine, the extra thrust of speed as a driver roared toward him. Shipley's grip tore at his arm, yanking him backward as a Mercedes sedan swished past.

Drew dropped down and did an acrobatic roll toward the lamppost. Shipley huddled on the sidewalk beside him. The determined driver shifted gears and raced backward toward them, jumping insanely over the curb and scraping the side of the traffic signal. A passenger leaned out the window; the spurt of a semiautomatic cracked through the night air.

Cars honked. People screamed. The Mercedes Benz careened wildly down the boulevard, swinging a wide right at the corner and disappearing from view. As Drew stumbled to his feet, he shoved off the concern of a passerby.

"We're okay," he said. "The driver lost control."

"Yeah," Shipley muttered. "Twice. I'm leaving, Gregory. I stay with you, and I'm sure to get myself killed."

"We don't know who they were after. *You* maybe, David."

"Your room got ransacked, not mine. They're after you."

"But aren't you the one who told Kaminsky my room was in shambles?"

"No . . . yes, I guess I did."

They staggered the rest of the way across the street and stood braced against a darkened window front. Shipley's breathing turned to erratic little puffs as he stared at the torn threads on Drew's coat. "How did that driver know how to find us?"

He had twenty blocks, Drew thought. *Twenty blocks worth of time since Warren Mackey placed his call.* "I don't know, but he never intended to kill us. The shots went over our heads."

"They were close enough. I thought they hit you, Gregory."

"But they didn't."

"Drew, I'm heading out to the airport."

"It may be closed. Planes won't take off in this storm."

"Yeah, yeah, but I'm not going another step with you."

He pressed Shipley's arm. "When will you contact me? And how?"

"About Breckenridge?"

"Can you get back to Xangtiene and let me know what you find?"

"I'll think about it."

"Contact me at the embassy in London."

"No, I'll let the admiral know. He'll get word to you."

"Not good."

"Then your daughter."

Drew rattled off the address. "Will you remember it?"

Shipley tapped his temple. "I've got a good memory. Phone numbers and addresses are stored up here."

Drew ran his gloved hand across his numb lips. "Good luck, Shipley," he said as Shipley limped off.

"You're the one who needs the luck."

Chapter 13

Drew found the nearest phone, dropped in the coins, and dialed 0. "I'd like to place a collect call. Yes . . . to Chadsworth Kaminsky in Georgetown."

He overrode the operator's singsong pleasantries and persuaded Chad's wife to accept the charges. His anger mounted as he waited for Chad to come on the line. Chad's delays were getting to be a habit. *It's your money, so take all the time you want.*

Three minutes later the bulldog growl came over the wires. "Yes, this is Chadsworth Kaminsky."

"Gregory here."

"Where are you?"

Drew rattled off the cross streets. "I'm at a pay phone, and it's freezing cold."

"Are you alone? No one around you?"

"Not even the guys in a Mercedes who tried to run me down."

Chad forced a chuckle. "What did you do, jaywalk?"

"I stepped off the curb."

"That's it?"

"The driver hit the accelerator, and I did a fast roll. Otherwise I'd be a John Doe in the city morgue right now."

"Probably a drunk. We have enough of them on the streets."

"This one was sober enough to reverse and try again. His passenger fired a semiautomatic. I thought maybe you sent them."

"You know better. We don't run down our own good men."

"So what's going on, Chad?"

"That's what we want to know." He tried ten seconds of silence. "We don't like the friends you're keeping, Gregory."

Shipley? The Breckenridges?

To Drew's surprise, Chad said, "That stranded motorist may have been a setup."

"How did you know about her?"

"We have our ways."

Mackey? "You're wrong, Chad. That motorist was stranded."

"And you were the Good Samaritan. You were always a sucker for defending women. And believing the underdog. We don't like your taking off without telling us, especially with David Shipley."

"What's with this Shipley business?"

"We had him followed for his protection and ours. He didn't leave the country as planned."

"He stayed over to talk with me."

"And you met him in Arlington."

"His idea, not mine. I just went. Oh, no! The old lady kneeling on the ground by Breckenridge's grave."

"Yeah, one of ours. Not as old as she looked. I'm warning you, Shipley is not a good contact. He denied knowing the Breckenridges, yet he drove you straight to their place."

"I wanted to meet the admiral and his wife."

"So why did Shipley go?"

"Curiosity maybe." *To deliver a wedding band. But I'm not going to tell you that.* On the street traffic had picked up. He kept his eye out for the black sedan, but his mind was on Luther Breckenridge's wedding ring nestled in his pocket. He wiggled it onto his own finger for safety.

"Gregory, Shipley and the Breckenridges intend to use you. Whatever their game is, we don't like it. Just keep us posted."

"Chad, our meeting at Langley fizzled out in fifty minutes. Then I was trapped into a miserable lunch hour with your Senator Summers and his less than charismatic personality. With the last bite, you sent me on my way. So why report back to you?"

Kaminsky grated his teeth. "Don't go

back to your hotel."

"Have to. My things are there. I'm freezing. Gotta go."

"Wait, hang in there until you see a taxi."

"Little chance in this weather. I just hiked twenty blocks, and there wasn't one empty cab."

"My wife called on the other line. A taxi is en route. We know about your ransacked hotel room. You could have been killed."

"I wasn't."

"Maybe the next time you won't be so fortunate."

"They've missed three times now."

"You're lucky the truck driver happened along the parkway, otherwise you'd still be in the snowbank."

"So Warren Mackey was one of yours, too?"

"Yes, he followed you from Ocean City."

"His call on the car phone — that was to you?"

"No, to Neilson. So we had your hotel room emptied out."

"Emptied out?" Drew exploded.

"Keep your cool. Everything was taken to Uriah Kendall's. We're trying to keep you alive."

"Is it this Breckenridge issue?"

"Can't say."

"Or won't?"

"Just get on over to Kendall's and stay put. We've booked you on an earlier flight out of Washington National. Porter's suggestion."

"You've been in touch with him?"

"Had to. We were worried about you. Actually, he called us. He's been trying to reach you. That led to Oscar Radcliffe."

"The pompous house detective." Drew was numb with cold, but he saw the taxi coming. "Then you know about Nell Ashcroft?"

"Yes, was she a friend of yours?"

"Never heard of her, not until two days ago. Kaminsky, a maid at the hotel can identify the man who ransacked my room." *And, God help him, I hope it wasn't my bro*ther.

"We know about Maria. She's been fired."

"That's crazy. She may be in danger and doesn't even know it."

"She's safe for now. Don't worry."

"Gotta go, Chad. The taxi's here. Number 4-8-Z."

"That's the one. Go straight to Kendall's."

"I assume the driver knows my destination?"

"Yes, my wife gave him the address. I'll be in touch."

"You do that."

"Have a safe trip back to Paris."

"It's been a long time," Kendall said as he opened the door.

"Your choice."

"Yes, you're right." He beckoned Drew inside and led him into the warm room where two winged chairs faced the roaring fire. As they took their seats, Uriah said, "I'm sorry. I let my friends go when Olivia died."

"That was years ago, Uriah. It would break her heart to see you still grieving."

"It was *the way* she died. Friends only remind me of her."

"We could have talked it out at Robyn's wedding."

"Again I'm sorry, but when I saw Miriam, it reminded me of how close she and Olivia had been. Miriam never forgave me."

"For burying the truth?"

"I've just accepted it as a hit-and-run accident, Drew. Nothing mysterious. But so final. So fatal for Olivia."

Uriah seemed to grow more weary with the words. *But who ran away from the accident?* Drew wondered. *Just the unknown driver of that car? No, Uriah, you're still run-*

ning from the memory.

As they sat quietly for a few moments, Drew felt the chill melting away — his body thawing — as the logs burned. He had forgotten the luxury of this home, the exquisite tastes that Olivia and Uriah had shared. He saw something of the Victorian flair in the fabric chairs on which they sat, yet felt the cushioned comfort that Uriah expected. Bookshelves on either side of the fireplace were crowded with leather-bound volumes: Dante, Longfellow, the Bronte sisters, and Dostoevsky. Copies of Olivia's novels lined two shelves. Warmed now, Drew allowed his gaze to travel from the delicate pastels in the sofa and ottoman — surely Olivia's choice — to the contrasting bold brilliant paintings that Uriah loved. Drew's eyes settled on the painting above the fireplace.

"That's a masterpiece, Uriah."

"It came from Miriam's gallery."

"Robyn tells me you own several."

"Four actually. I've donated the others to the museum in my wife's memory."

"Olivia appreciated art, didn't she?"

"She loved it almost as much as she loved to write."

They lapsed into another comfortable silence, their friendship rekindled. Uriah had to be in his early seventies, his sandy hair powdered a silver gray. Even in his maroon dressing gown, he looked well-groomed, the deep rich color like one of his bold paintings. His weight had dropped since Olivia's death, but Drew still saw confidence in his movements and, except for the grief lines around his dark blue eyes, it was a strong, proud face.

Uriah smiled. "Have I changed that much?" he asked.

"I was thinking how little you've changed. Tell me, Uriah, how did you get in touch with Kaminsky?"

"He got in touch with me. I left a message at your hotel the night your room was searched. Kaminsky remembered me from the old days. So he jumped to conclusions — figured MI5 was involved somehow." He stared at the fire, a sad smile on his serious face. "I was with British Intelligence years ago."

"I suspected as much."

"But you never questioned me."

"No, but I did some checking on my own. Our first meeting at the Metropolitan Museum of Art seemed contrived. That worried me."

"The museum was Olivia's idea — her way of trying to help Miriam. They thought I could persuade you to give up the CIA."

242

"You weren't very persuasive."

Uriah ran his long fingers through his hair. "I couldn't do that to you. Not when I wished I'd stayed on with MI5."

"Why didn't you?"

"They didn't want me — not if I married Olivia." He sighed as he eased back from his past. "Kaminsky is worried about you, Drew. He wants you hidden until your flight back to Paris. I suggested my place."

"He worries about the company I keep."

Uriah chuckled heartily. "Does that include me?"

"It does if you ransacked my hotel room."

Uriah stood and stirred the fire with a long iron poker. "I was there that night — to meet your brother."

"Aaron was at the hotel?"

Uriah sat down again. "We were to meet in the lobby. He had called me, quite agitated about his firm putting him on probation."

"They can't. He's a partner."

"An unhappy partner. He was outnumbered. The other lawyers told him to get his act together or resign."

"And he's blaming me?"

"He didn't say. He asked me to speak to you about selling the family farm to him."

"We're not exactly friends."

"You never were close. But as much ill will as he shows toward you, he would never destroy your things. What is it between you two?"

"An inheritance."

"Have you considered letting him take over the farm?"

"Never."

"That's a long time."

"Uriah, my brother played a major role in art fraud."

"How well I know. I purchased one of the forgeries from Miriam's gallery. Since then Miriam and the insurance company made the sale good — at great financial loss to Miriam, I'm sure."

"And you were still willing to meet with my brother?"

"He sounded troubled. I was foolish enough to think he might want to make amends for the forgery. But when I got to the hotel lobby, no Aaron. I left word at the desk for you to call me."

"I got the message."

"And you've wondered if Aaron is responsible for the damage to your room? I don't think he fits the description."

"When Kaminsky called, did you mention Aaron to him?"

Uriah turned in his chair. "He didn't give

me time. He wanted to take me up on my offer to house you. But you're not my only guest. Maria arrived earlier this evening."

"The hotel maid? Here at your place?"

"She needed a place to stay — at least until you're safely back in Paris. Maria is a frightened young woman, but the man she described — the man who robbed you — couldn't be Aaron."

"Who then?"

"Someone muscular. Handsome. Maria notices those important things," he said chuckling. "And she's certain he had an accent."

"What kind of an accent?"

Uriah's eyes held a tiny twinkle. "Foreign, she tells me."

"Only a few people even know I'm in the States."

"And on your way out tomorrow evening," Uriah reminded him. "By the way, I'm to persuade you to forget Captain Breckenridge."

"Kaminsky's order? Neilson's? What does it matter? How can one dead marine cause me so much trouble?"

Uriah stared at the fireplace. "I've always thought Olivia's death was the result of some secret she knew. Death silenced her. Perhaps it's the same with your marine. What secret could he have carried with him to his grave?"

"He was accused of passing top secrets — not of being buried with them."

"There's renewed interest in Breckenridge. That's why Kaminsky is concerned about your safety." He extended his hands toward the fireplace, palms to the heat. "I'd say that someone who knew Breckenridge still wants to keep things silent, wouldn't you?"

He glanced at the picture of his wife on the mantel, his grief rising poignantly again. "Sometimes things are best left buried."

Drew checked his baggage at the airline desk with forty minutes to spare before his flight to Paris. Using his credit card, he placed a call to Miriam. The sweet fragrance of the rose in his lapel reminded him of her.

"Hello." She sounded sleepy. "Hello," she repeated.

"Miriam, I'm sorry to call so late. I just had to hear your voice before I flew back to Europe."

"Drew, are you all right?"

"I'm fine."

But he had hesitated for a second too long. "I don't believe you."

"Really. Truly. Two legs. Two arms. Two eyes." *And one head that almost got blown off.*

"Why are you so worried, *Liebling?*"

"Floy awakened Sunday just past midnight and prayed for you. She said you had to be in danger."

Drew calculated the time difference. Floy might have been praying as a bullet whizzed overhead. *Good timing,* he thought. "You know that's not my thing, but thank her for me anyway, will you?"

"Then you were in danger?"

"It's over now. Just some crazy Washington driver." *The ones with the windows rolled down and guns in their hands.* "No need to worry."

She laughed. "But I'm so good at worrying."

"Miriam, I called to tell you I'm at Washington National. I'll be in the air in another thirty minutes. Safe and sound."

"Then I'll really worry. Are you heading to Robyn's place?"

"Paris first." *For a report to Porter. And a few answers from him.* "Then Robyn's and then back to the embassy in London."

"Did you get the answers that Robyn wanted?"

"Not the ones she wanted. Things were more complicated than we figured. Classified files and keep-out signs. But Robyn's good about facing the truth."

"Then you won't pursue it any further?"

"You know her better than I do. Will she take no for an answer?"

"Hhmm, I think that's the Gregory in her."

And I don't intend to take a no from you, Liebling. "She has a bit of your pluck and determination, too," he teased.

"What a combination. Poor child. Do keep in touch with her."

"Every chance I get. My phone bill will be sky high."

"Mine, too. She'll keep me posted on how you're doing, too."

"I hope so."

"Drew, before I forget it, Tran Industries opened an account with me. Duc Tran says he's a friend of yours."

"Definitely not. Don't get involved with him."

"Does he work for your Company?"

"No, Miriam. Close the account. Forget him."

"I can't do that — he was very polite."

I can imagine. "Miriam, did you get my flowers?"

"Yes, I love them. Floy counted them several times." Her voice filled with laughter. "She insisted that I call the florist and complain that a dozen means twelve, not eleven red roses. I just had to tell her, Drew, that you always send eleven roses — that you keep the twelfth one. Did you this time?"

He grinned and sniffed it again. "Yes, I'm wearing it in my lapel. I'd better go, Miriam. They're boarding my flight."

Wistfully she said, "Drew, stay safe. You know I do care."

Chapter 14

In Arlington Uriah Kendall's chauffeur-driven limousine pulled to a stop in front of the exclusive men's spa, fifteen minutes ahead of his scheduled appointment. The health and fitness center stood on the border of town, flanked by snow-laden evergreens. The sidewalk had been shoveled clear, leaving snow mounds along the walkway to the glass entry.

"Should I wait, sir?" Ned asked as he helped Uriah from the car.

"No need, Ned. You'd freeze out here. Go enjoy breakfast in some warm cafe, but be back in two hours. I should be ready by then."

As the chill of the wind hit him, Kendall felt the miserable restrictions of an arthritic spine. He steadied himself with a cane. He rarely used one, but in the winter months the weather played havoc with his bones, making him feel older than his years.

"I'll see you up the steps, sir," Ned offered.

Uriah shook his arm free. "You'll do no

such thing. You may have to carry me out, but I'll walk in."

It was the same cane that Olivia had used when she fractured her leg; it gave Uriah a sense of warmth touching it, flooding him with nostalgia and longing. The years without her had been unbearable. He squared his shoulders, trying to hide the slump that had accompanied the years of growing old alone.

He nudged Ned's muscular arm and smiled. "You should be going in there this morning, not me."

The chauffeur's amiable grin matched his own. "Are you sure you don't want me to stick around just in case you need me?"

"I promised to come alone."

"And you're always a man of your word." Ned glanced at his watch, a gift from Uriah. "I'll be back at eleven. No later. You wait inside. And if you're not there, sir, I'll charge through that facility like there ain't no tomorrow."

Another quick nudge for the young man who would have made a better son than his own, and Uriah set out, stepping cautiously with Olivia's cane. The doors at the top of the steps swung open. He entered a swank atmosphere of highly polished furnishings, a room resounding with lively music piped in through the paneled walls.

The tempo was faster and more contemporary than suited his taste. He shrugged and went straight toward the reception desk to the pretty young woman in skimpy sportswear — white shorts and a blue polo top emblazoned with Lyle's Health and Fitness Spa. Her own name was scrawled in cursive letters across the pocket.

Kelly sported a short mop of curly hair, even teeth, and long slender legs. She grinned her welcome, a bright chipper smile filled with youth and vitality. "Good morning," she said. "I'm Kelly Mederia. Welcome to Lyle's athletic club. How may I help you?"

He wanted to say, *Help me out of here.* "Yes, good morning, Kelly. I'm to meet Glenn Summers here."

"Then you must be Mr. Kendall, Senator Summers's guest."

She hesitated, looking at his cane.

"I suppose you're thinking about a release form," he observed. "But my cane is just for show." To prove it, he swung the crook of the cane over his arm and took three high steps to the music. The jerk in his spine served as a warning. He gripped the shiny desk and grinned sheepishly. "I guess I'm a bit out of shape."

Kelly's quick burst of laughter cheered him. He liked this girl — as Olivia would have liked her — for the wholesome tease in her voice and eyes and her quick acceptance of him.

"Let me check your coat here, Mr. Kendall. And if you like, we have a safe deposit box for your valuables."

I'll keep them with me, he thought, but before he could tell her she said, "You're to meet the senator in the steam room."

He had expected to go snail's pace on the stair-stepper or to ride an exercise bike at his own speed. But he didn't dare risk passing out in a steam room or a sauna bake. Kelly seemed to guess his concern. "Senator Summers thought it would be good for you, but if you're not up to it, I'll send word to the senator."

He felt a smoldering rage at Summers. *Not up to it, indeed.* The man was only six years younger. "Don't do that, Kelly. If he thinks the steam room would be good for me —"

She came around the desk and helped him slip out of his overcoat. "There's a buzzer inside the room," she whispered. "If you don't feel comfortable, someone will come at once."

He swallowed his pride and thanked her. Then he followed an athletic young man named Paul back through the club toward the steam rooms. In spite of the weather, at least thirty men — the club's elite, he decided — had already checked in and were using the state-of-the art equipment. Mirrors lined both walls offering ample opportunity for the sweaty men to check their body mechanics as they strained against weights and machinery.

The workout music sounded even louder here, blocking out the grunts of the body builders. Paul bounced along in his cross-trainer shoes and spotless white socks, cheerfully shouting, "Good workout, Jim . . . watch those shoulders, Lou . . . Add five pounds, Ben."

Uriah had expected metal lockers in the dressing room, but again the fancy paneling prevailed on the lockers. Paul handed him a terry cloth robe and two thick bath towels. "As soon as you're ready, sir."

Moments later Uriah stepped reluctantly into the steam room. As the door closed, steam vapors rose around him. He groped for a spot on the tiled bench and then slapped a towel over his thighs.

As his eyes focused, he became aware of two men in the room with him. He recognized Summers — scrawny and lean, his dark eyes squinting without his glasses on. Uriah had not expected the other man who slipped down from the higher bench to sit beside him.

"Neilson," the man said. "Harv Neilson."

Yes, they had met at Langley. Neilson was CIA. High up, if Uriah remembered correctly. Chad Kaminsky's friend, he was certain.

"I asked Glenn to arrange this meeting. The exclusive use of the steam room was his idea, private and unobserved. So thanks for coming."

Summers made no effort to move from his comfortable spot on the top of the three-tiered bench. "And, Mr. Kendall, thanks for housing Gregory."

"He got off on time?" Neilson asked.

You should know, Uriah thought, but he managed a polite, "Of course, on time. He should be in Paris by now."

"Not in Busingen with my daughter?" Summers asked bitterly.

"He didn't mention Busingen."

"But he did mention my daughter?"

"Yes, as his daughter's friend." *And Luke's widow.*

He didn't like Summers. Never had. Probably never would.

"Any problems with Gregory?" Neilson asked.

Uriah felt the first prickles of sweat forming on his body and found himself enjoying the warmth of the steam against him. The mist veiled Neilson's face one moment, revealed it the next.

"Any problems?" Neilson pressed.

"Drew and I are old friends. We mostly reminisced."

"Did Gregory mention Nell Ashcroft?"

"Who's that?" He stared at the man beside him, a well-built man with sweat pouring down his face and over his hairy chest.

"Her passport said British."

"But you don't think so?" Uriah asked.

"No, Mr. Kendall, we don't."

"Well, Drew never mentioned any woman except Miriam."

"She's past history," Summers mumbled from the upper deck.

"Not with Gregory. And if there were other women in his life these last sixteen years, he never mentioned them to me." Uriah thought of Drew's animated expression as they spoke of the old days when Miriam and Olivia were still part of their lives.

"We need your help, Kendall. Did Drew know Nell Ashcroft?"

"How would I know?" Uriah asked. "What's the problem?"

"The woman was murdered in the hotel where Drew was staying."

"Oh, my! I don't recall reading about her in the paper."

"We managed to keep it out of the news."

"Come on," Summers interrupted. "He was with you for two days."

"A day and a half. And he didn't mention any Nell Ashcroft."

Neilson wiped his face dry, but the steam soon drenched it again. "Gregory works at the American embassy in London. For his sake, have British Intelligence look into Ashcroft's background."

"Pick up the phone and contact them yourself." Fortunately, the steam hid his smile. *Who are you fooling, Neilson. You've already been in touch with London. But why me? How do I fit in?*

Neilson sounded tight-lipped as he urged, "Kendall, you still have friends there. Talk to them for us. A quiet inquiry. With Drew in London, we prefer to avoid scandal."

I bet you do. "Tell me about Ashcroft."

"Like I said, she carried a British passport and registered at the hotel the day after Drew did. Supposedly, she came in from London that day, but she detoured by way of the Russian embassy."

Gregory, old friend, what are you up to? As his heartbeat raced, Uriah felt for the buzzer beneath the bench and pushed it. "I can't stay in this steam any longer. I'm beginning to feel ill."

Summers swung off the bench. "Let's get you out of here."

Paul opened the door and extended the robe to Uriah. "Here, Mr. Kendall," he said. He took Kendall's elbow, and this time Uriah welcomed the strong arm. The young man led him to the massage tables and allowed him to stretch out on the middle one, face down with a warm bath blanket over him. The heart palpitations had eased, but he felt exhausted. He chided himself for giving in to weakness at the moment when he needed to be attentive. Drew was in trouble, and he had no way to warn him.

"Are you all right, sir?" Paul asked, his broad hand firm on Uriah's shoulder. "May I get you some juice."

"Yes, please." *And get me out of here before they ask me about Maria.* He tried to move, but felt too weak. He lay still, counting the miles to Drew's farm in upstate New York. Maria would be there by now. Drew's idea. Drew's arrangement.

"Maria will be safer there, Uriah," Drew had said as they sat by the fireside. "She can stay with the Quinwells and work off her room and board. Aaron won't risk going back up there."

"And how long do you plan to hide her there?" Uriah had asked.

"Until this whole thing blows over. If necessary, she can enroll in a nearby community college next semester. That would make any long stay look legitimate. The Quinwells will work with me."

And you'll pay whatever it costs, Uriah thought. Anything to protect the young woman. There was always a good side to Gregory, a cunning side too. Gregory took pleasure in outwitting Neilson and Kaminsky, swiftly making his arrangements by phone and sending a frightened Maria by car in the snowy predawn hours.

Paul was back, kneeling beside him, orange juice in hand. Uriah sipped the juice through a straw. "Good, sir," Paul said as though speaking to a child. "Rest a bit. Then I'll help you up."

Uriah kept his eyes open as Neilson and Summers took the tables on either side of him. "Hold off on the rubdown," Neilson told Paul. "Give us a few moments alone first."

When Paul's cross-trainer shoes disappeared from view, Uriah turned toward Glenn. "What kind of trouble is Gregory in?"

Summers had his glasses on now, his thinning hair combed. He'd been a lawyer early in his career before his political aspirations took over. Summers smiled drolly. "Obstruction of justice, for one. We know that Maria is no longer at your place."

"She was gone when we got up, but I was asking about Gregory."

Summers's shrewd eyes darkened. "Neilson won't own up to it yet, but the FBI is investigating a suspected mole in the Agency."

"They're twenty years too late," Neilson snapped.

"Not according to the FBI. As far as they're concerned, the second oldest profession in the world is tainted again. The mole hunt is a tedious task, but they'll find their answer."

"It's taken them fifteen months already," Neilson said.

"Touchy," Glenn answered. "But it's true. And the Senate Intelligence Committee, which I chair, expects some answers up on Capitol Hill. Soon."

"You blow this one wide open, Glenn, and you will have a wiggling can of worms all over you."

"What kind of a threat is that, Neilson?"

"Push it, and the scandal against your son-in-law will explode."

They seemed to have lost sight of Uriah

between them. Or did they want him to hear this? He stiffened with pain, the tension in the room adding to the spasms at the base of his spine. They wanted him to walk into British MI5 and contact his old friends, maybe even ask them to search the files for Nell Ashcroft. But mostly they wanted him to doubt Gregory — to suspect him as a mole, a double agent.

Uriah tried to rally his old loyalty for Drew and felt it shaken as the mumbling voices of Summers and Neilson rose and fell in the stuffy room. Yet he knew that Drew had been on to something. Uriah had sensed it that night in the library. And Luke Breckenridge, Senator Summers's ex-son-in-law, was somehow involved. But how? Breckenridge had been dead for twenty years.

"Gentlemen," he said, turning stiffly toward Neilson, "I must leave. My chauffeur is waiting for me."

"Don't," Neilson urged. "I told you we need you."

Summers agreed. "Hang in there, Uriah. The massage will do you good. They'll work those shoulder muscles so you'll feel better."

But I won't feel any different inside. "I can't help you. I haven't been with British Intelligence for years."

"We know," Neilson said. "You gave it up for your wife."

"It was worth it. We had some good years together. Neilson, I know how it works. We've had our own scandals, Philby and crew chief among them. But if you do have a mole, you already have your list of suspects. I trust Gregory isn't on it."

"He is. Our station-chief in Paris insisted on it. But as far as I'm concerned, Gregory's at the bottom of the list. He's been a good officer, a man of integrity."

Summers's voice came across thinner than his lean face. "Don't be shortsighted, Harv. He's got the right qualifications: passed over for promotion, demoted to the embassy, a ruined marriage, and money for whatever he wants. CIA salary doesn't set him up like that."

"Why, you —" Uriah curbed his anger. "Gregory inherited his wealth, and you know it."

Neilson nodded. "When we look for a mole, we look for somebody who has compromised other agents. Drew doesn't fit the pattern. He was compromised himself in Croatia. It almost got him killed."

It would be a clever way, Uriah thought. *Compromise yourself and throw suspicion elsewhere.* It was something to consider, but not with a man like Gregory.

"Drew is an idealist," Summers taunted. "Like my ex-son-in-law."

"But Gregory is not a traitor."

"He's an unhappy man."

"Stoic, but loyal," Uriah defended.

"He's pushing this Breckenridge issue," Summers said bitterly.

"Maybe somebody has to." Uriah rolled over on the narrow table and sat up, the bath blanket still draped across his lap.

Summers cleared his throat. "Gregory keeps a Swiss account."

"So does your daughter."

"Why not? She lives there."

"Gregory lives in Europe, too." Uriah glared back over his shoulder at Neilson. "I assume you've searched his flat in London."

"We had to, but it was clean. What about it? Will you help us?"

"I'll be visiting my grandson in London soon. I'll see what I can find out." *For Gregory's sake.* "But you keep your bugs and your men out of my private life. If I find wiretapping or anything that indicates that you crossed my property line, you'll wish you hadn't overstepped your rights." He shot another glance at Glenn. "That goes for both of you."

"Fair enough," Neilson said as Paul appeared in the room.

They watched Kendall walk from the room, a slight limp to his gait, Paul's firm hand on his elbow. "Thanks for getting us together, Glenn," Neilson said.

"Do you think it did any good?"

"We planted a few seeds. He'll help us."

"Are you sure? He and Gregory go back a long way."

"Their friendship cooled for a while."

"It did when Uriah lost his wife. I've been wondering, Neilson, did your boys have anything to do with that one?"

"No. I think it was a straight out hit and run. Pity, too. His wife was quite a successful woman, I hear."

"Maybe she had enemies."

"We all do."

"Yes, the mole in your Agency for one. That's high-level stuff, Neilson. Do you really think it's Gregory?"

"His station-chief in Paris does. Drew wanted that job. Maybe the loss of it soured him. He's missed some of the prime CIA posts — once because of his wife, another time when he was injured. And then that job in Paris. It's not easy to be passed over, especially when you're fully qualified. Gregory has held some top-level assignments with access to a lot of intelligence data."

The masseur slipped in unannounced. Angrily, Neilson tossed his sheet aside. "Forget it, Matt," he said. "I'm in a hurry. I have a briefing with the President in an hour."

Matt left as quietly as he had entered.

"Do you think he overheard us?" Summers asked.

"Not enough to put it together." He bent to tie his shoes. "This trip in, Gregory pushed for a transfer back to Langley for a high-tech job. Kaminsky and I worried about that one. It would have given him access at an unbelievable top level."

"You recruited him, didn't you? Straight from the military."

Neilson stood and knotted his tie. "No, my father did. Years ago."

"If he's your mole, Neilson, why would he be so interested in my ex-son-in-law? Seems like he'd steer clear of that one."

"Unless there's a connection, some secondary motive. Maybe Breckenridge's old contact —" He let the words drop.

"The possibility of a mole in your ranks has been rumored for years. The President has known about it for months. The White House is pushing us. Our committee is pushing you. It's time to expose the mole, Neilson. Arrest him."

"We will when we know for certain. You know we have an inter-agency task force at work on it. We've locked horns with the FBI before. Push us now, Glenn, and the guy may bolt."

"Where would he go? Russia? Hardly. Or Iraq? He'd never be welcomed there. My committee won't wait much longer. We'll go public."

"And ruin it for the Agency? I'm warning you. Keep a lid on that intelligence committee of yours. We don't want any double agent to run, no matter who he is. Quit pushing us. If you don't, this whole thing will blow up in your face. Do you understand?"

"You can't link my son-in-law with today's troubles."

"Don't be so sure."

"Why didn't you tell Kendall what we know about the Ashcroft woman? He didn't flinch when you mentioned the Russian embassy. Is the man deaf or something?"

"He heard us. He'll put it together sooner or later."

"How? We haven't put it together ourselves."

I have, Neilson thought. *She was Drew's contact. But so blatant.* He shoved the curtain back and left the room. He didn't look back at Summers. The man had always irritated

266

him intensely. Yes, they had a mole in the Agency, two maybe. And he didn't want to lose them. Personally, he wanted to be on hand as the net tightened. Damage assessment to the country and the Agency was astounding: top secrets out, critical operations uncovered, America's security system compromised, years of hard work wasted, and his own position threatened. The next thing he knew, the President would be asking for his resignation.

The Company was Neilson's life. Unless this thing got settled soon, they'd be the laughing stock around the world, to say nothing of admitting to dead agents in Bosnia, dead agents in other parts of Europe, two agents executed in Russia. And the latest star on the wall at Langley for one of their own. Everything the direct result of betrayal within the ranks.

He'd had enough stuffed down his gullet to infuriate any man. Right now, it seemed that no one recognized that he'd spent a lifetime defending the integrity of the Agency. How, then, could he admit to treason within its ranks again?

More than anything, he didn't like Porter Deven's accusations. *Not Gregory.* They'd known each other superficially for years. Chad Kaminsky swore by him.

For a moment, Neilson hesitated. Should he risk everything and go back and tell Glenn that his ex-son-in-law might have lived long enough to escape Laos? The shock could send Glenn into cardiac arrest. And it would destroy Summers's daughter. As annoying as Breckenridge's widow had been from time to time, Neilson pitied her.

No, he'd keep that nasty old rumor about Luke's escape to himself, at least for a little longer. He didn't want to risk public disfavor or stir up a greater furor about a grave site in Arlington National Cemetery.

Chapter 15

Victor Wilson stood facing the harbor of Monaco, his arm around Nicole as they watched the yachts glide over the azure blue waters of the Mediterranean. Wide sails caught in a gentle breeze, and stark white sea gulls flitted like tiny clouds against the brilliant sky. The smell of sea water and scaled fish rose from the dock, mingling with the fragrance of the mimosa's pink-feathered leaves and the tangy odor of eucalyptus.

For the first time in weeks, Vic felt free, scot-free, even from the petty annoyances that had disturbed him hours ago — the pressure of the crowds and endless noise on the narrow streets choked with traffic and exhaust fumes. He drew Nicole closer, wondering if she felt his euphoria. From this vantage point, he sensed no fear of time running out for him. But should he admit to her that he was short-circuiting through life, his health on a downward spiral? How else could he ask her to befriend his cousin — to be Brianna's best friend when he could no longer do so?

Tourists in sunshades walked barefooted across the sandy beach, some hand-in-hand, some clutching their shoes. The pungent odor of rosemary leaves and fresh basil and thyme filled the stalls at the nearby open market. And then the alluring scent of Nicole's perfume caught his attention again.

He smiled down at her. "I could stay here forever."

"At least until tomorrow," she answered lightly.

She knew him so little, yet so well.

"Vic, come back before May — before it rains again."

"Will you be free then?"

"I think so."

He looked away, up toward the palace perched on the limestone cliffs, the Grimaldi coat-of-arms above its arch. The flag fluttered from one of the medieval towers, indicating that the prince was in residence. The prince's private yacht bobbed in the harbor. Vic scanned the waters again searching for the *Monique II*.

"Nicole, do you come here often?" he asked.

"Not anymore." She freed herself from his embrace. "And you, Vic? Why did you ask me to drive you here today?"

Yes, she knew him so well. "You remember Drew Gregory?"

"The older man? The silver-haired tennis player?"

"He'd hate either description. We're heading to Spain as soon as Drew gets back from Washington."

"But not on vacation?"

"I'd spend that with you." He risked her reaction. "Drew and I want to join a mercenary army."

"Hired soldiers in Spain? Never. I know the reputation of the Guardia. They patrol the frontiers and countryside and ports of entry. You'd better look for your merc camp on the other side of the Pyrenees."

He laughed outright. "Does bribery work better on that side?"

She shrugged her thin shoulders. "You're impossible, Victor Wilson. I thought you were happy with your present job."

He considered Porter Deven. "Not always." On impulse he urged, "Join us. You like adventure. You'd make a good cover for us."

"Take Brianna."

"I can't. She worries about me."

"She shouldn't waste her time."

"She's my cousin, my best friend."

"It took me months to believe you are really cousins."

"Nicole, we could bluff our way into camp if you went along."

"I don't know the first thing about guns."

Vic gave her a frank appraisal. "You wouldn't need to."

He lifted his binoculars to peer at the sleek elegance of a luxury yacht cutting toward the shore. "There she is," he said. "What a magnificent vessel!"

Nicole frowned as it glided gently toward them. "That's the *Monique II*. It sails into Monaco often. The skipper acts like he owns it, but it really belongs to a rich widow."

"You sound jealous."

"Do I? I'll never own anything like that. Or even get on board. The closest I came to the yacht was touching the bow. The skipper almost tossed me in the harbor for nosing around."

"Were you?" Vic teased.

"Salvador thought so." She smiled. "So I nosed around some more. He does charter runs, but he guards the comings and goings of his passengers. Makes me wonder who they are and what they're up to. So what's your big interest in the boat, Vic? The owner?"

"Believe me, Nicole, until two weeks ago I didn't know the yacht existed. I was searching for a military camp along the Pyrenees close enough to Andorra to still be neutral. Then a man in Barcelona linked the *Monique II* to the merc camp."

"I've heard rumors, too, but I'm telling you, check out the other side of the mountains and leave the Spaniards alone."

"Nicole, does the skipper gamble at Monte Carlo?"

"Mostly he talks to strangers." She laughed. "Maybe Salvador is recruiting men for that imaginary merc camp of yours."

"I'd know soon enough if I could just get on board."

The skipper stood on the dock now, offering his hand to an attractive passenger with shiny dark hair. Vic would have known her anywhere — Monique Dupree, Harland Smith's widow, beautiful in a stylish lavender suit, a print silk scarf at her slender neck.

"Nicole, introduce me to the skipper."

"And risk his fury again?"

"Then wait here. I'll introduce myself."

Vic walked alone down the pier until he reached the captain, a strong muscular man in his thirties. Long strands of sun-blond hair fringed the blue-visored cap. Salvador whirled around as Vic approached, his wide eyes cold and unfriendly beneath the bristly brows. A faint fuzz of hair covered his upper lip and chin.

"Nicole isn't coming?" the man asked.

"No. She didn't think you'd remember her."

Monique Smith smiled at Vic, a faint questioning look in her enormous brown eyes. He extended his hand. "Vic Wilson."

The puzzled frown grew. "Do I know you?"

"I'm Drew Gregory's friend."

She brushed a windblown lock of hair from her face as the skipper edged toward Vic. "It's all right, Salvador," she said. "Come aboard, Mr. Wilson. We'll talk inside. Privately."

Monique led Vic across thick carpets into the paneled salon, a bright, airy room with sycamore walls and a floral motif. Rich, plush furnishings stood against the walls, and a spinet piano filled the space beneath one porthole. She eased into a soft chair, crossed her legs beneath her, and smiled at his boyish curiosity.

"I see you like my yacht," she said.

"This is one slick vessel."

"Yes, it is. We have five staterooms and a crew of six with space to house ten guests comfortably. Plus the sauna and game room. My late husband entertained on board frequently, foreigners mostly. He liked to meet in international waters."

"Did he?" *I can imagine,* Vic thought. *The wealthy guests buying arms for third-world countries — in the sleek pleasure vessel moving innocently along the coastline.*

Sharply, she said, "I remember you now. You and Mr. Gregory brought me word about Harland after he was killed."

"Yes," Vic acknowledged.

"That's not a pleasant memory. My son saved Mr. Gregory's life at the cost of his father's. But Mr. Gregory never came back to see Anzel as he promised." Quickly she regained her composure. "But you didn't come here to talk about Anzel."

"No," Vic admitted, "but tell me how he is."

"He's in a medical clinic an hour's drive from here." She ran the palms of her slender hands together. "Anzel hit a milestone last week when he played a few notes on his violin. Then he dropped it and ran from the room crying."

"Drew says he plays well."

"Well enough to qualify for the Conservatory of Music in Bern someday. But Harland's death may have snatched that dream away from us unless Anzel can come out of this." She offered a fragile smile. "What did you want to see me about, Mr. Wilson?"

"I'm interested in your castle in the Pyrenees."

"And not our home in Seville? Or our chalet in Switzerland?" She studied him for a few moments amused. "It seems that several people are interested in Harland's vast fortune. The Surete in France, some of Harland's creditors — perhaps you're one — and his old friend Porter Deven in Paris. Do you know Porter?"

Vic forced surprise out of his expression.

"The castle?" she mused. "I just met with Harland's friends in Barcelona. They're anxious to purchase it from me, but I'm not ready to sell."

"Is it wise to keep the old place?"

"It's well furbished. Harland enjoyed going there with his friends." She chuckled — a light, mocking laugh. "They want to use it as a hunting lodge. I don't believe them. It's poorly located and expensive to keep up. I don't even know what kind of game exists in that area. Or what kind of game they're really playing."

Vic looked around the salon again and felt the gentle bob of the yacht on the water. "Perhaps I could help you find out, Monique, if you'd introduce me to the man in charge at the castle."

"I'm afraid not. The brigadier is most unfriendly."

As she tilted her head back, he fixed his gaze on her long white neck. Cautiously, he said, "I understand that the brigadier recruits men at the casino for training at the castle."

Her lips, lovely a moment ago, drew taut. "What kind of training are you talking about, Mr. Wilson?"

"Militia. I'd know if I could get inside."

"I don't know what the brigadier does. I've only met him once — a few weeks after Harland died. And then only by chance. He's a comparatively young man, fortyish, tall and muscular with a jagged scar from his ear down his neck." She shuddered. "But his coldness frightened me. He seemed glad that Harland was dead, yet sympathetic toward the boys and me."

"He may be training terrorists at the castle."

Monique pushed herself from the chair. "I think you'd better go. I don't like what you're suggesting. And I won't let my sons suffer further shame about their father."

Vic stood. "Nor do I want that," he said kindly.

At the sound of the skipper stomping about on the deck above them, she smiled, a charming full smile that softened the pain in her eyes. "Perhaps Salvador can help you."

277

But up on the deck, her voice cooled as she said, "Salvador, Mr. Wilson wants to meet the brigadier. Now if you'll both be so good as to step aside, I'll leave. I must get back to my sons."

They watched her sashay down the pier with quick, graceful steps. She passed Nicole without a glance. As she disappeared into the crowd, the skipper ran his rough hand over the sleek white rail. "So you want to meet the brigadier?" he asked.

"Yes. My friend and I are hunting for a job. We have references." He pulled a thick envelope from his hip pocket. "Here's some background on my friend and myself." *And I hope the Pentagon has our mock-up records on file by now. Or, Porter, did you foul up on that one, too?*

Salvador slit the envelope with his nail and scanned the pages. The cynical gray eyes narrowed. "Your friend has had a long military career, but didn't Mrs. Smith tell you? We're running a hunting lodge at the castle now."

"I still think you could use us."

"Army intelligence for you, too?" Salvador asked.

"No, antitank weapons with the infantry," Vic lied, thinking of his navy days. "I'm good with rifle-propelled grenades, too."

Salvador tapped the papers against his clamped fist. "We have ways of dealing with those who lie or cheat us." He faced Vic squarely. "Wilson, what's your association with Monique?"

"I knew her husband."

"He never mentioned you."

"Funny thing, skipper, he never mentioned you either. I thought Mrs. Smith owned the castle now and handled recruitment."

"She just owns it — until we can persuade her differently."

Vic offered his best sardonic grin and felt his face pucker with the effort. "Give me a shot at that. I'm quite persuasive."

"Mr. Wilson, I'll be at the casino in two weeks. I'll leave word for you at the desk."

"Nicole would like to come with us."

"No, don't bring her."

"She's teachable. Good behind the wheel, too."

"Can she handle a Hum-Vee like a man?"

"Teachable," Vic repeated.

Salvador tapped the papers again and handed them back. "I won't be needing these references. Once you are with us, it's first names only. It's a very exclusive hunting club."

No, it's a secret cabal run by powerful men

and politics, Vic decided. *In spite of what Porter wants, we're going in and take the American out alive.* "In two weeks then," he said cheerily, extending his hand.

Ignoring it, Salvador crooked his finger at a crew member.

Vic whistled as he sauntered down the dock toward Nicole, knowing that the sailor would tail them at a safe distance. He wrapped his arms around Nicole's shoulders, brother-fashion, and grinned. "Sweetheart, can you get me out of Monaco fast?"

"I thought you wanted to stay forever."

"Not anymore. I just volunteered our services to Salvador."

Vic felt her shudder beneath his grip. "You don't have to go," he said, "but I bet Brianna would jump at the chance."

"I don't think so, Vic. Not if Brianna had seen the devious look on that woman's face when she passed me."

Chapter 16

A rushing stream of discontent that no bridge could span separated Drew and Porter. Three hours of argument in the Neuilly office had only widened the chasm. Their lives seemed as divided as the city of Paris with its Left and Right Banks severed by the River Seine. Porter stood by a window in the granite and steel tower, both hands thrust deep into his pockets, those crystal blue eyes fixed moodily on sights beyond his office window.

"You disobeyed my orders, Gregory. I told you to lay off the Breckenridge file when you went to Washington."

"I just asked a few questions."

"And it exploded in your face. Your involvement with the Breckenridge family goes against Company policy."

"Breckenridge's widow and my daughter are friends."

"Then it's up to you to end that friendship."

Drew resented talking to Porter's back. "Then you'll be glad to know I asked Neilson for a transfer to Langley."

"I sent you to Washington to talk about mercenary camps."

"That wasn't his favorite topic."

"I'll discourage any transfer."

"I figured you'd welcome it." Drew left the chair across from Porter's desk and walked over to stand beside him. "I'd be out of here that way. Aren't you sick of our arguments?"

Porter's question shocked him. "What came between us, Drew?"

"Our political views over Vietnam and Croatia."

"And not my promotion to station-chief?"

Yes, Drew thought. *That, too. Even the DCI at Langley knew I was better qualified.* "I was surprised when you got it."

"This is my city. You'd never appreciate her like I do."

Paris was a spectacular place with centuries of history and architectural heritage spread out before them. One could easily lose himself within the boundaries of this city as Porter had done. In many ways he blended with the culture so well that he seemed like a Frenchman — self-contained and aloof, philosophical and intelligent. Yet Porter lacked the style and flamboyance of the Parisians who strolled on the Champs-Élysées.

Porter sighed. "That's a magnificent structure, isn't it?"

Which one? Drew wondered.

Before he could ask, Porter said, "I go into the cathedral now and then and light a candle and listen to the anthems. The building is immense, but I enjoy sitting there watching the sun stream through the rose windows." A crooked smile lifted his handlebar moustache. He tugged at the corner with the tips of his fingers. "What do you think of Notre Dame, Drew? Is it all trinkets for sale and tourists with cameras? Or something more meaningful?"

Drew reflected on the architectural achievements, on the forest of flickering candles, and the solemnity of worshipers who knelt there. "Sorry," Drew said. "I'm the wrong man to ask. I do more browsing at the book stalls outside Notre Dame."

"You never think about peace and your own mortality?"

"I did when the ambassador died."

Porter pressed the bridge of his nose, his eyes closed. "Sometimes I wish I could go back in time to erase the blunders and right the wrongs. Don't you, Drew?"

Yes, he'd like to go back sixteen years and right all those mistakes with Miriam and Robyn. Or go back to the farm and sit at his

283

mother's death bed. But he had no intention of sharing these regrets with a man like Porter.

"Oh, God," Porter cried, "if I could just wipe out the past."

Drew sensed the solitude of the man beside him, a man who spent his lonely hours with a basset hound and a glass of wine. Permanent scowl lines lodged between his bushy brows. A bottle of antacid tablets and a well-used emery board protruded from his shirt pocket. He sounded distant, empty. "Drew, did you know I lived with the Taoist monks for a few weeks?"

"Yeah. You were lost on a night patrol, weren't you?"

"Lately, I've thought about going back to Vietnam and trying to find them. They were a simple lot, living in harmony with one another. If it weren't for them, I'd be dead." He nodded toward a book on his desktop. "I still read the *Tao Te Ching*."

"Does it help?"

"Nothing helps."

Porter seemed sober enough this morning, yet he rarely talked about anything remotely religious without three stiff drinks under his belt. For one crazy moment, Drew wanted to suggest that Porter talk to Robyn and his son-in-law Pierre about God. It might save

Porter a trip to Vietnam in search of peace.

Beyond the closed window, they heard the mournful toll of a church bell ringing in the noon hour. As it tolled, Porter said, "There's another mole in the Company, Gregory."

Drew felt as if he'd been hit with mortar. "A turncoat?"

Porter popped an antacid. "We think so. In Europe this time."

"Has he been arrested?"

"He will be. We've had denials from Moscow and Madrid. But someone has been putting classified material into the wrong hands for a long time. What would you do, Gregory, if a man you served with for years proved to be a double agent?"

"I'd court-martial him."

"That's too merciful. I'd take him out with the first shot."

"Is that what you would have done to Breckenridge, Porter?"

"Arlington Cemetery was too good for him."

Porter's melancholy seemed contagious. Drew stared toward the patches of storm clouds that grayed the horizon. "Do I know the man?"

"You will soon enough. And when you do, you'll ask yourself if any woman or bank account was worth it. What about you,

285

Drew? Would you have betrayed your country for Miriam?"

"Never. And she would never have wanted me to do that."

"You really loved her."

"Still do," he admitted.

"A pity. A woman can destroy you. I know. I met a girl near a Buddhist temple in Thailand once. Thought myself madly in love with her — like you were with Miriam. Going inside Notre Dame often reminds me of her."

"You?" Drew chortled. "A girl. You surprise me, Porter."

"Don't mock me, Drew. Isn't anything sacred with you? It wasn't with her either," he said bitterly. "I was on R&R, and she flattered me with a smile, so I offered to take her picture in front of the temple. She snapped mine instead."

"Sounds serious."

"I thought so for a time. Months later I arranged to meet her in Tokyo, then Manila. And after that I used my rank for additional leave time and arranged one rendezvous after another. She was beautiful with deep-set brown eyes and thick, dark hair. One tiny ringlet always curled on her forehead."

Drew risked a glance at Porter. "Was she Thai?" he asked.

"No, Caucasian. But she had a hint of a slant to her eyes, long lashes, and a tempting well-shaped mouth. I would have done anything for her — until she told me she was married."

"Why didn't you just forget her and marry someone else?"

Porter slammed the wall. "Why didn't you forget Miriam?"

You're losing it, Drew thought.

Suddenly, a grossly twisted grin shadowed Porter's face. "I just painted you a picture, Drew. The makings of a spy. That's what we think happened to Luke Breckenridge. A woman. A foreign agent."

"That's ridiculous."

"Is it? His own marriage fell apart. He volunteered for a third tour of duty. He didn't even have a full year at home before going back. Breckenridge was attractive to women. We're looking for the same kind of man again."

"Did you know Breckenridge, Porter?"

"I know all I need to know about him. He disgraced his family and country when he sold secrets to the enemy." Porter shook his head, a confused expression on his face. "Luke broke faith with the Corps. A marine destroys his soul when he betrays his country."

Drew put his hand firmly on Porter's shoulder. "What's wrong?"

Porter pulled free. "What makes a man betray his country, Gregory? Yes, I want that American traitor in the mercenary camp."

"Neilson and Kaminsky are adamantly opposed."

"Neilson changed his mind. It's unofficial, but we have his okay. Vic Wilson took care of the initial contacts while you were gone. Everything is ready." Porter had stepped into a safe zone, his voice matter-of-fact now, his gaze back on Paris. "You saw the reports. The smaller merc camp closed during the last ten days. Someone on the inside is filtering warnings to them. We can't wait for that to happen to the larger garrison."

"Burdock in Madrid should handle this. It's his territory. What if we go in and he finds out?"

"Of course, he'll find out. He gets the same satellite reports. We're waiting to see what he does with them. The man may be our mole, Drew."

"Colin Burdock? Impossible. He's a good man."

"An American is running the merc camp, and Burdock may be looking the other way, even instructed to do so from Moscow or somewhere. He's had some major financial problems lately, Drew."

"Does that surprise you? His divorce set him back ten years."

"And he hasn't been the same since."

A divorce does that, Drew thought. He tried to remember the last visit in one of those fancy restaurants in Madrid — Porter, Burdock, himself. Burdock had drowned his sorrows with drink after drink, saying, "I'll get even with my wife someday."

But, Colin, you don't get even selling out your country.

Porter's face hardened. "We'll keep our eyes on Burdock — and spread the net a little further around him. You forget Burdock. Your objective is to take out the leader of that merc camp."

"We're to bring him out alive?"

"That would be too merciful. Kill him. The man is preparing a group of hit-and-run terrorists, perhaps for strikes against the Palestinians. We can't wait for that to happen."

"So we join an army of malcontents," Drew mused.

"Yes, you and Vic should fit right in."

Porter walked back to the desk and picked up an envelope. "Wilson sent this along."

Drew took it and opened it. In bold scrawl, it read: "Meet me beneath the marble goddess."

Drew crumpled the note, shoved it into his pocket, and caught the first Metro en route to the Louvre.

The museum stretched out in a long gallery, a world of art and beauty that would have delighted Miriam. Drew glanced at the priceless statues and paintings as he waited impatiently beside the armless *Venus de Milo*. Just when he had decided to go back to the hotel, he saw Vic on the other side of the corridor intently studying a picture as though art were his favorite pastime.

"Hey, Vic. Over here," Drew called.

He watched Vic stroll toward him — a slender man in casual attire moving with a nonchalant gait and flashing a cocky smile. Vic always lived for the present, his time frame limited to his next conquest. He seemed content with an address book full of first names: Nicole. Fran. Audrey. Madeline. Glamorous women who helped him forget his failed marriages. He looked relaxed and unhurried, a pound or two lighter maybe, but his eyes were bright, color fair, his cocksure smile spreading from ear to ear.

He gripped Drew's hand. "Come on, ol' boy, we might as well check out the musty paintings while we're here."

Drew fell into step, confident that his own vitality and muscular strength matched Vic's, maybe surpassed it. "Thought we were meeting at the embassy, Vic."

"The embassy walls have ears."

Minutes later he paused in front of the Mona Lisa, but his gaze remained fixed on Drew. "I got into Paris about a week ago. Porter found me a cubbyhole for an office so I could map out the plans for Spain. No surveillance cameras. No bug on my phone. Everything plain and simple — desk, chair, file."

Your face is too narrow, Drew thought, but he kept listening.

"I stuck to my own desk. No extra chatter with the regulars."

Drew grinned. "Except the pretty maidens."

"They're always an exception, but last night someone checked out my wastebasket. You know the rules. Baskets emptied before we leave the office. Papers shredded. The axe if we don't."

Vic glanced cautiously at people nearby. "I'm a stickler on empty baskets, Gregory, on anything that might break cover or expose my plans. So I know that waste container was dumped when I left. I'd only been gone an hour when I remembered a memo I'd left

291

on the desk, and I raced back."

He lowered his voice. "There was trash in that basket."

And there was anger in Vic's eyes as he added, "Bits and pieces of a report I didn't write. Trade secrets that wouldn't have landed in my basket. I shredded them fast and got out of there."

"Am I privy to the memo?"

"Scuttlebutt about Burdock and the Breckenridge file."

"So it had an Oriental ring to it?"

"An Asian trap is more likely, Drew. What do you and Burdock care about this Breckenridge? The kid's been dead for twenty years."

"Rumors about him are still alive. Maybe he got a bum rap."

"Would you say the charges against Burdock are a bum rap, too? His love for Flamenco dancers and bullfights is understandable, but explain his Spanish villa and fancy car."

"Is that what the memo said, Vic?"

"Yes, they have Burdock's name at the top of a list. They're watching him for some reason. Our names are on the same memo."

"Somehow that doesn't surprise me."

"Yes. I think Porter wants us out of Paris."

"Out of the Breckenridge files sounds more like it."

They ambled toward the exit, their voices low. "I've laid out a plan, Drew."

"So Porter tells me."

"According to the satellite reports, there's only one merc camp left, the one run by an American known as the brigadier."

"And Porter thinks Burdock may be his contact man."

Vic shrugged impatiently. "We have two targets then?"

"So it would seem. What do you have on this brigadier?"

"He's cautious. Capable. Elusive. Well-respected by his men. He took up arms at least twice himself — in South Africa and Bosnia."

They stopped in the courtyard and faced each other. "Drew, I've made two trips to Spain. Before he died, I think Harland Smith may have been priming the brigadier for leadership."

"Harland Smith," Drew exploded.

"The castle in the Pyrenees foothills — where the camp may be located — belonged to Smith. It's Monique's now. His widow — remember?"

"Yes, poor woman. Harland showed her the glittering world of Paris and gave her a permanent migraine. Unfortunately, she looked the other way when it came to his business deals."

"But those sons of hers, they're her whole life. Anzel is still feeling the shame of killing his own father. Have you forgotten, Drew? The kid saved your hide."

"I've sent money."

"That won't give Anzel back his peace of mind. Neither will inheriting his father's possessions." Vic picked up a pebble from the ground and tossed it. "There's a motor yacht named *Monique II*, part of Smith's vast holdings. It's involved with the camp somehow. So I made contact with the skipper on board."

"What about Mrs. Smith?"

"I saw her, too," he said grudgingly.

"I figured as much. Is Monique Smith involved in the camp, maybe carrying on her husband's work?"

Vic's tone sharpened. "I don't know. She goes by her maiden name — Monique Dupree. I think she's okay. But she's French, and there's a rumor the camp is being moved across the Pyrenees."

"Then Burdock may be warning the brigadier — or Monique?"

"They may be connected. Monique and Burdock move in the same social circles. But she wouldn't know he was CIA — probably thinks State Department."

"Quite possible," Drew agreed.

"And if Burdock has sold out, Harland Smith may well have been one of his contacts."

"Vic, we need a Frenchman to work with us. Jacques Marseilles knows Monique and he knows the Pyrenees. When he served with the Free French back in the war days, he helped Allied airmen escape over the mountains. I'll ask him to help us."

"He's a bad choice, Drew. He'd ruin the whole operation."

"No, he wouldn't want to muck up a third time."

"Forget him. We're due at Monte Carlo next Tuesday. After that, you call the shots. But I'm not working with Marseilles."

"I'll need a day in Geneva before I can leave. Robyn and my son-in-law are expecting me. And Sauni."

"Breckenridge's widow? Porter won't like that."

"I don't plan on telling him."

Vic frowned, narrowing his face even more. "Then I'll meet you in Monaco on Tuesday. If we're lucky, the *Monique II* skipper will give us a boat ride to Spain."

"That's better than swimming," Drew said. But he wondered if they'd end up on Jacques Marseilles's side of the mountain.

Chapter 17

The road to Vendome became familiar as Drew reached each landmark — a sparsely populated village, a railroad crossing, an empty store front, sheep grazing near a rickety barn — sights that he had noticed months ago on his first trip to the Marseilles chateau. Back then, he had needed information to convict Jacques Marseilles of treason. This time he sought the man himself.

Drew recognized the village as soon as he saw the spires on the cathedral and the magnificent sixteenth-century mansion perched on the hilltop above it. For generations the Marseilles family had looked down on the struggling farming community in the valley. Drew made a left on the lane that curved around the church and rose in steep hairpin turns to the chateau.

He half expected Stephan Marseilles and his aged friends to be in the courtyard challenging each other in a game of boules and basking in the friendship that had seen them through a war fifty years ago. The French

Resistance had drawn them closer. The war's end had sent them back to their village alive and well, unlike some of their comrades.

Now age had crept in, doing what the war had not done — bending their backs, thinning their hair, dimming their vision. Three men huddled together around Stephan — wearing their same dark baggy pants, zippered sweaters, and visor caps. One man stooped down, squinting at the ground in front of him. The chubbiest of the men folded his hands on a midline pouch, his fat-wrinkled face bulging like his belly. And the third friend, with rimless glasses riding the tip of a wide nose, leaned on a walking stick. Stephan stood erect, the same commanding figure that had first impressed Drew.

Stephan's nephew was not with them. Drew's hands tightened on the steering wheel. Had Jacques survived the judgment of these men? Or had they done as Stephan had threatened and put Jacques in front of a firing squad for his cowardice, ridding themselves of the disgrace of a man who had failed both the family traditions and his country as well — not once, but twice?

Stephan frowned as Drew drove the car across a dry patch of lawn and stopped.

Drew stepped out and extended his hand. "Monsieur Marseilles, I'm Drew Gregory," he reminded him.

"I have a good memory, Gregory. What is it this time?"

"I'm looking for your nephew."

The old man glowered back. "You were looking for Jacques the last time you were here. And you ruined him."

"I kept my word. His name didn't appear on my report."

Pride straightened Stephan's shoulders. "This was his courtroom."

Drew felt chilled. "You didn't —"

"Execute him? No. But your coming to see him should amuse Jacques. Is it another article for your tabloid, Mr. Gregory? Writing, eh? You and Jacques should get on well then."

"No articles, sir."

"What then? Oh, never mind. Go through the kitchen. You know your way. You'll find him in the sitting room bent over his computer. Alone as usual."

Drew found Jacques hunched at the desk, the laser printer beside him spitting out pages. He looked older. His posture spelled despair as though he wore the word *traitor* across his chest.

"Bonjour, Jacques. I'm Drew Gregory."

He answered without looking up. "Yes, I know. I saw you arrive. Have you come to take me away? Is that my uncle's plan for me now?"

"Only if you want to go with me."

Jacques turned then, his face forlorn. "Since when would a man choose prison? Or have you come to tell me Harland Smith is tracking me down again?"

"Harland Smith is dead, Jacques. No one knows you helped him."

"You know. My uncle knows. So why have you come?"

"I need your help to locate a merc camp in the Pyrenees."

"Use a map."

"It's not that simple. Rumor has the training camp located in Spain, but it may be on the French side in an unpopulated area."

"Foreign mercenaries? I'm not interested, Gregory."

"Not even if the property belonged to Harland Smith?"

Skepticism replaced the pensive gaze. "You said he was dead."

"He is. But Smith had investments worldwide. Wouldn't you like to topple part of that kingdom?"

"No."

Drew leaned forward, map in hand. "We've checked on you, Jacques. We know you've been writing articles on old chateaus and monasteries. No one would question your surveying some of the old ruins along the Pyrenees."

"And why would I want to do that?"

"For your country. For yourself. For money. We'd pay you."

Drew refolded the map, exposing the mountainous border that separated France and Spain. He ran his finger along the coast and over the waters toward the French Riviera. "It's a diagonal run from Barcelona to Monaco," he said.

"Do you plan to swim over?"

"The mercenary brigadier uses a pleasure cruiser."

A glimmer of interest flashed in the tired eyes. He made room on the desk for the map. "If I had a yacht," he said sadly, "I'd find Annamarie again and be gone from here — forever."

The mistress? Drew wondered. *Ah, yes. The one who loved opera and pretty clothes. The one who dined at the Amitie when Jacques worked there.* "There are few islands where you and your Annamarie could escape, Jacques."

"True, and my conscience would be a sorrowful companion."

"Help us. We'll compensate you enough to buy your way out of this chateau and back into favor with Annamarie."

"She likes extravagant things, Mr. Gregory."

"So does the camp director. He spends considerable time in Monte Carlo. At least the skipper of the *Monique II* does."

"Gambling?"

"He seems more interested in the contacts he makes there."

"Recruitment for foreign armies?" Jacques mocked.

"We think so. Some of those contacts leave Monaco aboard the *Monique II* and head across the Ligurian Sea. Lately, there have been some landings south of Narbonne on the French side. They may be transferring the camp there."

"Along the Pyrenees? That's where you want me to look for the ruins?" Again interest flickered across the morose face. "But mercenaries keep a low profile, Mr. Gregory. They don't use a fancy yacht to announce their presence."

"On the contrary, I find it a clever decoy. The skipper does charter runs with an odd assortment of wealthy passengers, men who may be funding the camp. Who would question the transport of men and equipment aboard a yacht that sails on friendly waters?"

"The boat must belong to Smith's lovely widow. Does Madame Smith own the mercenary camp in the Pyrenees as well?"

"Yes, but she has no idea what it is being used for."

"Don't be so certain. She used to dine at the Amitie Cafe with her husband when I was maitre d'. She's a clever woman." He shoved the map off the desk as though it were venomous. "I want no part of the Smiths."

"But you'd make an excellent guide, Jacques. I know about your work with the French Resistance — how you led Allied airmen across the mountain to freedom in spite of Franco's government."

His beady eyes darkened with memory. "A few pilots," he said modestly. "Brits and Americans. They'd get shot down in occupied France, and we'd smuggle them across the Pyrenees. I was young then, trying to prove myself to my uncle — to my country." His voice filled with resentment. "What thanks did I get? No, I want no part of infiltrating that camp."

"A coward to the bitter end?" Stephan Marseilles asked from the doorway. "Maybe I should go with you, Mr. Gregory. I was a much better warrior than my nephew."

A mask came over Jacques's face. He kicked at the map and glared at his uncle. "You never let up, do you? But even the humble Galilean was without acceptance in his own family. You do know about the Galilean, do you not, Mr. Gregory?"

Drew smarted at the strange reference. Embarrassed, he said, "Yes, my son-in-law speaks of Him often."

And if Pierre considered the Galilean a friend, then he could not fault Jacques for doing the same. He glanced across the room toward Stephan Marseilles. "We need a man like Jacques."

"A coward?"

"A soldier."

Stephan turned away in disgust, but he stopped at the door. "You offer Jacques the chance to restore his honor. Other men would die for such an opportunity. Not my nephew. He's afraid."

When they were alone, Drew said, "I can't make you any promises, Jacques. The job is risky, but you'd be paid well."

Jacques pointed to the elegant tapestries and furnishings. "I have no need for money. My uncle is right. Honor is important to my family, even to me."

"Then join us," Drew urged.

"It's too late. I rarely leave the grounds

304

these days. I've become a journalist of sorts. This is my life now."

"Think of the story if you locate the merc camp for us."

Jacques stood slowly, one hand braced on his desk. Drew folded the map, convinced that he had tried to recruit the wrong man. But suddenly Jacques smiled. "In a way I'm indebted to you, Gregory, for bringing me news of Harland Smith's death. Perhaps I can help you by contacting friends in the Basque regions on both sides of the Pyrences — former patrons at the Amitie. If there are any merc camps along the western foothills, they'll know."

Drew pressed the map back into Jacques's hands. "I've marked our locations on the map. Keep in touch with me."

Drew shook hands and left. The cold chill of the stone-walled chateau followed Drew into the courtyard. He nodded toward Stephan, climbed into the rental, and careened his way back down the hairpin turns to the village.

Sauni Breckenridge tried to compose herself as she placed the tray of cookies and tea in front of Robyn and Drew. The herb tea was steamy, the cookies freshly baked, but her slender hands felt like lead as she sat down and faced Robyn's father.

"Do you have news about Luke?" she asked.

"Not the kind you want."

She lifted the teapot to fill his cup. Robyn reached over. "Let me do that for you, Sauni."

"Don't spare me, Drew. Tell me what you found out."

"At Langley? Denial. But Luke is still a hot issue back there. If he hadn't been, I would never have met Glenn Summers."

"Dad!"

"Yes, at Langley. The meeting was arranged. We didn't get on."

"I never meant for it to go that far. Did Dad ask about me?"

"He suggested that I could help you both by not interfering."

"I'm sorry." Her hands steadied as she rested them in her lap.

"I met your in-laws, too — through a man named David Shipley. Don't look so worried. He's not CIA. David's work takes him into the villages of Laos and Vietnam. He's been to Xangtiene twice."

Sauni felt like a porcelain doll thrown violently against the sofa back — its hands translucent, its eyes staring blankly into space. Even her voice sounded lifeless like the doll when she whispered, "Then Xangtiene does exist."

Drew swallowed the tea and placed the cup back on the saucer. It tilted precariously on the edge, all three of them eyeing it intensely. Gently, he said, "According to Shipley — and he knows the language well — Luke lived in the village for a period of time. Shipley swears that Luke was alive during two monsoon rains."

"How could he have been, Drew? Luke was already buried in Arlington Cemetery before the rains came."

He watched her as she ran the tips of her polished fingers over her bottom lip. She knew she had paled beneath the makeup, that her taut face was ridged with disbelief. "Do you trust Mr. Shipley?"

"Not altogether — not at first. Actually I met him the same day I met your father. I disliked David and labeled him one of the arrogant new breed at Langley."

"But, Dad," Robyn protested, "you said he isn't CIA."

"He isn't, Robyn. He spent years searching for our missing men in Vietnam. Neilson and Kaminsky at Langley —"

Sauni winced. "Yes. I've met both of them. More than once."

"They called Shipley in two or three times,

trying to convince him that Xangtiene didn't exist. Maybe they wanted to know what Shipley knew, but he didn't tell them everything."

Robyn slipped her hand into her father's. He seemed comfortable leaving it there. With his free hand he removed a tissue-wrapped parcel from his pocket. "Shipley gave this to Luke's parents."

Sauni pulled back, whispering, "What is it?"

"Open it. Your in-laws sent it on to you."

Her fingers felt stiff as she took it, her motions precise as she removed each layer of tissue. She stared down at the wide gold band for a moment before picking it up and reading the worn inscription. Like the porcelain doll, her jaw seemed locked. Hoarsely she stammered, "How dare that man take my husband's ring. What was your Mr. Shipley doing with this? It's Luke's wedding ring — the one I gave him the day we married."

"Sauni, David found it in Xangtiene on one of his search missions. One of the Hmong leaders was wearing it."

The thought of Luke's wedding band on someone else's finger infuriated her. "Are you certain the marines didn't send it home with Luke's personal effects?"

"I saw David give it to your mother-in-law."

Sauni's skin prickled. "Did Luke die in that village?"

He hesitated for only a moment. "It's possible."

The old wound tore open. Clearly now she recalled Harv Neilson saying so long ago, "Mrs. Breckenridge, your husband left classified secrets by a downed aircraft in a Laotian village."

She kept her eyes on Drew, trying to block out the memory of Harv Neilson's angry face. Neilson. Gregory. Men from the same Agency. The Agency that had sent Luke to his death.

"Sauni, while David was still in the military, he filed a report with his commanding officer about a downed aircraft and the death of its pilots in Xangtiene. According to Dave, his C. O. substituted the name of the village, changed the location as due west, and blacked out the line that another American was held there."

Drew's monotone voice droned on. "It was on David's second trip to Xangtiene that he saw a Hmong wearing Luke's wedding band. He bartered for it with *kip* and a lot of rice."

She touched the ring again and smiled

through her tears. A warm smile for Luke. "It was worth a lot more."

"Shipley is fond of the people in Xangtiene. He said the village is quite peaceful now, the landscape green and mountainous."

"Luke always loved the mountains." She cried, wracking sobs, for several minutes. Finally she stopped and blew her nose. "Drew, Shipley's dates are all wrong."

"Do the dates really matter, Sauni?"

"They do to me. If only someone still believed in Luke."

"Like Luke's friend, Allen Fraylund?" Drew chewed on a cookie as though it were a tough morsel of steak. "Forget Colonel Fraylund. I tried to contact him. He's stationed in Washington now under your father's influence. Allen refused my calls." He paused. "Sauni, why didn't you tell me Fraylund was no longer your friend?"

"I was afraid you'd turn against Luke, too."

Drew reached over, squeezed her hand, and smiled. He had a nice smile, a pleasant, kind face. His eyes seemed trustworthy, but she braced herself as he added, "Your husband was in Xangtiene, Sauni, and we don't know why."

"He was on a CIA mission."

"That hasn't been confirmed. Washington wants to keep the files closed. But the news media stirs the ashes. Don't keep torturing yourself, Sauni. We may never know the whole truth."

He sat quietly for a moment, then looked up. "You asked me to trace Luke's final hours. I believe they were in Xangtiene."

"And you want me to let him rest there — not in Arlington."

"Let him rest wherever he is — *and go on with your life.*"

Drew stood. "Sauni, David Shipley has an aunt living near Schaffhausen. She's keeping some photos of Xangtiene for him in a safe deposit box. If I could get those pictures, you could see the mountains and the beauty of the Hmong people. I think it might comfort you to visualize the place where Luke died."

She held up the ring. "This is better. This was part of him when he was alive." *Part of him when we were in love.*

Drew slipped his arm around his daughter. "I'll be gone for a few weeks, but keep in touch with Robyn, won't you, Sauni?"

Seeing the concern on Robyn's face, Sauni smiled. "Of course. And you be careful, Drew."

Those piercing blue eyes held hers as he reached the door. "You didn't know a Nell

311

Ashcroft, did you?"

"Should I?"

"I thought she might be a friend of yours."

"Is she important?"

He opened the door. "Not really. When I get back, I'll try to reach David Shipley again — he lives in Bangkok. Maybe he'll give me his aunt's name and address then."

"I'd like that," she said.

As the Gregorys left, Annabelle Vandiver walked through Sauni's kitchen door, her usual bubbly smile missing, her face tight with worry. She dumped her books on the sofa, collapsed beside them, and stared mournfully at the empty cookie dish.

"I didn't hear you come in, Annabelle."

"I came in through the back door — before I realized you had company. When I heard Mr. Gregory mention Bangkok — and David Shipley's name — I stayed on and listened. I'm sorry."

"It's all right. You're always welcome."

Annabelle looked more miserable as she met Sauni's gaze. Pushing her books aside, she cleared a spot. "Sit down," she said softly. "I think we need to talk."

"About Luke?"

"No, about a safe deposit box in Schaffhausen."

Chapter 18

In London Uriah Kendall sat in a leather chair facing his old friends in British Intelligence. He rested his cane across his lap and took the steaming tea offered to him. Over the brim of the cup, he eyed Dudley Perkins, a grim man with listless eyes and pachydermal skin; he seemed framed by the faded wall map behind him.

"It was good of you to see me, Dudley," Uriah said.

"Always nice to have friends drop by."

Me — a friend? Perkins had never liked Olivia. His prying into her background had ruined Uriah's chances to move up in MI5.

Patiently Perkins said, "You mentioned British security when you called last night, so I invited these gentlemen to be on hand."

Uriah nodded. He took another lingering sip of tea and studied the other men in the room. Miles Grover, the friendly face in the crowd, had joined MI5 back in the Cold War days. Grover, it seemed, had been reduced to a scribe; a pen and open note tablet lay on his lap, his bony knees pressed together for a table. Grover's welcoming smile faded as he thumb-brushed his thick gray moustache. Lyle Spincrest, thirtyish, with analytical eyes behind those thick glasses, appeared overly confident. *Perkins's boy,* Uriah concluded, *being groomed for promotion.* Smugly, young Spincrest lifted the teapot and offered Uriah a refill. Thornton Alton sat farthest from the desk. Younger than Perkins, he was always subordinate — and dressed as usual in one of his wide pinstriped suits, as out of fashion as the room.

"Where did you go last night, Uriah? I tried to call you back."

"Out to dinner with my grandson," he lied. "Ian took me to one of those upbeat places not far from Hampton Court."

Perkins smiled thinly. "That can be checked, you know."

How well he knew. Uriah scanned the drabness of Perkins's office: a plain desk and hardback chairs, an umbrella and coat rack, three five-drawer file cabinets, and a massive metal safe in the corner. The colorless room offered no chance for Uriah to fix his sights on a flowered chair or an Impressionist painting.

He eyed the file cabinets again, wondering whether Perkins had kept a folder on Olivia and perhaps even one on himself. The red phone on the desk rang, the light blinking persistently.

Perkins jammed the receiver against his good ear. "He's on hand . . . Shortly, sir. We're having a spot of tea first." The disgruntled face twitched. "Of course, sir. I suppose it does. Yes, we'll get on with it." More frown ridges underscored his irritation. "You might say that, sir. The old school tie. We were in MI5 together — years ago."

He cradled the phone with care, but rage smoldered in his eyes. "I've been summoned to Downing Street, Kendall. So let's get on with this visit. You said it was important."

And you believed me, Uriah thought. *Or this elite gathering would not have been necessary. And the Prime Minister wouldn't have called.* Uriah lifted his thick gray brows, sickened by his own message. "There's a mole in the American CIA," he said calmly.

Perkins spun around in his swivel chair, his lanky hands braced on his knees. "Why are you coming to us, Uriah? Are you working for the Americans now? Spreading false information?"

Uriah avoided Perkins's prying gaze and fixed his eyes on the man's rough tweed jacket. His thoughts raced back to dining at Gregory's flat last night. Accusations had flown wildly; then two hours later Uriah told

315

Drew, "I have no choice but to see MI5. I can't risk the old rumors against Olivia surfacing if I don't cooperate with them. I owe that much to my family."

"Kendall, have you lost your hearing?" Perkins asked. "Or should I ask you again? Are you working for the Americans?"

Misery gripped Uriah. "They sent me to enlist your help — to warn you that their spy may be stationed here in London."

"Someone in high position?"

"He moves in embassy circles." Uriah hesitated, then begged, "I need your help, Perkins. The Americans suspect a friend of mine."

"And you want us to smoke out the real defector? Why?"

"I still believe in my friend."

Thornton Alton's cup rattled as he put it down. Miles Grover adjusted a button on his vest, his gray eyes crossing slightly as he looked at Uriah and asked, "Who is he?"

Again Uriah stalled. "Drew Gregory. Drew Wallace Gregory."

Lyle Spincrest whistled. "One of the attachés. I've played tennis doubles with him a time or two." He drew back, seemingly embarrassed at his own admission. "He's in our files as CRISSCROSS."

Perkins glowered at the younger man.

"Sorry, sir. You told me to keep contact at the embassy."

Perkins turned on Uriah. "Have the Americans picked him up?"

"They're still building their case against him."

"And we're to sit tight?" Grover asked. "Is it to our advantage to help the Americans?"

The chair squeaked as Perkins swiveled again. "Of course, it's to our advantage, Miles. Anything that gives us leverage with them is important. But there's more, isn't there, Uriah?"

"There's a woman —"

"There usually is."

Uriah ticked off the facts: Nell Ashcroft. British passport. Murdered in Washington. Strangled in the hotel room beneath Gregory's.

"All right. Go on. Age? Occupation? Acquainted with Gregory?"

"Sorry, Dudley. The statistics were withheld."

"Held in the CIA files, no doubt." He turned to Miles Grover. "Take that notebook of yours and dig up anything you can about Nell Ashcroft. Call Interpol if you have to. Spincrest, you check out that tennis-playing attaché. But leave your racket at home. We'll have trouble enough when the media tracks down your association with him. Go on — get on it right away."

Spincrest looked annoyed, but he was already at the door.

"That's a good lad, Lyle," Perkins told him. "And see what you can find out about Gregory's Russian contacts."

"He was never assigned to the Russian station," Uriah said.

Alton picked up his cup again, balancing it precisely between his thumb and two fingers. "He must have contacts there. Why waste time? If he's one of Langley's senior officers, then order an immediate expulsion and send him back to the States."

"We'll do no such thing," Perkins told him, "not without the Prime Minister's approval. I'll get that shortly. So we'll take it from here, Kendall. Good of you to come by."

Dismissed by MI5. In the same way that he had been turned away three weeks before he married Olivia Renway. His stomach churned as he remembered something else that Drew had urged him to say. "There may be a link with an unsolved act of treason back in the Vietnam era."

Perkins's head jerked like a whiplash. "The old Breckenridge case? That's been hush-hush the last two decades."

"It raised its ugly head lately." He used his cane to stand. "I'd best be pushing off. If you need me, I'll be at my grandson's."

"Like last night? The P. M. thinks you were with an American. Drew Gregory perhaps? You said you were old friends."

Uriah took Perkins's unfriendly handclasp. "Very old friends." He nodded toward the gray phone. "May I call my grandson?"

Perkins shoved the phone toward him, staring coldly as Uriah dialed the numbers and waited. Silence. Then Uriah smiled slowly. "Ian must be out."

He cradled the phone and offered an empty smile to the men left in the room. "Good luck," he said, and strangely enough he meant it.

As he left Perkins's office, he heard Thornton Alton ask, "Dudley, does Kendall really have a grandson in town?"

Uriah kept the door cracked and listened.

"Yes. Ian's a cyclist. Raced in the Tour de France last year. Kendall's quite proud of him. But I don't trust him. He's secretive like his grandmother Olivia."

"You never liked her, did you?" Grover asked.

"We'd had our fill of defectors and spies in the ranks — of men like Burgess and Maclean, Philby and Blunt." His voice rose

319

in disgust, clearly reaching Uriah's ear as he stood by the cracked door. "And too much publicity about colleagues like Peter Wright trying to blacken the reputation of Sir Roger Hollis."

"Wright wasn't the only man who doubted Hollis," Grover said. "And Hollis wasn't the only man whose career was ever in question."

"So you think I'm like Peter Wright?" Perkins asked. "You think I darkened Uriah's career? Well, you're right, Miles. I did. Kendall was blinded by that woman. That's why we couldn't keep him on in intelligence, not when he married her."

"I know. A political scandal had to be avoided."

"So why do you look so worried, Miles?" Perkins asked.

"Perhaps Kendall is getting even with us after all these years."

Outside the room, Uriah smiled. He shoved open the door and reached for his coat still hanging on the rack. "Gentlemen, sorry," he said. "The weather's a bit nippy for going without this."

He flashed a triumphant grin and left them again. He didn't bother to secure the latch, but tapped his cane lightly over the carpet as he limped away. *My dear Olivia, you would be pleased with me,* he thought. *You always defended our friend Drew Gregory.*

Drew Gregory avoided the glittering social life and tourist traps like the bubonic plague. Now, thanks to Victor Wilson, he'd spent two days wandering around the tiny principality of Monaco and still hadn't caught a glimpse of Wilson.

No need to check the calendar. He'd checked and rechecked already. This was the day, the casino the place. Three P.M. straight up they'd have their answer from the skipper of the *Monique II*. But how had Vic eluded him?

Drew kept to himself, not risking friendly chatter with the local people or tourists, but browsing alone through the narrow streets in the old quarter. He took his meals at tiny cafes that might have appealed to Wilson and spent hours at the Oceanographic Museum. This morning he had feasted on fresh fruit at the market and by noon had already checked the harbor twice for the *Monique II*.

What he found was the *Firestar*, a powerful motor yacht with a fresh coat of blinding white paint and a bulletproof, seaworthy hull — the yacht a sure contender for any international regatta. Bobbing beside it lay the *Thunderstorm* with its triple-spreader sail

321

ready to challenge the wind and the sea; yet the boat was dwarfed by the *Firestar*. Drew stopped to admire them both and was immediately challenged by crew members from the larger vessel. His curiosity whetted, he ambled along the dock chatting with people until he learned that the *Firestar* sailed under a foreign flagship. Though he found foreign yachts by the dozens, he hadn't spotted the one that belonged to Monique Dupree.

In his wanderings over the narrow streets, he found himself charmed by Monaco and the beauty of the Blue Coast. His thoughts turned without warning to Miriam. He felt like a giddy sixteen-year-old smitten with his first romance as he had once been with Carla Montroe back on the farm.

The allure of Monaco held him, but not the casino. Drew was not a drinking man, and, unlike his half-brother Aaron, he refused to waste a dime inside Monte Carlo — except for the nominal entry fee. He'd blown that twice already looking for Vic. Now, waiting outside on the promenade walkway, he stared up at the nineteenth-century casino — a white palace made more spectacular by its terraced gardens and swaying palms. The clock on the building reminded Drew of his 3:00 P.M. appointment with Vic.

He knotted his tie and entered the huge

atrium with its massive paintings hanging on the wall, passed the theater where the concerts were held, and made his way into one of the main gambling rooms. *Was it here,* he wondered, *where his brother Aaron had lost money again and again? Was it here that he had decided to turn to art forgery to pay those debts?* Discouraged by thoughts of his brother, he decided to have a cold glass of water and lemon.

As he sat there, seeing Aaron's gambling spirit in the faces around him, a young waiter arrived to take his order. "Your first visit, sir?" he asked.

"You might say that. I've been down by the harbor for hours."

The precise expression lit with excitement. "Did you see the *Firestar*? It belongs to that gentleman over there."

Drew's gaze followed the young man's cocked head to a table of four by the window. The ship's owner and a blond-haired Italian — his skin bronzed by the Mediterranean sun — were arguing heatedly, their lips barely moving. The blond became more adamant, the older man more defensive. Abruptly, the owner of the *Firestar* shoved back his chair and stomped from the casino, his turbaned assistants a polite few steps behind him. The Italian smiled cunningly, tossed money on the table, and went after them.

Drew had been so caught up with the strangers that he almost missed Vic sauntering out of one of the private card salons. Vic kept a rapid pace out of the building over the terraced walkways, fast on the heel of the Italian with the sun-kissed skin and brawny shoulders.

Drew cursed himself for not noticing the man's face as he passed by. Salvador? Yes, this had to be the captain of the *Monique*. The man put his white sailing cap on his head the moment he stepped from the casino and set out resolutely toward the harbor.

Drew frowned as he passed the *Firestar* and walked another three berths to the *Monique II*. Vic had been right — it was an elegant vessel, almost as impressive as the *Firestar*. How had he missed it? He'd walked this same dock only three hours ago.

Salvador, Argus-eyed and sullen, made no attempt to stop Drew as he followed Vic on board. Instead, the skipper led them to the lounge chairs on the upper deck that faced toward the *Firestar*. He proved witty and quick, his sharp gaze cagey, his speech centered on seagoing vessels. After two drinks, he paced along the rail, lifting his binoculars periodically. A chary smile crossed his lips as the *Firestar* crew hauled in the ropes.

Drew shaded his eyes, admiring the elegance of the vessel as the yacht backed from its berth and moved toward the open waters, its flag fluttering proudly now.

Finally, Salvador turned and came back to face them. "Gentlemen, do you still want to go with me?" he asked quietly.

Drew nodded. "That's why we're here, Captain."

Drew stretched out in the chair, legs extended, his face turned to the late afternoon sun. As the warm rays beat against Drew, Salvador signaled the crew. They snapped to attention and moments later, the powerful engine roared beneath him. Gregory's excitement mounted as the *Monique II* slid from its moorings. Waves slapped at the jutting sea rocks as they glided into the Mediterranean, the *Firestar* setting a foamy path for them.

Lulled by the rhythmic motion, Wilson dozed beside him. Salvador whistled in the wheelhouse above them. In this perfect setting Drew's thoughts turned again to Miriam, to Robyn, to the lost years without them.

Suddenly, a deafening explosion ripped through the waters. The ship's mast splintered and toppled into the sea. The yacht shattered and fragmented, a thousand pieces of blackened rubble spraying the cloudless sky and then spiraling to a watery grave.

Smoke. Fire. The smell of death.

Silence.

Chapter 19

Jacques Marseilles relived Drew Gregory's visit night after sleepless night. Return to the Pyrenees with Gregory? Never. He hit the delete key on his computer and wiped out the page he had just written. Gregory had ruined Jacques's career at the Amitie Cafe, his safe haven for decades.

Haven? Was that how he really viewed the family restaurant in Paris where he had risen from kitchen detail to maitre d' — where he had been respected by the elite diners of Paris, his past hidden? No, those last three years became a nightmare once Harland Smith learned of his past collaboration with the Germans.

Other Frenchmen had paid for their disloyalty in front of a firing squad. Jacques — barely eighteen back then, an old man in a boy's shell — had escaped because of his uncle's influence.

He had cried out, "Stephan, I stole food for the family until the Storm Troopers threatened me with death."

"Get out, Jacques. You've disgraced us all."

He had whined like a child then. "We were hungry, Stephan. Was that collaboration with the Nazi?"

"Betraying your neighbors in exchange for food was."

Jacques repressed the bitter truth that his family had died anyway. He didn't even have the words to bring up his fight against the Nazis — his two years with the Resistance fighters, pouring his life into hit-and-run raids and smuggling Allied fliers safely through the Pyrenees to freedom.

"I'll go away," he offered. "I'll become a journalist."

Stephan had roared with laughter. "No one wants to read the words you write. But I'll give you one more chance to prove yourself. Leave here and work for me at the Amitie. It'll be food in your belly and a roof over your head. It's more than you deserve."

Jacques ran his thick fingers over the computer keyboard, his jumbled thoughts trying to describe the old monastery in the foothills of the Pyrenees — the one that had been destroyed during the war. Gregory's visit had renewed Jacques's interest in the old brambled ruins where he had once hidden two British fliers in the tangled undergrowth.

The monastery had been rebuilt after the war, only to be wiped out by an avalanche ten years later.

Jacques saw himself like those brambled ruins — only partly standing, only partly remembered. No, it was not Gregory but Harland Smith who had destroyed his reputation by making the Amitie Cafe a point of contact for terrorists. But he could not blame Smith — nor even Gregory — for Annamarie leaving him. No, Uncle Stephan had arranged that, as he had arranged every moment of Jacques's confinement at the chateau.

The day after Drew's visit, he tried to call Annamarie in Paris. He yearned to be with her, to find comfort in her arms. But when a man answered the phone, Jacques slammed down the receiver.

Now for several days Gregory's request for help had haunted him. He stared at the monitor and began to form new paragraphs. The computer had become his comfort zone, an escape from isolation. His last hope for recognition lay in a series of articles on the old chateaus and monasteries in France — on the ruins coming to life. Weekly, he took the steep path down to the village to post an article. Three times in these last few months there had been a check, small recognition that at last the words of Jacques

Marseilles held meaning.

From his window, he could see the spires of the steepled church where he often visited with the priest. He left the computer on, not even realizing what he was doing, and went to his room.

Taking out the worn satchel, he filled it with a change of clothing, an extra sweater, toiletries, and Gregory's maps. On top he placed his revolver and the prayer book the priest had given him. He slipped into his overcoat, tucked a wool scarf around his neck, and then trudged outside to the courtyard. He tipped his hat politely to his uncle's friends.

"Ah," Stephan said, "my nephew has readied more of his infamous articles for mailing."

The mocking laughter sent Jacques hurrying down the winding path toward the village. Pebbles caught beneath his slick shoes; he fought to keep from stumbling, his decision final. Jacques had failed his country twice. Perhaps this was his hour, his chance to find the mercenary camp and rid France of more terrorists. Driven by the need for acceptance, he set his sights on the ruined monastery where he had once hidden two frightened airmen. And after that — once he had data for his article — then he would follow Drew Gregory's route to honor.

The priest in a long robe walked prayerfully in the church yard. "Good morning, Father Frederick," Jacques called.

"My son," the priest called back. "Come in. Let's visit."

Jacques hesitated. He longed for the old priest's handclasp, his words of encouragement. But Jacques knew his own weakness. He must not allow the priest — or anyone — to persuade him to change his course. "Later, my friend. Not now," he said.

"Then visit me on your way back."

Disappointment filled the priest's voice. He was alone in his parish, just as Jacques was alone and cut off in the family chateau. Jacques hurried off before he changed his mind. It would be an hour before Father Frederick knew he was not coming back and two hours before Stephan realized that his nephew had gone away.

In Washington Harv Neilson sat gloomily in the back seat of the heavily armed limousine, an Agency driver at the wheel. On his lap lay a briefcase with some of Washington's top secrets locked inside. Chad Kaminsky squirmed beside him, his fat hands hanging limply between his knees.

Neilson turned and glared out the tinted

window. Taking Chad to the Oval Office for the daily briefing with the president had been an unfortunate error. Behind his warm smile, the president had been surly. He declared himself weary of opposition from Congress, of pressure from the U. N. about the maneuvers of men and planes, and of complaints by other countries that American aid was never enough.

As the president mentioned Senator Summers's latest grievance, Neilson laid another report on the desk. "The British media won't let go of this one either," he said.

The president stared down at the report and laughed good-naturedly. "So we're testing another new Stealth aircraft?" He pushed the article aside. "Neilson, the American media concerns me more. A newspaper is prepared to run an article tomorrow exposing the existence of a double agent in the CIA. Under Tracy Mathison's byline."

"We need more time, Mr. President."

"So a spy can bolt? Mathison has pinned it down to the European Division. He'll break the story if we don't."

"We're tightening the net. We have it down to four men."

"So does the newspaper."

The president stood, looking tall and handsome as he ran a hand through his thick, well-groomed hair. Neilson understood the pressure on the president. On himself. The usual handclasp was forgotten.

"Neilson," the president said quietly, "the reporter agreed to wait a few days in exchange for the full story when it blows. Can you promise him that? If you can't settle this before then, I'll find someone who can."

Rage ripped through Neilson, his jaw clamping tighter than the president's. *Replace me?* Humiliation right here in the Oval Office in front of Kaminsky. This was Kaminsky's department, *his* man who needed to be picked up. He shot a glance at Chad. Surprise, expectation, a chance for promotion showed in his face. *If the president replaces me,* Neilson thought bitterly, *you'll go with me.*

Now, still rankled, he blocked out the noise on the George Washington Memorial Parkway and reached for one of the car phones. Without a word to Kaminsky, he dialed the newspaper office and demanded to speak to the publisher, one of the regulars at the Arlington health and fitness spa.

"Harv Neilson here. I need to talk to you . . . Today . . . What about lunch in the director's dining room? Say twelve-thirty?"

The publisher's gravelly laugh boomed over the line. Harv could picture him leaning back in the leather chair, winking at his investigative reporter. "I'll bring Tracy Mathison with me," he said. "You'll no doubt want to talk to him, too."

Neilson's free hand went protectively to the briefcase. "Good," he said. "I'll expect you both around noon."

"What are we going to tell Porter Deven?" Chad asked.

"It's too late to tell him anything. Gregory and Wilson left Paris for that merc camp a couple of days ago."

"You authorized the mission?"

"Unofficially."

"You'll hang when the president hears that."

"Not if we produce the double agent. You know it's been narrowed down to four men. Don't worry, Chad. We have someone on their every move."

Chad chewed on an unlit cigar with its band still on it. "Then how come we don't know where Gregory and Wilson are right now? Is that a Porter Deven blunder?"

Neilson grabbed the cigar and tossed it out the window.

"Hey, that was a good stogie."

"I don't like the smell of it, lit or unlit."

As their driver pulled into the underground garage at Langley, Neilson said, "Kaminsky, I had a fax from Gregory after he reached Paris. He really wants that transfer to Langley."

"Drew must be crazy. Doesn't he even suspect that we're on to him? The deeper he goes in —"

"I thought he was your friend, Chad. What happened?"

"So is Porter. Neither one of us can face the possibility that Drew would sell out his country."

At his private elevator, Neilson pushed the black button. "Now you know how Admiral Breckenridge felt when we told him his son was a traitor."

"What brought that up?"

"Not what — who. The president did. Weren't you listening? Seems that Glenn Summers tried to block the admiral's reservation to Zurich."

"That's not the senator's business."

"Summers doesn't want Luke's parents anywhere near his daughter. And that's exactly where they're heading, at Mrs. Breckenridge's invitation." Neilson set his briefcase down as they stepped inside the elevator and rode in silence to his carpeted office on the seventh floor.

Sauni Breckenridge and Annabelle Vandiver sat in the corner of the Schaffhausen

335

tearoom — their favorite place for a Sunday afternoon.

"You seem more peaceful these days," Annabelle said.

Sauni smiled. "Luke's mother used to tell me, 'Saundra, you can't fall too far, not when the eternal God is your refuge and underneath are those everlasting arms.' Mother Breckenridge was right, Annabelle. She was convinced that nothing could shatter our faith."

"Not even Luke's death?"

"You come to accept death after a while. It's rather like coming out of a dark and painful tunnel into the brilliant sunshine." She fought the lump in her throat, her fingers lacing around the locket Luke had given her so long ago; now his wide wedding band hung on the chain with it.

Moments later she took a large manila envelope from her handbag and sorted through the photographs once again. Her eyes settled on the picture of Luke in the baggy pants and shirt of a Hmong, his arm draped around the shoulders of a much smaller man. Luke looked ill, at least twenty pounds lighter than she remembered. Empty eyes stared at her from the black-and-white photo, yet he looked handsome even in illness.

She placed it beside her saucer and went

through the other pictures. "Xangtiene is a beautiful place," she said. "Luke loved the mountains. I'm glad he lived and died there instead of in some muddy, forgotten valley."

Saundra stacked the pictures together and placed Luke's photo on top before slipping them back into the envelope. She avoided Annabelle's eyes as she slid the packet across the table. "I won't need these any longer."

"You don't want the one of your husband?"

"That isn't the Luke I remember. I don't want his parents to see it. Prisoners —" She fought for control. "Prisoners don't put their arms around their captors."

Annabelle stirred her coffee, poured in some sugar, and stirred again. "David's photographs don't prove anything — only that Luke was in Xangtiene — *not why.*"

"Whatever happened, the Luke I knew would never betray his country. But he was anxious to go back to Southeast Asia the last time I saw him. He seemed more at home there, more at peace with himself in that part of the world. Perhaps he really did choose to stay there. I've come to terms with that these last few days."

"And not return to his wife?"

"We were divorced by then."

"Sauni, what will you tell his parents?"

"Must I tell them something, Annabelle? I just wanted them to come over and spend some time with me. It's been five years since our last visit. I'm all the family they have left."

Annabelle hesitated. "You're certain about the photos?"

"Yes. Put them back in the lockbox — before your nephew finds out you showed them to me. Now I really must go. I'll be late as it is."

"Let me drive to the airport with you."

"No, it's better if I meet them alone."

Sunday traffic on the road to Zurich forced her to drive at a slow-and-go thirty. She would never get to the airport in time. Tourists in rentals, families on their way home from weekend outings, and Saundra — all heading in the same direction. The young man in the car ahead shrugged and made comical grimaces at her through his rearview mirror. She stopped tapping her long nails on the steering wheel and started humming.

She hoped that the flight from New York City would arrive late. After parking the car, she did a zigzag sprint through the crowds toward the arrival gate, but the plane had touched down three minutes early, putting her eighteen minutes behind schedule. She found Amy Breckenridge sitting alone in the empty waiting area clutching her purse.

"Mother Breckenridge, I'm here."

Amy rose slowly, one hand on the arm of the chair, the other brushing the pleated skirt of her rich brown suit. Her gray hair curled softly around her face. Luke's generous warm smile came alive as they tumbled into each other's arms. "Where's Dad?" Sauni asked. "He came, didn't he?"

The smile widened. "Of course. You know the admiral. Impatient as always. He's off to the turn-around to rescue our suitcases. We're to meet him at the baggage department."

Sauni took Amy's thin, age-flecked hands in her own. Five years had made a difference. Her throat tightened at the thought of Luke's mother growing old. The peppery spirit seemed fringed with age, the blue eyes lighter in color. Saundra kissed the wrinkled cheek and heard Amy's soft voice saying, "It's about Luke, isn't it? This sudden invitation to be with you."

"Sudden? For the last five years I've asked you to come."

"And you insisted on it this time."

She thought about the photographs of Luke in Xangtiene. "I have come to accept the truth about Luke."

"Not his guilt?" Amy's chin quivered, her eyes brimming with tears.

"Mother Breckenridge, it's time we let all the rumors go. The Luke we knew and loved was a wonderful man. That's all we need to know."

"You did love him, didn't you, dear?"

"I still do."

Amy nodded. "Sauni, when you see Luther, don't mention your father either. The senator's rejection has been so painful for us. He even tried to stop our coming here."

"Someday Dad will understand. He'll come around." *Once the votes are in again,* she thought.

Luke's mother sighed as they headed for the main terminal. "Promise me, no talk about unpleasantries around the admiral."

"I promise." She tucked Amy's arm in hers and set her pace to her mother-in-law's, strolling with unhurried steps down the crowded corridor. "Unless the admiral has questions, we'll just talk about the Luke we knew. Now, how long can you stay?"

Timidly, Amy suggested, "A week?"

"Absolutely not long enough."

"Luther said we'll spend the first week with you and then — well, at our age it's doubtful we'll ever be back, so he insists that we really see Europe. He has it all mapped out right down to the last hour for at least sixteen days." She sighed happily. "Luther acts like he's back on the ship and in command. Then we'll come back and stay the final week with you in Busingen if that's all right."

"Sounds great."

Saundra spotted the admiral standing by the luggage, his eye on his watch. He had maintained that straight, proud stance. His silver hair was still surprisingly thick.

"Dad," she called. "Dad Breckenridge, welcome to Switzerland."

A wide grin cut across his stern expression. Forgetting the three suitcases lined up side by side, he struck out on his lanky legs toward her. Those bright dark eyes so much like Luke's brimmed with tears as he reached her.

"Young lady," he said, "you are late."

"Predictable, just like always, Admiral," she teased back.

He crushed her against his broad chest. "Sauni, Sauni, Mother and I have missed you."

Chapter 20

The blast from the explosion still rang in Drew's ears. He shaded his eyes searching for survivors. But nothing of the magnificent *Firestar* remained. Only splinters of the hull and fragments of the flag floated in the water. One lone piece of mahogany wood still burned, waves washing over it. Before the *Monique II* could reach it, the flame sizzled and died out.

Drew glanced toward the wheelhouse. "What happened, Skipper?"

Salvador let his binoculars fall against his chest. "They lost a bet," he said fiercely.

The siren of the fire cutter echoed in the distance as she pulled anchor and set out on a futile search and rescue. Nearby, a young man stood on the deck of the *Thunderstorm*, his back to the windblown sail, his face dark in the fading sun. The *Monique* circled the area once more, creating a tiny whirlpool where the *Firestar* had gone down.

As the fire cutter pulled alongside them, the sea gleamed a silvery blue in the waning light. Salvador waved. "We didn't find any survivors," he called. "Must have been the engine . . . she was riding smoothly, and then she blew. Blew into nothingness."

As the *Monique II* reset her course, Drew saw Wilson standing behind the deck chair, a life preserver still in his hands. "Hang it back up," Drew said. "We don't need it."

A crew member came on the run. "Señors, you are to go below at once. Captain's orders."

The sailor ushered them into the spacious lounge and locked the door behind them. Vic stormed to the portholes; they were bolted securely. He turned on Drew. "What's going on?"

"Salvador told the skipper on the fire cutter that the *Monique II* is traveling with crew only."

"What now?" Vic asked.

"We'll know as soon as we reach the merc camp."

"If we reach it." Then Vic shrugged, regaining his cockiness. "Right now my bet is on Salvador, not some unknown American running the camp. Salvador is Italian. Comes from one of the powerful families near Milan. He's not the type to be subordinate to a foreigner, especially an American."

"He didn't get on with the owner of the *Firestar* either."

"I know, Drew. But I didn't expect what happened just now. I don't know how, but I think he just blew up the *Firestar*."

"I think you're right. Something must be terribly wrong in the cabal. And we're walking right into it."

"A power play," Vic suggested. "I heard them talking near the roulette wheel. They seemed determined to break off any association with Salvador. They threatened to cut off all funding if the camp moved into France."

Drew whistled. "So that's what they were arguing about."

As their ship moved smoothly in the water, a rhythmic hum to its powerful engine, Drew stretched out on the bunk, his hands behind his head. He forced himself to concentrate on the gentle swells beneath them. Even with the portholes locked, the smell of the sea reached him; the sway of the vessel lured him.

"Vic, why would a merc camp run an extravagant vessel like this? Better to keep a low profile and avoid attention."

"Why not? It makes a nice cover. Gives acceptance into places like Monaco. No one will link the explosion to this yacht or connect her to a merc camp in the Pyrenees." He sat down at the spinet, slowly running his fingers over the keys.

"Do we dock in Barcelona?" Drew asked.

"The town's heavily populated — a hundred miles from the French frontier. We'll go in along the Brava Coast, away from prying eyes."

"Where were you, Vic? I spent two days looking for you."

"Meeting with Salvador. I took a couple of runs with him. It's bigger than we thought, Drew. I cracked a supply crate. Rifles. Ammo. The kind you'd use on hit-and-run missions."

"You take too many risks."

"I don't have long to prove myself."

Drew cocked his head.

"Brianna made me another medical appointment in Paris."

"You sick?"

"She thinks so. It's this virus thing."

Drew frowned, but Vic had looked away, his attention drawn to the creaking sounds of the ship plowing through the water.

"On those trips with Salvador, we had live cargo — locked in the lounge like we are. I offered to take coffee to them."

Drew knew he should press for answers on health, but he pushed his concern to the back burner. "What did you find out from those men?"

"Three of them hired on because of an ad in a London paper. 'Wanted: healthy men for short-term travel. Family allowance. Military experience preferred. Benefits.' "

"Mostly death benefits."

Vic ignored him. "They were all tough, seasoned soldiers. Military background mostly. One of them said he'd been signed on for six weeks. Another for two months."

"Wow, specific targets and barely enough time to train them."

"Yeah. The youngest kid was nineteen. And scared. Said Salvador had forced him to sign a will before boarding. He asked me how I had been recruited. Told him I volunteered." Vic ran his fingers over the bass keys again. "When I got back on deck, Salvador quizzed me. Wanted to know why it took me so long. So I gave it to him word perfect — figured he had the lounge bugged anyway."

"So we're filling his ears right now."

"Nope." Vic grinned and pointed to the bug in his hand. "Once we hit the castle we may not get too many opportunities to talk. I just hope we go ashore together. The question is whether the raft takes us in on the Spanish side or lands us in France south of Narbonne or Perpignan. Once we're near port, it's over the side for both of us."

"We're to swim in and climb some sheer cliff?"

"We enter in total darkness in a four-man rubber raft. No passports needed that way. After that, you'll be calling the shots."

Drew actually laughed, but his smile faded as he realized that the engine had stilled. "We've anchored."

"We haven't docked. We're swaying too much for that."

An hour later Salvador ordered them to dress in skin-tight wet suits, stow their own gear in water-sealed duffels, and grease their faces and hands before going ashore. Wilson adjusted a web belt securely around his narrow waist, gave a cocky salute to the skipper, and dropped agilely into the raft bobbing in the current. Two muscular crew members held the raft in position, waiting impatiently for Drew to join them. He tossed the duffels to Vic one at a time and then swung over the rail and secured his footing on the rope ladder.

"Good luck, Gregory," Salvador said, his sneer disconcerting. He took two crumpled cables and shoved them into Drew's hand. "You had messages at the Monte Carlo. I had them picked up for you."

"Why, you —"

"You work for me now. I intercept all

correspondence. There was nothing for Wilson."

Drew felt his Beretta against his back, bulging securely beneath the wet suit. Clenching the letters in his teeth, he pushed off, rappelling down the rope. As the yacht pulled anchor and sailed into the darkness, waves swirled around the raft. Drew crouched low and turned on his penlight.

"Douse that light, you fool," Enrico cried.

Drew had already read his mail. Robyn's note ended with: "Mother is trying to reach you. Vietnamese client from Tran Industries insists on finding you. Advise."

Duc Thuy Tran. If Duc was being pursued, as he claimed, then Miriam was in danger. The second note sounded just as alarming: "Found monastery ruins in foothills. Archaeological dig in progress. High caliber weapons and missiles for equipment. J —"

The skipper of the *Monique* had read both messages. *Jacques,* Drew thought, *you've mucked up again.*

As they neared shore, Enrico announced, "You go in from here alone. Half mile or so, you'll see the Pyrenees road sign. Wait there for our minibus."

They swung from the raft, caught their balance in waist-deep water, and waded ashore, duffels of dry clothes held high above their heads. Moving cautiously over the sharp rocks, they reached the slippery cliffs without mishap. Vic scaled the smallest one and then extended his hand to Drew. "We should duck out while we can. I don't like the way things are going."

"Neither did Porter. That's why he sent us."

Small roads and a railroad track followed narrow gaps between the mountains and the sea. As the minibus left the scenic cliffs and inlets of the coast and bumped along the rough country roads, the shadowed ridges rose into a rugged mountain range. In the distance Drew saw the outline of the central Pyrenees where the peaks seemed permanently snow-covered. The crest of the range formed the dividing line between two countries. He guessed that they had covered less than half of the 270 miles between the Mediterranean and the Bay of Biscay.

To stay awake, Drew counted the villages and Romanesque churches scattered along the thinly populated foothills. White-washed houses glowed in the dark. The pungent odor of vineyards here and there tickled his nostrils. After running out of villages and olive trees, they still had thirty miles of bleak countryside and cramped muscles before they reached their destination.

Harland Smith's Moorish castle sat on a rocky escarpment overlooking the wooded hills and lower slopes of the Pyrenees. In the night shadows, it looked imposing with its massive gatehouse and square towers. Except for the wild cries of animals and a mountain stream rushing by, the place was cloaked in silence. A caretaker led them to the open courtyard, handed them bedrolls, and left them as quietly as he had come. The mountain air cut through Drew, but exhaustion lulled him to sleep.

When he awakened, Vic was coughing, looking peaked and unrested. Drew kicked their bedrolls against the stone wall and glanced around. Even at dawn the massive structure appeared formidable with a solid circular keep and tall conical turrets, a well-fortified manor that could still withstand any attack.

He realized that he had awakened to gunfire — shots coming up from the valley in fast bursts that sounded like small automatic weapons. The target range had to be nearby. Beyond the walled courtyard camouflage netting concealed the minibus, a Hum-Vee, and a dark pickup truck with a flat tire. A lone guard with a rifle and a snarling police dog kept watch by the vehicles. But there was no plane for a fast departure. Drew caught a branch of one of the towering trees and swung high enough to look down toward the valley.

A rifle range lay flush against the hills. Black and white targets stood at what he guessed to be 200, 300, and 500 yards from a row of men in military fatigues. Taking a rough count, twenty or twenty-five men at most, he let his gaze rise to the snow-covered peaks, the endless barrage of gunfire still rumbling in the valley.

Vic was beside him now, swinging like a monkey. "They keep that up," he said, "and it might cause an avalanche."

"No worse than the snow cannons they use to break one up. Besides, the targets are pretty much in the open. I think it's part of the image of an exclusive hunting club."

Vic dropped to the ground and led the way into the castle. Inside, a pretty young woman cut across their path, a tray of dirty dishes in her hands. Vic gave her a smile, and she answered with arched brows. Her jet-black hair was pulled back from a slender neck, her soft Spanish complexion darkened by the sun.

Behind her a burly man appeared in the open arch, his skin and features dark, his boots mud-caked. The combat jacket failed to hide the weapons on his belt — a pistol and two sharp knives. "You're late," he said. "We get up at 4:00, not at sunrise. Breakfast is at 4:30. Nothing until noon after that."

He turned, and they followed him through the great hall with its high vaulted ceiling and deeply recessed windows. Hunting trophies decorated the walls. In the main living quarters, a Van Dyck painting hung over the stone fireplace, and a seventeenth-century tapestry covered one wall. Renaissance furniture filled the room. Close to the fireplace sat a soft leather chair that might well belong to the brigadier. But the man ahead of them was definitely not an American. He didn't look like a person to cross or question, but Drew risked it. "Are you the brigadier?"

"I'm Rabcal. The men call me Tiger." He led them into an empty dorm lined with pillowless army cots; wool blankets lay folded at the foot of each one. "You'll take the end two beds," Rabcal said. "You may have to fight it out with Carlos later. But you'll spend most of your nights in the woods on maneuvers." Apparently amused, he gave them a beastly smile. "You bathe daily in the river. Just one hot shower a week up here."

For the next three weeks they spent sixteen-hour days with a motley crew of misfits and renegades, swindlers and romantics, mostly ex-military men unaccustomed to living at peace. Vic took the youngest man under his wing, the nineteen-year-old who had feared writing his will. Trevor had cropped red hair, a baby face, and a rap sheet in Scotland for stealing. Candy, mostly. The rest of the men were tough and experienced — some Brits and Germans, a cheerful Irish boozer, a Turk with two months free time, a Hungarian who had led a previous mercenary coup, and Pepe, an Italian who didn't care what color the flag was as long as he could carry a gun.

In spite of their differences, Drew found himself bonding with these men, caring about them as they marched together, crawled through the woods on night patrols, and stripped and cleaned their weapons in the dark. Drew had always been an expert marksman, good with AK-47s and any combat weapons that Rabcal threw at him. But he faced stiff competition. These men had chosen to make their living as soldiers of fortune. Most of them would never see a dime for their effort, but would die fighting in somebody else's war.

Within days the riffraff became a working unit, twenty-two look-alikes in reversible camouflage fatigues and combat boots, each man bent on his own survival. But their headgear varied: an old army helmet, a Munich beret, a bush hat, and a boonie and balaclava reminiscent of the Vietnam War.

Their trainers, particularly Rabcal the Moroccan Tiger, were devoid of kindness. Rabcal demanded rigid discipline and silence at mealtime. Drew lost track of the schedule. They spent hours in self-defense and infantry maneuvers and even more time in the film room studying maps, tactics, and coded communications twice daily. They practiced climbing and rappelling down ropes with bare hands.

Twice Rabcal sent the men out in the darkness to detonate mines. He wanted quick-strike forces — execution squads that were experts with small arms and grenade launchers, men skilled at spanning rope bridges and handling explosives, alert minds that could deal with thermal imaging and scouting in unknown territories. They'd fall exhausted on their cots; two hours later Tiger doused them with ice water and sent them on night patrol, actual hit-and-run missions as far away as the Basque region in the western Pyrenees.

But Drew and Vic saw no one who fit the description of the American brigadier. Finally, on their twenty-first day at camp, a new man walked the firing line checking each target. That evening, in spite of being wasted with sleepless nights, Drew rolled off his cot and made his way outside into the courtyard. At the far end the stranger leaned against the wall staring up at the Pyrenees. He stood motionless in the moonlight, his strong profile chiseled in bitterness — a lonely, solitary figure with a .45 automatic strapped on his right hip.

Drew approached with caution, calling out so the man would not turn on him. "Sir, good evening."

The stranger turned — a very tall, well-built man with fine features hidden in part by sideburns and a one-inch stubble of beard. Strands of his hair strayed in every direction as though he had forgotten to run a comb through it. He wore black "Bata" boots and a dark field jacket over his *cammies* with a single silver star on his lapel and his large wristwatch fastened through a buttonhole.

"Having difficulty sleeping?" His voice was stony.

"Sooner or later Rabcal will have us up again anyway."

"Not this evening. I've told him to ease up."

"And will he, Brigadier?"

"For now." His eyes, even in the moonlight, were empty, expressionless like the hazy, sightless eyes of a blind man.

"I saw you checking the targets earlier this evening, sir."

"You're an excellent shot. A good marksman like the shepherd boy who took out the giant with a slingshot and a stone. I can respect a man like that . . . I have giants of my own."

He turned and faced the peaks again. "The shepherd boy said that the mountain peaks belong to God. Provocative thought. But then the Pyrenees are majestic, aren't they?"

"They're that, all right," Drew said. "Rabcal takes great pleasure in making us climb them at all hours."

"Does the young man climb them any better than he shoots?"

"You should send Trevor home before he ends up dead. He's a good kid, but he'll ruin any mission."

"They're all good men," the brigadier said sadly. "Tomorrow. Next week. Next month many of them will be dead in some country or village whose name they can't even pronounce." He thrust his broad hand against his forehead and massaged his temples. "Places that are so small they aren't even marked on the map."

"It sounds like you've been to some of them."

"I have. Too often. I seem to gather the malcontents of the world around me." He ran his finger down the jagged scar on his neck. "I'm like the psalmist that way. I gather in those who are in debt and distressed over life. But I have no brothers to come and do battle with me. David the psalmist did, you know."

The brigadier stared out into the shadowed darkness again, ignoring Drew as he mentally named the stars and thought back to the brilliance of the Laotian sky. The stars had been his companions in his bamboo cage in those long years of captivity. He couldn't walk or exercise in the cage, but he could turn his head to the Winged Horse and the Big Dipper and set his sights on the North Star no matter where his captors moved the camp.

"Wise men watch the stars," his mother had always said.

He tried to see God in the distant stars, tried to find hope and do mental gymnastics when his cramped body could barely move. Day after day. Month after month. Waiting as the years rolled by for his country to come and rescue him.

Only the woman came to taunt him. He called her the Dragon Fly when she handed him a cup of watered-down soup and forced him to swallow. He spewed it out into the round face of the prison guard.

"Captain Breckenridge, that was a very foolish thing to do," the Dragon Fly said as they dragged him from the cage. "All right, Ivan. Teach the captain some manners."

A leather belt came down across his shoulder and neck, shredding the baggy Hmong shirt that hung on his back and tearing into his flesh.

"Air America," Ivan said. "Tell us about Air America."

Luke only remembered the plane that had carried him over the mountains toward the village of Xangtiene.

"Tell us about the troop movements . . . the battleships anchored off the coast . . . what about the red herring — the withdrawal from Saigon. Your country is running, Captain."

"They left you behind, Captain Breckenridge," the Dragon Fly said as she forced him to look at the pictures of the Hanoi prisoners of war marching toward the planes that would take them home.

She slapped a photo on the table in front of him — Sauni standing with someone else.

"Your wife is married again," she said softly. "The day after her divorce became final."

He tried to lunge at the Dragon Fly — to hurt her as she was hurting him. Another photo landed on top of Sauni's. His parents. "They know about your treason, Captain. You've disgraced them."

Her grapevine had been international. He vomited then across the crude table, a projectile emptying of his gut. When he fainted, she kicked him and splashed his face with stagnant river water.

When he awakened at last, he was back in the bamboo cage with no space to move or turn, lying in his own excrement. The torn picture of Sauni lay on the floor of the cage beside him.

All around the castle the night images still rose in craggy mountain peaks. Trees clung to the cliff like an uneven column of marching men, as distant as the images in Laos. Distant and unfriendly. He had fought a psychological warfare and come out scarred and bitter.

Now the man beside him was playing this same game with him.

"Why don't you quit, Brigadier — get out now?" Drew asked.

"I have nowhere to go. I'm a military advisor. I just do my job." His eyes remained empty, bereft of feeling. "This is a well-guarded fortress. And when we move our camp to the other side of the Pyrenees — and we will — there's no way out there either."

To the brambled, tangled ruins Jacques had found? Drew wondered. *Was Jacques dead or alive at the archaeological dig?*

Harsh regret filled the brigadier's voice as he said, "Sometimes we have to live with the choices we make. Once you work for men like Tiger and Salvador, you don't leave. Not Trevor. Not you. Not me. I could fly out of here, but where would I go? Tiger and Salvador have contacts worldwide, a network of men who could track me down sooner or later."

He folded his arms deep in thought. "I've climbed mountains all my life," he said. "If I left, I'd go over that mountain range and maybe find a little village and lose myself there. It might work."

"I'll get you out," Drew offered.

"You and your friend Victor?" The cold, calculating eyes blazed in the moonlight. "Do you think we stand here unnoticed? No. Tiger knows our every move. I could walk in there now and say, 'I'm through, Rabcal. I'm leaving.' They'd let me take out the

Monique II, and they'd blow it up."

"Like they blew up the *Firestar?*"

"Yes, if they thought the operation was compromised. They'd shut down here and begin again elsewhere without me, Mr. Gregory."

"I thought we were on a first-name basis here."

"With my men? Yes. But you are an intruder, Mr. Gregory. I know who you are. One of the Langley boys. But I'm not certain why you're here."

"I've been looking for you, Brigadier."

"How did you think you could get away with it, Gregory? Do you and Mr. Wilson plan to take me out alive?"

"Actually we were sent here to kill you."

Chapter 21

The brigadier stood alone long after Drew walked away, his thoughts turning back to the country he had once served, the life he once lived, the girl he had married. He tried to imagine how she might look now, but he could only remember her lovely china-doll face with flaxen hair falling softly around her shoulders, her well-shaped lips, and those dazzling blue-green eyes dancing, teasing, pleading.

She had been wearing red the day he met her — wearing red the day he took her home to meet his family. They had stood on opposite sides of his shiny new Thunderbird, the car doors open, peering at each other across the rooftop. He was so proud — so in love with her. For a moment he was afraid the memory would fade. No, he clearly visualized her refusing to get in the car — plucking at a dangling red earring, a bulky red sweater hiding her slender arms, her golden hair pulled back into a ponytail. Those gorgeous eyes were apprehensive. "Will your parents like me?"

"Mom will. You'll have to work a bit harder to win Dad's favor." If the car hadn't been between them, he would have swept her into his arms and whisked her off to Elkton to elope. He had loved her so very much.

Thoughts of the old home on Asbury Avenue came crashing in — the house where his mother had been born. That wonderful, warm-hearted person who had shaped his early life. Or did she lie beside his brother now at the Seaside Cemetery? Flashes of those yesteryears twinkled brilliantly like the stars — running over the Jersey shore with his brother, splashing in the cold waves of the Atlantic. Hot dogs on the boardwalk with the surf pounding beneath it. Saltwater taffy at Shriver's — the memory so real his mouth salivated. The Sunday school where he had first heard about David and the slingshot. And that poignant trip with his dad to the lighthouse in Cape May a month after Landon died.

The stillness of the night air wrapped itself around him. Nothing of the young man he had once been remained. His features had turned harsh, his facial muscles rigid, his life hopeless. When he looked in the mirror, he saw what he had become: grim, rancorous, desolate, dead inside — robbed of life by the very government he had served. How many years he had hung on, waiting for his country to find him. Now two strangers had come to this merc camp, not to welcome him back to America, but to kill him.

America! Ten years ago he had tried to find his way home. When he had called his mother from a public phone near her house, she gasped at the sound of his voice, her words fading away. The line went dead. He stood at the corner near the fire station and watched the ambulance race away with his mother, sirens wailing.

At the hospital he snatched a pair of surgical greens from the linen cart and walked brashly into the cardiac care unit. He found his way to the C-3 cubicle and stared down at his mom's ashen face, tubes attached to her body, the oxygen prongs jammed in her nostrils. He took her limp hand in his and squeezed. From out of that groggy, medicated sleep, she fought to open her eyes. Those eyes dulled by medicine and illness met his. "Luke, Luke."

The cardiac monitor went wild. A nurse approached running. He grabbed the laundry hamper and began moving away.

"You're new around here, aren't you?" she asked as she checked the EKG leads.

"Yeah." He waited and left the cubicle with the nurse. "The lady there —" He could hardly get the words out. "Will she make it?"

"Mrs. Breckenridge? I think so. She's a fighter, that one. She keeps calling for her sons, but they're both dead now."

"Dead?" he asked.

"The younger one disgraced the family — accused of treason back in the Vietnam era." She made it sound eons ago. "It's no wonder the woman collapsed. Some prankster called and pretended to be her son. Doctor says another shock like that will kill her."

"She looks terrible."

"They've sent for her husband."

He turned for one more glimpse of his mother, not daring to go back and kiss her goodbye — not with the nurse watching him. *Oh, Mom, I want to come home, but another shock would kill you.* He stumbled blindly from the unit in the borrowed surgical greens and hitchhiked to the Seaside Cemetery, stopping on the way to buy a kite for Landon.

He sat by Landon's grave site for an hour and finally cried when the kite caught on the tree limb. At dusk he stole back to the house on Asbury Avenue, took the key from under the flower pot and went upstairs to his old room and slept until morning.

The next day in a desperate attempt to find

answers, he finally reached Allen Fraylund in Washington. "Hey, old buddy, it's Luke. It took me a dozen calls to track you down."

"Breckenridge? Where are you?"

Not, *You're alive?* Not, *It can't be!* But, *Where are you?*

"Just outside Washington. I need to see you."

A pause, a long, deliberate one. "That's impossible, Luke."

Just like that. Stranded by his best friend. "What's wrong, Allen? It's really me. I'm not dead. My country left me behind as a dead man. But I'm here. I'm alive. I've got to see you."

"I can't meet you, Luke. I've got my own future to think about. I've got a family now."

"I thought we were old friends."

"We were."

"Past tense?"

"Yes. I didn't think you'd end up in so much trouble."

"Meaning treason?"

Another "Yes." Strangled this time.

"Help me prove my innocence, Allen. I've nowhere else to turn. I can't even go back home until this mess is cleared." He swallowed what little pride he had left. "I'm broke, Allen. Let me come out to your place and talk with you."

"I'll meet you somewhere. I'll bring you some money."

What I want is a friend, he thought. "So you think I'm guilty, don't you?"

"I've never thought that. But there's no way we can prove it. Believe me, I've tried. I can't get involved anymore. Look, I'll have my wife leave an envelope at the T.W.A. desk at Washington National."

"That's it? You won't be there to talk with me?"

"Luke, I don't dare. Rumors are circulating in Washington that you escaped. If they find you, you'll hang."

"The CIA?"

"Don't ask. Just catch a flight to Europe and disappear."

"Thanks, old buddy," Luke said bitterly. "I owe you one."

The brigadier gave allegiance to no flag now, yet he cared about these men at the castle as he had once cared about the soldiers who had served under him in Vietnam and Laos, in Africa and Bosnia. Death and dying stalked him in the faces of his men. Emptiness and darkness. He cocked his ear to the sound of Rabcal's footsteps behind him and turned.

Rabcal was a big man, strong and violent,

tigerlike in his actions. "I have divided the men," Rabcal said quietly. "Only half of them are going on to the new camp."

"And the rest?"

"Salvador arranged for two strike teams for the Caribbean. I'm sending Pepe with them. If anyone can come out alive, he will."

"And the young man Trevor?"

"I'd like to send him and be rid of him. But I won't."

"Tiger, we need to be out of here in the next few days. The Dominton Monastery is almost ready."

"And not in utter ruins?"

"There's plenty of land for tents and maneuvers with no villages or towns in the vicinity. It's safer than here. You know the castle was never intended for anything more than our strategy sessions — our legitimate hunting club."

Rabcal's horse laugh was jeering. "It's served us well since Smith's death. As soon as we persuade Mrs. Smith to sell out —"

"That's exactly what she did when she met with Colin Burdock at a party in Madrid. Burdock took a liking to her. Mutual, I think. She has no intention of losing her yacht and this castle to Salvador or to any of us."

The brigadier laughed inside, a soundless laugh. He had prepared the ground work for a new camp, but Salvador and Tiger had no intention of him ever reaching it again. Yes, he could try to escape — fly out even — but no matter where he went Salvador or Tiger would find him. But he wouldn't allow these men to cut his life short, not until he found the person who had betrayed him so long ago. He knew now that his betrayer was still alive. How else could Langley have found him here? He would take the young man Trevor with him, protect him as he would have protected Landon from the deadly cancer cells.

"Rabcal, ease up on those beatings on Jacques Marseilles. I need him. He's combed these mountains in the past, and if anyone can take the men on to the new camp, Marseilles is the one."

"And Gregory and Wilson?"

"Leave them to me, Tiger. I'm the one they're after."

"An old score to settle?"

"A very old score. Gregory and Wilson are good at maps and tactics. I'll ask them to join Jacques and me in the morning and work out some maneuvers that will get us to the crest of that range and safely into France."

Early in the morning, a young peasant girl with woeful, dovelike eyes led Drew and Vic into the strategy room. She smiled when she saw the brigadier. "I did as you asked," she said sweetly. "I took a breakfast tray to the prisoner."

"Was he all right?"

"His face is swollen. He's frightened."

The brigadier strolled to the narrow recessed window and looked out toward the Pyrenees. "Did you take care of the radio communications, Sophia?"

Sophia moved on birdlike feet and stood beside him. "I used a sledge hammer like you said. Tiger can't call out."

In spite of the men watching him, he touched her face. She seemed so childlike, so trusting. He had been kind to her, unlike the other men who passed through the castle.

"I want to go with you when you leave," she begged.

"You stay here with the caretaker. Mrs. Smith will be good to you when she comes. The men with her will ask you questions."

"I won't tell them anything. I'll show them the hunting trophies in the great hall."

He turned to Wilson and Gregory. "I want Sophia protected."

Gregory nodded. "Then send her to the nearest village."

She shrank from him. "I won't go."

"Not even for me, Sophia? Now go along.

Fetch the prisoner for us. We need a way through those mountains," the brigadier said.

He turned and pointed to the contour map, a large table model of the mountain region between France and Spain. When Sophia came back a few moments later, they were still poring over the map. "Jacques," the brigadier said. "Come in."

Marseilles limped into the room, his face swollen and bruised, one eye at half mast. He almost fled when he saw Drew.

"Jacques," the brigadier said, "we need your help to marshal men and equipment through the mountain passes."

Jacques slumped into a chair, wincing as he favored one hip. "It's not like the old days. There are trains and roads. Use them."

"We need to get to the Dominton Monastery."

Jacques forced his swollen eyelid open. "The Surete will be waiting for you. I got word to my uncle."

"How?" the brigadier stormed. "We watched your every move once we found you."

"My article —"

"The one you mailed to the priest? But I read it."

"Father Frederick is a friend. He loved the

old monastery. He'll read between the lines and get word to my uncle."

"And Stephan Marseilles is a powerful man," Drew said.

"But I scanned the article. Nothing but historical facts about the destruction of the place — the need for renovation."

"Father Frederick will see the inaccuracies. The monastery was destroyed in World War II and then later by an avalanche. Not by an earthquake, Brigadier."

Drew smiled. "Brigadier, I think Jacques has outwitted you. If he got word to his uncle about the archaeological dig, Stephan will check it out. Stephan Marseilles despises his nephew, but he will believe him."

"Then it's over." The brigadier's calm voice startled Drew.

"You have your private plane. We could fly out in that."

"That's ten miles from here. We'd never get that far. Tiger has no intention of any of us leaving. Nor do I." He straightened, adding an inch to his height. "Tell me, Mr. Gregory, how long has Langley known I was alive?"

Drew tried to piece the words together and came up empty. "You've lost me, sir."

"And me," Vic agreed.

"Does the name Luther Breckenridge jog your memory?"

"Breckenridge?" Drew stammered. The brigadier was fortyish: the right age, the right height, brown-eyed. But Luke Breckenridge was dead. Why would anyone impersonate him?

The brigadier ran both hands through his hair, disheveling it even more. "You really didn't know, did you?" He leaned back and laughed bitterly. "I am so important to Langley that they sent you to get rid of me. And you didn't even know who I am."

The peasant girl moved closer to the brigadier, her dovelike eyes trustful as she searched his face. "You have a wife?"

He looked at her, surprised to see her still standing there, surprised at her question. "I did — a long time ago, Sophia."

Yes, Drew concluded, *this young girl is in love with him. But is it mutual?* He turned back to the brigadier's flint-hard gaze. Luke Breckenridge? No, the eyes belonged to someone else. They were not the ones Sauni had described or remembered. Or had a widow's blindness painted a more gentle face?

Luke took a torn picture from his pocket and shoved it toward Drew. "That's a picture of my wife."

Drew picked it up. Saundra Breckenridge!

The scar on Luke's neck bulged as it pulsated. "I've spent weeks compiling statistics on you, Mr. Gregory, trying to find your connection to my wife and family — and you didn't even know who I am. Salvador was wrong. He beat Jacques for nothing."

"Let Jacques go. He can take young Trevor with him."

"I wish I could do that."

"We'll take the three of you with us," Vic said fiercely. "If you're really Breckenridge, where have you been all these years?"

"In prison camps waiting for my country to find me. And for the last ten years here in Europe."

"Oh, you just walked out of the Laotian jungles and moved to Europe?" Vic's words grew more biting. "What kind of fools do you take us for?"

Luke shook his head. "I didn't walk out on my own. Someone made certain I arrived in Europe safely."

"Is that a crack at the CIA?" Drew asked.

"Salvador was uneasy from the moment he met you two. So we checked. That's when I figured that I was your target."

"You were," Drew admitted. "But for running a merc camp."

"But you were sent here to liquidate me."

Vic glared back. "That was never *our* intention."

"You're forgetting something, gentlemen. I was sent on a mission more than twenty years ago and left to die in the jungles of Laos just to cover the trail of a turncoat, a mole. No, the Agency will not take me. How can they? I'm already dead."

"Not to your family. They've lived with your memory day after day. For their sake we're going to take you in, Luke."

"Why all the *desperate haste to succeed,* Gregory? Why this *desperate enterprise?* You can't win. You can't take me in."

"You sound like you're mouthing Frost or Wordsworth."

"No. Thoreau. When my brother died, I memorized some of the poems he loved. Made me feel closer to him." Luke rubbed the back of his neck. "Dad used to say, 'Forget Thoreau, son. It's going to trip you up — blow your cover wide open in the military.' Dad didn't want to be there when it happened. But poetry didn't destroy me. A fellow American did."

Drew thought about his own past. He'd known every football score in the NFL. "Every man has some habit, some giveaway. You don't belong here, Breckenridge. Thoreau is out of place here."

"I don't belong anywhere. I'm wanted for treason, remember?"

"Your *drum's off-beat,* Brigadier," Vic said.

"*I step to the music I hear.* I have ever since I met Harland Smith at the Monte Carlo. He slaughtered French — just enough so I could peg him as a New Yorker."

"And you struck up a conversation?"

"No, he did. Over a cocktail." Luke stared off into space. "Smith seemed to know all about me. He was confident that I'd listen. 'I hear you need a permanent job,' he said. Desperation kept me from sprinting."

"So he hired you to run a merc camp?"

"He asked me about my military background. I lied. He smiled and told me if we could do business, he'd order me another drink."

The neck scar kept pulsating. "Some of the men sitting around the table that evening were rich philanthropists. Men who wanted to fund wars and take out governments that they didn't like. They were making arms deals with Smith right there in the casino, as relaxed and unworried as any men could be."

"So you bought into it?"

"Not with money, Gregory. I didn't have any. But with my skills. I trained men and kept my nose clean. Smith liked it that way.

It was a way of life for me — food, shelter, usefulness."

"Training other men to kill?"

"I didn't see it that way. Being a military advisor was all I knew. Many of the men were castaways — like I was. Our own countries didn't want us."

"What brought you to Spain, Luke?"

"Circumstances. Rabcal created trouble in Africa. We left while we still could. So Smith had me check out the fortress. I gave him some pointers, some ways we could use the place. But he had something new in mind. Scouting parties."

"Terrorists?"

"Even more. Quick hit-and-run missions. All I had to do was train the men. Smith took care of the funding with his worldwide contacts. Countries pay big bucks for well-trained men."

"And that's all you wanted?"

"What I wanted was to stay alive long enough to find the man who ruined my life. Everyone I trained was money in my pocket. But that didn't mean that much to me."

"Brigadier, do you really expect me to swallow all of this?"

"Believe what you want, Gregory. You asked for a summary. I'm giving it to you." The shaggy, gray-streaked beard clouded his smile. He lapsed into silence. Gregory waited.

"When we first got word that Smith had died in a plane crash, I figured the garrison would fold. Salvador insisted that we try to purchase the fortress from Smith's wife. I advised against buying it after meeting Colin Burdock at the casino."

"Burdock?" *Burdock involved?* Drew felt sick.

"Yeah, one of the Langley boys. Of course, he didn't present that way. But I learned to spot them. Burdock was heavy in debt and drinking too much. It loosened his tongue. Salvador tried to recruit him. I tried to sober him."

Luke's hollow eyes remained empty, expressionless. "It took quite a bit of black coffee before I realized Burdock wasn't really drunk. Monique Smith had been in touch with him. She wanted him to check out the hunting club at the castle. I didn't dare tell Salvador. But I told him we had to relocate."

"To the other side of the Pyrenees?"

Jacques looked up from his long silence. "Smith didn't die in the plane crash."

Luke showed genuine surprise. "But I read the news clippings."

"He died a couple of months ago in Switzerland," Drew said.

"You seem confident."

"I was there."

"You killed him?"

"No, his son Anzel did."

Drew turned abruptly and stared out the window. Down in the valley, Tiger was forcing the men through more maneuvers. Suddenly, there was an explosion, a flash of blinding light. One uniformed body blew into the air and tumbled to the ground. Lifeless. Drew's lips went dry. "That was the young kid Trevor."

Luke was beside him at once nodding. "He didn't have a chance."

"You won't either, Brigadier, if you don't leave here now. That plane of yours is your last hope — our last hope."

"What do you want me to do — fly until the gas runs out?"

"No one is leaving." Drew whirled around. Salvador stood in the doorway, his captain's cap shoved back on his forehead, his revolver gleaming in his hand.

Jacques pushed up from the chair and started running, his feet unsteady as he bumped into Sophia. Salvador aimed his revolver and fired a round. As Jacques fell in front of her, Sophia screamed.

"Get back, Sophia," Salvador warned as he reloaded. "It's the brigadier I want."

Luke walked calmly toward the door. "Sorry, gentlemen," he said. "It looks like you won't be taking me alive."

"But we will," Drew told him. "Mark my word."

"Why? So you can hang me for the traitor you believe me to be? Looks like Salvador will save you the job. You might as well tell Langley I'm sorry to miss the showdown."

"Langley? No, we'll take you to Schaffhausen so I can find out whether you're still the man your family believes in."

Luke's dark eyes softened momentarily. A sudden movement on Drew's left caught his attention. He spun around and saw Vic lunging for Salvador. Another shot winged past Drew's head as Salvador toppled.

"Come on, Drew. Let's get out of here," Vic urged.

But Drew had already reached Jacques and knelt beside him. "Hold on, Jacques. We'll get you back to your uncle's chateau."

The eyelids fluttered. He groped blindly. Drew gripped his limp hand and leaned down, trying to hear Jacques's words.

"Father, forgive me . . ."

Drew's grip tightened. "Can you hear me, Jacques?"

The man's lips moved, his words barely audible. "Holy Mary, mother of God . . .

pray for us sinners."

"Give me something, Vic," Drew demanded. "I've got to stop this flow of blood."

Vic grabbed a table scarf and tossed it. "You're wasting your time, Drew. He's bleeding out."

"Help me then."

Luke stooped down eye-level with Drew. "He won't make it," he said. "Tiger and the men are coming back. Get out while you can. Take the Hum-Vee."

"I'm not leaving this man behind."

"Gregory, I'll stay with him. Go."

Vic called from the doorway. "Drew, are you coming?"

"Not without Jacques."

Vic pounded the door casing. "Look, the man's dying."

Jacques opened his eyes again without seeing. "Father, forgive. Forgive me . . ."

Drew was sweating, too. He touched Jacques's cold damp brow. "Vic's going for help," he told the man.

Vic hadn't budged. He shook his head. "We can't get help soon enough. You know that, Drew."

Drew nodded. He tried to remember a prayer and fell short. Then he thought of Captain York. Normandy. Eons ago. "The Lord is your Shepherd, Jacques."

Jacques turned at the sound of the words. He gurgled the words, "Shepherd . . . forgive."

"He leads you beside still waters, Jacques." Luke was quoting the words with him.

"Er — er —" His eyes rolled back.

Gregory couldn't remember the rest of the words of the psalm. But there was no need. Jacques seemed at peace, his gaze fixed. Drew lowered the limp hand to the floor and stood.

"What did you tell him, Drew?" Vic asked from the door.

"The truth."

"Truth?"

"I told him the Lord was his Shepherd."

"Guess he needed to hear it."

"So did I."

"Don't go soft on me," Vic warned.

Drew ignored him, his eyes on Breckenridge. "Will you help us?"

He tried to lift the dead man from the floor and felt Luke supporting Jacques's body from the other side. "Sophia?" Drew asked.

"We'll drop her off at the village. You're certain we need to take Jacques?" Luke asked.

"I promised his uncle I'd get him back to the chateau."

They hurried out of the castle into the

courtyard, stumbling toward the Hum-Vee, their feet dragging under the weight of Jacques's body. Vic raced ahead, a sharp hunting knife in his hand. When they reached him, the guard was out cold, the dog dead.

As they lowered Jacques into the jeep, Drew wondered how the news of his death would be received. Stephan Marseilles had waited a long time to bury his nephew.

Robyn dashed to the door when the bell rang, hoping that her father had returned. She smothered her disappointment, but not her surprise. "Uriah Kendall, what are you doing here?"

"I'm worried about your father."

"Pierre," she called.

"I'm here, sweetheart. I heard." His arm went tightly around her. He nodded to Uriah. "Come in, sir."

Kendall turned slightly and stared across the street.

"Did you come in that car, sir?"

"No, by taxi, Pierre."

He followed them up the stairs and into the apartment, pacing nervously as he reached the living room. Pierre went at once to the window. "The car is still there. Who followed you, Uriah?"

"The British? The Americans? What does

it matter? It's Drew I'm worried about. It's all over the news — that attack on the old Dominton Monastery in France."

He frowned. "They found a supply depot and a mercenary training camp at the ruins. A French antiterrorist squad moved in at dawn. They took a few prisoners, lost a few others, and confiscated weapons."

"What does that have to do with my father?" Robyn whispered.

"When did you hear from him last?"

"Three or four weeks ago."

"He'll be okay, sweetheart. He's in Spain," Pierre told her. "He mentioned trying to see Colin Burdock in Madrid while he was away on this trip."

"But I don't really think he went there."

Pierre grinned. "What do you mean?"

"He wanted it to sound safe. Darling, please call Paris for me. Ask Porter where Dad is. Surely Porter knows."

Chapter 22

The Hum-Vee bounced over a ten-mile back road with Luke at the wheel and Jacques's lifeless body propped against Drew. Sophia gasped as Luke squealed to a stop long enough to let her out. She began running the minute her feet hit the ground, the dust flying as her sandals stirred the rubble.

"Will she cause us any trouble?" Vic asked.

"In this village? Not likely. Folks here barely eke out a living. If it weren't for us, they'd starve."

Drew sized up the handful of houses, the ground that would take a miracle to produce crops. He saw the makeshift hangar standing innocuously at the far end of the village, barrels of fuel lined up in front of it. "Three planes. Busy airport."

"We're off the line of commercial runs. Safer that way. The Pilatus Porter is ours."

"An old model."

"Yeah, Drew. A PC-6, but she's in mint condition."

"Who's your competition?"

"I don't ask."

"That Piper Cherokee could carry contraband."

"I told you, I don't ask."

Luke pulled along side the Pilatus Porter, a high-wing monoplane with a turboprop engine. The plane faced toward the jagged mountains. Open, barren land lay in the other direction. Drew eye-balled the landing strip hacked out of the rubble and fringed with tall, dry grass. Two football fields at most. *My kind of challenge,* he thought.

"Can we make it?" Vic asked.

"No problem," the brigadier said confidently. "She's a STOL. Short takeoff and landing. Safe and reliable. Besides, who likes the alternative? Rabcal will be on our tail any minute."

Vic cocked his head, grinning. "Not without effort. I disconnected the batteries on the other vehicles."

The thought seemed to please the brigadier. "Let's get our cargo on board before someone sees him. Then I'll go inside."

"I'll go with you," Drew said as they propped Jacques in a seat and strapped him there. "I've got to place a call."

"Not in that bloody shirt, Gregory."

Vic tossed his sweater to Drew. "Who're you calling?"

"He's not phoning anyone," Luke said cheerfully.

"I have to notify someone about Jacques."

"Let's just drop him at the nearest strip and forget him."

They were inside the battered old hangar now, Drew using a shortwave radio to contact Father Frederick. He heard grief in the priest's voice as he told him what had happened. "Can Stephan use his influence and meet us?" Drew asked. "It's hush-hush . . ."

Luke scowled as Drew said, "No, we're flying in. Yes, Father Frederick. I remember the place. We'll land there instead. I'll check the charts. It doesn't matter where we are right now . . . No Surete," Drew warned, "or we won't even stop . . . Yes, I'm sorry, too. Really sorry."

"Come on," Luke demanded. "It won't take Tiger forever to get those vehicles running again."

Vic climbed aboard the Pilatus. "Drew's a pilot. He might as well sit up front with you."

"Really? Commercial?"

"Small aircraft mostly. Actually I flew one like this a few times before I gave up flying."

"When we get up, I'll let you take the stick."

Drew studied the instrument panel, the old excitement of the takeoff pumping his adrenalin. He gulped. "Luke, we've got company."

His adrenalin raced even more as he pointed to the yellow Hum-Vee bouncing full speed over the dirt road toward the PC-6, a weapon mounted on its rear, an angry Rabcal at the wheel. "Luke, if that's a missile aimed at us, we've had it."

Luke's hands were chalky on the controls. "It's you or us, Rabcal," he said as he headed down the tarmac toward the jeep. The rat-a-tat-tat of ground fire exploded around them. Bullets poked holes in the fuselage. The plane shuddered as Luke swooped over the Hum-Vee, flying so low that even the gunner ducked, his weapons misfiring into empty space.

Moments later Luke's laugh filled the cockpit as he dipped his wing in farewell and turned east.

"Everything under control?" Drew asked.

"Seems to be. But this thing was built for flying, not target practice. I thought for sure they hit the aileron, but the controls seem okay now. Hey, Wilson, anyone dead back there?"

"Jacques," Vic said sourly. "And if I've been hit, I'm too numb to know it. But I'm sure they hit the back of the plane."

"Just skinned it a bit. All I've got stored

back there is radio gear. We're okay. There's no fuel spewing from the wing."

"What's the flight plan, Luke?" Drew asked.

"Straight out of here. Unfortunately, Rabcal knows every landing strip I use."

"Go for one he doesn't know. I promised Father Frederick that we'd transport Jacques to an airstrip near Tours. They'll drive in from Vendome and meet us."

"I don't plan on being met by a six-man antiterrorist squad. No, we'll fly low to the Mediterranean and avoid a direct flight over the Pyrenees. We'll refuel at a private airstrip outside of Lyon, France, and then go on to Smith's old place near Montreaux."

"Switzerland?"

"Plane's registered there. Everything's legit. Smith had a fleet of planes — seven once. Under the company name Smithsonian Air Service. Clever, eh? How American can you get?"

"How'd he get by with that?" Vic asked.

"He had many interests — vintage planes and air shows included."

The sea rippled below them, blue-green and peaceful. Luke turned inland and flew north to Lyon. After refueling, he grew agitated as they waited on the tarmac for clearance to take off again. "I don't like the cargo we're carrying," he said.

"Then head to Tours, and we'll deliver it."

"Never." Luke's jaw clamped, the same Breckenridge defiance that Sauni had once described. The glare of the late afternoon sun hit the windshield, glazing the hardened eyes even more.

On a signal from Drew, Vic thrust himself forward and secured his arm tightly around Luke's neck in a carotid restraint. Within seconds the brigadier slipped into unconsciousness.

The traffic tower responded immediately as Vic dragged Luke from the controls. "What's all the commotion?"

"No problem," Drew said as he switched to the pilot's seat. "Everything's in good order. Yes, ready to go."

"Then it's time to roll. You're cleared for takeoff."

By the time Luke regained consciousness, his hands were tied behind him. He cursed as they roared down the runway and headed for Tours. "You play rough," he said angrily.

"Just be grateful Vic didn't shatter your trachea."

Eagle instinct took over. In spite of the five years since Drew's license had lapsed, he felt at home at the controls. Now he wondered why he had given it up. Never did he feel more free, more peaceful than when he was winging through the sky, drifting with the clouds.

As they neared Tours, Luke said, "I should have left you back at the castle, Gregory. Tiger would have had great sport with you."

"Or with you — had we left you behind."

"Why didn't you?" Luke tugged at his arm restraints as they shouted at each other above the hum of the engine. "What's your plan B? I'm still alive. Do you drop me off at Langley?"

"Schaffhausen first. There's someone there who would like a mighty big explanation, Luke."

And she's waited two decades to hear it, Drew thought. But would it break Sauni Breckenridge's heart? Or had Luke done that twenty years ago?

Uriah Kendall's warning bothered him even more. "Neilson and Kaminsky are up to something. And right now, Gregory, you're in the way."

In the way of what? Truth?

The urgency in the traffic controller's voice grabbed his attention. "PC-6, please come in . . ."

"Yes, I seem to be off course," Drew admitted. *But don't worry about your radar* screen. *I've got my destination in sight.* Aloud he said, "Sir, I'm declaring an emergency."

A pause. "Your nearest emergency strip is the Anglican Seminary . . . Please advise."

"Nice to have the tower agree with my plans," he said as the grassy strip came into view. "Father Frederick calls this his old alma mater."

For a few seconds, the landing turned rough. Just short of the gardens Drew bounced to a stop. He made final contact with the tower. "Safely down." He switched off communications.

Vic groaned. "Gregory, if that priest breaks his promise with us, we won't make it out of here."

Drew stepped from the plane. "You have your revolver; we'll go down fighting, but I believe the man will keep his word."

"You don't even know him."

"I trust him. I was an altar boy a long time ago."

"You?"

"Yes. Sounds out of character, doesn't it?"

Again Drew glanced at the back fuselage peppered with bullet holes. Even the wing tip had been grazed, narrowly missing the aileron. "So far our luck's holding," he said.

His confidence waned as the sun set and twilight threatened. Finally, five men came toward the plane, two of them pushing what could well be a mortuary cart. "At least a couple of them are priests."

"I trust that's all they are," Luke said tight-lipped.

"Don't worry, Brigadier. Frederick is a man of the cloth." But Drew felt a little unsure as the group came closer.

The priest in the foreground walked briskly. As he reached the plane, his feet seemed to drag as though he dreaded what lay ahead. Frederick's face looked old as Drew gripped his hand. "I'm Drew Gregory."

Frederick's silver-white hair blew in the evening breeze. Under the black brows sad, dark eyes brimmed with tears. Without a word he climbed on board, glanced briefly at Vic, and then cried out in pain as he looked down on Jacques. "He's been shot."

Frederick reached out to touch Jacques. "Old friend, it has come to this." Gently, he anointed him with oil and prayed.

Outside, Drew asked, "Sir, may I use a phone?"

The wide brows arched as Frederick's companions lifted Jacques's body from the plane. "We could trace the call."

"But you won't, not if you keep your word with me."

Frederick beckoned to one of the younger men. "Take this man to the library. Put the charges on my account."

Drew felt as if he had entered an ancient cathedral with a vaulted ceiling. A crucifix and icons hung on the walls. Robed figures moved mutely ahead of them. The place was soundless except for his own footsteps echoing loudly in the sacred hall. Politely, the young priest pointed him toward the library.

A portrait of Pope John Paul looked down on Drew as he sat on the edge of the desk and dialed. "Come on, Robyn. Pick that thing up."

And then her warm *"Bonsoir"* reached his ear.

He grinned up at the pope's picture, but he was seeing Robyn — looking all too much like the Gregory side of the family with wisps of auburn hair falling over her forehead, the pudgy nose that gave her fits, the soft complexion that was as lovely as Miriam's. And those brilliant sea-blue eyes and bubbly laughter that delighted Pierre.

"Bonsoir," she said again, her voice rising.

"Princess —"

"Dad, where are you? Are you all right?"

"Just listen. I'm fine. I've been eagle-bound again."

"Flying?"

"Smart girl. I need your help. I'll be at the airport near Montreaux. Three of us. *Three*," he repeated.

As she gasped, he gave the time and location. "We'll need a safe escort out of there. And transportation to Zurich."

"And not Schaffhausen?" she whispered.

"Pierre and I will meet you."

"We'll need a safe haven at Zurich, Princess."

He heard her respirations growing shorter. "What about the man with the cast?"

"Good girl." *Good girl,* he thought. Heinrich Mueller's old *zimmer frei* would be perfect. "He might not approve."

"I'll persuade him. I love you —"

"Honey, do you remember me talking about Colin Burdock?"

She hesitated. "Your old friend in Madrid?"

"Get a call through to him. Tell him *to go for the castle.*"

"What?"

"Tell him to go for the castle in the Pyrenees. He'll know what I mean." He tightened his grip on the phone. "Honey — Miriam?"

"Mother is worried about you."

"Good," he said. "At least I'm in her thoughts."

He wiped his fingerprints off the phone, then cradled it. *Good girl. My girl!* The boyish young priest led him back to the Pilatus Porter where Father Frederick stood leaning against one wing.

"Thank you," Drew said. "Sir, did you get Jacques's article?"

"The one on the Dominton ruins? I passed it on to Stephan."

"Then it's up to him to finish what Jacques started. It was a good beginning, an honorable one."

"At first Stephan wanted to do nothing."

"Didn't he believe there was a mercenary camp on French soil? Tell him to go there. I think he'll find ample evidence."

The priest's smile was understanding, kindly. "He was afraid Jacques had shamed the family name again. It took two days before I could persuade him to look into it."

"And?"

"He went to the American embassy in Paris first." The dark eyes narrowed. "They referred him to an office in the Neuilly district."

Drew groaned inwardly. *So Porter Deven already knew what was going on. But he didn't know about Luke. Not yet.*

"The American at Neuilly denied knowing your whereabouts. That seemed unlikely, so

Stephan went to French Intelligence."

"Then it's up to *them* to finish what Jacques started."

The priest frowned. "Haven't you seen the headlines? I guess not. Stephan was quite effective. There'll be no merc camp at the Dominton ruins. And now I will keep my word with you, Monsieur Gregory. Jacques's body in exchange for a few more hours of silence."

He rubbed one eye with his knuckle. "I didn't know Jacques as a boy, but it seems he bore a guilt that should never have been his. Stephan knows that now, but in all my years in the village parish, Jacques was never really accepted. Now," he said sadly as they rolled the stretcher away, "he's free."

"Sir, he — he was praying for forgiveness when he died."

"Good. That comforts me. I was not there to pray with him." He glanced at Luke. "Is that man in there your prisoner?"

"Like Jacques, he's been a prisoner far too long. But for the rest of this flight, he'll be our pilot."

"I won't ask your destination."

"It's best that way." *Then you won't know our revised flight plan.*

"In another three hours, Stephan will know what happened."

397

"We'll be across the border by then. Will you tell Monsieur Marseilles I'm sorry? Really sorry."

"He won't believe you, Mr. Gregory."

Drew nodded. "But he'll be glad that it's over for Jacques."

"You're wrong. There was no time for reconciliation."

"Sir, they had fifty years."

Frederick shook hands with Drew and stepped back. "It's only been in the last few days that Stephan saw a need for amends."

After forty-eight hours in Drew's custody, Luke felt more hopelessness than anger. As he showered in lukewarm water, he thought sadly of the men, the malcontents who had gathered around him for the last ten years. So many of them were dead. He especially felt the loss of Trevor — a mixed-up kid who should have stayed in Scotland. In a way Trevor reminded him of Duc Thuy Tran, the Vietnamese soldier who had served under his command in that secret war in Laos. He wondered what had become of Duc. And he thought of Neng Pao in the village of Xangtiene, a man who barely came to his armpit, the man who had saved his life. Then he thought of his brother Landon and wept.

Luke had never shed a tear as the brigadier, but in this no-man's land between training mercenaries and taking back the identity of Luke Breckenridge, the traitor, he felt like giving up. Yet quitting was against the Breckenridge tradition. Escape had been within his grasp when Drew slipped off to the water closet at the end of the hall, but Luke hadn't bolted. Sooner or later Langley would find him again. But why had Gregory delayed his surrender? If Drew held him much longer, Rabcal, the Moroccan, would outwit them. *So why leave?* he asked. *I'm hemmed in from all sides.*

When he stepped from the shower, Gregory was waiting for him. "Heinrich Mueller has breakfast ready for us," Drew said. "After that we're driving to Schaffhausen."

"Then let's have brunch there," Luke suggested.

In Schaffhausen Drew insisted on taking seats on the outdoor patio of the Schweizerhof not far from the bridge that spanned the Rhine River. Other customers had gone inside, unwilling to fight the brisk spring wind. They sat on the outer edge near a flower box budding with early spring colors, but the shade trees above them added to the dampness.

Drew looked around gazing periodically

toward the bridge.

"Expecting someone, Gregory?"

"The waiter."

"No one else?"

"Yes. My daughter Robyn and her friend."

"Oh!"

Luke took in the winding streets, the frescoed buildings, and the people passing by. "Is this our Langley contact point?"

"I haven't been in touch with Langley yet."

"Really? Then where's Wilson?"

"He's reporting in to our station-chief."

"About me?" Luke shrugged as the waiter brought their meals. He attacked his food with a burst of enthusiasm. "A few more hours of reprieve then." He ate hungrily, gulping the wine down and then pouring himself another drink. "Have some, Drew."

"None for me."

Luke pushed the glass aside. "I'm not much for drinking either. I just figured it was a condemned man's meal."

He eased back in his chair as two women came over the hump of the bridge strolling leisurely as they approached the cafe. The younger woman wore sunshades and walked in a carefree manner. The one with the shoulder-length blonde hair wore a raincoat over her bright red dress, a handbag over her shoulder. She moved gracefully, her high heels emphasizing the narrow ankles. As they came closer, his attention went back to her oval-shaped face.

Something stirred inside him. He couldn't take his eyes off her. He would know that lovely face, those tender sensitive eyes anywhere. *Sauni. Sauni. Sauni. Time has been kind to you.*

He gazed unflinching, his expression impassive as they took a nearby table. "I'll get some coffee," the younger woman said.

As Robyn left her, Sauni braced her head with her hand, one elbow resting on the table, her expression so pensive that he wanted to cry out, "It's Luke. It's Luke."

But he remained rigid and immobile. And then he saw the heart-shaped locket around her neck. She reached her fingers instinctively around it; their eyes met. The muscles in her face contorted, robbing Sauni of her beauty. The trembling lip and wounded gaze said it without words: *Why? Why? Why?*

Even when Robyn came back with the coffee, Sauni didn't take her eyes off him. From where Luke sat, he could see the tears in Sauni's eyes and knew that she had recognized him.

His extremities went numb; his throat constricted. Slowly the women pushed back their chairs, stood, and walked away, their coffee untouched. Still he could make no sound, no move. He watched them cross the bridge. When they were out of view, he turned on Drew. "Curse you, Drew Gregory. Why?"

"I had to know that you were really Luke Breckenridge."

"My word wasn't good enough? You had to put her through this?"

"We told her you were alive. She had a right to see you."

Luke stared toward the bridge. "Why? She married someone else."

"You're wrong. No one else quite measured up to you, Captain."

Luke felt cold inside. "She was better off thinking me dead. Why didn't you leave me in Spain? Why did you save my life, you —"

"For her. I did it for her."

Chapter 23

Saundra walked rapidly back over the bridge, her shoulder bag banging against her slender hip, her fists doubled. Robyn touched her elbow; she resisted the comfort.

"I don't have to ask, do I, Saundra? It really was Luke."

"You doubted it?"

"Dad had to be certain. I'm sorry we did it that way — but you begged to see him."

"Not on some street corner in Schaffhausen. I wanted to see him alone. Just the two of us. And you wouldn't even give us that."

"Luke didn't want to see you."

The clicking of her heels on the bridge ceased as she whirled and faced Robyn. "Did your father arrange that, too?"

"My father has risked his career, but Luke spurns his help. There's nothing left to do but turn him over to Langley."

"No. Can't you see? Luke has suffered enough. I saw it in his face, in his eyes. Emptiness. Despair."

"Sauni, all I see there is harshness and cruelty."

She was walking again, leaving the bridge and cutting along the path beside the Rhine, her thoughts flowing swiftly like the river. "You don't know him, Robyn. I remember the man he once was."

"He's changed, Sauni. He's a different person."

Brushing at the tears, Sauni ran ahead a few yards to a tree and tore at the bark with her bare hands. Waves of nausea rolled through her stomach, the sour taste of vomit trapped in her throat.

When Robyn caught up to her, Sauni lashed out again. "He's dead inside, Robyn. What have they done to him? Something awful has happened. With that ugly beard, I couldn't see the dimple in the cleft of his chin."

She felt faint, but fought it. "I used to run my finger over that dimple, and then he'd kiss my fingertips. Please, let him go free," she begged. "Don't turn him over to Langley. They'll have him court-martialed, maybe even hung."

"But Luke refuses to account for those missing years."

"He will now." A calm washed over her. "I may never have him again, but I'll storm

404

the American embassy on Luke's behalf. Tell your father that I'll battle with the military or crawl up the steps of the White House and beg. And I'll bombard Heaven with my prayers — anything to see Luke free again."

"Luke lost a treasure when he lost you."

"He never really lost me." She stopped by the water's edge and faced Robyn again. "Back there at the cafe, I saw Luke focus on my locket. I promised him once that I'd never take it off until we met again." She reached up and undid the chain and pushed the locket and Luke's wedding band into Robyn's hand. "Give these to Luke and tell him I kept my promise."

"But, Sauni —"

"Robyn, hide Luke for a few more days until I can talk to him and hear from his lips that he betrayed his country. If he tells me that, then I will understand what Drew must do."

When they reached the house on campus, Sauni flung herself on the sofa.

"I'll make some tea," Robyn offered.

"Don't bother," came a cheerful voice from the kitchen. "It's already made. So let's celebrate."

Annabelle Vandiver came from the kitchen, tray in hand. "Where have you been, Sauni? I have such good news. David —

that's my nephew — wants to come for a visit. He hasn't talked to Namlee yet — Oh, Robyn, I didn't know you were here."

She set out the cups and saucers and rambled on. "David hinted that the family would want to come. Well, you know what that means, 'Auntie Annabelle, can you pay Davey's way?' He's my very favorite one, you know . . . their oldest boy . . . oh, yes, the baby's due any day now. I'm anxious to see them all. And, Sauni, if they come, your in-laws can meet them. Wouldn't that be splendid?"

"Yes, that would be wonderful," Sauni agreed.

"Saundra, what's wrong? You look terrible."

"I'm not feeling well."

Robyn said worriedly, "And I have to leave to meet my dad."

"Go on, Robyn. I'll stay with her," Annabelle offered. "I'm so sorry. Talking about my family like that. Come on, Sauni, let's get you to bed. Then I'll make some soup."

The nausea grew worse. "I'm all right."

"You look like you've seen a ghost."

"She has," Robyn said.

As the front door closed behind Robyn, Sauni whispered, "Annabelle, I want to buy those photographs of Xangtiene. I'll pay you whatever you want. Just get them for me — today."

"You're kidding, of course. You know I can't do that. David says he may have to turn them over to someone in Washington."

"To the highest bidder?"

As Heinrich Mueller served his customers lunch, Gregory and Breckenridge sat in the back room of the *zimmer frei*.

"Try and remember the man's name," Drew demanded.

"It's too hazy, Gregory. We were in a war."

"Yeah, at the end of a long war."

Luke scratched the back of his head, stirring the unruly mop of peppery hair. "The pilot who flew me in on that mission called him DeVol. Devlin. Devore — something like that."

"You don't remember the man's name, yet you obeyed his orders."

"He outranked me. A major."

"I'll check." Drew considered Kaminsky, but he wasn't certain where Chad's loyalties lay these days. He did a mental rundown — back to his years in Washington. He came up with two men who had clout at the Pentagon. He'd ask them to do a search for someone stationed in Southeast Asia at the close of the Vietnam conflict, captain or above, army or marines. He needed a check-list. But why? Why was he putting stock in a man like Luke? Because of the admiral's wife in Ocean City? Or the grass widow in Busingen? Maybe it was more personal; he still blamed this Breckenridge affair for the ransacked room in Washington. Or was that one really Aaron's work?

"I don't know the man's name. You've got to believe me, Drew."

But I don't, Drew thought.

"He flew into our base camp by chopper while my men were out on night patrol. My commanding officer brought the guy to my tent. Look, the major kept saying his name wasn't important. It was too risky for me to know in case something happened. Said the assignment was classified, top secret, straight from the President. Why ask me, Gregory? Why didn't they quiz my C. O.?"

"Hank Randolf? He died a few days after you left the camp."

"A sniper?"

"Suicide, I believe."

Luke slipped deeper into his dark mood. Perspiration spread across his forehead and trickled down to his stubbled beard. "No, Randolf wasn't that kind of person. He was a tough one."

"Think. Think. Try to recall the major's

habits. His looks."

"It was nighttime in the jungle, Drew. We were outside my tent, his features hidden by shadows. He didn't want to be seen. There were times when I thought I knew the voice, but imagination runs wild sometimes. The moon peeked in and out of the clouds, but the major kept ducking into the shadows."

Luke lifted his head defiantly, his lips twisting as though remembering would destroy him. "He wasn't very tall. His *cammie* shirt was a size too small, so his flabby neck bulged over the collar. He was young enough, maybe a few years older than I."

"That would make him about fifty today."

Luke nodded as though it didn't matter. "Younger maybe. He's probably lounging comfortably at a desk job in Washington now."

"Or maybe he doesn't exist." Drew poured them both a cup of coffee. "Cream? Sugar?"

"Black."

Luke twirled the steaming liquid and took quick gulps without flinching. "There was one other thing. The guy kept running an emery board over his thumbnail."

Drew didn't move. "You said you couldn't see him."

Luke fought back. "I spent twenty or twenty-five minutes with him in not exactly the brightest of lights. I couldn't pick him out in a mug shot. But I tell you, he kept filing his nail."

Heinrich Mueller entered the room without knocking and took a seat. "Why did you take that assignment, Captain?" he asked.

Luke gave a disgruntled snarl. "Did I have a choice?"

"Drew tells me you weren't well. The peace talks were going on in Paris. There were rumors of a Nixon pullout. Why didn't they send a national in your place?"

Pride squared Luke's shoulders. "It was a rescue mission. I was the best man for the job. I'd climbed mountains all my life. I knew the area, spoke the dialect. We'd heard rumors about a helicopter evacuation. Americans left behind would be mistreated. My gut feeling said I might not make it back in time. I told the major I was worried about my family. It was my life, my risk, my family, and all he said — calmly, mind you — was, 'What about them, Breckenridge? If something happens, we'll notify your parents.' "

Anger edged his words. "But I knew the Agency wouldn't tell my parents I'd been sent on special assignment."

"You were under marine cover. It had to remain that way."

"I know, Gregory. But I didn't want my

folks to think I died running, died as a traitor. My dad was navy. He'd understand the need for secrecy, but I never told him about my connection with Langley. My folks never knew."

"They guessed as much when your name didn't appear on the Vietnam Memorial Wall in Washington. Your folks fought that one. After all, you'd been buried with military honors."

"An empty box? For love of God, for love of country," he mocked. "So my folks know about my CIA connection?"

"Never clearly stated. They put the pieces together when Washington linked your name to treason. Your dad backed off then."

"Is that what you plan to do, Gregory? Back off?"

"Luke, you never saw the major except that one time? You didn't meet him at the Farm during your training?"

"Not that I recall. Just in Laos. He was edgy. In a hurry. He told me I had to be off long before dawn — before my men came back from patrol. He had mapped out an escape route, but I still didn't like the odds." He shifted. "I understood the need to rescue that missing station-chief and the disposal of a foreign agent, but I didn't get why I was to plant a microfilm in Xangtiene."

Gregory sucked in his breath. "Then why did you do it?"

"You want to know why I did it? It was an order, man. I was trained to obey from the time I quit wetting my pants until the day when I slipped into the jungle alone." His intensely cold eyes met Gregory's, his words dripping with bitterness. "Man, I believed in my country. Then that guy stowed his emery board in his pocket and gave me a fish handshake. As he walked away, I asked, 'What about my wife? Will she know the truth —' "

"I thought you were divorced," Mueller interrupted.

"The major said the same thing, but a piece of paper didn't break my vows to Sauni. In my eyes, she's still my wife." Luke pounded his fist on the table. "I was being set up by my own country. And I never found the missing station-chief."

Drew glanced at Mueller. "He was never missing," Drew said.

"So you think I made that one up? America wasn't winning that war. We were deeper in than we needed to be. But there was another kind of a war going on, and the Agency was right in the thick of it. Training an army of its own and transporting men and equip-

412

ment via those fly boys with Air America."

"Go on."

"Someone made a mistake, Gregory. Maybe someone in the Agency was running a double agent."

"Working with Laos?"

"Laos. Vietnam. The Russians. Does it matter?"

"And you believe a mole in the Company betrayed you?"

"Isn't that what they branded me all these years?" His eyes turned to burning coals. "What's the use? It's my word against —"

Mueller's voice boomed out. "Perhaps you never wanted to take the escape route. Or maybe you made a mistake, a wrong turn."

"I had it memorized, Herr Mueller. It was engraved in my brain. I got off before dawn like I was instructed. I did the first lap of the journey with one of those Air America jocks. The pilot sat in his fixed-wing plane, wearing khaki shorts and nothing but sandals on his bare feet. He had combat flying in his blood and a fuselage still riddled with bullet holes."

Luke's empty gaze encompassed both men. "I didn't ask his destination; he didn't ask mine. But I had a feeling the sacks in the back were not intended as food for the hungry. My bet was on 'hard rice' — ammunition for the rag-clad soldiers."

413

His memory of the flight seemed vivid. "We flew under cloud cover, not unusual for the weather conditions there. I figured he'd dump me out along with the 'rice.' His flight pay would be the same. The whole time in the air my coughing got worse. 'You're in no condition to trek that jungle alone,' he told me. 'I could take you back once I drop that payload in the rear.'

"Below us was steaming jungle, but he picked a strip out of that maze and set me down. Even shook hands as I got out. 'Good luck,' he said doubtfully. 'See ya around in a few years.' He didn't have any idea how many years."

Drew pitied Luke's empty expression — almost believed him.

"I followed the river bed for miles," Luke said, "then cut across a narrow path. It was more thicket than trail and slow going, but it meant less chance of capture. At daybreak I hid. At dusk I set out again. Because of my fever, I'd run out of canteen water. I couldn't risk boiling muddy river water, nor did I have the strength to do so. My lungs were giving out."

"No enemy patrols along the way?" Mueller asked.

"A couple came close. But I finally reached the place where I was to go forty steps north, then due west to a downed American aircraft. I was to leave a message at the wing tip, one of those old cloak-and-dagger jobs. That plane had plowed straight down, its nose burrowing out a small canyon in the earth. One twisted wing protruded above the ground."

"You're certain it was the right plane?"

"It had the right markings. I'd secured the message, hellbent on getting out of there alive, but I was too sick to move. Oh, the major had been accurate to the step. But he made one mistake. It was a guerrilla base all right, but not one of the friendlies. There wasn't even time to take the capsule."

Luke slammed the table again. "A woman was waiting for me. 'I've been expecting you, Captain Breckenridge,' she said."

Drew's anger flared. "You expect me to believe that a Laotian woman was in charge of a military encampment?"

"She was a Russian agent."

"A Russian woman in the middle of the Laotian jungle?"

"If it matters to you, Gregory, she was attractive in a cunning sort of way. I called her the Dragon Fly. Yeah, a Company man sent me right into her hands — that major probably. And I've wanted to know why for a long time."

"You still haven't accounted for the other missing years."

"They're gone, Gregory," he said. "Gone."

"And you won't account for them?"

Luke's scorn took in both men. "The woman kept expecting someone else. When he didn't come, she took pleasure in telling me that the war had ended. That the American troops had gone home. Weeks later she spoke about the POW release from the Hanoi Hilton."

He struggled with the memories. "When the woman, Lisha, and her guerrilla band pulled out, they planned to take me with them. I was having another bout with pneumonia, so they had to leave me behind. 'But we'll always know where you are,' she told me. I was left to the mercy of the roving Pathet Lao troops."

With the same deadpan expression he said, "Beatings. Caged like an animal. Humiliation. Lying in my own excrement. I tried to escape more than once." He turned and yanked his shirt over his shoulders. Deep scars lined his upper torso. "They would have killed me if it hadn't been for a fellow prisoner."

"Another American?"

"I think some were there, but I never saw

them. No, the man who befriended me and saved my life was a Hmong. When we finally escaped, Neng Pao took me back to his village near the downed aircraft. So find the man who sent me into the jungle, and you'll find out who betrayed me and why I was allowed to escape ten years later. I didn't get to Europe on my own. Maybe the CIA gave me a free ride," he said bitterly. "Or maybe the Russians did."

Sadly Luke added, "Someone in the village was Lisha's contact."

"Neng Pao?" Mueller asked.

"No, he was my friend."

"I'll be honest, Luke," Drew said, stretching his legs. "I'm not sure I believe you. But for my daughter's sake, I must do everything in my power to find out if you're telling the truth, and if you are — to clear your name. Most people think you're a dead man. That buys me some time."

"But even if you cleared me — and God knows how you could —"

"According to Robyn and Pierre, God is the only one who can."

Luke ran his hand through his hair in a boyish gesture. "My brother always figured a way to get us both out of trouble. When Landon died, I had to do my own surviving."

"You've done quite well," Mueller told

him. "But I have men posted outside. So don't leave the *zimmer frei* on your own."

They watched Luke storm from the room. "What do you think, Drew? Could he be telling the truth?"

"If he is, he deserves a chance at freedom. But if he refused to take the escape route mapped out for him, then the spirit of the real Breckenridge died in the jungles of Southeast Asia."

A half hour later Robyn found Drew sitting alone twirling his empty cup. "I've been looking all over for you, Dad."

"I've been talking with Luke. But don't get your hopes up, Princess. I don't know how it's going to come out."

"But Pierre and I are praying."

"And your God will work a miracle?"

"Can you, Dad?"

"Do what?"

"Work a miracle?"

He sighed. "I'm better at other things."

She touched his cheek. "You're so certain Luke is lying. You just can't accept betrayal in the ranks, can you, Dad?"

"Finding the person who may have betrayed Luke is a long shot. Time's running out with Porter coming here tonight with Vic."

"From Paris? Then Porter knows Luke is here?"

"He just knows the reports on Spain are incomplete. At least the ones he expected." Drew didn't risk explaining except to say, "There's an American mercenary not accounted for."

"Luke?"

"Yes, but Porter doesn't know him by that name."

"Pierre doesn't trust Porter, Dad. Should we?"

Drew choked on his answer. "Porter's a good man."

"That's a new line. I thought you were archenemies."

"We're Company men, and I've stretched the limits far enough, Robyn. We've got to let Porter know what's going on."

"I'll keep my fingers crossed."

"I thought you specialized in praying."

She grinned sheepishly. "I do both."

"Princess, tomorrow I'll arrange to breakfast with Porter downstairs. I want you to come by and tell me you're going to be with the Breckenridges for the day."

"Dad, I won't lie for you, but I am meeting them. I promised Luke I'd drive him back to Schaffhausen in the morning. I'm going to whip your prisoner right out from under your nose."

"I can't let you do that."

"You can't stop Luke and Sauni from meeting. Besides, sweet Daddy, you want Luke gone when you talk with Porter."

He agreed with that. "I don't like you traveling with Luke."

"Neither does Pierre. But he's in Geneva."

"I'll ask Mueller to have one of his friends tag you."

"Not too closely. Luke and Sauni trust me. This may be their last chance together, and we're not spoiling it."

Chapter 24

Breakfast sizzled on Mueller's stove as Robyn rushed into the cafe and waved at Porter. She leaned down and kissed Drew on the cheek. "Dad, I'm spending the day with the Breckenridges."

"Luke Breckenridge?" Porter asked as she left them.

"Aren't you the one who said he didn't exist?"

"I qualified that."

"That's right. From nonexistent to dead."

"Cut the garble, Drew. I wasn't happy with the blunders in Spain. Vic tried to bluff it, but all the reports in confirm that the American got out safely before Burdock arrived."

"That's what I read. Fast action, eh?"

"Not fast enough. The place had cleared out except for a caretaker and a girl we picked up in the village. Where is he?"

"The brigadier?" Drew asked.

"No — Luke Breckenridge."

Porter's pause had been minuscule, but Drew had caught it. He mulled it over, trying to determine why Porter had ordered the mission. But the man was more mystical than the religion he delved in. Drew glanced at his watch — time enough for Robyn to be on the road to Schaffhausen, Luke at her side. He relaxed. "I'm surprised that Burdock didn't move in while Vic and I were there. We lost a couple of good men."

"Yes, you left one young man dead at the firing line."

"Have they put an I. D. on the kid yet?"

"His father was Scottish clergy."

"Then how did Trevor ever get into a mess like that?"

"Maybe the same way Jacques Marseilles did."

"Porter, I didn't recruit Trevor, but if it hadn't been for Jacques, they wouldn't have cracked the merc camp on the French side."

"You still recruited the wrong man. Stephan Marseilles has stirred up trouble all the way to the White House."

"Just guilt," Drew said. "He and Jacques didn't get on."

"And *we're* not getting on right now. You were sent into that camp with a specific order. Instead you brought the man out."

"Correction. He brought us out in his PC-6. Great little plane. Otherwise, we'd be dead on the firing line, too."

"So that's how you outwitted Burdock. Where's the brigadier?"

"Robyn just told us. His widow lives nearby."

"And his parents? We know they're in Europe."

"For a visit, not a family reunion. They still think their son is dead. Tell me, Porter, how long has Langley known Luke made it out of Southeast Asia?"

"Just in the last few years."

"Ten maybe? He's been in Europe that long."

"You've been on the Breckenridge run long enough, Gregory. You're to back off — Neilson's orders. The Agency takes over now."

"Give me a few more days, Porter. I'm waiting for a checklist from the Pentagon. You can help me sort out the answers."

Porter yanked at his shirt button, releasing the choke hold on his flabby neck. A deep crimson ran from his jugular to his jaw, blotching his cheeks. "No bargaining," he said coldly.

"A few more days," Drew repeated. "I'm convinced Breckenridge was betrayed. Once he hits Washington, he doesn't have a chance."

"No compromise."

Drew pushed his advantage and dropped a verbal grenade. "I read some reports on Luke when I was in Washington. You signed some of them, Porter. Strange. You told me you never heard of him."

Porter's clear blue eyes looked like hard crystals. He took his emery board from his pocket and ran it against the tip of his nail. As he chipped away, he stood. "I'll call Neilson," he said angrily, "and ask for a Breckenridge escort back to Washington."

Drew considered the liquidation order on the brigadier. It might still be in effect. If so, Breckenridge would never make it across the Atlantic. "Tell Neilson that Vic and I will escort the captain back to Washington. But I think you should meet with Luke first and hear his story."

"So you do have Breckenridge?"

"You've known that for several days; otherwise you would not have had me followed. You've made no effort to have him picked up. Why not? There's been opportunity."

"I want you back in London. Now. This Breckenridge affair is off limits to you. America withdrew from Vietnam years ago. I should know. I was on one of the last helicopters out."

"Luke wasn't."

"A lot of men weren't."

424

Drew risked it. "Tell Langley they definitely had a mole high in the Agency back in Breckenridge's day, but it wasn't Luke Breckenridge." He said it so adamantly that he believed it. "If that turncoat is still alive, they need to find him."

"Forget Asia. I want you on the plane to London today."

"I won't leave until Luke is safely back in Washington. I need your guarantee, Porter. There's an Asian connection in this affair. One man. And I want him."

Luke came to the Busingen road sign after a brisk walk from Schaffhausen. Never had he longed to see Sauni more, yet tentacles of worry coiled around his heart. He glanced back at Heinrich Mueller's man, lingering on the footpath to light a cigarette. Luke could overpower one man and escape across the border deep into Germany. But how many other watchdogs were following him?

Moments later he reached the gray frame house on the campus. He ran up the steps and was startled to see Sauni in the doorway, her knuckles tight against the doorknob, her color draining as she saw him. "I've been expecting you," she stammered.

He felt a sudden nauseating blindness as he remembered the woman's voice so many years ago: *I've been expecting you, Captain Breckenridge.*

"Luke . . . would you like to come in?"

What he longed to do was take Sauni in his arms and never let her go again. He wanted to reach out with a Herculean grip and keep her from falling — the way he had done on the steps of the Capitol the day they met. How lovely she had been — the sun favoring her good looks and brightening her gorgeous eyes. Again he realized that the years had been kind. She was still a beautiful woman.

"Luke," she said, gently, "would you like to come in?"

He hesitated at the thought of being alone in a room — just the two of them. Smoldering embers of longing ignited as he looked at her, memories of love chipping at his bitterness. "I thought we could just go for a walk. Is that all right, Sauni?"

She looked away. He caught the scent of Arpege perfume — and cookies baking. "Of course," she said. "Just let me turn off the oven and grab a wrap."

"Let me guess."

"What?"

He almost smiled. "A red sweater."

"Yes, that's what I should wear — for old times' sake."

He stepped inside to wait. Sauni's touches were everywhere: colorful throw pillows, Renoir and Monet paintings, a spring bouquet in a Dresden vase. *Die Schweizer Alpen,* the history of the Alps in three languages lay on the coffee table, a small book of poems beside it. His gaze encompassed the whole room again as he waited. He had always waited for Sauni to get ready. Then he saw their wedding photo on the end table and remembered how often she had quoted Sir Thomas Malory, "The joy of love is too short."

When Sauni came back, he was still holding the picture. Her cheeks flushed, the red blending with the thick knit sweater.

"I usually keep that in the bedroom," she whispered.

Afraid that they might linger, he quickly asked, "Shall we go?"

He considered taking her hand as they went down the steps, but he stayed inches from her, his heart pounding so abnormally that his ears ached. As they reached the sidewalk, neighbors greeted them.

"Guten Morgen," from a muscular blond.

A *bonjour* as fresh and crisp as the weather.

"That one hasn't turned in her term paper yet," Sauni confided.

"Good morning, prof," from a jogger with

a British accent.

"Good morning, Dr. Breckenridge. Spring is surely here." Said with a hint of a Scotch brogue.

Sauni seemed to know everyone. Some glanced curiously at Luke; others barely noticed him. From the open window on the second floor of the yellow house, a woman called, "Will you be back by one?"

"I'll call you when I get back, Annabelle."

A cheerful wave and the woman disappeared.

"That's Annabelle Vandiver. We usually have lunch together."

"Does she know who I am?"

"She knows about you; she doesn't know you're still alive."

"Then you'll have some explaining to do."

"No, I often walk with my students to talk about literature or life's destiny — or about God's love for them."

He backed away, suddenly faced with an unfamiliar Sauni.

As they left the campus and strolled toward the footpath along the Rhine, Luke said, "Saundra, I never meant to hurt you."

"Then why did you stay in Southeast Asia?"

"I was a prisoner, Sauni."

"That's not what they said in Washington.

They said you betrayed your country."

"Sauni, is that what you believe — that I betrayed America?"

"I wouldn't even let myself think that until I saw the pictures of you alive in Xangtiene wearing Hmong clothes."

"I had no clothes of my own."

She stopped by the edge of the river where several crude rowboats bobbed in the water. The surface water rippled as it slapped against them. A sixteenth-century fortress crowned a hillock in the distance, overlooking Schaffhausen.

"I must hear it from you, Luke. The truth. Did you really carry secret documents into Xangtiene?"

He thought about the microfilm he had left at the wing tip. "I was told I was carrying false documents that would free a fellow American . . . Am I guilty of treason? No. Can I prove it? No."

Sauni began walking upstream again, almost running. When he caught up to her, she asked, "Where's Robyn?"

"At the tearoom in Schaffhausen. I gave her my word that I'd be back in two or three hours."

"Then we don't have long, do we?"

He glanced over his shoulder at the watchdog keeping a steady pace behind them.

"We've never had very long."

"Luke, don't you want me to send for your parents?"

"No. I won't hurt them anymore."

"Luke, you've put them through such pain. They buried you with military honors, but they never buried their love for you."

"What about my pain, Sauni?" he asked bitterly.

As they talked, he saw contempt in her eyes one moment, betrayal another.

"Your father wept at your funeral. He was weeping for you, Luke. I never saw him so broken. And your mom had to drag me from your closed casket. I was so ashamed of the divorce, so afraid you had gone to a Christless eternity."

"You thought that?"

"Yes. I've changed, Luke."

"You've gone religious? That should have pleased Mother."

"I was more interested in pleasing God."

Again he backed off, his anger almost peaking as he said defensively, "I phoned Mom once — ten years ago."

Sauni stared up at him. "Ten years ago? Amy kept saying she had talked to you — that she recognized your voice on the phone. That's when a heart flutter put her in the hospital; we thought she was confused. Oh,

Luke, even before that your dad took an early retirement just to be with your mom." Sauni's voice remained surprisingly calm. "What made you give up everything and not come back to us?"

"A traitor? What kind of a welcome would I have had? No one believed there were any POWs left. They were wrong. I wasn't the only one left behind." He longed for her to believe him, but he knew that she didn't. He spared her from hearing about the prison camp or the beatings or how Neng Pao had saved his life. "Someone wanted me out of Laos and back in the States. Langley maybe or the Russians. I don't know. Someone has controlled my whereabouts for twenty years. My giant I call him." His voice hardened. "I swore to Gregory that if I ever find that man again, I will make him pay for the lost years of my life."

Behind them the hillsides were filled with spring flowers and red geraniums and the scent of newly mown grass. Ahead lay the bridge that would take him from this peaceful side of the Rhine into picturesque Schaffhausen with its narrow cobblestone streets and timbered, frescoed guildhouses. Luke was afraid to move and rob them of this moment of standing together, perhaps for the last time.

Mist obscured the summits of the distant mountains. Fern leaves shrouded Sauni's face as she crouched by the gnarled tree roots to watch the mute swan circle gracefully along the water's edge — its long curved neck held proudly, its orange bill bright in the hazy sun that reflected on the rippling river.

As Luke helped Sauni stand, he took the locket from his pocket and held it out to her. "Sauni, Drew told me about the wedding ring — how a friend of his bartered for it in Xangtiene. I want to keep my ring, but I want you to have the locket as a keepsake from our better days."

She touched it, smiling. "Yes, I had grown rather fond of it."

As he fastened it around her neck, he felt his own heart thump wildly again. She turned and looked up at him. "They were happy days, weren't they?"

The toll of a village church bell broke their silence. "We must not keep Robyn waiting any longer," Sauni said.

She fell into step with him, the stranger still walking behind them. Should she mention the man? No, Luke was surely aware of his presence. Luke was a prisoner even here on the footpath along the Rhine. There was no escape for him. *You're innocent, my darling,* she thought, *but you will be tried for treason.*

She slipped her hand into Luke's icy one and felt warmth go from her own body. He curled his fingers around hers, but he had already drifted back into his somber mood before they reached the bridge. She wanted to talk to him about God's love, but the words twisted on the tip of her tongue as she remembered how much he had hated God for taking his brother Landon. And now she had missed the opportunity to remind Luke that Jesus still loved him.

"Luke," she said quietly, "for all these years, I've wept over divorcing you when you needed me the most. I'm so sorry. Is that why you went back to Vietnam for a third tour of duty?"

"I went back to win the war."

"Win the war? We were already losing."

"I know, but before I rotated home that second time, we were in Saigon celebrating getting out of there alive. Actually I was drowning my sorrows. One of my best friends had just been killed."

He stepped aside to allow a young couple to run by. "There were fifteen of us. I didn't even know the men at the other end of the table. All I could think of was my dead buddy. What had he died for? Washington had been dragging its feet. We had the greatest military strength in the world, and we were losing to a bunch of commies with inferior weapons."

His one-inch beard hid the Breckenridge jaw line. "One of the officers at the other end of the table talked about the secret war still going on. 'We can win this conflict,' he said. 'We don't need the military.'"

Luke looked embarrassed. "I was three sheets to the wind. That's what happens when you're not used to drinking. The man boasted about a way to win by funding a secret army. I toasted his army and told him I was glad someone could win."

"Who was he, Luke?"

"I don't know. He could have been CIA, but he wasn't in civies. He had a marine uniform on. He came up to me afterward. I could barely stand, let alone see him. But the guy gave me a phone number — told me to call when I got back to Washington. They needed men like me, bent on winning in Southeast Asia."

"Why didn't you tell me? We could have talked it out."

"That was part of it — a code of silence. I was to train for nine months. But Nixon was anxious to end a lost cause in Vietnam.

If he pulled out the military, it was unlikely I could get back in."

He freed her hand. "I hated losing that war."

"Did you hate losing me?"

"More than you'll ever know. I didn't think you'd go through with the divorce. I wanted us to spend the rest of our lives together."

They were halfway across the bridge when Sauni stopped and leaned against the rail. "I can't go any farther."

"It's getting late. I should walk you back to the school."

She peered up at the afternoon sun. "Dark is a long ways away."

"Darkness is always with me," he said.

She touched his hand. "When they take you back to Washington, do you have any chance at all?"

"None. At best it would be the rest of my life in prison."

"Then don't go back to Zurich."

He glanced at the man behind them. "I can't hide from them, Sauni."

She turned as if to leave, then faced him again, tears on her cheeks. "I don't want you to give up without a fight. Now go on. Robyn will be worried. She and Pierre are your friends."

"I thought Pierre tolerated me for your sake."

She blushed. "We've been friends for a long time."

"How serious was it?"

"Does it matter?"

He sighed. "Yes."

"He was my student. I was lonely. Yes, I cared about him."

"And I'm putting you all in danger."

She nodded. The harshness of his face had softened again. As he smiled down at her, his dark eyes came alive once more. She reached up and ran her hand over the scar on his neck. "It's April. Did you know that, Luke?"

He glanced at his calendar watch. "So it is. The third of April." He reached out, his fingers barely brushing hers. "I promised you I'd come home again in April. Remember?"

"I know — in time for your birthday."

He looked as though he had forgotten about birthdays, as though life had already burned out for him. "I didn't think it would take me forever to keep my promise, Sauni."

"You're here now," she whispered.

"But I have to go away again."

The river breeze chafed her skin. "Must April always be forever?" she cried. Then, in spite of the ugly beard, she touched the dimple in his chin. "Luke, no matter what has happened I still love you."

Tears moistened his eyes. He caught her hand in his and kissed her fingertips. "Forgive me, Sauni?"

She ran from him, but she stopped long enough to blow him a kiss. Then she stumbled on as he trudged, head down, into Schaffhausen.

Drew was waiting for Luke when he reached Mueller's *zimmer frei*. "Porter Deven wants to see you," Drew said.

"One of your Langley boys?"

"Our station-chief in Paris."

"So what's he doing here?"

"He came back with Vic Wilson. Wants to make certain you know the shortest route to Washington."

Porter stood as they entered, hands behind his back, those crystal blue eyes studying Luke with contempt. "Gregory wanted us to meet before your flight to Washington."

"I wanted you to hear his story," Drew said. "Sit down, gentlemen. Let's make this meeting as easy as possible."

Drew didn't like the look on Luke's face nor the sound in his voice as he summarized his mission to Xangtiene. He seemed to be leaving large chunks unsaid as though the truth didn't matter. The visit with his wife had surely gone sour.

Porter's usual self-assured tone was missing, and his voice seemed high-pitched, his annoyance with Breckenridge apparent. "Gregory here thinks you're an innocent man. The records speak differently."

"I bet they do," Luke said. "Langley should have thought twice before they sent a casket home in my name."

"Don't blame that on Langley. You know mistakes were made; IDs of KIAs were not always accurate."

"The Dover Mortuary prides itself on accurate identification."

Porter glared at Drew's interference. Then he turned back to Luke. "Admit it, Breckenridge, you deliberately betrayed your country."

Luke seemed equally determined. He kept referring back to the helicopter on a night run and the major who wouldn't give his name. "I always figured he was a coward," Luke said pointedly.

The suggestion infuriated Porter.

"Someone from Langley betrayed me," Luke said heatedly.

"Most unlikely," Porter snapped.

In his anger Porter reached for his emery board and rubbed it vigorously across his thumbnail. For a moment Luke fixed his gaze on Porter's hands. Then slowly contempt, fury, disbelief hardened Luke's face.

Drew thought Breckenridge would lunge toward Porter like a lion attacking its prey, but a strange smile crossed Luke's face. He leaned back in his chair and listened to Deven's rantings until Heinrich Mueller appeared in the doorway.

"Overseas call for you, Deven," Heinrich said.

As Porter lumbered from the room, Drew turned to the fireplace and added two logs to the fire. He watched them crackle and pop and burst into flames. Still he kept his back to Luke.

Silence. Complete silence.

Finally, Drew turned. The room had emptied. When he stepped into the hall, he heard Porter on the phone at the other end of the *zimmer frei*. Vic Wilson stood there grinning.

"It worked," he said. "Luke's en route to Geneva. Your daughter's buying you a little more time."

"She's buying me a lot of trouble."

Chapter 25

When Robyn Courtland answered the apartment intercom, a commanding voice on the other end said brusquely, "Admiral Breckenridge here. Trust we aren't too early."

She gasped and then mumbled, "I'll be right down."

Pierre frowned. "Must you run downstairs to open the door?"

"Oh, Pierre, I promised Sauni we'd show Luke's parents around Geneva. In the excitement, I forgot all about them."

She nodded desperately toward the smaller bedroom. "Luke's asleep in there. We can't let them see him."

"He's their son, Robyn. Now go on. Our guests are waiting."

She felt calmer as she climbed back up the stairs with Luke's parents. The austere man behind her frightened Robyn, but she felt warmth toward Luke's mother. Pierre welcomed them with a hearty handclasp for the admiral and a light kiss on the cheek for Amy Breckenridge. As he beckoned them toward chairs, the bedroom door swung open and

Luke appeared, his hair sleep-tangled, his mouth gaping as he saw his parents.

Before Luke could reach his mother, she collapsed on the floor. He leaped across the hassock, cradled her in his arms, and carried her to the divan. When Amy awakened, Luke was kneeling beside her, his dark, desolate eyes brimming with tears.

"Luke! Luke! Luke!" she agonized. "Where have you been?" As she studied his face, she cried out again, "It's really you."

"Yes, Mom. I'm so sorry."

"You — you've changed." Amy's fingers rested on Luke's cheek. "I never liked you with a beard, son."

"Isn't that why you gave me a new razor every Christmas?"

"She should have given you stamps." The admiral's color drained as he mopped his face with a folded handkerchief and allowed Pierre to ease him into a chair. "How could you do this to us, Luke?" His voice slipped to a hollow moan. "We thought you were dead. Why? Why?"

"Dad, I —"

"There's no excuse for a Breckenridge to hide for twenty years. How could you betray us like this?"

Amy traced the scar on Luke's neck, then cupped his cheeks. She shook her head sadly as though she would awaken and find him gone. "You've been dead for so long," she said, confused, bewildered.

"Why didn't you bury me by Landon?" he asked hoarsely.

"Dad wanted you at Arlington."

"The government wanted him there," Luther said.

"It doesn't matter now. You're safe." She looked as though she would faint again. Her hands trembled. Luke clasped them.

"I'm so sorry, Mom," he repeated.

"For betraying your country?" the admiral cried. "You didn't do that, did you, son? You didn't do that to us."

"And ruin the Breckenridge tradition?" Luke asked.

"Please," Amy begged, "don't hurt each other."

"Why? I was always there for you, son. No matter what."

"Really, Dad? Then how come you missed all those father-son banquets and my high school graduation?"

"And you missed my promotion to rear admiral. We were a military family, Luke. Remember?"

"How well I know."

"I thought you understood."

"I didn't. Neither did Landon. But what

does it matter now?"

The admiral searched the cold, hard eyes of his son, his own tearing as he studied Luke. "Dear God," he cried out as he tried to regain his composure. "What's happened to you?"

Luke met the rebuttal with silence.

He's built up a barrier, Robyn thought, *withdrawing into his shell like a loggerhead turtle. Only Sauni had cracked that shell and caught a glimpse of the tenderhearted Luke that he had once been. If only his father could do the same.* "Don't push your son away," she said softly. "You need each other more than ever now."

"You never thought about coming home?" his father asked.

"All the time. My captors showed me pictures of the POWs being released from the Hanoi Hilton not long after I was captured. Lisha — she was in charge — told me, 'See, Captain Breckenridge, your country has left you behind.' "

Amy touched his scarred neck again. "Oh, my poor boy."

"Later they told me my wife had remarried and that I was wanted for treason. But I really gave up when they said my parents had denied me publicly." A sneer lifted the corners of Luke's mouth. "Go home after that — when no one wanted me?"

The admiral stiffened. "Your family wanted you."

"So did the CIA, Dad."

"That doesn't make sense, Luke."

"It does if you want to eliminate a dead man."

"I wish you would stop referring to yourself as dead."

"What else? Everyone I ever knew thinks of me that way, and most of them call me a traitor."

"Stop it," Robyn said. "All of you. Someone still wants Luke dead. If we didn't believe he was innocent, we wouldn't be hiding him."

"Only cowards hide," the admiral said sadly.

"You've got it wrong," Pierre defended. "But he's in danger if he stays here. There's a mansion in Germany. He'll be safe there."

The admiral clutched his chest, his breaths coming in tight little gasps. Luke reached out and placed his hand on his father's knee. "Dad, someone betrayed me. You've got to believe me."

The admiral nodded. "We tried so hard to clear your name, son, but the doors in Washington slammed in our faces. In the end all we had were our memories of you."

His voice cracked as he whispered, "Son, I've relived our trip to the Cape May Lighthouse a thousand times in the last twenty years."

"Me, too, Dad. Me, too."

Robyn left the room, popped some broth in the microwave, and brought it back. She handed a cup to the admiral, the second one to Luke. "This is for Amy, Luke. Do you want me —"

He brushed her aside, but there was tenderness in the way he offered his mother sips of bouillon. Tears kept washing his face, running jagged streams through his beard. "I called you once, Mom. And I went to your hospital room —"

"Then I didn't dream it," she whispered.

"No. I was there, but I couldn't stay. The nurse said another shock would kill you. Mom, I never meant to hurt you. But Pierre is right. I can't stay here. It won't be safe for you — knowing I'm alive."

"I refuse to let you go again."

"You must, Mrs. Breckenridge," Pierre said. "Once we get Luke settled, we'll arrange something. But right now we can't risk British and American Intelligence converging on our apartment."

Pierre walked to the window and peered through the curtain. "Our watchdog is still on duty. He's looking for Luke, but we'll leave by the back entry as soon as it gets dark."

Again Amy looked faint. "Will we ever see you again, son?"

"We don't have twenty more years to wait." The admiral's voice broke. He hid his face in his freckled hands and wept.

Luke rose slowly and went to him. "I'm accused of treason, Dad. I didn't want to shame you by coming back."

"But you said —"

"That I'm innocent? I am. But I may never be able to prove it — unless the man who betrayed me confesses." He pulled his dad from the chair and hugged him. "I wanted to come home, but I couldn't face all those lies about me. Dad, for years I kept hoping that my country would find me. They never even tried."

Pierre took Robyn's hand. "Honey, get our coats. Please." To the others, he said, "We'll be gone for an hour or two. It's all the time we dare give you."

"I'll be ready when you get back," Luke promised.

He glanced at his parents. "Come on, you two," he said gently. "We've got at least one glorious hour. Let's make it one we'll never forget."

★ ★ ★

At the mansion the following day, Luke wandered through its rooms marveling at the aristocratic surroundings. He came at last to the living room where Felix von Tonner sat alone in his wheelchair. "Good morning, Baron," he said.

The old man merely nodded toward the paintings on the wall.

For several minutes Luke studied the portraits of Felix and his wife. The senile old man in the wheelchair seemed a far cry from the strong face that stared down at Luke. The lovely baroness was dead. Luke knew little else about her.

He tried to imagine his own portrait hanging there with Sauni's beside it. The contrast would be unbearable. His face chiseled in stone these days, hers like a fragile china doll. His gruffness, Sauni's gentleness. His empty eyes, his wife's trusting ones. Luke's militant stance — her gracefulness. They had once made a handsome couple. But not now.

The man in the portrait looked down on him; the fragile old man in the wheelchair looked up, his watery blue eyes hazy. Impulsively, Luke gripped the baron's shoulder. *The admiral will grow old like this someday,* he thought. *And I won't be around to help him.* He tried to imagine his father accepting help, tried to picture him frail and confined like the baron. Overcome, he patted Felix's hand, then turned abruptly, and made his way out the double doors to the magnificent view of the Rhine and the German country-side.

In the stables he leaned against Monarch's stall. He felt drawn to the chestnut stallion with its shiny coat and muscular shoulders. The animal neighed at Luke's intrusion, its nostrils flaring. The baron and this horse would be the only reasons Luke would stay on at the mansion. The old man needed him; Luke needed the horse.

Luke moved on to the empty foaling stall and flung back the opening to the tunnels. Yesterday he had toured them with Pierre. Now he'd go back and find a safe spot where he could toss his sleeping bag and remain isolated.

The Courtlands found him there twenty minutes later.

"We've been worried about you," Robyn told him.

"Were you afraid I had escaped?"

"Not really. Albert keeps the electronic gates locked."

Pierre said coldly, "I've told Albert you're free to walk out whenever you want. This is not the jungles of Laos." His irritation abated. "You can fight us all you want, Luke, but my wife and I are convinced we're ministering to a weary pilgrim — somebody who lost his way for a little while."

"The prodigal son bit? You sound like my mother."

"There's a bit of the prodigal in each of us, Luke."

"Then I'd be doing you a favor if I turned myself in."

"For what?" Pierre asked. "Betraying your country in Vietnam? Or for being a mercenary? Like Drew says, what offense have you committed against international law? In my country it is against the law to hire out as a foreign soldier. But in your country — or this country — what precise offense could we charge you with?"

Luke rubbed his beard, his eyes on Robyn now. "So what do I do? Spend the rest of my life hiding out on the Rhine."

"You could help here at the museum," she answered grinning. "Or help take care of the baron. You seem to get on with him. We could bring Sauni here from time to time to see you."

He lunged at her with words. "Don't do that, Mrs. Courtland. How long do you think I could bear seeing Sauni and not want to hold her and love her?"

Robyn flushed, but she met his attack, saying gently, "Sauni's still in love with you, too." She rested her head against Pierre's shoulder. "Luke, nothing will happen to you. Albert and Hedwig will see to it. Besides, the Klees have decided to introduce you as Felix's new caretaker. Come along, we'll show you the baron's art treasures."

Pierre led the way farther down the damp, dimly-lit corridor into the vault where most of the art collection was stored. "If Robyn has her way, all of these paintings will have to be carried upstairs and displayed on the walls of the ballroom and the top two floors. She really plans to make a museum out of this old place."

Robyn shook her head as she forced the lid from a steel drum. "The museum is Pierre's dream, too. We still have to catalogue these paintings. Good job for a new caretaker."

"I could do that," Luke agreed.

Pierre helped Robyn lift out the first two Rembrandts. Then she tugged cautiously at the red cloth surrounding the third painting. She freed it at last and gasped as it unfurled.

All three of them stared at the flag with its ugly black swastika in the center. Pierre choked out, "It can't be."

Robyn gripped his hand. "What is it? I

mean, what does it mean? Oh, Pierre, the flag of the Third Reich — not the baron?"

Pierre kicked the flag toward the wall and looked helplessly at her. Quietly from the doorway, Albert Klee said, "It means nothing." He picked up the torn flag and folded it. His red-rimmed eyes stayed steadily on Pierre. "Should I burn this, sir?"

"It should have been burned long ago."

"Yes, it would have been if I had remembered. But don't come to false conclusions, boy. It doesn't belong to the baron."

"Then why is it here?" Pierre demanded.

"We flew it over the mansion for several months during the war."

"Fancy that," Breckenridge said. "A merc camp right here on the von Tonner property. Did the Germans build these tunnels?"

"No," Albert said fiercely. "They were built long before that. The baron and I played in them as boys — as you did, Pierre, when you were young."

"But the flag?" Robyn insisted.

"It belonged to one of the Storm Troopers, Hitler's elite."

"One of Hitler's dogs?" Pierre snapped.

"It was wartime, boy. The military was confiscating castles and old mansions to billet the men. I was second in command of a small group, so I suggested taking over the von Tonner mansion for a headquarters. I thought the baron might protect us — protect me."

Luke chortled. "That puts us on the same level, Herr Klee."

Albert's deep facial grooves ridged with worry. "I was in on the attempt to kill Hitler. A minor role, but when it failed, I knew I'd be discovered in time. I'd been assigned to an engineering unit — masterminding the destruction of enemy bridges and the fortification of German buildings so we could hold out longer."

Pierre slipped his arm around Robyn. "The baron detested Hitler and all he stood for. But he would have died to preserve the von Tonner art collection. I expected the baron to expose me. Instead, he allowed us to set up quarters on the first two floors; he retired to the third floor with only his young housekeeper Hedwig to serve him. As soon as we moved in, I realized the paintings were gone, the walls bare."

A smile swept over his wrinkled face. "Felix said Goering or Bormann had stolen them. But Felix was too clever for that. He always had been." Klee clutched the flag against him. "Only the baron and I knew about the tunnels. There was only one entry back then — through the parish wine cellar.

I guessed what Felix had done; he had hidden the paintings right under the noses of the soldiers he despised — even as he despised me at that moment."

Robyn said softly, "Albert, the war's been over for fifty years. Don't torture yourself so."

He shook his head. "Let me settle it for Pierre now. I went to Felix and confronted him with the truth, even threatened him. In the end I begged him to hide me in exchange for my silence. I wouldn't reveal the whereabouts of that vast fortune in paintings in exchange for a hideout in the tunnels. So we faked my death."

"Yes," Luke said, "we have a lot in common, Albert, but don't expect the Courtlands to believe all of this."

"You're wrong, Herr Breckenridge. Pierre has trusted me all his life. I have no reason to lie to him now. Hedwig and I are old, but we want to stay on and care for the baron."

Robyn asked, "Your name is not really Klee, is it?"

"I'm a distant relative of Goering's wife. My real name no longer matters. Felix gave me a new name. I gave him my allegiance."

He turned to Luke. "It never pays to give away your loyalty to serve another flag. Can you agree with that?"

"Then burn the flag," Luke said. "Get rid of it."

Albert wiped his eyes with the back of his hand. "When the war ended, Felix left the art collection hidden. He was embarrassed because his neighbors had lost everything, but I persuaded him to bring a few paintings back into the mansion. Hedwig and I stayed on; after all, I owed Felix my life. I'd deserted the military. If they discovered me, there would have been no mercy."

Luke said scathingly, "Did you show mercy as a Nazi?"

Albert's shrewd gaze settled on Luke. "No more than you have, Brigadier, with your mercenary soldiers."

Luke glared at Pierre and Robyn. "I won't stay here with him."

"Where else will you go?" the old man asked. "I understand you. I was forced to hide once myself — to deny my identity."

"You're all fools," Luke said bitterly. "Why try to salvage me?"

"For reasons beyond your comprehension," Pierre told him.

Robyn touched his wrist. "For Sauni, for one."

"It's too late — too many years lost. I've changed. So has Sauni. She's different now — talking about God and prayer like my mom does. No, let me disappear from her life again. That's best."

"Wrong, Herr Breckenridge," Albert said, his beady gaze meeting Luke's. "That's the easy way out. You're safe here as I once was. You'll have a solid roof over your head — like I did. And Hedwig's good cooking." He offered his roguish grin. "And I'll expect your strong arm with the baron."

"Luke, if you leave here," Pierre warned, "expect a bloody battle. Porter wants you dead. Or if Salvador and Tiger get to you first, they'll kill you on sight. You've wrecked their whole operation."

"What about me, Pierre? My life was wrecked in Laos."

"My brother's life was cut short in the same war."

Stunned, Luke's attitude softened. "I didn't know."

"There's something else you don't know. Your parents agreed to cut their holiday short and fly back to New Jersey — to throw off suspicion. We've promised that if something happens, we'll call them immediately. They'd fly back."

"Were they okay, Pierre?"

"They're strong. They plan to take flowers to your grave in Arlington. Your dad thought that would be a nice little decoy, but your mom's going because somebody's son may be buried there."

Luke went silent for several minutes. He ran one hand over his whiskered jaw, defensive again. "Robyn, does Sauni know I'm here?"

"Not yet. She can't confess what she doesn't know."

"But Sauni has a marvelous imagination."

"I know. She's called the Klees twice already to ask about you. I'll invite her to come back with me this weekend, so if you're staying on, you'll need shaving gear and clean clothes to make a good impression."

They were almost through the tunnel. "Use my clothes," Pierre offered. "If they don't fit, Albert will send the stable boy shopping. He's Hedwig's nephew. He'll keep a buttoned lip."

"I'll stay for a while, but I'll need something to read."

"Looking for any book in particular?"

"Something on David and the giants he slew."

"The psalmist?" Pierre asked in surprise.

"Yes, I guess that's what they called him. But I'm more impressed with his military skills and campaigns."

Pierre grinned. "I've got just the Book for you."

They made their way up the steps to the foaling stall in silence. As Pierre closed off the entry and covered it with sawdust, they heard the stallion whinnying.

"Monarch doesn't take to new riders," Robyn warned Luke.

"But I like a challenge."

Albert chuckled. "They just might be good for each other."

Chapter 26

Harv Neilson brushed past the secretary and barged into Glenn Summers's office unannounced. Quick strides took him to the desk before the senator could scramble to his feet. He slapped the morning paper on the desk and pointed to Tracy Mathison's column: CIA SCANDAL UNCOVERED. "Glenn, why did you leak this information to the press?"

"Who said I did? That's just scuttlebutt."

"The President doesn't think so." He dropped into the chair and sifted his fingers through his hair. "Couldn't your intelligence committee have given me a few more days?"

"Why should we?" Glenn yanked off his glasses and wiped them with a monogrammed handkerchief. His nearsighted eyes remained fixed on Neilson. "I don't like depending on the *Washington Post* — or any other news media — for my reports. Now I have to depend on the evening news to discover the agent's name in bold print."

"You won't like that, Glenn."

"You're right. I don't even like it now."

"I have seventy-two hours to clear up this mess. If I don't, the President wants my resignation." His voice cracked. "Washington is my life. If I go down, Senator, I'm taking you with me."

Glenn's glasses were on, his gaze more transparent. "Don't threaten me. You've had months to uncover the mole in your Agency, perhaps longer. So is Drew Gregory the man who sold us out or not?"

"It's Porter Deven, our station-chief in Paris — a man with a long successful career. But we've got to keep it under wraps. There's too much at stake in the European Division, too many operations that could be compromised." He sifted hair strands again. "We've got everything but Deven's confession and, unless we stop Gregory, we'll have that too. He insists the records speak for themselves — the dates secrets were passed, Porter's availability."

"Deven. Porter Deven," was all Summers could say.

"Don't worry, Senator. We'll remove him from his position and send an immediate replacement. I have an appointment today with Tracy Mathison. I'll give him a different name for his column."

"To save your face? You're a fool. Mathison is thorough in his investigations. He won't be deceived by the wrong name. And I've been in office too many years to betray my voters now."

Harv laughed in spite of himself. "A man of integrity, eh? Well, we have another option. I'm prepared to turn over the name Breckenridge to Mathison with convincing statistics to go with it."

Glenn's knuckles blanched as he gripped the desk. "Leave my son-in-law's name out of this. Working with you against Luke has ruined my relationship with my daughter. I won't hurt her any more."

"Not even for votes?" Neilson leaned forward and dropped a file on the desk. "That's current information on your son-in-law," he said. "According to the latest intelligence reports, Luke is still very much alive."

The blanching reached Summers's cheeks as he thumbed through the report. "You've known this all along? For twenty years?"

"Haven't you? We tracked him out of Laos ten years ago. We lost him after that, with only periodic sightings. Now he runs a mercenary camp that trains hit-and-run death squads. Tracy Mathison can meat-grind that one for the evening press."

Glenn slumped into his chair. "This will kill my daughter."

"And ruin your career, Senator?"

"My wife doesn't want me to run again."

"Even your daughter wants what's best for you and this country."

"You'll never convince Sauni that Luke was a traitor."

Neilson smiled. "I'll get proof soon enough. I'm sending a search team to Laos. I'll ask David Shipley to accompany them to Xangtiene. They're not to come out until they have proof that Luke Breckenridge lived with the Hmong as an enemy agent. Do you want me to send one of your intelligence committee with my delegation?"

"Yes, Charles Canfield . . . did Porter know my son-in-law?"

"He betrayed him according to Gregory, but it's best to expose Breckenridge and avoid another long investigation. We'll just have to sweep Porter's treachery into the locked files."

"My daughter — will you sweep her away, too?"

"You should have thought of her a long time ago, Glenn. She's seen Luke — and hidden him. We're going to smoke him out — at the sacrifice of your daughter if necessary. And we're going to send him back to some merc camp to die in one of his foreign wars."

"And the real double agent goes scot free?"

"We'll retire Gregory and close the files on Porter Deven. Perhaps we'll exile Porter to some island with no means of escape. We might even send that old basset hound with him. And a revolver. If Porter gets depressed enough —"

"But my son-in-law may be innocent after all."

"Yes, but don't try to stop me, Glenn. If you do, we'll involve your daughter in the conspiracy. And the admiral and his wife — let's spare them any more grief."

"How? With Luke's name in bold print in the evening news?"

"Thanks to Vic Wilson we have some photographs of the ruckus that went on in the merc camp. A couple of men have died. As far as the media is concerned, Luke will be listed as one of them."

"But Saundra —"

"Chad Kaminsky left last evening for Europe. He'll arrange a dinner with your daughter. Then he and Gregory will confront Porter and ask for a written confession — for our files, of course."

Neilson took the Breckenridge report out of Summers's hands and locked it in his briefcase. "I don't intend to lose my job at Langley, and I rather think you like it here in Washington. Your daughter will get over this. She'll come around — she'll cooperate."

"And Luke?"

"According to Gregory, Luke will do what's best for Saundra. And Langley must keep Deven's betrayal internal. Deven has been drinking heavily lately, making poor judgments. In the morning briefing, I'll announce the need for his replacement."

"You'd deceive the President?"

"I must do what's best for the intelligence community. The White House will have your son-in-law's name as our mole. Deven goes off the Soviet payroll. The passing of top secrets comes to an immediate stop." He sighed. "The man has caused untold damage."

"And Luke will be further scandalized to save your face?"

"To save my job and yours. We have a reputation to maintain, Senator. We can't risk more disfavor with the American people, or the world for that matter. I want what's best for this country."

"You're sick."

"I'm thinking quite clearly. By the way, Senator, Duc Thuy Tran, Luke's old friend, keeps trying to get in touch with Gregory. I've asked that Tran's back income tax records be checked. A tactical delay to keep his interest off the Breckenridge affair."

He offered his hand and for a moment thought Summers would spit on it. "Let's just keep this meeting between ourselves, Glenn."

"I'm going to fly to Zurich to be with my daughter."

"Don't. Luke's parents may still be visiting her."

"I should be," he said sadly. "My wife warned me."

"Your voters always took first place, didn't they?"

Neilson felt much more confident as he left the room. As he passed Glenn's secretary, she glared at him, her feathers still ruffled. "Good day," he said pleasantly.

And the day was improving for him as the plans took shape in his mind. Yes, he did want what was best for the country. *And myself*, he had to admit. But didn't the two merge as one?

Glowering, David Shipley disengaged from the long distance phone call with Langley. As he unraveled the tangled cord, Rockboat barreled barefooted across the room and tumbled into his father's arms. David's agitation gave way to a smile. He tossed the boy in the air, holding him at arm's length.

"Mo'e. Mo'e," the boy cried.

David caught him once more before throwing the child over his shoulder and slapping the well-padded bottom affectionately. Exhausted by the phone call — comforted by the child — David slid to the floor and rolled on his back, the boy still in his arms.

"David. DAVID!" Namlee stood in the doorway looking terribly, terribly pregnant, her swollen feet squeezed into open sandals. In slow motion she rested her hands on her bulging belly and leaned against the door casing. He sat up, legs outstretched toward her and smiled. Rockboat balanced contentedly in his lap.

"Did we wake you, Namlee?"

"Not really. You know I'm not resting well these days."

"Sorry, honey. Come sit with us."

She smiled at that. "I'd never get up again."

"Are you okay?"

"You look at me and ask that?" She shook her head. "I'll be all right. Your phone conversation woke me."

"I should have taken the call in the other room."

"And risk me answering it? Was it Mr. Gregory?"

After fifteen years her directness still surprised him. "It was Harv Neilson this time. From Langley. He wants me in Geneva, but he asked me to take a small delegation to Xangtiene first."

Again her eyes smiled back. "The village that doesn't exist?"

Not your concern, dear Namlee. "I volunteered to go. We'll have Laotian officials with us. I'll be safe there."

"And then you're off to Geneva — before the baby comes?"

"I'm sorry." He went mute, as he often did these days when he thought about Xangtiene and Breckenridge. Neilson had given it to him straight: "Shipley, we want you in Geneva with a full report on Breckenridge's life in the village. This Breckenridge affair will be headlines again if we don't close this case."

Gregory had expressed the same concern a week ago. Searching for the remains of missing men depressed David more each day, but to go and find proof of a man's betrayal overwhelmed him. Slowly, he met Namlee's worried gaze.

Her sigh crossed the room to him. "Don't get involved, David."

He blew her a kiss. Namlee was one of the good happenings that had come out of the

Vietnam conflict. Her father had been an American flier on R&R in Bangkok, her mother pure Thai. Namlee had her mother's rich complexion, the same black silky hair, the graceful mannerisms — except for this clumsy period with their unborn child.

She accepted his silence as she often did when it concerned his work. "Did you see the toys?" she asked.

"I trip over them all the time."

"No, no. The *new* ones." She pointed toward his rattan chair where a wastebasket overflowed with wrappings. With Rockboat riding his legs, David scooted across the room on his buttocks. He tore at the parcel paper and found Admiral Breckenridge's name in the corner — with a Busingen address and Swiss stamps.

"They're spoiling the children," she said softly.

"It looks that way."

"Twuck," Rockboat said. "Fi'e twuck."

Namlee sighed. "It's already in need of repair. It took him all of five minutes to separate the ladder from the fire engine." She didn't wait for David's question. "Davey's in his room — with all the parts of a ship model spread out. He wants your help. And Maylene is sulking in her room disappointed with another doll. She wants to know why they didn't send her a Swiss chalet."

"I'll call the Breckenridges. Tell them no more presents."

"No, David. They would be hurt. But our children can't take the place of their sons."

"I know." She was standing beside him now. He touched her swollen ankle. "It won't be much longer, Namlee."

"Then don't go away until after the baby comes. I saw your boots and backpack under the bed. You've been planning this trip ever since you talked to Mr. Gregory a week ago."

He pushed himself up and faced her, wondering how she had bent low enough to see them. "I'll be in Laos three or four days."

He swooped Rockboat back into the air, then nose-dived him headfirst for a crash landing. In his mind's eye, David pictured the American aircraft nose down in Xangtiene. Barely an inch from the floor, he sent his giggling son airborne again.

"Enough," David said as he set Samuel down.

"David, why can't you send someone else?"

"It's my job." His fear of something happening to Namlee or the children on the back streets of Bangkok reared its ugly head. Going back to Xangtiene threatened the reputation of the admiral's son, maybe threatened his own safety. He wanted to warn Namlee about the photographs hidden in his aunt's safe deposit box in Schaffhausen — especially the ones he had bought from the Hmong. Those very pictures might betray Luke Breckenridge.

He pulled Namlee to him and rested her head against his chest. "Honey, maybe I'll find your father's remains this time. Maybe that's why he never came back for your mother."

"In Xangtiene?" She touched the cleft in his chin. "My father is only a name, David: Lt. Derry Conan from Idaho. He just wanted Mother to spend his leave with him. Not a permanent commitment."

"I wish he knew about you — knew how lovely you are."

"How much longer, David? You know, I'm worried about Davey. What happened to all our dreams of living in your country?"

"Our country," he corrected. He shared Namlee's worry. At fourteen Davey showed a growing interest in the Buddhist temples where his friends worshiped. "We'll go as soon as my replacement comes."

It seemed the wrong moment to mention that he had been asked to stay on in Bangkok for another year. "I was thinking about us vacationing in Paris — in Europe."

"With four children? I wouldn't like that."

"But it's springtime there — and Anna-belle wants us to come."

Namlee gave him a wistful smile. "If you go to Geneva, you will miss the baby's birth and midnight feedings."

"I want you to go with me. The Company is paying my way — air fare, hotel, everything." As he held Namlee, he felt the baby kick — a reminder that what he was suggesting was indeed insane. "My aunt said she'll pay Davey's fare if we can scrape the rest together. We can visit her and go to her church retreat again."

Namlee's laughter muffled against his shirt. "We didn't have children then, and you were stationed in Germany, not Bangkok."

"I could finish up in Geneva in time for the spring retreat."

"*Lauterbrunnen!* You're crazy, David. We can't afford that."

"But you loved the Alps and the water-falls."

"Yes," she whispered. "But what I really loved was falling asleep in your arms. But four children — ," she protested.

"I'd arrange for a larger chalet." He ran his thumb gently over her lower lip. "We'll work it out."

Lauterbrunnen. A five-day honeymoon in

the snow-covered Alps — just the two of them in a tiny chalet that his aunt had rented. The retreat had changed their lives and given their marriage a godly foundation. If something happened to David, Namlee would never get back to Lauterbrunnen, and the kids would never see how easy it was to touch God at a mountaintop.

"What's wrong, David?" she asked, pushing away from him.

He studied the worry line wedged between her penciled brows. "I'll talk to Annabelle again. We'll work it out so you can meet me in Geneva as soon as the baby is born."

As the plane lifted and circled Bangkok, David still bristled over the last-minute rush to get papers and clearance for Senator Canfield. Canfield had arrived as part of the U. S. delegation, but his close association with Neilson and Summers annoyed David.

David peered down at the city, lit now by the glints of dawn reflecting off the golden spires of Buddhist temples. Within the hour traffic would gridlock while monks in saffron-yellow robes serviced the temple and women in blue smocks and straw hats floated their long, slender boats up and down the murky canal selling vegetables and silver fish. And finally — reluctantly — even Namlee and the children would awaken.

The pilot turned north, flying above the forested peaks. Crossing the border between the two countries, he followed the Mekong River to Luang Prabang, the old royal capital of Laos. A three-man Laotian delegation met them as they deplaned. Tao Thongsouk, the squattiest of the men, gripped David's hand. Tao surveyed the others, accepted introductions, and then turned back to Shipley. "It's so long since you came."

Once they began the ascent up the rugged mountain, David set a fast clip through a rain forest filled with broadleaf evergreens. The hot sun beat down on them, adding to their misery, but he pushed on, challenging Canfield to keep up. Five hours after leaving the city, they reached the downed American aircraft.

Canfield grabbed his camera and rapidly used up a roll of film. Wiping his brow with the back of his hand, he scowled at Shipley. "Why here? Was the pilot off course?"

"Maybe," Shipley acknowledged. "He might have strayed this far after one of the bombing raids over the Ho Chi Minh Trail."

"You've been here before. Why didn't you have the plane buried?"

"Couldn't, Senator. It's a cultural thing.

Two Hmong boys died here when the plane crashed. To bury this aircraft would displease the spirits of those children."

Canfield stared hard at Shipley. "That's utter nonsense."

"Not to the Hmong."

The senator slid down on his back and wedged himself beneath the broken wing. "No spirits here," he said mockingly. Again he aimed his camera as David crawled down beside him.

"It's a rusty mess. Why the picture, Senator?"

"There's a name scratched beneath the wing: LANDON. Guess it's a message from the pilot. LANDON — odd name."

Landon Breckenridge. David stiffened. Why had Breckenridge scrawled his brother's name in this Godforsaken place? In those last hours of his life, had Luke wanted his brother's forgiveness — or was he confessing his betrayal to his best friend? David stood and brushed the blades of grass from his hands. Whatever Luke had become, David did not want to stir the ashes. He fingered the rusty wing of the plane, touching it as he would a headstone — a memorial to pilots and children and two brothers from New Jersey.

"Come on, Senator," he said gruffly. "We

473

haven't got all day."

Canfield turned to Thongsouk. "We'll want a joint U. S.-Laotian excavation of this site. And soon."

Politely, Thongsouk said, "We returned the remains of your men."

"I know. I know. It's the third man we want. And we want this plane buried out of respect for those pilots."

David adjusted his backpack. "There were two pilots, Senator."

"I'm aware of that, but there were *three* Americans."

When they reached the eight-thousand-foot elevation, a deer crashed through the thicket, four Hmong right behind it. All of them wore pajamalike pants and shirts, the woman more distinctive with her tufted headdress and silver-bangled necklace.

She shook her fist at David. "You flew the airplanes?"

David mimicked the tonal sounds of the language. "No. Others flew the planes." Turning to the men with him, he said, "Strangers aren't welcome here. This woman remembers the bombings that almost destroyed these hillsides."

She gave David a puzzled glance before recognizing him. Then a smile deepened her wrinkles. She led them the rest of the way to the wood-hewn houses nestled under a canopy of trees. Chickens cut across their path as they walked toward a lean man with thick black hair; he was wearing a bright pink shirt, unlike the rest of the villagers.

"Who's that?" Canfield asked.

"Neng Pao, the head of the clan. At fifty-three he's the oldest man in the village; that makes him chief."

The chief who once wore Luke Breckenridge's wedding band, David thought.

Before David could stop him, Canfield started clicking the shutter, taking photos of everyone. The women and children shied away from the camera and ran into their homes. "Stop what you're doing, Canfield," David warned. "You're frightening the people."

"What's wrong? Am I infringing on their religious life?"

A quirk of a smile played at the corners of Neng's mouth. He thrust the camera away from his face and led them into his house. Neng paraded them past cooking pots and the family altar and invited them to sit on the floor mats at the far end of the room. As the meal was served, Canfield refused to eat the rice and boiled vegetables until David said, "Have the courtesy to eat, Senator."

"And risk dysentery?"

"Yes, rather than insult these people. Be careful how you treat Neng Pao if you want their cooperation."

"Is he that important?"

"His word is final. Neng was one of the Hmong recruited by the CIA to fight against the North Vietnamese. When the Americans pulled out, Neng spent three years in a re-education camp. It was a costly war for him, so whatever you came here to find out, he's the one to ask. I'll interpret for you."

"Then ask him where the other American is buried."

Neng listened to David's question respectfully and answered it. Then David turned to Canfield and said, "He speaks of several people — skin like ours. Uniforms —"

"Prisoners?" Canfield asked.

"No. Neng says they controlled the village for a while."

"Does he mean Breckenridge?"

David repeated Neng's words. "A woman expected the American."

The questions shot back and forth — accusations, denials — David interpreting, Neng Pao growing more mute in response to the senator's arrogance. Finally Neng shook his head. "I was not here when the Communists first took over the village."

"The Pathet Lao? The North Vietnamese?"

He pointed to David's skin. "People like you from far away."

"But the American?" Canfield persisted. "Where is he buried?"

"We have no remains," Pao said finally. "Just the pilots."

But what about Breckenridge? David wondered. On his last visit, Neng Pao had spoken warmly of the other American, *the tall one* — they had been prisoners together, friends, Neng had said. As Neng stood to dismiss them, Canfield turned to Thongsouk. "The plane must be totally demolished, Mr. Thongsouk."

David slept fitfully that night on a thin floor mat. Across from him Canfield snored loudly from a hammock, his camera bag hanging on a peg above him. In the moonlit darkness that came before dawn, Neng's son stole quietly up to Canfield.

Before David could call a warning, Vang lifted the camera case from its place and slashed it with a knife. Deftly, he opened the camera and exposed the film. The tip of his knife brushed David's bare toe as Vang slipped away as quietly as he had come.

In the morning David arose with the animals — his body stiff from the uncomfortable mat. Outside, Neng shaped a silver bowl with his hands. As he smoothed the outer rim, he looked toward the mountaintop. "Tell Mr. Canfield that he will not find us here when he returns. We must lead the spirits of the boys away."

David allowed his gaze to rise toward the forest-lined hilltop. Would Neng ever be freed from the spirit world? Would he ever find the one true God? David tried to form a cross with his hands, but Neng interrupted. "You are different, my friend. Like the tall one. Will you ever come back to see us again?"

David thought of Namlee and the children — of their plans to settle out west. "My family and I will be moving soon," he said.

Neng held up the bowl for inspection. "You did not tell your senator everything I said about Captain Breckenridge?"

"Not everything."

"It is best," Neng said. "We are both protecting him."

Chapter 27

Drew and Vic sat in an embassy office in Paris writing their reports on Spain in triplicate. The facts looked as hopeless as Drew felt. The *Monique II* now drifted lazily in the Monaco harbor with no evidence of a captain named Salvador. Colin Burdock was still following up on that one at the Monte Carlo and coming up empty. Yes, guests at the casino knew Salvador. He did pleasure cruises for high-paying guests. Ill health had taken him back to his home in Milan. Yes, quite recently. The rundown on Tiger the Moroccan had hit another snag. In fact, it had slammed against a brick wall. Tiger had his fingerprints on file at Interpol and mug shots that barely looked like him. But no one had talked. "Terrorists have a way of getting even," they said.

"What about Italian Intelligence?" Vic asked.

"Negative. Same with the Moroccans. No one admits seeing them."

"They'll be back in business soon enough. It's a shame Luke can't give us a lead on those who funded the camps. Salvador and Tiger always handled that end of it."

Drew ran his pen lightly over the report. Several people at the casino and four businessmen in Madrid remembered the brigadier. Some placed him at fifty, others more accurately at mid-to-late forties. He was described as both terrifying and harmless, bitter and kind, handsome and nondescript. But an American? No, the man didn't claim any nationality. Oh, yes, they all recalled an ugly scar down his neck. The caretaker at the castle defended him militantly; the village girl who had loved him, with tears in her eyes.

"Vic, I wish we could keep Luke's full name off the report."

"Why bother? Porter knew it before we hit the merc camp."

"But did Langley?"

"What do you think?"

"I guess you're right, Vic. With Laos and the merc camp against him, neither record shows him as a man worth remembering."

"At least Burdock smoothed it over for Monique Smith."

Drew smiled wryly. "She put up a fuss when Spain took over the castle temporarily, but her yacht is still bobbing safely in the harbor. Spain didn't have jurisdiction to take over the boat, and the Prince of Monaco isn't available for questioning."

"Monique is too busy for yachting anyway. She's at the clinic with her boys, refusing to talk about her friendship with Salvador."

"Smart lady," Drew said. "She knows what a scoundrel he is."

"So was her husband." Vic tossed his part of the report across the desk. "All of this is a waste of time. How far do you think these papers will go? They'll need Porter's approval."

Drew felt as weary as Vic looked. "I'll pass them on to Kaminsky. He can take them back to Washington for us."

"Will he?"

Drew capped the pen. "Highly unlikely."

"Has Kaminsky seen Porter?"

"No, Porter's not taking calls. I reached his brother Zach, but they're out of touch, too."

"We have no proof without Porter's confession —"

"Vic, he knows that we know. How long can he live with that?"

Vic sneered. "He's lived with it since the Vietnam War."

"Kaminsky is getting pressure from Washington to let Luke go. You know what that means? We're to send him back to his war games so he can get killed."

"Breckenridge never had a chance, did he?"

"He won't unless Porter admits the truth."

"You're on shaky ground. You can't hang Porter for treason just because he files his fingernails."

Drew saw the incongruity of it. "What about the statistics from the Pentagon? It's not everything, but if Washington would consider our findings, we'd get our foot in the door."

"Fat chance."

"Then let's convince Senator Summers that we have enough proof to clear his son-in-law."

"Sure, sure. What's our proof?"

"Porter's access to classified data. His genius with computers. His frequent presence at Washington and Parisian cocktail parties."

"So he drinks at the international level. So does Summers."

"But Porter often travels without Agency approval."

"So have we."

"He's made bad friendships. Smith, remember? Yes, Deven's the one free to traffic in sensitive data — not Luke Breckenridge."

Vic roared with a mirthless laughter. "You'd have better luck with a newspaper reporter than with the senator. What about that young investigative reporter back on the Post? Tracy somebody. Mathison. He's great at opening a can of worms. Pass on the statistics to him. Let him play with it."

"We don't have that much time, Vic."

"Well, I'm out of it. I'm heading back to London."

"Is that why Brianna flew over — to escort you back?"

"She came over to make certain I kept my medical follow-up."

His strained voice startled Drew. "What's going on, Vic?"

"That phone call I had earlier today — I'm HIV positive, Drew. Thanks to my second wife or one of my girlfriends. Can you beat that? Vic Wilson going down with a lousy blood test."

Drew's mouth went dry. "I'm sorry."

Vic averted his gaze. "It was a private lab — here in Paris. It'll be a while before Kaminsky or the Company knows. Once they do, I'm out on the count of ten. They'll dump this Company boy in a minute. That merc camp may have been my last big assignment, and we can't even wrap it up without Porter's confession."

He glanced anxiously at Drew now. "Why couldn't it have been Porter instead of me?

He deserves a disease like this."

Drew considered Vic's lifestyle, a girl in every city. "Does your cousin know?"

"Brianna made the appointment. When I told her the results, she cried." He turned, his narrow face tight with rage. "Imagine, someone really cares what happens to me."

Gregory wanted to say, *So do I.*

"I've been straight, Drew. You've got to believe me."

"We'll work this out. Get a second opinion."

Vic made a gallant attempt at his cocky smile. "This was my second opinion. It's funny. I don't have any war record or memorial wall where I'll be immortalized. It'll all be summed up, 'he lived; he died.' No wonder it affected Sauni so much when they left Breckenridge's name off the Vietnam Memorial."

"You're not dead yet, Vic. It's not full-blown AIDS."

"Yeah, but you might as well say I've got a death sentence."

Drew picked up the pen and twirled it. As he struggled for the right words, the phone rang. He grabbed it in relief. "Yes. All right . . . Where? About an hour?"

Drew cradled the phone. "That was Porter. Says he's ready to talk. He's meeting me at the Eiffel Tower."

"I'll go with you."

"No, I'm to go alone."

"Risk that and you've got a nine-hundred-foot free fall."

"If he plans to kill me, he wouldn't pick a public place. But he did mumble something about his pagoda."

"What?"

"The tower always reminds him of the steel pagoda he made when he was a kid. His father toppled it with his boot."

"Hey, that sounds crazy. You're not meeting him alone."

"I've got to. I need the man's confession." He stood and clapped Vic's shoulder in a warm embrace. "Hang around a few more days, and I'll fly back to London with you."

As Drew left the metro station on the Champ de Mars, he faced the antenna-tipped Eiffel Tower. The latticed girder was a masterpiece of engineering. It tapered upward, tons of iron and steel riveted together, a forty- to fifty-ton paint job. To Drew it was both immense and awe inspiring, ugly and beautiful, plain and magnificent. For a hundred years it had been idolized and tolerated, visited and marveled at — a floodlit landmark at night and by day a bronzed silhouette against the sky.

He set out briskly to keep his appointment with Porter, a niggling doubt in his own mind about the wisdom of taking the elevator to the top. He tried to remember his previous visits and reassured himself that there were guard rails and protective fences.

He saw Porter standing as rigidly as the tower, his eyes more crystal blue than the sky, his jaw set, his hands fidgety, his trench coat open. "Does anyone know you're meeting me?" Porter asked.

"Vic knows."

"And my brother?"

"There wasn't time to call him. But he's worried about you."

Porter searched the crowds, his face expressionless.

"I came alone," Drew said.

A smirk touched the chalky lips. Had Porter come to barter? Or to make certain that Drew would never turn him in?

They rode the elevator in silence, pressed in by tourists as they soared toward dizzying heights — past the first two platforms and on to the top, nine hundred feet above Paris.

As they stepped onto the observation deck and leaned against the rail, Drew was startled to see Brianna with two hot dogs in one hand and an Eiffel Tower lollipop in the other.

She brushed past him and hurried over to the narrow-faced young man with his back to the wall. Vic wore a thick leather jacket, dark sunshades, and a cocky grin that said, *I have the wings of an angel.*

Yeah, Drew thought. *Either a fast-driven taxi or an embassy limousine.* But he found Vic's presence comforting.

Porter's moustache drooped like his spirits, the breeze from the open walkway blowing his thinning hair. The wind made a strange hissing sound from this height, like the wail of farewell. A mourning cry for Gregory. Porter shoved his hands into his pockets and felt the cold handle of his loaded pistol. For three days he had planned this ride to the Eiffel Tower, this final moment with Drew Gregory. He would have preferred pushing him over the rail and watching Drew spiral down to his death. But there were no openings, only guardrails on the observation platforms.

He had come to despise Gregory — an impressive man with gray-blue eyes like the shades of the ocean and a trickle of laughter that hid his dry sense of humor. Porter's grip tightened around the gun; the silencer would deaden the blast. He calculated the time it would take him to cover the 1652 steps from the summit to the souvenir shop on the ground level. An insane plan for any other man, a challenge to Porter.

He looked out over the panoramic view. "I come here often. When I'm up here, I always think of my toy pagoda."

"The one your father kicked over."

"I've told you about that, eh?"

"Many times. But we didn't come up here for the view."

Slowly, Porter removed his hands from his pockets and formed a pyramid with his fingers. "I'm at the pinnacle of success, Drew, and you're trying to topple me. I can't let you do that."

"It's all over, Porter. There's no place left to hide."

Porter tried to light a cigarette, his hand trembling. When the third match blew out, Drew reached over and lit one for him. Porter inhaled, exhaled — the smoke forming miniature ringlets that drifted away like the clouds cutting across the sky.

"You used to tell me I acted like a man with something to hide," Porter said. "I thought you knew then."

"I never even guessed. But I pitied the way you came out of the Vietnam conflict so scarred."

"I was never wounded."

"You were emotionally. It affects everything you do. You still act like defeat in Vietnam was your personal loss."

"I did lose something, Drew. My honor."

"Then give Luke Breckenridge a chance. You betrayed him."

Porter lit another cigarette, successfully this time. "You can never prove that, Drew."

"I've been gathering statistics. Dates. Times. Places. *You* had access to top secrets. Luke didn't. What happened, Porter? You had a good record in the beginning."

Porter tried to remember when it all began. His hands were back in his pockets again, his finger twitching against the safety catch. The stairs. Would he have the strength to run down them?

"You had it all," Drew said. "Annapolis. The Marine Corps —"

Porter's fingers relaxed. "I was recruited for intelligence work back at Annapolis even before graduation."

"And when did Lisha recruit you for the KGB?"

He felt the buzzing in his head, the same blinding guilt trip that had haunted him since Vietnam: *I sold out my country for a woman.* He grabbed the rail to steady himself.

"Luke told me about Lisha. About her charm and her cruelty. She had him beaten

489

because of you, Porter. More than once."

"I had no choice, Drew. I had to save myself. It was only a matter of time before the government discovered that I had passed numerous secrets into her hands." He glanced at Drew. "Lisha was the wife of a KGB colonel. She bugged the rooms where we stole so many hours together. I hated her for that."

"No wonder you were glad when the Soviet regime collapsed."

"Yes," he admitted. "Especially the downfall of the KGB. I counted on them destroying their records so I'd finally be free."

Porter lit another cigarette, his thoughts briefly on Notre Dame and the strange hold the cathedral held on him. But did he want to go on talking to Gregory? Yes, the need to confess his guilt — to brag about his deception — overpowered him.

"I kept hoping they'd force Lisha to swallow one of those deadly little capsules. She used to call them her security."

"Was she really worth it, Porter?"

"Not in the end. She had ordered me to meet her once more by the wing of a downed American plane. But with the cease-fire in Vietnam imminent, I feared being left behind." He twisted the tip of his moustache. "If I didn't take the documents Lisha wanted, she threatened to expose me. Things were not going well between us. Her feelings had cooled — if she'd ever had any at all."

"So you decided to send someone in your place?"

"I sent word to Lisha that it wasn't safe for me to go, that Captain Breckenridge would take my place."

"But why Breckenridge?"

"He was at a remote camp in Laos — harder to trace. He knew the language and area, but I hadn't counted on him being ill. I knew Lisha would never let him go, and then word filtered back that he had been buried in enemy territory." Matter-of-factly, Porter said, "The records identified him as our mole, the Asian connection. We sealed his files, notified the family of his death, and his body was presumably returned for burial."

"In a hermetically sealed casket."

"My orders," Porter said. "We didn't have Luke's body to send."

"You have no idea how much grief you caused that family."

"I thought it was a special touch — to bury him in Arlington."

"Was it all really worth it, Porter?"

"I liked the money. Altering Luke's records was the easiest part. It bought me enough time to convince the Agency that Luke was our double agent, a man I had trusted."

"But Luke didn't even know you."

"He didn't remember. But we toasted the secret war in Laos before he rotated home that second time. I changed the records to say that he was listed under my command."

Porter turned against the sudden chill. "I thought it would only be a year or two before my Russian handler attempted to contact me again, but ten years passed. By then I'd been promoted. I didn't know that Lisha had arranged to keep Luke alive as her guarantee that I would be useful to them again."

The things Porter hadn't been told still angered him even now: Admiral Breckenridge's unrelenting search for answers, rumors of Luke's survival, the opening of Luke's files for review, the Russian involvement in Luke's escape from Laos. Finally Kaminsky announced that Luke had been tracked to Europe.

Months after that Porter's new Russian handler knocked at his door, a beautiful woman who looked like Lisha beside him.

"Lisha — my mother — sent me," Nell had told him.

"Drew," Porter said, "Luke's survival pressed me back into the role of double agent. I searched the continent for him."

"And Kaminsky and Neilson never suspected?"

"No. It took them almost seven years to realize a mole had surfaced again — and all the time since then trying to identify me. I'd pass documents to my Russian handler in Paris one day and be in on a confidential session with Langley the next. But you worried me, Drew. I thought you suspected, so I sent you to Croatia and compromised your code name."

"And you tried to frame me in the hotel in Washington?"

"Nell was like her mother. She threatened to expose me."

"And you had her killed?"

Suddenly, Porter felt as trapped here in Paris as he had been that day on the fall of Saigon. The end of April. Spring, like it was now. Saigon had been totally surrounded, rockets and artillery shells pounding the city. *Now* he stood at the top of the Eiffel Tower; *then* he had stood on the rooftop of the American embassy in Saigon as marines tossed canisters of tear gas at the crowds seven stories below.

Air America's compound lay in shambles. A North Vietnamese A-37 Dragonfly jet soared in the distance. U. S. ships waited forty miles offshore for the Operation Frequent Wind helicopters to reach them. Porter had crawled into the whirring Sea Stallion. Eleven frightened marines scrambled on board behind him. The door closed, and the last helicopter out of Saigon lifted from the rooftop, leaving hundreds of high-cheeked Vietnamese marked for death.

Saigon. Paris. Thoughts of escape still filled his mind. South Vietnamese refugees hindered his flight from Saigon. Drew threatened his freedom now. Porter's timing had to be perfect. One moment they stood alone; the next, people moved into the space around them. Porter moved to his right, running his hand along the rail, repositioning himself closer to the stairs. Drew followed.

Porter only half noticed a young couple move to the spot they had vacated — a man in a leather jacket with wide sunshades and the girl attractive, but too old to be sucking on a lollipop. He chose to ignore them and fixed his gaze on one of the distant cloud patterns that had grayed at the edges.

Aloud he cried out, "Drew, you've ruined me. You and Lisha."

His head roared. He fumbled in his pocket for his high-powered Browning, pulled it free, and aimed it at Drew.

"Look out, Drew," a woman screamed.

"Porter has a gun."

The shot reflected off the rail. He fired again, hopelessly off target. The crowds shrank back. Drew and the man in the leather jacket lunged for him. As he crashed the semiautomatic against Drew's jaw, he recognized Vic Wilson. He stumbled on toward the stairs. Firing wildly at his pursuers, he pushed his way toward freedom.

The roar in his head exploded as he raced down the steps, two at a time. The pulsation felt like a blood vessel erupting. One hundred steps, three hundred, five hundred, eleven hundred to go. He braced against the narrow banister and gasped for air. The seconds ticked into eternity as he shoved the Browning back into his pocket. Three tourists eased past him, fear in their eyes, but Gregory and Wilson had been detained.

Two hours later he met his Russian contact by the familiar drop, a book stall along the quayside of the River Seine. "I want to defect to Moscow," he told the man, trying to calm the desperation in his voice. "I need passage at once. In the last forty-eight hours I've sent several coded messages —"

Coldly, the handler said, "You've been warned about that."

"But, Theo —"

"Take no risks. I'll contact you with instructions."

"Here? Today? Tomorrow morning? I don't have much time."

Theo smiled cunningly. "We're aware of that."

The man turned and walked away, rapidly crossing the bridge to the other side of the Seine. Porter knew as he disappeared that the decision had already been made, his request denied. Porter Deven's usefulness as a double agent had just run out.

Chapter 28

Thursday breezed in at a cool fifty-two degrees with the sky overcast and the prospect of meeting Chadsworth Kaminsky disheartening. Chad disliked Paris; he liked it less when it rained. And he hated having his schedule altered. His return flight to Washington had been canceled. Neilson's orders.

Drew watched Kaminsky lumber out of the taxi and make his way toward the embassy door. Chad moved slowly, bogged down by weight and worry, his suit wrinkled from an all-night train ride, his scowl sending its own warning. Chad's tone sounded as gravelly as his mood when he returned Drew's less than cordial greeting. "Oh, Drew. There you are. Let's get on with it. Where's Porter?"

Drew's jaw cracked as he said, "At his apartment we trust."

Chad paused in the hall, caught his breath, and sneezed. "We trust? What's that supposed to mean?"

"I met with him for an hour yesterday. That's how I got this bruised face. Porter admitted everything, but he told me we'd never take him alive."

Chad's countenance fell even more. "Neilson won't be pleased if you've given Porter time to defect to the Russian embassy."

Or catch a flight to Moscow, Drew thought. "The ambassador is loaning us his car so we can drive out to Deven's now."

Kaminsky sneezed again. "And if he's locked in his room?"

"I'll pick the lock if necessary. Or if you prefer, his brother Zach lives in the same complex."

In the back seat of the limousine, Drew asked, "How did your visit with Mrs. Breckenridge go?"

"I never found her. I walked three miles to Busingen in the rain; she was off to a faculty retreat in Lauterbrunnen. So I trudged back to Schaffhausen — drenched to my undershirt — and took that long ride to Lauterbrunnen for nothing. She was gone."

"It doesn't sound like Sauni not to keep an appointment."

"I didn't call ahead. Wanted to surprise her. She's with that husband of hers, you can be sure. And Neilson is convinced that both of you know where he is."

Drew didn't argue that one. He took a sudden interest in the outside traffic and rode the remaining five miles without talking.

Porter's apartment complex was a narrow three-story building built of honey-colored stone that gave it an earthy quality. Its plain outer facade had been relieved by colorful shutters, wrought-iron balconies, and a high-gloss turquoise door on each apartment. The entire place was gated, but their credentials impressed the security guard to give them rapid entry.

They walked up the sweeping communal stairs to the second floor, leaving Kaminsky winded with the effort. Drew led the way to #8. When continual knocking failed to gain admittance, Chad insisted on checking with the manager. "Mr. Deven may be ill," he told the middle-aged man. "He hasn't been to work for several days."

The manager hesitated, considered Kaminsky's credentials a second time, and then went reluctantly to unlock the door. Gregory followed him into the apartment, struck at once by the closed curtains and stuffy smell of an unaired room. Light from a single lamp reflected off the 9mm Browning lying on the floor.

Drew knew before he involuntarily glanced around the room that Porter had won. He felt the gnawing sense of personal defeat and

Porter's triumph in this final act. The room was familiar: three whitewashed walls with traditional wallpaper on the far end by the fireplace, comfortable furnishings, oak floors with throw rugs, a yellow kitchen to the left with heavy crockery on a shelf. Through the room on his right was the brass bedstead — beyond that, the sound of the toilet still flushing, its handle jammed.

"Oh no," Kaminsky said.

He stood frozen beside Drew, his eyes riveted on Porter's large leather chair that faced the fireplace. An untouched glass of wine and a small framed photograph lay on the end table beside it.

Now Drew forced himself to see what he had tried to block out — the top of Porter's balding head showing above the chair back, his large torso slumped to the left, his hand dangling toward the floor, the rigid fingertips almost touching Jedburgh. The dog — Porter's only real friend in Paris — lay stretched out beside him, its black nostrils and long sleek body splattered with blood. The old basset hound was as dead as Porter.

"Do you need any more proof?" Drew asked.

"What proof?" Chad hissed. "We have no written confession unless we find one here."

He turned and called across the room to the manager. "Mr. Deven was an American diplomat. We'll handle it."

"But the police?"

"We'll call them."

His tone boomed so authoritatively that the manager backed out of the apartment. Chad shut the door behind him.

Again Drew allowed himself to look down at Porter's rigid body. Porter sat in the chair still dressed in the trench coat he'd worn at the Eiffel Tower, blood stains on his polished Italian shoes. His face looked distorted, bruised and puffy almost beyond recognition. A single bullet had entered at the right temple, the kickback from the explosion so violent that it had sent the pistol skidding across the shiny floor.

Drew picked up the picture from the end table — a beautiful woman against the backdrop of a Buddhist temple. She had black hair and the deep-set eyes and well-shaped mouth that Porter had described and a tiny curled ringlet on her forehead.

"Who is she, Drew?"

"Lisha, the Russian agent who caused Porter's downfall. I think you'll find that she was Nell Ashcroft's mother."

"You're trying to link Porter with that killing?"

"Maybe he arranged it. Or maybe her own people ordered the hit. Ashcroft would have been a threat to Porter's usefulness if our Agency traced her back to the Russian embassy."

Chad grabbed Porter's wine glass.

"Don't risk drinking that," Drew warned. "Porter may have considered more than one option. If you need something, there's a whole winery in the kitchen."

Chad sneezed, his eyes watery from the miserable cold. "We've been friends since Vietnam. I never thought he'd come to this. Start checking. Take anything that links him with Langley or this woman."

Drew walked to the desk. "Chad, Porter's the one who first accused Breckenridge of espionage. Didn't anyone question that?"

"I was uneasy. Some of his reports didn't add up, but then they said Breckenridge was dead. They wanted to close the case."

"And you went along with them? You never wondered if Luke's records had been altered to throw suspicion on him?"

"Why would I? As far as we knew, no other sensitive data was funneled to the enemy. Then the war ended, and I rotated home."

Drew opened and slammed drawers, scooping papers and computer disks into a sack. "Kaminsky, when the rumors surfaced that Luke was still alive — that he had escaped Laos — what then?"

"Now and then a classified document would pass into enemy hands. Some of our foreign agents disappeared. But we didn't know Luke's whereabouts or his method of delivery."

An empty drawer crashed to the floor. "What's wrong with you, Kaminsky? Luke didn't have access to classified documents, not without someone passing them to him. Didn't the Company ever face the possibility that the mole had never been found?"

"We considered it." He turned his back to Drew. "I'd better put through a call to Neilson for instructions."

"What about Breckenridge?"

"He's run out of loopholes. Porter was his last hope."

Lyle Spincrest from MI5 bounced into Dudley Perkins's drab office, his hazel eyes glowing like an Abyssinian cat. "Have I got news for Uriah Kendall. Where is he?"

"He flew back to the States. So what's the big news?"

Lyle grabbed a chair, uninvited. "Kendall's friend Gregory is in the clear." His grin broadened. "Gregory is the one who nailed it down. Imagine. Porter Deven, their chief-of-station in Paris, turned out to be the double agent. He's dead. Killed himself and all the proof of his skulduggery is gone with him."

"You're certain?"

"Yes. Why don't we call BBC and beat them to the headline?"

Perkins's long fingers flattened on the desk. "We'll do no such thing. We've been there before — trapped in all the humiliation and shame. Years before your time, Lyle."

Spincrest stiffened, the glow in his eyes dimming. "I thought you'd be pleased, Dudley."

"At another man's downfall? I have friends in the CIA."

"Are you going to notify Mr. Kendall?"

"Uriah will know soon enough."

"You're not going to tell him about Nell Ashcroft either?"

Dudley's annoyance turned to a thin smile. "Miles is still on that one. Let's wait and see what the Americans know — perhaps not much more than we do."

"And what is that, sir?"

"She was Russian born. Married one of our space scientists. Years older than she. Widowed three years later when he died in a car crash." Dudley's smile vanished. "After that Mrs. Ashcroft traveled under a British passport — thanks to her husband. Takes an annual visit to the Caucasus region near the Black Sea. But we've found little about her political convictions."

"No question marks until she went to Washington?" Lyle asked.

"That was the grand awakening. Until then she'd lived alone in a garden flat on the outskirts of London playing the role of a grieving widow. My guess is she's been an agent-in-place all along."

Lyle leaned forward. "On assignment to Washington?"

"Possibly. The Americans may know why."

Uriah Kendall and his chauffeur reached the turnoff to the Gregory Dairy Farm shortly after three in the afternoon. As Uriah gazed at the brilliant hillsides from the car window, he could understood why Drew Gregory loved springtime in upstate New York. The last of the winter snows had begun to melt, filling the streams and river with a rush of bubbling water. The fields were turning green, the flowers budding, the robins nesting in the back yards.

It had been a pleasant drive from Washington, unhurried and companionable, with Ned at the wheel and Uriah sitting up front beside his chauffeur — something that always displeased Uriah's son.

Ned pulled the limousine to a smooth stop and then bounded around to open the door for Uriah. "I'll see you up the steps."

"Good, Ned. Then I'll get you inside for a cup of coffee."

"And maybe a glimpse of Maria?"

Kendall smiled back. "Ah, you've taken a fancy to her?"

As they walked up the steps, the thought of Ned falling in love and moving away saddened Uriah. Ned had come into Kendall's life shortly after Olivia's death — an unlikely fan who had read all of her books. Doubly surprising since he was a school dropout who had bummed his way across Europe doing small jobs to cover his travels.

They had met at the cemetery, Ned running his hand over the Rolls Royce with envy in his dark eyes. "Yours, mister?"

"Mine," Uriah had said. Without thinking about danger or strangers, he had offered Ned a ride. He wondered at times if that meeting had been deliberate. He never asked, not even during their long evenings together over a chess game.

Ned rang the bell with one hand and slicked down his hair with the other. Uriah expected Loyal Quinwell to greet them, but he was startled when he found himself facing Aaron Gregory. Aaron's pallid skin had taken on a rosy hue, his intelligent brown eyes an apologetic glaze. He'd spent a lifetime hiding behind oratory and club memberships, exclusive fraternities and tailored clothes. But now faded jeans replaced his usual well-cut flannel slacks.

"Loyal told me you were coming," Aaron said. "I've been staying with the Quinwells — Drew's idea after you told him I was on suspension at the law office and running low on cash."

His smile was unexpected. "The Quinwell kids are marking off the days until summer. Stan's in the barn. Loyal is baking cinnamon rolls, and I've been helping Maria with math problems. I've found I'm better at math than I am at milking cows or mending fences."

As they followed Aaron down the hall, he stopped and let Ned rush ahead. "Kendall, I'm sorry about that fake painting you purchased at Miriam's shop a few months ago."

"Miriam and the insurance company made it good."

"I should have." The weakness in his face became apparent, the thin lips drawn. His mouth twitched. "Miriam won't speak to me now. And the Quinwells tell me that I should go back to Europe and face those charges of art fraud — so I can live with myself."

"The Quinwells can't make that decision for you."

"I know. I've been here almost a month. I keep waiting for them to throw me out."

"We're not going to," Loyal said as she stepped into the hall to meet Uriah. "Not as long as you keep your part of the bargain. Room and board in exchange for helping Stan with the chores — and church every Sunday."

"Slipping into that pew every Sunday is the tough part."

He avoided Uriah's eyes as they stepped into the kitchen. "Come on, Maria," he said. "Let's show Ned around the farm."

Uriah frowned as they left. "She's not afraid of him, is she?"

Loyal shut the screen door and looked quizzically at Uriah. "Why would Maria be afraid of Aaron?"

"She can identify the man who ransacked Drew's hotel room."

"And murdered the woman on the floor below?" Loyal asked. "Dear Mr. Kendall, if you were thinking Aaron — goodness! No. She's never been afraid of him. They've been good for each other."

Relief swept over Uriah. "Drew needs that confirmation. I'll tell him when I call him this evening. If things work out as Drew plans, Maria will be free to go home soon. That's why I'm here — to talk to you about Maria's future."

Loyal looked dismayed. "Tell Mr. Gregory she can't leave. The children adore her, and she wants to stay on with us."

"Ned might have something to say about that."

"He doesn't have a chance, not unless he finishes school."

As they waited in the Metro underground, Drew and Vic were on coffee overload, both of them tormented by Porter's death. Trains roared in and out of the noisy station, yet Drew felt alone as he wrestled with eternal issues. He was far from peace — still doubting the existence of God, the soul of man.

Vic caught his attention. "We've got a watchdog over there, one of the unfriendlies. Either that or the man's at the wrong station. He let every train go by for the last twenty minutes."

Drew shot a glance at the burly figure chain-smoking by an empty bench. "Maybe Kaminsky sent him to apologize."

"For what?"

"Labeling me as a double agent."

"All you'll get out of Kaminsky is a firm handshake."

"Got that already. You know, for a while I thought Langley was behind everything that happened to me. Or that my brother was; he hated me enough. But Porter set me up."

"Guess he warned his Russian handler that you were nosing around in the Breckenridge files. The rest is history."

"They were thorough, what with my ransacked room and that attempt on my life." He shuddered thinking about the Mercedes Benz trying to run him down. "Poor Nell Ashcroft. She was just excess baggage, a threat to Porter's usefulness. If they could blame her death on me, all the better," he said bitterly.

"Did you know Porter's replacement is en route to Paris — handpicked by Neilson? Troy Carwell has never been to the European Division; now he's going to run it. You should have had the job."

"I'm blacklisted, Vic. Kaminsky and Neilson aren't thanking me for Porter's death. They say I robbed him of his career and honor."

"That's what Porter did to Breckenridge. What do you really think, Drew? Does Luke have a chance with the Geneva committee?"

"With the brass of Washington coming?

There's only a slim possibility that he'll ever be a free man. I've let him down."

Another train slid to a stop. The automatic doors swung back. The passengers pushed their way to the platform — Kurt Brink-meirer, Pierre's uncle, towering above them. When he reached Drew and Vic, he stood beside them, a newspaper under his arm.

"Did Luke come?" Drew asked as the crowd thinned.

"He's at the hotel."

"Does he know the odds?"

"He's setting his own terms. A complete pardon or nothing."

A cunning smile lifted Vic's lips. "He has other options — staying on at the von Ton-ner mansion or defecting to Russia."

"Don't joke, Mr. Wilson," Kurt said.

They stood in a row like three strangers watching the trains come and go. Kurt's pro-file was sharp: a hooked nose from an old fracture, the square jaw stubbornly set, the broad bony forehead creased with wrinkles, his thick lips pressed against an unlit Marlboro. "Drew," he said, "you're involv-ing Pierre and Robyn in serious situations. I don't like it."

"That wasn't my choice. Luke is their friend. They know the risk. That's why Pierre asked you to help out. The rest of us are all under surveillance. If Luke had traveled here with any of us, he might not make it to the meeting tomorrow."

"He's safe. My wife and Luke registered at one hotel. Up the elevator to dump empty luggage in the room, then down the stairs for a five-block zigzag race to the second hotel where I'd already reserved connecting rooms." Kurt shifted his paper to his other arm. "The chamber maid arrived a few minutes later with fresh linen and a Federal Express package from New Jersey."

"Sauni?" Drew asked. "She's with him?"

"Yes, she makes an attractive maid. Your mercenary is in good hands with his wife and mine. Pierre and Robyn will pick the Breckenridges up in the morning and meet you at the United Nations." He thrust his fingers through his wavy gray hair. "Then Ina and I will check out of the hotel suite. But rest assured, Gregory, I want something in exchange for the captain."

"I owe you one," Drew told him.

"You're asking me to believe that Porter ruined the captain's life. That's hard to swallow. I knew Porter for a long time."

"We all did."

The burly stranger hovered nearby as Kurt paced a few steps and scanned the tracks like a passenger irritated with a late train. Kurt's wanderings came to a standstill beside Drew again. "I'm sorry about this thing with Breckenridge, but my concern is with your brother. We need Aaron in Europe. It's not just Interpol. Police from other countries and the International Art Loss Registry are still involved."

"Luke for my brother — is that it?"

Kurt shrugged. "It's a tough one, Drew. It's going to be difficult — if not impossible — to tie Aaron in with art forgery. But he was deeply involved. There's no question about it."

"And if they can prove it, what will my brother get?"

"Two, three, six years. Less maybe. They have to prove intent to defraud. He's sticking to his claim that he was just their lawyer."

And he was a good lawyer, Drew thought. *Lucky maybe. David Levine's kid. It didn't matter to Aaron whether his client was guilty or innocent; by the time they went to trial, Aaron had a 90-percent chance to win.* "Maybe I can persuade him to come back to Europe."

"How? The two of you hate each other."

"I've got what he wants." In the half-empty Metro station, he faced Kurt for a minute. "I was the older prodigal son, out of touch, yet I walked off with the bulk of the family inheritance."

Kurt spewed his unlit Marlboro across the platform. "Go on."

"Aaron wants the family farm in upstate New York."

"You'd give that up?"

"I have plenty of acreage. I could lease some land to Aaron for a dollar a year. If he gets a sentence for art fraud, I can at least give him a place to live when he's free."

"Have you gone religious or something, Drew?"

"No, I'm just convinced it's the thing to do."

A train rattled to a stop in front of them. "The Quinwells manage my farm. They're like Pierre and Robyn. They think God has a hand in everything. The Quinwells took Aaron in on a trial run. Room and board in exchange for chores."

"Can you trust him there?"

"In spite of what he's become, the farm is the only place Aaron has ever been happy. According to Pierre, God can forgive everybody. And according to Robyn, God can change people. My daughter keeps hoping I'll catch on sooner or later."

"They are rather persuasive, aren't they?"

As Kurt's train pulled into the station, Drew asked somberly, "What did you tell Luke about tomorrow?"

"That the Geneva meeting is his one chance to clear himself."

Kurt dashed for the train, the watchdog close on his heels. Vic lunged toward the stranger, pushing him away from the sliding door. "Sorry about that, sir," Vic told him as the door slammed shut and Kurt's train pulled safely away.

Epilogue

Drew waited outside the *Palais des Nations*, his attention riveted on the traffic. "Come on, Breckenridge," he said, tapping his Rolex. "Get with the program. It's too late to back out."

The hour hand settled at ten before Pierre pulled to the curb and waved. Drew caught his breath as Luke Breckenridge climbed from the back seat wearing full winter greens, a buffed polish to his captain's bars, a spit shine to the black shoes, a row of ribbons and service medals on his chest. Sauni slipped out and stood on the sidewalk beside him, obviously pleased with Luke's new appearance. The neatly pressed uniform added strength to Luke's bearing, self-confidence to his stance.

That shabby beard was gone, his hair cropped in military style. The clean-cut look put the emphasis on Luke's piercing dark eyes. Only a bit of slack showed in the winter green uniform, but his broad shoulders hid the weight loss.

Sauni's face had filled with such tenderness that Drew felt like an intruder. Gently, she brushed a strand of her blonde hair from Luke's sleeve. "Do you like the uniform, Drew?"

He shared her pride, but warned, "Luke, they'll axe you for walking in there in those Class A greens."

"I earned the right to wear them, Drew."

"Kurt Brinkmeirer's idea?"

"It was a good one. My folks sent it overnight express. Mom always kept everything even after I was . . . lost."

Drew remembered the room full of mementos. The admiral had to be crazy wanting his son back in uniform. What if the committee saw it as an act of rebellion? It could sway them against Luke.

Worriedly Sauni said, "You told him to dress appropriately."

"Yes, I did, didn't I? His folks would be proud."

Luke touched Saundra's cheek. "Wish me luck, Sauni."

As Drew tapped his watch, Robyn said, "Let them go, Saundra. They're already late." She reached out the car window and clasped Drew's hand. "We'll be waiting for you. Do your best, Dad."

"I will, Princess. Come on, Breckenridge. We've got to go."

Luke half saluted the Courtlands. He allowed Sauni to give him a quick hug, and then she touched his lips with her fingers. "I still love you, Luther Breckenridge," she whispered.

They were expected and passed through both the gate and lobby rapidly. Then they were led to the boardroom safe from tourist scrutiny. Two marine guards stood outside the door.

"Must be my escorts if things go sour," Luke quipped.

"Things might not go well for you in there."

"I know. Sauni warned me. You've taken quite a beating for my sake over this Porter Deven affair. Are you having second thoughts about my being here, Drew?"

"You were safer back at the mansion."

"Hiding won't get my name on the Memorial Wall. My wife told me that God's miracles pop up in the most unexpected places."

"I'm not much help in that department."

Luke shrugged. "I want to believe as Sauni does. I'd give anything for her peace, but I lost my faith when my brother died." A rueful grin cut across his face. "In those early years of captivity, I tried to pray. I wanted to see my wife again."

"Well, she won't think much of my friendship if we can't find someone in there who believes us. With Porter Deven dead, it's your word and mine against all of them."

"Gregory, I agreed to show up at this hearing for Sauni. You will tell her that for me if things go wrong?"

"We'll *both* tell her." Drew pointed to the shiny silver bars on Luke's epaulets. "We're here to restore your honor, too."

Luke barely smiled. "I'm ready, sir."

A marine guard swung the door open, his expression impassive as Drew and Luke entered. Thirteen unsmiling men focused on them, their rigid faces reflected in the high gloss of the conference table. *Luke's judge and jury.* Drew hadn't expected all the brass, all the uniforms. Kaminsky, Neilson, and Senator Summers had rounded up the top dogs. Luke Breckenridge didn't have a chance.

They headed for two straight-back chairs, walking stiffly past a stormy seascape hanging crookedly on the wall. The room offered no escape except for the guarded door and an expanse of windows that looked out toward snow-frozen Mt. Blanc.

Drew floored his briefcase. When he looked up, Luke was studying the men as if testing each one's integrity. Neilson and Summers were purposely absent, but Chad Kaminsky sat at one end of the table, his suit stretched taut against his bulky frame. The arbitrator at the other end was Swiss, a man with trifocals and a hint of a moustache gracing his moist lips. He was flanked with American military — two high-ranking navy officers on his left and Les Harrigan, a *full-bird* army colonel to his right. Ferguson Meyers, a lieutenant colonel, represented the Joint Chiefs of Staff. State Department had sent Scott Reymire, a tough overweight lawyer with an intense dislike for the military. Drew and Scott had tangled more than once over the years.

The room remained stock-still, everyone sizing up Luke in his uniform. The Spaniard from King Juan Carlos's cabinet stroked his pointed black beard. Drew had forgotten his name, but the man had obviously not forgotten the mercenary camp in his country nor the self-appointed brigadier who had run it. There were two surprises: Stephan Marseilles, a last-minute change for the French representative, and David Shipley with a wad of gum in his mouth and a forced grin on his face. Both men met Drew's gaze with intense disfavor.

Shipley stood to acknowledge Luke, his

voice nervous. "I'm Dave Shipley. Your parents and I are friends."

The stranger beside Shipley had to be Ivar Slavansky, the man sent by Russia. He was younger than Drew, solidly built with thick, squared glasses. His hair loss left him with a high brow that sharpened his features and emphasized the amused glint in his narrow, dark eyes as he looked at Breckenridge. The ache inside Drew's chest felt almost physical. Luke didn't have a chance.

Drew saw despair in Luke's eyes as his gaze locked with the marine colonel across the table. "Who is he?" Drew whispered.

"Fraylund. Allen Fraylund, my old classmate and friend."

There was no friendship visible now. The colonel sat rigidly in his chair, everything about him squared and professional: chin firm, shoulders back, face expressionless, uniform impeccable.

One empty chair remained, the one intended for Troy Carwell, the new station-chief in Paris. Drew felt grateful to see it vacant. That could be the one thing in their favor.

"Gentlemen," Drew said at last, "we're sorry we're late."

The Swiss arbitrator nodded politely. "I'm Karl Liene. We've been expecting Mr. Carwell from Paris. Apparently he's been delayed. Perhaps we should begin without him."

Liene proved himself quick and efficient. He spoke in a well-modulated voice, saying, "Captain, state your name, rank, and serial number."

"Luther Walton Breckenridge IV, sir . . ."

Karl Liene cleared his throat. "Your position?"

"Infantry, U. S. Marine Corps."

"And your position since the Marine Corps?" he asked.

"I've never left the Corps, sir. Never had the opportunity to do so. I've been dead, you see."

Liene licked his already moist lips and studied the notes in front of him. "In the interest of time, I'll give a brief personal history. Captain, correct me if there are any errors."

Luke sat erect as he listened to Liene tell the date of his birth, his schooling, his scholarships, and sports career, but his mouth twitched at the mention of his brother Landon's death.

"Valedictorian, Ocean City High School, Ocean City, New Jersey," Liene continued. "Valedictorian, U. S. Naval Academy."

One of the navy officers with gold braid

on his shoulders glared across at Luke. "He's a disgrace to our school and a humiliation to his own father, a retired rear admiral."

"Leave my father's rank out of this. He's not on trial here."

Luke flinched under Drew's warning grip as Liene droned on giving a rundown on Luke's first two tours of duty in Vietnam, his Pentagon assignment, his training at the Farm at Langley, and the questionable special assignment with the Agency under military cover when he passed into enemy territory in Laos.

Turning to Drew, Liene said, "Mr. Gregory, I understand you represent Captain Breckenridge, but you're not a lawyer."

"No, just a friend."

Karl Liene's gaze drifted lazily around the table to the faces of granite, his eyes settling on Fraylund. "Colonel, how long did Captain Breckenridge serve with the U. S. Marine Corps?"

A tic threaded its way along Fraylund's jaw to his throbbing temple as he thumbed the pages in front of him. "From graduation from the Naval Academy until he disappeared from the base in Laos."

"Kaminsky," Liene asked, "what was Captain Breckenridge's relationship with the Central Intelligence Agency?"

"He never served as a case officer under CIA."

Coldly, Liene pressed, "According to Mr. Gregory's report, Breckenridge trained at the Farm in Langley, Virginia."

"There is no record of that, Mr. Liene."

"You're a liar," Luke said. "You personally advised me twice during that training period about the risks. Remember?"

Kaminsky half rose from his chair, but with a sharp glance from Les Harrigan, he said nothing.

Chadsworth Kaminsky, your eyes give you away, Drew thought. *But no one here knows that. If one of Sauni's little miracles is going to pop up, it's got to be soon.*

Liene pushed his trifocals into place. "Captain, you are charged with acts of treason committed twenty years ago in Laos."

"Wait a minute," Gregory said. "We're here to discuss a full pardon for Captain Breckenridge."

Liene ignored Drew. "Captain, you face additional charges of mercenary activity in Spain. I can offer you asylum in this country until your innocence or guilt is determined. If we find you innocent, you will be free to return home or to seek temporary residence in another country. A determination of guilt will necessitate your immediate surrender to

Colonel Fraylund. Extradition to Spain on the charges there will be made between the two countries."

The drooping eyelids raised. "The decisions in this room will be reported directly to the American President and kept from the public and media. Release of information will be through the U. S. government. Is this clear, gentlemen?"

A rumble of assent followed.

Drew's thoughts ran wild. *Neilson and Kaminsky are playing for high stakes. They've used me to bring Luke out of hiding.* Drew saw no hope of a miracle in this room.

Liene's voice held steady. ". . . on that fateful day in January 1973, you left your base camp and went voluntarily into enemy territory."

"Another lie," Luke cried. "The CIA sent me on that mission."

Liene nodded toward Allen Fraylund who kept his eyes on the papers in front of him. Fraylund mumbled, "According to military record, Captain Breckenridge left the base camp without authorization. He was subsequently reported as absent without leave by his C. O."

"Then tell me, Colonel Fraylund," Drew interrupted, "why was Breckenridge buried with full military honors? Why that elaborate coverup?" He didn't wait for an answer. "And why was Captain Breckenridge first reported killed in action in Vietnam?"

"That location error was corrected, sir, to the jungles of Laos."

Drew persisted. "Weren't those early records based on reports by Captain Breckenridge's commanding officer, a man who committed suicide only days after Luke's reported absence? Thirteen days ago Porter Deven told me that he deliberately sent Luke to Xangtiene to cover his own acts of espionage. Gentlemen, the two men who could prove Breckenridge's innocence have both taken their lives."

He continued, "The records at Langley should be reexamined in order to trace the exact times when secrets passed into enemy hands. I believe you'll find that Porter Deven, and not Captain Breckenridge, had access to those secrets."

Scott Reymire whirled around in his chair and stared hard at David Shipley. "Mr. Shipley, you've been to Laos. You've even been to the Laotian village of Xangtiene, haven't you?"

"Three times."

"You have photographs of a downed aircraft there. What convinced you to release those pictures to this committee?"

Shipley eyed Kaminsky. "My wife's safety."

"She was threatened?"

"Wasn't she?"

"Mr. Shipley, pass those pictures around to these gentlemen."

Shipley glanced at Luke and reluctantly produced a packet of eight-by-ten blowups. As the pictures reached Luke and he held a photo of Neng Pao, a flicker of warmth lit his face.

"Mr. Shipley, besides yourself and those traveling with you, were there any other Americans in Xangtiene?"

"American pilots died in the plane."

"Aside from that. It's true, is it not, that Breckenridge is known to have been in that village for a period of time?"

Shipley avoided Drew's eyes. "I can only —"

"Yes or no, Mr. Shipley?"

"Yes, sir."

"Since you speak the language fluently, you were able to do some thorough checking. To your knowledge, was Porter Deven ever in the village of Xangtiene? Yes or no."

"No."

"What convinced you that Breckenridge lived there?"

Shipley's gaze settled briefly on the large

wedding band on Luke's finger. "Does it matter?"

"It mattered enough for you to hide these photos in a bank in Schaffhausen. You live in Thailand. Why did you choose a bank so far away?"

"My aunt held onto them for me."

"In case something happened to you? Her name, please?"

"Annabelle Vandiver."

"I understand she's a personal friend of Mrs. Breckenridge, that they are faculty members at the same school. Shipley, how long have you tried to hide the captain's presence in Xangtiene?"

"It's not what you think," David said miserably.

Reymire's face twisted to a cunning grin. "Thank you, Mr. Shipley. You've been most helpful."

Reymire turned on Luke. "Well, Captain?"

Luke kept his voice even. "Yes, I lived in Xangtiene — as a prisoner. I was sent there by Major Deven. You have my report, Mr. Reymire. You all do. My men were on patrol when my commanding officer brought a stranger to my tent. That man, Major Deven, sent me deep into Laos to rescue the missing station-chief from Thailand. I've spent twenty years in exile for Deven's betrayal."

Reymire tapped the report in his hand. "Captain Breckenridge, your men were on patrol. Your C. O. is dead. The station-chief in Thailand was never missing, yet you expect us to believe that Porter Deven risked a night flight to send you on a CIA mission to rescue him." He shook his head. "Didn't you leave your base camp with the intention of becoming a soldier of fortune worldwide?"

"It is my record in Laos that matters to me, Reymire."

Kaminsky's bulldog growl erupted. "Captain, Porter Deven is the one with the unblemished military career and outstanding service record with the Agency. We lost a good man when Porter died."

Colonel Fraylund turned angrily on Kaminsky. "It looks like we lost a good man, too." He retrieved another folder from his briefcase. "These are copies of Captain Breckenridge's records from the day he entered Annapolis until the day he walked into the jungles of Laos." He drummed his fingers soundlessly on the folder. "This was a good record, an honorable one, until we loaned him to your Company, Kaminsky, for special assignment in Laos."

"He volunteered," Chad said hotly.

"Breckenridge would," Fraylund declared. "How many of us came into this room determined to save face for Porter Deven? Ordered to do so."

"By whom?" Drew asked. "Harv Neilson and Senator Summers?"

"Sir, Senator Summers wanted to protect his son-in-law. But the rest of us were brainwashed, convinced that our country could best be served by covering Deven's betrayal. Luke," he said huskily, "I'd forgotten we were friends." He pointed to the Russian. "Mr. Slavansky, you could put this to rest for us once and for all."

Amused, the Russian looked around the room. "We know nothing of this man. Captain Breckenridge was never one of ours."

A low rumble spread through the room. "Quiet," Liene ordered. "Go on, Mr. Slavansky. You were saying —"

"Major Porter Deven was the one expected in the village of Xangtiene, not this gentleman. Major Deven was recruited by my country twenty-three years ago."

Drew stared in disbelief. Sauni's words rang in his ears, *Miracles pop up in the most unexpected places.* "Mr. Slavansky, would you swear to that?" Drew asked. "For the record."

"I just did, Mr. Gregory."

"Señor Liene," Franco Garcia said fiercely, "what about the charges of mercenary activity in my country?"

"Soldiering was my living, sir," Luke said. "I was trained as a military advisor in Vietnam. I had nowhere to go. No future. No country. No passport. Training men to fight was what I knew best. I don't care about international politics. But tell me, gentlemen, how can you make up for my twenty lost years?"

Silence filled the room for a few minutes before Liene said, "No one can restore those years to you, Captain." He turned to Chad. "Mr. Kaminsky, I need to contact your President regarding Mr. Slavansky's statements."

Kaminsky's expression seemed to say, *You've won, Breckenridge.* "Liene, my Agency likes to handle its own internal affairs. The files on Porter Deven will remain closed, but we'll arrange clearance of Luke's records in Washington. Immediately," he added.

"How?" Luke asked. "So that only a handful of men at the top — like yourself — will know that my record in Laos is flawless? The men I served with will not know. My family won't know. My file will still be top secret, won't it?"

"It has to be that way, Captain."

Reymire looked scathingly at Luke. "We're prepared to offer you the right to an American passport. We'll arrange a new name."

"You know my name, sir."

"But Kaminsky here and I believe it would be best —"

"Best for whom?" Luke asked. "My family? My wife? I must be fully pardoned, a public exoneration, sir. Nothing less."

Take what's offered, Drew thought. *Just get back to America.*

Luke's dark eyes were penetrating. "What about Porter Deven? Is he to be honored for his years of service, pitied for his suicide? Is his espionage to be kept secret just to keep the Agency's image clean and the country free from disgrace? No," Luke said sadly, "I am still a dead man — a man without a name, without a country."

Les Harrigan broke his silence. "Breckenridge, there is no place in my country for terrorists or for those who trained them."

"Luke is not a terrorist," Drew shot back.

"You seem quite certain of that."

"I have Luke's word."

"His word," scoffed Harrigan. "What an honorable thing to have."

Luke stood so abruptly that his chair tumbled to the carpeted floor. "It's no use, Gregory. As far as this committee is concerned, I'm better off dead. For them to admit that Porter Deven was a man guilty of treason would put a black mark against the Company, against the government."

"We have no real proof of Deven's involvement," Kaminsky thundered. "Only Gregory's word. And the word of this mercenary."

"And my word," the Russian said. "In my country, Captain, you would have been welcomed back as a hero." His bushy brows touched in a quizzical stare. "Captain, perhaps my country should expose Porter Deven to our *Pravda* paper as a double agent."

"There's no need to do that, sir," Luke said.

"He's right, Slavansky," Franco Garcia warned.

Slavansky's tough square face creased with amusement. "Señor Garcia, what has this man done to your country? Trained a few soldiers? Taught them how to fire straight? Did he put the weapons in their hands? Did he kill anyone in your country? I think not."

Garcia stroked his beard, too unsure to form accusations.

Drew kept his eye on the Russian. If Slavansky had three shots of vodka in his belly and another in his hand, he could not be more merry. His scorn toward this jury of men increased. "Gracia, tell your King that the *Pravda* will make headlines of that mercenary camp and a hero of this young brigadier."

Scott Reymire groaned. "I agree with Harrigan. There's no place in America for terrorists. Let Breckenridge go back to his mercenary camps. Let him start a new one in Africa or South America. Sooner or later he'll get himself killed."

Tears sprang up in Stephan Marseilles's eyes. "My nephew Jacques died for this man. And for what?"

"For what Jacques wanted himself," Drew shouted back, "a full pardon and more especially your forgiveness, Stephan."

Shipley stared blankly at the empty gum wrappers on the polished table in front of him. "If you came to Bangkok, Luke, I could give you a job working for me."

"Trekking the jungles of Vietnam and Laos so other missing men could come back to this hellhole? No thanks, Shipley. I lost more than years in those jungles. I lost my soul."

A dozen men lost in their own jungles stared back at him. "Let him disappear," Ferguson Meyers agreed. "Yes, let him mesh with the soldiers of fortune and die in the process."

Luke put on his garrison cap. "Yes, as long as I am a dead man in your eyes, then Porter Deven's records will go untarnished. Everything must be done, gentlemen, to preserve the honor of our intelligence community and the White House."

As Luke marched smartly from the room, Fraylund sat with his face in his hands, his shoulders convulsing. Quietly, Liene said, "Colonel, you should go after your friend."

"It's too late, sir."

One by one the men stood.

Drew knew that they had already voted in their minds. Like a row of dominoes collapsing spontaneously, these men were again ready to close the file on Luke Breckenridge, to deny that he ever existed. "Wait," Drew exploded. "This meeting is not over."

He glared at the top brass and Scott Reymire. "Captain Breckenridge is going to have his name cleared completely. We owe it to him."

"Don't be a fool," Kaminsky said. "We can't ruin the name of the Agency or the government for one man."

"One man cheated Luke Breckenridge and his family out of twenty years. How many of you have added to that shame by covering up for Porter Deven?"

"No go," Scott Reymire said. "Let it alone. Breckenridge made his choice when he left this room. We didn't stop him. As far as we are concerned, Captain Breckenridge died in Laos twenty years ago."

"I'm willing to risk everything for that forgotten man."

"You already did," Kaminsky shot back. "And Porter Deven is dead as a result."

The silence in the room floated on fear until Drew said, "Kaminsky, if America insists on this coverup — insists on maintaining that Luke is dead — then I'll go to every major newspaper at home. I'll go straight to the President if need be in order to see Luke's name engraved on the Vietnam Veterans Memorial Wall as a hero. A dead hero — a marine captain."

Kaminsky's fat face went scarlet. "Impossible."

"When they put that memorial up, Chad, they left space for any names inadvertently omitted."

"State Department offered Luke a passport."

"In another name! Luke wants a full pardon in his own name."

"Impossible," Kaminsky countered, "with the life he's led."

"No, we'll let the American people be the judge. And, Chad, I'll start with the *Washington Post.*"

"I knew you were trouble when you first asked about Luke."

Ferguson Meyers inched closer to Kaminsky and Scott Reymire and spoke in hushed tones to them. Then he turned back to Drew. "We'll fly to Washington in the morning and speak to the President. I'm certain something can be arranged."

"A full pardon," Drew insisted.

One by one the men filed out, the top brass first, leaving Drew and Slavansky in the room alone. Drew turned to the Russian. "Why, Mr. Slavansky? Why did you choose to help Breckenridge?"

"My son Nicholas was an idealist like the captain, someone who volunteered for what he believed in. He was crushed to death in Red Square when Gorbachev's power collapsed. He never tasted freedom, but like Breckenridge he sacrificed a great deal for it."

"I'm sorry. When you go back to Moscow, what will you tell them? Will you really expose the Deven affair in your paper?"

"Of course not. I was instructed to say whatever would best serve *my* country. I have done that. The negotiation table will be much easier now between our two countries. Your people will want to keep the Porter Deven affair quiet."

Alone, Drew walked slowly to the expanse of windows that looked down on the Avenue de la Paix, his eyes searching for Luke. On the other side of the boulevard, Sauni stepped from Robyn's car and started running across the street against the light. Luke raced out to meet her, cars weaving past them on either side.

Luke seemed to be arguing, Sauni pleading. Drew's pride in her rose. Luke's country might not want him, but the woman who loved him did. Again a miracle happened in an unexpected place as Luke leaned down and kissed Sauni, oblivious to the cars around them. They turned together, arms linked. As they crossed the street to Robyn's car, Pierre Courtland leaped out and opened the door.

Long after the four of them drove away, Drew stared out the windows. An overwhelming longing gripped him as he thought of Miriam back in the states. Turning abruptly, he raced through the empty room to the nearest telephone and placed a long-distance call.

Ring after ring! And then he heard Miriam's melodious hello.

"Miriam, it's Drew."

"Oh, Drew! Are you in town?"

He smiled at the welcome in her voice. "No, *Liebling,* but I can be there by tomorrow evening."

The employees of Thorndike Press hope you have enjoyed this Large Print book. All our Large Print titles are designed for easy reading, and all our books are made to last. Other Thorndike Press Large Print books are available at your library, through selected bookstores, or directly from us.

For information about titles, please call:

(800) 257-5157

To share your comments, please write:

Publisher
Thorndike Press
P.O. Box 159
Thorndike, Maine 04986